RHUBARBS A.

By Sally

Best Wishes

Published by Edwards and Lillie

ISBN: 978-0-9927927-0-1

About the author

Born in London, Sally has moved around the UK, enjoying the hustle and bustle of London, a quintessential English village in the Midlands, and the Hampshire seaside. She currently lives where the work takes her.

She has fond childhood memories of heady summer days in her parents' garden seated at a table learning to draw and paint. It was this period that moulded her career.

Sally's mother, a talented seamstress, taught Sally to knit and sew, so that by the age of thirteen, she was able to make her own clothes. This is where her interest in fashion and costume began.

Sally trained to be an engineering tracer and detail draftsperson, and ran her own company employing several tracers. She also designed record sleeves, adverts and worked on Marvel comic illustrations whilst raising three children. Subsequently, she was offered the chance to design costumes for a well established ballet school.

Her father also encouraged her artistic skills: his persuasion gave her the push to go back into full time education. Studying Fashion and Textiles, she later attained a BA and MA in Costume.

After the death of her mother, Sally's grief caused her to struggle with her creativity. During a period of isolation, she became inspired to write, and it was the intrigue of today's pursuit of material wealth and status by many, and the opposing contrast of deprivation in WWII that became the subject for this debut novel.

Sally is still a Costume Designer, as well as a Production Designer and Storyboard Artist. She is currently co - writing a new novel and screenplay.

DEDICATION

For my lovely mum, Hilda Annie Lillie, who inspired the story in the first place, and for Lenny.

And for the wonderful ladies of the
Air Transport Auxiliary

INTRODUCTION

If you had asked me way back in 2005 whether I would ever write a novel, I would have said no; I would run out of words and things to say within a few pages.

Well, that was until my lovely mum died at the grand old age of 88. I'm sure many of you can relate to how traumatic that was. I could no longer do my job as a Costume Designer. I would sit and talk to mum as though she were still on this earth, and on one particular evening I asked her to help me get back on my feet again.

That night I had a fragmented dream about WWII and modern day London. (By coincidence, mum had worked in a factory during the war, hand-stitching the fabric which was used to cover Spitfire rudders.)

The next morning the dream stuck in my thoughts, and I felt compelled to jot down a few notes. That same week, things to do with modern day London and WWII kept popping up everywhere; the internet, books, magazines, the news! I seemed inundated with it. Within the space of two weeks, I had the outline for a story.

I came across things I had no prior knowledge of: the two key things of interest being the female ferry pilots of the Air Transport Auxiliary in WWII and the Battle of Britain memorial on the Victoria Embankment, London. I have tried to extract the essence of the ATA, but it was incredibly difficult having to accept I could not include everything about them. Women in their twenties flew Spitfires, Hurricanes and Lancaster bombers up and down the UK with no radio and in often extreme conditions in order to supply the RAF with much needed planes. In my opinion these women have been gravely overlooked since WWII. In telling some of their story as well as that of the RAF, I have occasionally needed to manipulate the facts where necessary to aid the story, but have tried to do so as little as possible. Set during WWII and contemporary London, the story illustrates how life has changed between then and now, and how greed and loss can alter a person.

To this day I swear my mum was watching over me. As I sat at my keyboard, it seemed as though my fingers were typing free of instruction from me, often much faster than I am generally capable of. Several drafts later, and with selfless help from my editors Sian Tomlinson, Laura Johnson, and Lesley Brennan who started that process; here I am, hoping that you all enjoy my debut novel.

A big and eternal thank you also to my wonderful family for putting up with my obsession, my editors, the RAF for their support and backing, sculptor Paul Day (creator of the Battle of Britain memorial), Sue Sutton who has written a screenplay adapted from this novel, Richard Poad of the Maidenhead Heritage Centre, Joy Lofthouse and Mary Ellis (both female ferry pilots of the ATA), Andrew Sutton for his short film, Andy Marsh for building my Rhubarbs and Circuses Facebook page, Matt Heward-Mills for the front cover design, and everyone else who has encouraged me.

I'm bound to have overlooked someone - but you know who you are if I have!

About the title

"Rhubarbs" and "Circuses" were two terms used by the RAF for certain types of operational missions during the Second World War.

Chapter 1

London does not sleep. A fragment of time exists in the early hours of morning, when the streets are eerily quiet but never completely empty. During the day, deep under ancient roads, the underground carries its passengers through arterial tunnels around London or to the outer limits, where the beauty of England's countryside replaces bricks and mortar. Business people, tourists, students and families; a cosmopolitan sea of visitors and residents threatens to drown those without the strength to push their way through. Those who know it well regard the city as a living being with its own heartbeat, growing from the earth, thrusting itself skywards. The curiosity and desire to explore this city is inherent in most, with an occasional exception.

On this particular morning, Annie was one of those exceptions, showing no interest in her surroundings. Head throbbing, she had taken her time trying on different outfits until a crumpled heap of rejected items littered her bedroom floor. Shoes and handbags lay strewn across the bed.

'Blast,' she yelped, stubbing her toe on the corner of her bed. She kicked a discarded boot into a corner with the other foot. Deftly arranging her cascading chestnut curls with slender fingers, she cleverly created a look that would have been costly at most London hair salons. Finally, she left her glass-fronted apartment, which boasted spectacular views of the Thames and beyond, into the city, and made her way to the ground floor.

She was lonely. Of that there was no doubt. She had only a scattering of memories of her mother and father, who had both died when she was a teenager. She was subsequently raised by her grandparents until she had finished her degree, when she had chosen to leave the family home in Sussex at the age of twenty-two to pursue a career in advertising. London had seemed the obvious destination: it was, in her opinion, where all successful people worked and played. She had wrongly assumed that working her way to the top in a large corporation would numb the grief that twisted her stomach into knots. Thoughts of her grandfather's last moments were dominating her mind this morning, preventing her from focusing on the task at hand: her date with Tom. Endless hours spent at her grandfather's hospital bedside during the last fragile months of his life played havoc with every waking and sleeping moment. She wished she had paid her grandparents more attention when they had been alive; returned the phone calls, visited more often and, more importantly, told them how much she loved them. Now they were both gone it was too late. It did not help that Annie worked long hours at the office and had a few drinks each evening to try to stop these thoughts plaguing her. On her way to meet a man who could distract her, make her feel better about herself, she was too tired and hung-over to look forward to their date.

Lost in these recurring thoughts, she hurried along, but made a small detour to buy a bouquet of yellow roses from the flower seller in the doorway of the boarded up cinema. Tom would have to wait.

She opened the rusty iron cemetery gate, as neglected as the headstones in the far corner of the graveyard. Ancient oak trees bowed their branches in respect around the perimeter of a secluded spot, which nestled between the small church and a wall separating it from the river. The graveyard was serene and quiet. Stopping only briefly, she carefully placed the flowers at the foot of the white marble angel with its outspread wings, brushing away dead leaves and weeds from the family grave where her parents and grandmother also rested before standing up again.

'Sorry grandad, I don't have time to stay and talk today. I'll come again soon,' she added, including her parents and grandmother in her promise. She considered her excuses for a few seconds; they were no different to what the family had been used to.

Just as she turned to leave, a plump robin landed on her grandfather's grave, cocking its head to one side. It hopped closer, momentarily making eye contact with her. She wondered whether he thought his company might temporarily distract her from her grief. Taking one last look at the life-sized angel, she closed the gate behind her, noticing that the angel's face had suddenly been swathed in early morning sunlight.

Saturday mornings normally meant breakfast in bed, intense shopping expeditions, expensive restaurants, and occasionally rampant drunken sex with a rich Adonis. More recently, however, work had taken over her life, so the incredibly wealthy men with city homes in Mayfair or

Kensington had been put on the back burner. Visits to the graveyard had become shorter and less frequent.

Then there was her new boyfriend, Tom. As she spotted him in the distance, she tried to push thoughts of her grandfather to the back of her mind, but this morning she knew it was going to be difficult.

'Have you been waiting long? Sorry I'm late – had an argument with one of my boots,' she lied, trapping a high heel in a crack in the pavement.

'No, I've only been here a few minutes,' he replied, looking quizzically down at her footwear.

She wrenched her heel free and cursed quietly.

It was a crisp bright autumn day and the leaves had begun to change colour. Glorious showers of russet, gold and brown fluttered to the ground. Enthusiastic tourists, late in the season but eager nonetheless, were clustered around souvenir stalls crammed full of tasteless merchandise, where affordable goods jostled for space. Those visitors inspired enough sat on park benches writing postcards about their adventures and mundane weather reports.

'I gave up in the end,' she added after another minute had passed.

'Sorry?' Tom appeared confused by her remark.

'I gave up with the boots.'

'Oh I see. And tell me. Is there a reason I need to know the story about you and your angry boots?' He dodged the handbag that she swung at his head.

Tom was very patriotic. He was proud to be British and a Londoner, especially at this time of year. Winter would soon be knocking at the door, but for a while yet the parks would show off their neatly tended lawns, peppered with shiny new conkers. He reached down and picked up a particularly shiny specimen, playfully throwing it at Annie. She ducked and the offending object disappeared down the steps into Westminster tube station behind her.

'You're just a big kid, Tom.'

He laughed and stopped short of kicking an inviting pile of crispy fallen leaves.

'I despair. Are you ever going to grow up?'

The wind saved Tom the job, whipping up the leaves and creating a mini tornado. Discarded sweet wrappers seemed to have a mind of their own too, creating a myriad of patterns as they swirled in the wind.

'You look lovely by the way.'

'I know,' she jested, holding down the hem of her skirt as the wind tantalisingly tried to lift it. 'Can't help it - I inherited good genes.'

'Humble too.'

The weather had been unpredictable for several weeks so Annie had brought a coat, but decided it looked much better meticulously folded over one arm. On the other arm was the vintage handbag inherited from her mother. Her usual designer favourite lay on her bed: a status symbol and a reminder that she was one of the elite that could afford to frequent London boutiques.

'Where are we going?' she asked at last. 'This had better be worth giving up my morning.'

'Why, what else would you be doing, shopping? Anyway, I'm not telling you. It's a surprise.'

'Oh please let me guess - another boring war museum?'

'Not quite.'

'Jesus, Tom! Not again! I really needed to do something fun today.'

'You'll love it.'

'Spare me the details.'

'At least it will stop you blowing another grand on a handbag,' he ventured.

'It's none of your business what I spend my money on,' she informed him fiercely.

Tom was a fairly recent addition to her life. He had never seen her without makeup or with a head of tousled hair.

'How many handbags does a girl need?' he asked, scratching his head.

She huffed loudly, tempted to point out that the one she was using today was her mother's, but decided against it. She did not need to talk about things that saddened her today; she had Dr. Edwards for that. As the two of them moved on from Westminster Bridge, she looked out over the water. The wind dropped for a few seconds and she felt the heat of the sun, unusually warm for so late in the year. Despite being the weekend, the river was as busy as ever, boats of all shapes and sizes strategically passing each other by. Occasionally a warning bell sounded when one got too close for comfort.

She turned to look at Tom again. He was a real sweetie, according to her work colleague, Sophie, who had been the mutual friend who set them up. Sophie wanted nothing better than for Annie to settle down and marry a doormat as she had done.

Tom smiled.

'You look beautiful.'

'So you've already said.'

'I believe I said lovely the first time,' he replied, smiling cheekily.

'Is there a difference?'

'Well if you want an explana...ouch! That hurt.'

The handbag had reached its target. Unhurt, he smiled again and straightened his tie, which he wore loosely round his neck, his top shirt button undone.

'Sorry - it's just that your hair in the sunlight is so...'

'Get off. You'll mess it up,' she complained, flicking his hand away. She moved her bag to the other shoulder, thwarting his attempt to link arms.

'I never did thank Sophie for introducing us,' said Tom sarcastically.

'Neither did I - must have a word with her about that.' She took her mobile out of her pocket and began to text.

Sophie was the closest thing that Annie had to a real friend. She stood by her through thick and thin, despite Annie being generally unpopular with the other office girls. The office juniors had waged private bets as to how long Annie's relationship with Tom would last. The consensus was that Tom would undoubtedly end things - sooner rather than later.

To outsiders they might have been seen as a good match. Though Tom was older, the creases that had formed around his smiling eyes and the flecks of grey in his hair did not seem to age him. Most importantly, he had a good sense of humour; something many of the executives Annie had dated considerably lacked. Tom and Annie had started the day in playful combat, vying for power, each trying to take charge of the date and have their own way. Annie had soon realised she had met her match and Tom wasn't giving in any time soon: she was going to have to endure whatever he had planned and that was that.

Tom's unkempt wavy hair, youthful charm and casual clothes gave him a lackadaisical appearance that mirrored his long relaxed stride. For every step he took, Annie took two. She tossed her hair away from her face with her gloved hand, only to have it repeatedly fall over one eye.

'For God's sake Tom, slow down. Anyone would think we've got a plane to catch.'

Tom studied her flawless face. She was the most striking woman he had ever dated. He imagined the fearsome look of a crouching tiger lurking in her golden eyes whenever she threw him a withering stare, but when she softened and laughed, he could see the real her. For the second time he sheepishly attempted to brush her hair away from her eyes.

'How can you possibly see where you're going?'

She flicked his hand away again.

'I've already told you once - get off!'

'Don't want you tripping over now, do we?'

'For Christ's sake Tom, I'm perfectly fine thank you! I can walk just as fast as you if I want.' As she said these words, she caught the heel of her shoe in the crack of a paving stone for the second time. She grabbed his arm to prevent herself from falling.

'I told you! You should've worn sensible walking shoes – stout ones like mine.'

As she looked down at his faded suede footwear, a fleeting look of disgust spread across her face.

'Are you mad? Just because you dress like that doesn't mean I'm going to.'

Tom laughed.

'Ouch – that's twice you've hurt me today. I can see why the boots wanted to stay at home, Miss Grouchy!'

'Fool!' She marched on ahead but again Tom's long legs gave him the advantage. He skipped around her several times like a young child.

'C'mon Annie. Cheer up, why don't you? You seemed happy a minute ago, and it's such a nice day.'

She softened slightly at the sight of his antics.

'Shopping later?' She fluttered her eyelashes at him.

'Very well,' he succumbed.

'You know, you are a bit of an anorak,' she announced.

'An anorak? I'm not sure I know what you mean?'

Tom had increased his pace again and Annie's face was turning red. She huffed and puffed, attempting to catch her breath.

'Look at you – your clothes, your shoes, don't get me started on your hair, and you're obsessed with World War Two! And what bloody obelisk are you taking me to today?' She looked deep into his eyes hoping for a clue about the next few hours. 'Is it another museum, a decorated war hero, or the home where your grandparents sheltered from the bombs blah blah blah?'

'Doesn't my family history interest you at all?'

'Not enough to wear my shoes out tramping around London, or whatever else you've planned.'

They paused for a moment and Tom looked down at the ground like a scolded child.

'It might sound harsh Tom – but what's past is past. You can't change things. You can't keep looking back at what happened then, you've got to live in the present and get on with it.' As she said these words, she felt fleetingly hypocritical, unable to take her own advice when it came to her grandfather.

'I suppose this is where our age difference shows,' he remarked, oblivious to her mind wandering again.

'You're not that much older than me.'

He was in fact fourteen years older, with a very different type of upbringing. His family was close and his knowledge of the family tree was extensive.

Annie rarely discussed her family with Tom. It was something he still had to dig deep to find out about, as she was always very guarded on this topic.

'You can be so ruthless sometimes,' he retorted.

'That's a bit harsh! Anyway, you're wrong, and it's got nothing to do with age. I just can't see the point in looking back all the time.'

'As I said – ruthless,' he repeated.

'I'm not an ogre you know – just a realist,' she added. The truth of the matter was that she was everything he was not. Tom could talk for hours about his family, his memories and his childhood, but she preferred to keep these things to herself. She coveted all things material, rather than showing her heart to the world. Her large sum of inherited money fuelled many a shopping trip and her high-powered job in the city added to her financial security. Her grandfather, a former RAF pilot, was the person she rarely mentioned. Since he had died, she had struggled to come to terms with the fact that now he had gone, she had no family left. She had learnt to fly with him in her early twenties and these were the only memories she tried not to suppress. It was enough that she wrestled with her recent loss, which she chose not to share with Tom. Opening old wounds would not help. She did not discuss anything more intimate; only the practical elements of her life.

'Let's do something different one weekend,' said Annie unexpectedly. 'Get you away from stuffy museums for a bit.'

'What have you got in mind?'

'How about lunch at the Ritz, and a bit of shopping?'

'There's more to life than meals out at a posh restaurant and pretty things.'

'Really? What else is there then?' she teased.

Tom looked exasperated.

'I'll do that with you if you try and show some enthusiasm for the things I like,' he bartered.

She chose not to answer and continued walking.

'You know under that tough exterior I bet you have a heart in there really,' he laughed, clutching both hands to his chest. 'You can't get enough of me really.' His attempt at humouring her seemed to have no effect.

'In your dreams,' she replied, alone with her thoughts.

Seeing a therapist had become routine, a necessary part of her week. Tom could see by the look in her eyes that she was suffering, even if she would not admit it. Her expression could change in an instant from one of haughty indifference to that of deep sorrow. Nevertheless, he was tired of making allowances for her behaviour.

She had told Dr. Edwards about Tom; how she felt unable to give herself to him or anyone else. She felt empty; the world seemed devoid of colour. On waking in the mornings, there had been occasions when she had found herself not in control of her limbs, her mind convincing her that she could not move from her bed. This feeling would usually pass after a few minutes, but in the early days after her grandfather's death, the only way to break the imagined paralysis and reach the bathroom was to crawl on hands and knees. It had been a peculiar sensation, almost as though she had to be close to the ground to feel in touch with the earth: a comfort in itself.

She had also asked Dr. Edwards if he thought it reasonable that Tom spent so much time researching the lives of relatives long gone rather than concentrating on the living. Dr. Edwards had asked why Tom's interest in the past bothered her when she herself had not confronted the loss of her grandfather.

They walked along the Embankment, Annie looking out again across the wide span of the Thames. Its smooth surface glistened, reflecting the late autumn sun. The wash from a Thames tourist boat lapped against the banks of the river and the iron girders of the bridge as the boat chugged slowly underneath. A waft of diesel fuel lingered in the air after it passed by.

'We're so lucky, you know, you and me Annie,' said Tom. He waved his arms at the glorious blue sky framing the London skyline. 'I mean, look at all this.'

She finished his statement for him.

'It could have been so different if you-know-who had invaded.'

'How did you know I was going to say that?'

'Because you say it almost every day!' She turned away from him and continued to watch the activity on the river. A boat passed by, a group of small schoolchildren waving from the deck.

Tom chastised her.

'One day something will happen to you that'll change your outlook on life – forever.'

She changed the subject abruptly.

'Remember your promise - when we've finished here I need to buy some shoes!' She marched on ahead again, heels click-clacking sternly, with perfect balance, leaving Tom a few steps behind. 'Or maybe you can buy them for me,' she shouted back at him with a devilish grin.

He caught up.

Normally she walked like a dancer stepping onto a London stage: graceful, confident and poised. She overlooked uncomfortable fashion choices by knowing that she stood out in the crowd, her clothes a testament to her expensive taste. She had abandoned the black that she had worn for several months, choosing to wear bright splashes of colour in protest of the coming winter. Her glossy lipstick perfectly matched her cerise coat, and her purple angora jumper and knee length skirt hugged her figure as though they were tailor-made.

They were fast approaching the Battle of Britain memorial that Tom had been desperate to see. More showers of golden leaves fluttered down from the avenue of trees, as if heralding their arrival.

A large group of people had gathered around the sprawling bronze sculpture as they arrived. Some were deep in conversation or taking photos, others strolling from one end of its facade to the other, stopping occasionally to examine a point of personal interest. Young children, full of questions, impatiently pulled at the coats of adults accompanying them and shouted above the grown-up conversations in an attempt to be noticed.

'Even those kids seem more interested than you,' said Tom.

'Maybe they just want ice-creams,' replied Annie, trying to be witty.

Tom grabbed her hand and urged her on, ignoring her cynicism.

'Wow, this is amazing,' he exclaimed as they drew near the central section of the memorial, not realising that she was in a world of her own studying her mobile phone.

'I knew you'd love this,' he continued, pulling his camera from its case.

Annie rolled her eyes.

'Mmm,' she murmured, more interested in the contents of her messages.

'You should have seen the documentary on TV. It was a mission to transport it here you know,' he continued.

'Mmm. Yes. I'm sure it was.'

'Earth to Annie,' he said, tapping her on the shoulder in order to get her attention.

'I'm busy – can't you see?' she said, checking emails on her phone.

'You're working again. Don't you ever switch that damn thing off?' He moved a short distance away, a little disgruntled, and stopped by a large plaque to study a list of names. Annie continued as she was, with her back to the monument. Tom swapped an occasional comment with one or two enthusiasts walking from one end to the other.

The London Eye, turning silently at a snail's pace, dominated the south bank, whereas the bronze sculpture, standing around twenty-five metres wide, graced the pavement on the Victoria Embankment, a reminder of the heroism of young men who fought in the skies above Britain in the Second World War. A life-sized group of pilots, frozen in time sprinted to their planes. A series of sculpted montages illustrating different aspects of the war surrounded the central figures, which glistened in the sunshine much like the ripples on the river. Despite a few interested bystanders, many people passed by, the statue either unnoticed or just a familiar landmark on the way to their various destinations.

Still clutching her precious phone in case an email or message should demand her attention, Annie turned around to look at what all the fuss was about, unaware that she was very close to the group of central characters.

'Fuck!' she exclaimed, having turned, suddenly to be face-to-face with a fierce-looking bronze pilot.

Tom winced at her language.

'Stress,' he said to the man next to him. 'She's under a lot of stress.'

A mother had covered her young son's ears with her hands and glowered at Annie.

Annie shuddered, distracted by a subtle change in the air. A soft breeze seemed to whisper to her as she once again studied the lean face of the figure in front of her. His smooth face stared out towards the passing traffic, somehow purposeful. She let her eyes pass over his uniform and impossibly well-defined jaw line and nose, and met his gaze.

The whispering increased in volume as the breeze picked up, the words unintelligible, hissing like snakes. The air was suddenly icy cold. Annie was blasted by a high wind and she struggled to stay upright as it increased in intensity.

'Tom, what's going on?' she called out, but the words were instantly carried away on the wind.

Annie's eyes were drawn back to the central plinth. She gazed into the penetrating stare of the pilot.

'Who are you?' she half-whispered to him, barely moving her lips.

'Annie?'

She shook her head, waves of loose curls falling back over her eyes.

'Give me a minute.' Annie brushed her hair back fiercely and turned to follow Tom.

She stopped, feeling the air suddenly alive again with a warning wail echoing across the river. She glanced at the pilot and a light-headed, nauseous feeling knocked her almost off her feet, a sensation all too familiar since her grandfather's passing. Her eyes stung as she struggled to open them against the force of the wind. An acrid smell polluted the air and, coughing repeatedly, she covered her mouth and nose as best she could with the sleeve of her coat. She forced her head upright, responding to deep guttural rumbles coming from above. Huge shadows swept overhead, unfathomable shapes criss-crossing the stormy sky like angry bees. Annie dodged sideways and stumbled. She lay prostrate on the ground, terrified to open her eyes as she heard the thudding of boots on gravel pounding closer. An icy chill swept down her spine as she recognised the eerie sound of warning sirens and aircraft engines in the sky above her. Her hands scrabbled across the ground around her as she struggled to get up, but she felt nothing. The cold flat stones that pave the London streets seemed to disintegrate into harsh spikes of gravel. She searched for Tom, for something familiar, acid waves rising inside her. She clamped her eyes shut, frantically trying to ground herself and stop everything swimming around her. It didn't help, instead it merely intensified her other senses. Cars zooming past grew louder, heavy boots pounded dangerously near to her on the unforgiving gravel floor, closer, too close. Great, dark, winged shapes still swarmed above her through interrogative beams of intense bright light arcing up into the sky.

She fell to her side, holding herself. For a fleeting moment she thought she saw the face of someone she recognised running towards her. A blast of orange and red snatched him away, giving way to black, to stillness.

Chapter 2

'Annie? Annie, are you alright?'

Annie looked up at Tom from the pavement.

'What on earth are you doing down there? You look like you've seen a ghost!'

'Ha bloody ha! But you saw it too, right?'

He bent down and helped her to her feet. Her face was white, her eyes wide. A group of adolescent boys on skateboards smirked as they rode by.

'Saw what?' he answered, brushing leaves from her backside. 'Those men – they ran right through me,' she said, pointing vaguely in the direction of the statue.

'What men?' asked Tom, looking in the direction that Annie was pointing.

Curious onlookers had gathered round. The bustling noise of cars, buses and an airliner flying overhead filled the air once again.

'Come on, let's not make a scene,' teased Tom, smiling nervously, sensing all eyes on Annie.

'I'm telling you, I saw something!' she insisted, still stunned.

'You must have slipped on the wet leaves,' he replied, smoothing her hair down. 'Are you hurt?'

'Where did those sirens come from?'

'Now you're just being plain weird.'

From his puzzled expression, she knew Tom had no idea what she was trying to tell him.

'You're talking gibberish. You must have hit your head when you fell. Let's take you somewhere quiet and get you a cup of tea.'

'No, I'm fine!' she retorted, irritated by his refusal to admit that anything strange had occurred. She looked around with darting searching glances for the young men that had run straight through her. In their place were the three teenage skaters, jumping onto the platform of a moving bus. Still amused, they were laughing about her. Everything seemed back to normal apart from Annie's pallor and her inability to stand unaided.

'I knew I had too much to drink last night - I'm hallucinating.'

'You're shaking! Shall we grab that cuppa? We can come back another time,' Tom suggested.

'Not if I have anything to do with it,' she mumbled, looking over at the statue. 'I swear that statue has a life of its own.'

'What?' Tom burst out laughing.

'It's not funny you know. I called out to you but you didn't even look at me.'

Tom continued to smirk at her.

'Quick, run!' he shouted. 'There's a bronze man following you!'

'Very funny,' she growled.

She was good at shaking off impossible thoughts: she pushed her demons to the back of her mind where they belonged. At Tom's suggestion, and with her no longer being in the mood to put up any resistance, they took a detour via The Imperial War Museum en route, arriving at Tom's house much later in the day. Annie had sat in the museum coffee shop, distracted, flicking restlessly through magazines whilst Tom looked at the exhibits, so by the time they got back to Tom's it was starting to get dark. A rush of warm air greeted them as he opened the front door.

'Well all I can say is that I got off lightly today.'

'Sorry – you've lost me,' said Annie, glad to be out of the cold.

He pointed at her shoes as she took them off and put them precisely together on the doormat.

'You wanted new shoes didn't you? Not like you to pass on the chance to shop. Did you forget?'

'I had actually,' she answered, seeming perplexed as to how shopping could suddenly become so low on her agenda. She picked up her shoes: the heels were scuffed from where she had trapped them between paving stones earlier. 'Don't worry. I'll drag you along to Oxford Street next weekend.'

At this point, she was uncertain as to whether she should bring up her vision again, for fear of sounding like she was losing her mind. She decided it would be best to keep up appearances.

'You can buy me two pairs if you're feeling generous!'

'We'll see about that.'

He hung up their coats and reached down to kiss her. 'Have you got over that little incident by the river?' he asked, guessing her thoughts.

She made light of it.

'Like I said at the statue – I had too much to drink yesterday evening.'

'Are you sure that's all? Seriously, you had me worried.'

'You could've fooled me. It seemed like the highlight of your day!'

'You're right - I shouldn't have laughed. Anyway, what was it you said about it having a life of its own?' He kept his eyes on her as he moved around the lounge closing the blinds.

She hesitated a moment, wondering whether Tom would believe her, but decided it best to continue with the lie. It all seemed ridiculous now a few hours had passed.

'It was so weird that's all – a bit creepy if you ask me. It was their eyes. I felt like they were looking straight through me.'

'Well it is a pretty astounding piece of work, so I can see why you might think that,' he replied, falling for her revised version of events. 'It's bound to fire up the imagination.' He went through to the kitchen. 'Coffee? Tea?'

'I don't mind.'

He was quiet for a few seconds as he made the drinks. He seemed to be waiting for her to continue.

'Working late every night doesn't help,' she went on. 'I'm feeling really drained.'

'Anything else on your mind?'

All manner of things were worrying her.

'Well yes actually, but I'm trying hard to forget about it.'

'Go on. Try me.'

To tell him was like admitting they were closer, more serious as a couple. She was not sure she would ever see him that way, let alone share all her secrets with him.

'Come on – I might be able to help.'

Perhaps she should tell someone apart from her therapist: Dr. Edwards would not always be there when she needed comforting.

'Dreams. I've been having really bad dreams,' she said at last. 'More like nightmares in fact.'

'How often?'

'Almost every night.'

Tom hesitated as he considered her dilemma, stirring sugar into his tea.

'That must be tough to deal with. No wonder you're so edgy. You must be knackered.'

'Exactly. Sometimes I force myself to stay awake as long as possible.'

'What are they about?'

She hesitated; scared that discussing her demons was almost like breathing life into them.

'There must be something sparking it off,' continued Tom, trying to draw her out.

'They're very weird, almost surreal. Most of the time I'm being stalked by a red-haired man – it's like his hair is on fire.'

He listened intently still stirring his tea.

'Tom, you're so very together,' she said unexpectedly, leaning against the doorframe.

He passed her cup to her.

'Should I take that as a compliment?'

She went on.

'You don't seem to be spooked easily. Are you scared of anything?'

He thought for a few seconds before answering.

'Yes of course.'

'Well, go on – what exactly?'

He appeared to consider his response.

'I'm not too fond of wasps.'

'Is that all?' she laughed. Haven't you ever seen something you can't explain? Something that freaked you out, perhaps?'

He stopped stirring and turned to look at her.

'We're back at the statue again aren't we? What's bugging you?'

'Do you believe in ghosts?' She steadied the cup in her hands, deliberately avoiding eye contact. Her hands had begun to shake.

He chuckled.

'No Annie – I don't, and neither do you really, do you?' he replied, raising his eyebrows. He gently took her cup, placing it on the kitchen worktop. He pulled her towards him, holding her against his chest.

'But I do believe however, that you're still grieving. I'm no expert, but it would explain a lot. You need to let your feelings out. Why won't you talk to me more about the things that are bothering you?'

She let him hold her for a moment, fighting back the tears that were burning her eyes. Being in his arms was comforting; his body was strong and warm.

'Maybe you're right,' she agreed finally. She picked up her cup again and went to the window, sipping slowly, considering his words. A solitary hot tear trickled down her cheek.

'It'll take a long time to come to terms with losing your grandfather,' he said from the kitchen. 'I wish I'd known him.'

Another tear found its way down her cheek. She could not talk about her grandfather. It made the pain of her loss unbearable.

Leaving her unsettled for the second time this day, Tom began cooking dinner whilst she paced the lounge.

Tom's home was as showy and minimalist as Annie's apartment: painted predominantly cream, and dwarfed by a large television in one corner, which was flanked by two over-sized leather sofas. Annie felt a pang of guilt as she considered how similar they were. He had been kind; she should not be so hard on him.

She watched him through the kitchen door.

'I'm sorry about this morning,' she said. 'I wasn't very good company, was I?'

He looked up from the salad he was preparing. His smile demonstrated that he did not bear grudges.

'Don't mention it - it's forgotten.' He winked at her but it was useless: her thoughts had wandered yet again back to that morning's peculiar events. She seemed distant, confused.

'I hate seeing you like this.'

He entered the lounge and laid out wine glasses, a bottle of wine and a salad bowl on the coffee table.

Annie began to speak, unprompted by Tom.

'You probably think I'm a bit bonkers, but when I first saw those pilots – well, I could sort of imagine one of them was alive.'

'How do you mean, imagine?' asked Tom.

'I felt like I knew how he must have looked in real life.'

'Go on,' said Tom.

'The image of him just popped into my head while I was standing there.'

'Well let's just say you have a vivid imagination.'

'It was odd, almost like I knew him from somewhere.'

Tom took her hand in his.

'It's just a romantic notion, that's all.'

'Do you think that's all it is?'

'Undoubtedly, what else could it be?'

Thinking of the lifeless but staunchly upright figure that braved all the seasons year after year by the side of the ancient Thames made Annie feel sad. She consoled herself that at least he had his faithful bronze comrades with him to keep him company. She glanced at Tom, trying to imagine how it would feel to fall in love with him, but she was unable to hold the thought for more than a few seconds.

An image of the pilot flashed through Annie's mind. Rugged and strong, with hair the colour of a blackbird, his eyes were icy blue and penetrating like the sea on a stormy day.

Seating herself at Tom's desk, she searched the Internet for images of the memorial. She had the sudden urge to find out who the pilot was and why his face was haunting her. Picking up the piece of shrapnel that Tom used as a paperweight, she inadvertently twiddled it between her fingers as she flicked between images and information about the sculptor's vision. There were countless photographs and links: the initial brief from Westminster Borough Council, the competition between rival sculptors to win the commission, and the background to the final memorial. Nothing jumped out at her or pointed her to an instant answer. She began to read the pages on the sculptor's website, searching for anything which might offer an explanation.

'Open the wine. I'm nearly done out here,' called Tom from the kitchen.

'What's that?' she called back, distracted by the text displayed on the computer screen.

'Open the wine, please.'

'Okay,' she said, resuming her search.

Conversation between them was usually difficult. Today they had talked more than they normally did in a whole week. They both inhabited very different worlds and though she frequently thought about ending their relationship, she always stopped herself. After her grandfather's death, she felt she needed someone. Tom allowed his work as curator for the War Museum to spill over into his spare time. On this evening, he was for once very much in the present, trying to soothe Annie's worries away. This evening would turn out to be much the same as every other: dinner, wine and clumsy sex.

'Dinner's ready,' he called from the kitchen, continuing to sing in an attempt to lift her spirits. With her knuckles clenched on the desk in front of her, she was examining images on Tom's computer. The face of the bronze pilot stared back at her.

'I swear you moved,' she said, under her breath.

Juggling plates of food and cutlery, Tom stopped in his tracks as Annie jumped up from the chair, her face as white as snow.

'What was that you said?' asked Tom, standing in the lounge, plates and cutlery still in his hands. 'Who - what moved?'

Regaining composure, she cleverly sidestepped his question.

'I meant the memorial. How was it moved exactly?' She fidgeted with her hair, twirling it through her fingers nervously.

'I tried to tell you this at the statue, but you were busy on your phone.'

'I thought I'd find out more about it. It's very interesting.'

Tom smelt sarcasm, and muttered something about cranes and heavy lifting equipment whilst noisily setting the table and punching the sofa cushions into shape.

'I see you found my piece of shrapnel. I inherited it from my father. He dug it up in the garden.'

She shook thoughts of the statue away and cast the shrapnel to one side without any regard for Tom's attachment to it.

Tom was acutely aware that she was still not herself. He picked up the shrapnel, examined it and gently placed it back in its proper place.

'I'll open the wine shall I?' he said, noticing she had ignored his request.

They sat down together and chinked glasses. She began to relax as the effects of the wine took hold, and smiled at him warmly, looking up at him with large appealing eyes.

'You're far more amenable after a drink or two,' he observed, trying not to be annoyed about his precious piece of shrapnel.

'Look, I'm really sorry I made a spectacle of myself on the Embankment. I've got a session tomorrow. He'll sort me out.'

'Who?'

'Dr. Edwards.'

'Does he really help?'

'Well, yes actually. We can't all be as together as you are Tom.' She fiddled with her hair again and lifted her chin defiantly. 'I know you think I am away with the fairies but the sessions have been really helpful.'

'Sorry, I just thought that now we're an item you might want to talk to me instead.'

'An item?' She was surprised at his suggestion. 'Maybe you're right,' she added, seeing the hint of dismay in his eyes. 'How are you going to make me feel better then?'

Putting her glass down, she straddled him with her slender legs.

'You know, I may be more amenable after a glass of wine, but you are extremely attractive after a few drinks.'

'Only after a few drinks? Charmed I'm sure!'

She began to unbutton his shirt.

'What about dinner?'

'Let's have dessert first,' she suggested, undoing the belt of his trousers.

Chapter 3

The next morning, the menacing shadows of the previous day seemed to have disappeared. Waking very early, Annie lay next to Tom and tried not to let her problems take hold. The bedroom window was partially open and she noticed there was a warm breeze, unusual for the time of year.

She savoured the safety of Tom's warm bed. Rolling over to face him, she studied the line of his back. Now she was sober, any passion she had fleetingly felt for him had flown away with the night. Perhaps she would enjoy settling down, but no matter how hard she tried, the thought of a lasting marriage, babies and a conventional life scared her more than being alone. She wondered whether at this stage in their relationship, it would be kinder to just say goodbye and give them both the chance to meet a potential soul mate, despite not being ready herself at this moment in time. She scolded herself for being callous, and for considering giving up on him so soon. He looked after her.

At this point Tom seemed to sense her critical scrutiny, stirring from his sleep.

'Do you want tea, honey?'

'What's the time?'

He fumbled with his alarm clock.

'Just after eight,' he murmured. He stretched and turned towards her.

Closing her eyes, she rolled over to face away from him, letting out an artificial sigh.

He slipped quietly out of bed, kissing her lightly on the shoulder.

'I'll leave you a bit longer.'

Drifting off into a half-sleep again, thoughts of the day before filtered into Annie's semi-conscious state. She held onto the image of the pilot from the monument, realising that he made her feel both comforted and unsettled at the same time. She wondered whether this image would ever fade. Thoughts of the pursuer in her childhood nightmares unexpectedly popped into her head, his face merging with that of the face of the pilot: his red hair resembling a flickering orange halo of flames engulfing his head.

Slipping into deeper sleep, Annie's night terrors paralysed her. Her dream shifted to another scenario. An unseen force had pushed her into a cavernous black hole, which served as her underground prison. Looking up through gnarled tree roots, she scrabbled to find a way out. The more she struggled; roots grabbed and entwined their sinewy coils around her powerless body. Her fingernails tore and the tips of her fingers bled profusely.

She was suddenly aware she was not alone in the dark pit. Someone was pressed closely against her, his presence filling her with terror, starving her of oxygen. Her life was draining away as mud weighed down on her. There was no escape. Her mind was going round in circles. Was this the end?

'Annie, wake up – you're having another bad dream! Wake up!'

Her eyes flickered open but her floundering arms continued fighting against the invisible force.

'It's me - Tom. I'm here. Nothing's going to hurt you.'

Tom supported Annie, cradling her in his arms, his warm breath on her face. Finally, he eased her out of the darkness, wiping the beads of perspiration away that had formed on her forehead.

'It's okay - you're awake now. Have a sip of tea. You'll feel better.'

She sobbed and nestled into his welcoming bare chest.

'Don't let me go back to sleep, will you?'

'No, not if you don't want me to.'

'Stay here with me.'

The sound of Tom's strong heart beating against her flushed face was comforting and she realised that she needed him. She offered her lips to him and allowed him to slide back under the covers with her again, resuming where they had left off the night before. She succumbed, masking her distress and pushing the bad dream back into the farthest corner of her mind. She wanted to be in that moment and forget everything else. Tom's lovemaking was tender, slow and considered.

Chapter 4

Leaving Dr. Edwards' office the following morning, Annie hesitated for a moment, clutching the polished brass door handle. As she turned to head back to the outside world, her whole body sighed silently and she came to rest against the door of the psychiatrist's office.

On the streets outside, passers-by offered nothing but disinterested glances as they went on their way. Annie wondered why she had to pay someone to listen to all her problems when there were so many people in this city. She never felt so alone as when she was surrounded by commuters in their hundreds and thousands. Joining the throng, she adopted a stoic expression, wondering how many of them were happy with their lives. She contemplated the hour-long session she had just had, unsure as to whether lengthy consultations aggravated or alleviated her problems. It was still only ten o'clock in the morning yet she was emotionally exhausted.

It was bad enough that Tom thought that her insistence on regular counselling was self-indulgent. She withheld the nature of her appointments from her boss, Sir Frank, for fear it might compromise her senior role. Sir Frank came from a military background, and Annie was certain that he would consider that anyone in her position of responsibility should be free of emotional issues that might distract them. The purely professional relationship she sustained with her department meant that no one knew she was anything other than at the top of her game. She feared walking into the office with her usual confidence diminished and a delicate state of mind. She was not indispensable. At least one or two of the younger women in the office were capable candidates to step in should she flounder. She viewed the women in question as vultures waiting for her demise.

Today everything was devoid of colour and she was conscious that the late roses in the park had no noticeable scent. Through the narrow gaps in the wrought iron railings of the park, she could see squirrels were gathering food in anticipation of a cold winter yet to come. Congregating in large numbers on the pavements were bedraggled pigeons; thin and tatty, grey as the sky, hopping around on deformed feet.

Even more bizarrely, passers-by seemed more alien the further she walked. They had begun to ignore her completely as though she were invisible. She was used to admiring glances and their indifference irked her. Taking her compact mirror from her bag, she checked her makeup for smudges. Reassured that she looked her usual well-groomed self she continued, stopping every few minutes to look in shop windows.

She did not feel the need to hurry. A fabricated story about extensive dental treatment would be sufficient. Her colleagues would be too disinterested to question her. Sir Frank Butler was the boss of the whole firm. Even he would only query her absence if she were to fall behind with her work, but Annie prided herself on her ability to juggle and multi-task anything and everything that was put in front of her.

Sir Frank was an upright man, in his late sixties: sparse grey hair, combed back to cover his balding head, with small grey eyes that scrutinised Annie when he peered at her over the top of his wire-rimmed glasses.

She soon reached work, aware that her stomach was churning and that the familiar building she was approaching seemed strangely intimidating. She paused a few yards away, thinking that if she was in that much need of therapy, then maybe she should return home to where she felt protected from the outside world. She took a deep breath and exhaling slowly, continued walking. The huge façade of the art deco entrance, constructed from glass and steel, loomed magnificently in front of her. She climbed the marble and granite steps, breezing past the uniformed door attendant holding open the door to the foyer.

'Morning ma'am.'

She ignored the doorman. If asked, it would have been doubtful as to whether she would have remembered a single thing about old Samuel, devoted to his post for forty years. Like a faithful dog protecting his owner from a horde of hungry hyenas, he stood waiting for people to start their day's work. He had seen many people and companies come and go, and had never asked employees about any of these issues. It was not his place to do so. He doffed his top hat as professional men and women arrived or left, and shined his shoes on the back of his trousers. Shifting his weight from one leg to the other, he resembled a flamingo foraging in shallow water at the edge of a lake. He prided himself on his smart uniform adorned with several rows of shiny medals earned in the war. 'Cold today ma'am.'

Annie ignored this comment too, disappearing through the revolving doors without a look back. The most he could expect from this vixen was a sideways glance as she strode confidently across the highly polished mosaic marble floor and past reception to the lifts. During most of the time that Samuel had spent at the foyer door, he reflected on his long life. Rosy-faced and cheerful, he stood outside the great ornate deco doors. Each night at eight, he returned to his small upstairs flat in Nightingale Lane near Clapham Common.

The uniformed reception staff and lift attendant received the same dismissive treatment Annie had shown for Samuel. She passed them by and entered the lift.

'Eleventh floor, miss?'

The lift was slow and noisy. The attendant hummed the same song every day whilst Annie watched the floor numbers change on the flickering display above their heads. Unusually, she broke the silence.

'When are they going to replace this old crate?'

He turned to look at her, any surprise hidden well.

'No idea, miss. I've heard nothing to suggest they will,' he replied courteously.

'Well it's about time they did. I haven't got all day.'

Confined spaces bothered Annie, but climbing the eleven flights of stairs in her tight pencil skirt and high heels was not an option. The lift jerked to an abrupt stop and the double doors opened sluggishly.

'Eleventh floor. Have a good day, miss.'

She stepped out into the corridor, choosing not to respond, click-clacking heels on the shiny floor marking her arrival. She wanted to cover the distance between the lift and her office: silently, invisibly, quickly; so that she would not have to endure jealous eyes boring into her back. She made a mental note to wear soft-soled shoes the following day. Each morning was becoming harder as she performed the ritual of psyching herself up to walk past the junior employees, aware of whispers trailing behind her. This day, the shiny floor that led to her office door seemed longer than usual, a glossed treadmill sent to test her. She continued to control her breathing and with a fixed smile, counted the steps until finally, she reached the safety of her office. Closing the door quietly behind herself, she breathed normally.

Moments later, her assistant Sophie brought coffee, post and a selection of morning newspapers.

'Morning Annie. Not much post today.'

'Thanks,' said Annie, sifting through circulars and important looking envelopes without looking up at Sophie.

In colouring and build, the two women were similar, but there the likeness stopped. Sophie sat at her desk, performing her normal duties, making polite conversation with Annie.

This Monday was much like any other Monday in the office of one of the largest advertising companies in the City of London. Sir Frank operated Carlotti's to a tight regimented schedule, like the tightly coiled springs of a very accurate clock.

Mondays were always the day for briefings. Sir Frank was already in the boardroom with senior management when Annie arrived. She could hear him long before she approached the conference room door. She felt flustered, and smoothed her hair before entering the boardroom.

'It's about deadlines,' he roared. 'Deadlines, deadlines, deadlines.'

'Good morning, sir. I hope I haven't missed anything.'

'Oh good - you're here Annie. Whip this lot into shape will you?'

'Of course, sir.' She removed his old maps from the wall and turned on the overhead projector.

Sir Frank continued to pace backwards and forwards. Annie handed out documents and closed the blinds. Reminiscent of a Sergeant Major, Sir Frank drew himself up to full height and puffed out his chest, finishing with the same statement he used every time, before handing over to Annie.

'I will leave you in the safe hands of my second in command, she knows the drill.' He left the room, mumbling under his breath about targets, strategies and such-like.

When the day was finally over, Annie was still working when all the other staff were long gone. The only people left were a lone security guard, the ground floor receptionist and the door attendant Samuel, who generally never left until the last employee had departed.

As she was getting ready to leave, Annie remembered that Tom was picking her up, having mentioned live music. She looked down to the street below. Parked in the usual place, the roof down on his car, he was tapping his fingers on the steering wheel, in time to some classical music. Her phone bleeped.

Hurry up. I don't want a parking ticket.

She deftly applied hot pink lipstick and piled her hair up loosely on top with a large tortoise-shell clip. The eleventh floor, still bright with harsh strip-lights, was deserted. When she reached the lift, the attendant had gone. Closing the brass doors behind her, she pressed the button. The lift started to move with a harsh jolt.

'Bloody thing,' she mouthed, hesitant but defiant, checking herself in the mirror as the lift began its creaky descent. 'Feeling good,' she pouted, banishing all negative thoughts. She was suddenly set off-balance as the lift shuddered and squeaked. The lights blinked and went out.

Stopping abruptly, it groaned and creaked as it hung tautly in its dark shaft.

'Shitshitshit...'

Suddenly, a whoosh of cold air descended on her from the lift hatch above. Faint narrow chinks of light filtered weakly through a tiny gap between the doors, piercing the black confines of her prison. As the temperature in the lift began to drop, a sense of unease gripped her.

'Okay this isn't funny,' she shouted at the CCTV camera. The tip of her nose and the ends of her fingers were already cold, but inwardly she was flushed and hot. 'Hello – can anyone hear me?'

She fumbled in her bag for the mini torch she carried.

'Come on you morons. You must be able to see me on your damn screen.'

The light of her torch cast a thin blue beam into the darkness, but then it slowly dimmed. She shook it violently. It flickered for a few seconds before going out altogether. Her heart pounded. The lift cables in the shaft above and below vibrated again, the lift seeming to sway very slightly from side to side.

Childhood fears of claustrophobia washed over her as she hugged her arms to her chest for comfort and warmth.

'Think,' she said aloud with nobody to address. 'Use your head!' The words trailed away into ominous shadows.

Somewhere on the control panel, there was a red alarm button. She reached forwards, feeling for the walls of the lift, her mouth beginning to feel dry. Starting to edge slowly around, her fingers skated across the smooth mirror that she checked herself in daily. She started to hum random notes to distract herself from the fear and began to understand the reasoning of the lift attendant and his incessant humming. The lift protested and threatened to plummet at every slight movement of her feet. Acutely aware of the contrast of the soft and velvet-flocked wallpaper to the mirror and brass doors, she closed her eyes and relied on the sense of touch. She wished now that she had studied her surroundings more thoroughly.

She ran her fingers along the edge of the control panel to where she was sure the alarm button should be. Somehow, it felt different to how she remembered. She tentatively touched it again.

'Shit.' She jumped back. She had not found the lift buttons, but the bulbous metal buttons attached to a jacket or coat. It was then that she heard breathing. 'Oh my God.'

Her scream reverberated around the confined space, echoing until fading away into dark corners. She fell backwards, banging her head on the handrail.

'Who's there?'

The breathing continued.

'Answer me – I can't see you!' She began to sob uncontrollably, punching wildly at the invisible presence. 'Get away from me!' Wrapping her arms around her head for protection, she huddled on the floor in the foetal position, waiting for whatever was in the opposite corner to attack. The lights flickered on.

She squinted through half-closed eyes. There was nobody there. The lift jolted again, starting to move shakily downwards and finally bumping abruptly as it reached the ground floor.

The lift doors opened smoothly and silently for the first time in years, as though they were mocking her. Any strange happenings were between Annie and the dark space that had just entombed her. She stumbled, falling sharply onto her knees, and stared back at her own face reflected in the cold foyer floor. Her knees throbbed from landing heavily on the marble tiles. Glinting brightly on the marble floor, a single brass button was spinning towards her. Snatching it up, she scrambled to her feet and marched purposefully across the foyer, slipping the button into her jacket pocket.

'Did you not see me on the monitor, you idiots?' she bellowed.

The security guard put down his queen of hearts with the rest of the playing cards spread out in front of him.

'Sorry love.'

'Oh, I see why now.' She swept the cards off the desk in her rage. They fluttered to the floor. 'Get that lift sorted out by tomorrow morning. And don't call me love.'

Leaving the guard open-mouthed, she stormed across the remaining few yards of the foyer, swearing under her breath.

Chapter 5

Oblivious to the rapidly falling temperature, Tom had been observing the night sky from his car. The rectangular windows and geometric pillars of Annie's workplace stretched upwards into the darkness, overpowering everything situated at street level. Stars were beginning to appear, twinkling like thousands of diamonds in the deepening indigo sky. Tom wondered how many people bothered to look up at the heavens, and out of those that did how many were observant enough to spot flashing aeroplane lights, shooting stars and satellites in orbit. He watched for a few more moments, before reluctantly closing the roof. Annie would object if the temperature were anything less than tropical.

He still had to tell her that they were stopping by his mother and father's home, but knew she would not be too happy with plans being changed at such short notice. He was wondering how to broach the subject when she appeared suddenly through the revolving doors of the office building, leaving the doors rotating behind her like a mini-tornado. He gritted his teeth and waited for the sound of skidding tyres on tarmac as she stormed onto the road. Jumping back on the kerb, she adeptly avoided an angry motorist, losing a shoe in the process. The driver of the speeding car lowered his window, shouted some abuse at Annie and sped off.

Annie picked up her shoe and waved it defiantly.

'Bastard!' She hopped the last few yards.

Tom braced himself for her wrath.

'Oh dear, not a good start to the evening,' he muttered to an empty car.

She threw open the passenger door, causing Tom to cringe at the thought of the hinges snapping. The car bounced on its suspension as she thumped down into the seat, slamming the door shut.

'Bloody hell, Tom, it's freezing in here. You've had the roof down again, haven't you?'

'Had a good day?' he asked, with a touch of sarcasm.

'Well, since you ask, no. I haven't had a good day.'

He stifled a laugh as he turned to face her. Her aggressive manner was a striking contrast to the comedy of her appearance; the tip of her nose the only visible part of her face, poking through a dishevelled mass of hair.

'What's so funny?' she snarled.

'Here, let me.' He gently brushed her hair away from her eyes. Her face was ashen.

'What's happened? Are you okay?'

'No, I'm not okay. There's something bloody strange going on! First, the bloody memorial, and now this.'

He tried to calm her.

'What are you talking about?'

She faltered, her anger diminished, her speech suddenly becoming distinctively fragmented.

'The lift...the bloody lift... stuck. Dark. Cold,' she whimpered.

'You've lost me. Calm down and take your time.'

Her eyes widened as she tried to offer an explanation. Tom had never seen a woman so terrified before.

'There was someone...'

'Go on.'

'Oh never mind, you won't believe me if I tell you,' she continued, trying to regain some composure.

He made a clumsy attempt in the confined space to put an arm around her.

'You're getting yourself all worked up.'

'Look, forget I said anything. Just drive!'

'I'm sorry Annie, but we're not going anywhere until you tell me what's going on.'

She took a deep breath.

'You have to promise not to laugh.'

'Okay, I promise.'

There was a frailty about her that he had never witnessed before.

'I keep seeing people that aren't really there.'

Tom looked into her troubled eyes. He felt no desire to laugh as she sobbed openly with no attempt to disguise her emotions.

'Go on. I want to help.'

She wiped the tears from her eyes with a tissue.

'There's nothing you can do.'

'At least let me try to help.'

She looked across at the revolving doors, which were spinning slowly.

'I was scared senseless when the lift got stuck.'

'I'm sure you were.'

It was pitch black in there, and my torch didn't work.'

'Christ! You poor thing!'

'I managed to find the alarm button, only it wasn't the alarm button.'

'Uh?'

'And then I heard breathing.' She hesitated. 'I was the only person in there and it wasn't mine.'

Tom took her hand in his.

'You were terrified. It was obviously your own breathing. You must have been having a panic attack.'

'You're not listening. You don't get it do you? The button I touched; wasn't the alarm, it was attached to someone's jacket. I could feel their breath on my face.'

Tom squeezed her hand and rationalised her explanation.

'Annie, this is just yet another symptom of your grief. None of it's real - surely you know that.'

'I want to believe you Tom, really I do. A few days ago I would have laughed if someone had told me what I'm telling you.'

'Then hold on to those thoughts. You will start to feel better soon. I promise.' He wiped the tears from her face and kissed her hand.

'You don't think I'm crazy then?'

'Of course I don't. Anyway, how about we take your mind off it for a while - talk about it later? You'll see things from a different perspective after a good night out.'

She offered no resistance.

'If you think that's best.'

'My parents have invited us around for a bite,' he dropped into the conversation. 'On the way to the gig. Is that okay?'

'Sounds good to me,' she lied.

'You'll be pleasantly surprised then. Mum's a whiz in the kitchen.'

The half hour drive began; neither saying much, Annie subdued and emotionally drained. Nevertheless, by the time they reached Tom's parents' home, she had seemingly forgotten whatever had caused her strange behaviour.

'Are you feeling any better now?' he asked, stepping out of the car.

She shivered at the memory.

'Yes, a little better now I think.'

'Report the lift problem in the morning when you go in.'

'Don't you worry about that. It'll be the first thing I do!'

He helped her out, and wrapped her coat around her shoulders.

'Try and forget about it for now.'

They linked arms. The shingle drive crunched under Annie's feet, reminding her of the seaside, the beach and happier days.

Tom's mother, Maureen, opened the bright red front door. She hugged Tom affectionately. Her wide smile welcomed them both.

'Oh it's so good to see you Tom darling, and to meet your friend too.' She hugged Annie as warmly as she had hugged Tom. 'Hello dear.'

'Hello Mrs Blake, thank you for inviting me.'

'It's our pleasure. We've been dying to meet you. That's why I asked Tom to bring you along too.'

Vying for space behind Maureen, Richard, Tom's father was eagerly trying to get a good look at the young woman on the doorstep.

'Hello Annie – I'm Richard.' He welcomed his son with a strong handshake and offered his hand to Annie.

Annie whispered to Tom as he shepherded her into the hall.

'This is the moment every new girlfriend dreads.'

'Don't worry - I've done this a thousand times.'

She spun round and scowled at him.

'Only joking – you're the one and only,' he said, holding his hands up in surrender.

For a fleeting moment, Annie wanted his statement to be the truth. She wanted to be the only one he had ever loved.

Maureen closed the front door.

'I've heard so much about you. Tom talks about you all the time.'

'Really? All good things I hope,' said Annie glancing at Tom for affirmation.

Tom shrugged his shoulders and winked at her.

Annie was convinced. It would be no time at all before they would start asking questions about what the future might hold. Nevertheless, the uplifting welcome by

Tom's parents cancelled out any preconception on her side. Ushered into the lounge by Tom's mother, cooing like a mother hen, the tension of the day dissolved.

'Here you are dear,' said Maureen, plumping up the sofa cushions.

Annie found herself enjoying being fussed over, sinking into the sofa, likening it to sitting on a fluffy white cloud.

'Now you just sit there dear, and treat our home as if it were your own.'

Maureen's mothering took Annie back in time. A wave of grief briefly swept over her.

'I'll make some tea while you relax, dear.'

'Sorry?' replied Annie, jolting herself back to the present.

Tom, a few steps behind, was sharing a joke with his father as they entered the room.

Richard excused himself.

'I'll go and help mother in the kitchen.' He shuffled off in ill-fitting slippers, leaving Tom and Annie together on the sofa.

Tom smiled.

'See, they're harmless enough. Great parents. I can see they like you already.'

'They're acting like we're married. God knows what you've been telling them.'

Tom went bright red.

Annie studied the contents of the lounge. Belongings looked out of place. The over-sized furniture, decorative vases and oil lamps looked befitting of a stately home. Crowded with framed photographs of Tom: as a baby, as a teenager wearing rugby kit and on his graduation day, every available surface was covered with images of him. Annie had never thought to ask whether he had brothers or sisters. The photos suggested there were no other siblings.

Muffled conversation wafted through from the kitchen, alongside the sounds of chinking china and laughter. Annie concluded that theirs was a happy family. A touch of envy pricked her heart.

'I like your parents,' she said, unprompted.

'They're a couple of softies.'

'You're very lucky.'

'Tea and biscuits alright then?' he asked, distracting her from the sadness spreading across her face. 'I can ask mum to fix you a sandwich if you're hungry.'

'No thanks, tea and biscuits sounds nice.'

There was no time to change her mind.

Richard and Maureen appeared from the kitchen, both carrying large trays that barely fitted through the width of the doorframe.

Richard placed his heavy tray on the coffee table.

'Here we are. This should keep the wolf from the door!'

'Oh my goodness, you shouldn't have,' exclaimed Annie, her mouth watering at the sight of the spread that had been prepared. 'You've gone to so much trouble!'

The trays were laid out traditionally; teapot, matching cups, sugar bowl and jug on one tray, an abundance of food on the other. Different treats were precariously balanced, high enough to compete with the tiers of a large wedding cake. Sandwiches had been cut into pretty shapes, reminding Annie of a gingerbread baking set she had owned as a child.

Annie debated what her weight would rise to if she ate one of everything, and shot a concerned glance at Tom, who was smiling boyishly back.

Maureen anxiously wrung a white linen napkin between her hands.

'Now are you sure dear, that this is enough for you?'

'Oh yes. This is so kind of you.'

'Tom likes his food dear. Do you like baking?'

Annie looked at Tom, choking briefly on a piece of sponge.

'Actually Mrs Blake, Tom does all the cooking. He finishes work before me most days.'

Maureen looked surprised.

'When we're together that is. I cook for myself of course,' Annie continued, wondering whether Maureen would consider ready meals qualified as cooking.

Tom struggled to hold back his laughter.

'Annie's an amazing cook mum. I can't keep her out of the kitchen!'

Annie discreetly dug Tom in the ribs with her elbow.

'She's especially good at roast dinners,' he went on, sniggering.

Annie's eyes widened with horror.

'I doubt my culinary skills are a patch on this Tom.' She pushed a scone in Tom's face to stop him elaborating further. 'Eat up - your mum's fresh scones will get cold.'

He winked affectionately at Annie. Melted butter dribbled down his chin.

'Mmm, yummy.'

Annie wiped his chin with a linen napkin. She could not remain cross at him. His humour was endearing. Eating until she thought she was going to burst, memories of childhood tea parties entered her mind. Tom's parents picked at the food like two little sparrows, studying Annie as they ate. After copious cups of tea, Annie excused herself and made her way to the bathroom, the lift episode forgotten for a while.

In the hallway, a mahogany cased grandfather clock jostled for space amongst other furniture in the narrow hallway. A large gilt frame on the busy wallpaper opposite Annie, housed a concave mirror, reminiscent of those at fun fairs. Annie's distorted reflection twisted into strange shapes as she passed by to climb the stairs. Once in the bathroom, she retouched her make-up and rearranged her hair. She studied her face in the mirror above the basin. Her expression was one of tension. She prodded the fine lines around her eyes.

A faint rustling sound from somewhere close-by caught her attention. Looking upwards, she pinpointed its whereabouts to the loft. She left the bathroom and hurried downstairs. Reaching the cosy living room once more, laughter from Tom and his parents greeted her. She sat down next to Tom.

'Thank you for such a lovely tea.'

Maureen offered Annie another sandwich.

'Would you like to take some cake with you dear?'

Annie clutched her stomach.

'No thanks, I'm fit to burst. Oh, by the way, there's a strange noise upstairs. I think its coming from the loft.'

'I was investigating that earlier,' said Richard. 'Damn rodents woke me up again last night. I didn't fancy my chances on that old ladder though.'

Tom jumped to his feet.

'Don't worry dad, I'll check on it.' Without another word Tom disappeared upstairs.

Maureen encouraged Annie.

'Eat some more cake dear, it'll only go stale! I'll go and make a fresh pot of tea.' She disappeared into the kitchen leaving Annie politely nibbling at the cheese scones, thinking that if these visits were to become regular, she would have to get out the baggy jumpers from the depths of her wardrobe.

Richard struggled to make conversation.

'Tom hasn't brought a girlfriend home before. He must like you a lot.'

Annie choked again on a mouth full of scone.

'How long have you lived here?' she asked, quickly steering the conversation away from her and Tom.

To ask Richard about the house was a sound decision. Instantly animated about all the decorating he had done, he barely came up for air. His conversation seemed a long way away as Annie's thoughts drifted elsewhere.

She had been trying to work out whether Tom looked like either of his parents, but it struck her that there was no resemblance whatsoever. Richard was of slightly portly build: short grey hair, brown eyes with rosy round cheeks. Maureen was tall, fair-skinned, blonde and slender. Annie wondered whether she had been a dancer in her youth. She was poised, and moved quietly around the house, making no sound on the carpet.

Annie wished Tom would come back. Conversation with Richard was running dry. He fidgeted nervously opposite her, coughing occasionally as if to clear his throat.

Annie spoke first after a moment had lapsed.

'Tom's been gone a long time.'

An awkward silence ensued.

'I'll go and see if he's found anything,' she continued.

Richard stood up.

'Alright love. I'll go and help mother with the tea.' He scurried off to the safety of the kitchen.

When Annie reached the top of the stairs, she called out to Tom.

'Tom. We ought to go soon or we'll miss the band.'

No reply.

'Tom, can you hear me?' She studied the dark void above. The scratching noise had ceased. She hesitated and then slowly climbed the wooden loft ladder, gripping tightly onto the cold metal handrail.

There was still no response. There was no visible light above, only a black hole. She spoke to fill the silence.

'I bet you've found some old comics or toys.'

With no warning, Tom's face, obscured by a child's superhero mask, appeared unexpectedly from out of the shadows. Startled at his sudden appearance, Annie lost her grip of the handrail and toppled backwards.

Reacting instinctively, Tom grabbed her wrist.

'I've got you. Grab the handrail. Try and find a foothold.'

'I'm not a mountaineer,' she yelped, panic in her eyes.

She hung in space for a few seconds, swinging like a giant pendulum, before finding her footing on the narrow rungs. She glared up at him. Forgetting Tom's parents were in earshot, she screamed at Tom.

'You stupid bloody idiot.'

He sheepishly descended the ladder as Annie climbed the last few rungs to the floor before him.

'Sorry. I didn't mean to scare you,' he said, still sporting the mask.

'Sorry?' exclaimed Annie, yanking on the mask and causing the elastic to ping on Tom's ears.

Tom removed the mask.

'You're right. It was stupid of me. I never meant for you to fall.'

A concerned voice came from downstairs.

'Is everything alright up there?'

Tom put his index finger to his lips as if to tell Annie to keep her voice down.

'Everything's fine dad, we'll be down in a mo. I'm just putting the ladder away.'

Annie stood with her hands on her hips.

'Really Tom, I can't believe you did that, especially after what happened earlier,' she hissed at him through clenched teeth.

'I'm really, really sorry. I'd forgotten about that.'

'Well I hadn't.' She stared at him. 'I think we'd better go.'

Tom tried to disguise the incident as they entered the living room. 'We won't stop for any more tea, mum. We ought to be on our way.'

Richard and Maureen looked at Tom quizzically. He put his hands in the air.

'Sorry mum, dad, just clowning around. I made Annie jump.'

Annie raised her eyebrows.

Tom playfully kissed her on the cheek.

'Is he always like this?' asked Annie. Feigning amusement, she attempted to step on Tom's foot. He jumped up and down on one leg pretending to be hurt.

Maureen laughed lightly.

'Precocious and a touch disruptive is what most of his school reports said.'

'That sounds about right,' agreed Annie, giving Tom a knowing look.

Richard changed the subject.

'I hope you pop by again soon.'

They all made their way to the front door.

'It's so good to see Tom has found his perfect match,' added Richard, with a slight glint in his eye.

Annie pretended to kiss Tom's neck.

'He sure has found his match.'

Tom's hurt expression had a comedic value to it.

'Sorry,' said Tom for the umpteenth time, looking at her like a wounded puppy.

She whispered to him as they walked down the path in the dark. 'You'd better sleep with one eye open tonight.'

He was infuriating but infectious. Maybe it was the fact that he had been so concerned for her welfare earlier in the evening, or maybe it was because he had that boyish streak. Whatever character trait it was that Tom possessed that sometimes endeared her to him, she could not remain angry for long. Increasingly, he was there when she needed comforting. She wondered whether one day she might grow to love him.

Chapter 6

The weather had changed again. Pockets of fog hung in the damp air; clinging to houses, hedges and parked cars, slowing Tom's progress as he drove through the city.

'I couldn't resist it.'

'Resist what?' said Annie, distracted by a song on the radio.

Tom wiped condensation from the windscreen with a gloved hand and peered out into the gloom.

'Jumping out at you like that,' he went on, still feeling protective towards her.

'You don't need to mention it again. Anyway, it could have been worse. I could be in hospital now with a broken ankle.'

'You're not cross with me anymore then?'

She applied fresh lipstick.

'It's not genetic you know. Your parents are actually quite lovely!'

'Oh, so the ice queen is melting,' he teased. 'You liked them then?'

'How could I not? They made me feel like part of the family, plus your mum is a great cook.'

The fog was slowly clearing, replaced by a thin veil of drizzle. Rivulets of rain meandered their way down the car windows, creating irregular muddy patterns in the accumulated London grime. Darkness enveloped Tom's car. Annie closed her eyes.

'Bloody weather, I hate it,' she complained. 'I need to get away.'

The memory of the last few days began to filter into her thoughts again, making her head begin to throb relentlessly. Recent events seemed surreal when compared with the normality of her familiar working day. Her experience at the statue seemed more bizarre the more she analysed it, as did the incident in the lift at work. She concluded yet again that Tom's view was probably a reasonable assumption; her ripe imagination was just playing tricks on her troubled mind.

Annie made a concerted effort to push these thoughts away, focusing on work instead. As they approached the music venue, she weighed up the pros and cons of staying at Carlotti's: promotion lay easily within her reach, especially with the firm having recently expanded. Business interests within the Arab states meant that over the next few months she would need to travel overseas regularly to accompany Sir Frank when he flew out to meet potential investors. This appealed to the part of her that liked change and a challenge. The constant hostility between her and jealous colleagues also needed to be addressed. Time away from the office in a fresh working environment would no doubt alleviate the situation, at least temporarily. The strain of remaining calm and efficient was becoming too taxing with her mind preoccupied. She threw herself headlong into her work to distract herself from personal issues, but the thoughts just kept finding a way through no matter how hard she tried to bury them. Perhaps the weird dreams she was having were her body's way of making her pay for repressing these feelings.

She reflected briefly about the incident on the landing at Tom's house. The possibility of falling uncontrollably from the loft ladder suddenly reminded her of a frightening dream from a few nights previously: one that had completely been forgotten until now. In the dream, she had jumped out of a burning single-seated aeroplane and become tangled in her parachute. She hurtled towards the earth, completely out of control. Falling out of bed had woken her; confused and disorientated she found herself bound up in her king-sized duvet, struggling for air.

Suddenly a stone hit the windscreen of Tom's car, thrown up by the wheels of the vehicle in front, bringing Annie back to the present, the drone of passing cars on wet roads having rhythmically lulled her.

Tom glanced across at her.

'You look like you're elsewhere. Are you okay?'

He continued, trying to strike up a conversation.

'I hope you like this band. One of the guitarists is a good friend of mine. They play mainly rock.'

'Oh Tom, not heavy metal. You know I hate that stuff. I can just see you and me, trapped and crushed amongst a bunch of sweaty bodies!'

He laughed.

'It's not that sort of gig.'

'I bet it is. It'll be head-banging, a mosh-pit and idiots playing air guitar.'

'I promise you it'll be fine. I hate that sort of gig too.'

'You'd better be right. I'm not up to anything heavy, it's been one hell of a week.'

'Don't worry. Joe isn't into heavy metal either.'

Feeling slightly more optimistic, Annie looked out of the window again. Heavy rain had replaced the drizzle. She pushed her dark thoughts away and tried to look forward to the live music.

When they arrived at the club in Fulham, Tom parked in a sheltered corner of the busy car park under an ancient oak tree, which was battling with the wind. The last remaining autumn leaves were struggling to hold on to its swaying branches. The mild autumn had now passed, making way for winter. As they walked across the car park, huddled together for protection against the elements, Tom and Annie negotiated small piles of rotting wet leaves and deep puddles.

Situated in an imposing Victorian building, large stained glass windows complemented the club's red brickwork. Above the heavy crimson front door, the club's name had been beautifully crafted into coloured glass: The Gentleman's Castle.

'Strange name,' Annie commented, eager to get into the warm.

Tom opened the heavy front door and held it open for her to pass through.

'Used to be a brothel,' explained Tom, as they entered the busy lounge bar.

'Maybe I could do some moonlighting here then,' joked Annie.

'I said it used to be a brothel,' said Tom, playfully smacking her backside. 'Though I expect you'd make a killing with a body like yours.'

The interior boasted a vaulted ceiling painted with murals of curvaceous semi-naked women and strong muscular men, barely dressed to protect their modesty. The painted figures reclined, coiled around each other in erotic poses. Supported by solid marble columns, embellished with Roman scrolls and fig leaves, the ceilings arched high above them. Intimate booths, carved in solid oak with scarlet seat cushions invited them to sit and revel in the luxurious surroundings. Over the tables, elaborate oil lamps hung on sturdy brass chains. A large group of people was standing in front of a raised stage at one end of the lounge. Annie noticed the interior had not been touched for many years: faded art nouveau wallpaper and heavy draped curtains complemented each other. Annie chose a booth and waited for Tom to return from the crowded bar.

In a far corner of the lounge, an oak staircase curved upwards behind heavy red velvet drapes. The banisters culminated at the bottom of the staircase with a beautifully carved newel post in the shape of a voluptuous woman, who looked more like a figurehead on a ship's galleon.

Annie's mind drifted off to a bygone era when corseted women led their prospective clients through the plush curtains and up the winding staircase. Imagining anticipation in the eyes of men and women, hearing the laughing and flirting of a time gone by, Annie was fantasising about being seduced by a prospective lover when Tom returned.

He bowed like a nobleman as though fitting his character to their surroundings, and chinked glasses with hers.

'Your drink, m'lady.'

Annie's lover faded into the mists of time and she brushed off Tom's play-acting.

'This is quite a venue. How did you hear of it?'

'One of my regular haunts, and packed as usual. We're lucky to get seats.'

People were jostling for space at the bar, as the band's roadies were busy setting up and sound testing. Annie settled into the soft cushions of the booth, the red wine taking effect quickly and coursing through her body like fire in her veins. She began to feel a little more relaxed, her worries slipping away as the band started up; a warming glow comforting her.

'Which one's your friend?'

'The hairy one.'

'They're all hairy – except the backing singers!'

Tom pointed out the other band members, whilst Annie listened and sipped her wine. The two feline backing singers teased the audience with provocative moves from their position at the side of the stage.

Tom sat facing Annie, on an equally welcoming cushion. Her expression had softened. In the mellow lighting, Tom observed how any arrogance and feistiness seemed to have abandoned her, replaced instead by deep sorrow in her golden eyes. When she looked across the table at him, he once again had an instinctive feeling that she needed looking after, and that he wanted to be her protector. He studied her full, rose-coloured lips and became lost in the moment, not hearing the music or the crowd.

Annie unconsciously ran her fingers through her chestnut hair as she spoke, brushing the thick waves away from her perfectly proportioned face. She looked over towards the people mingling in the club; oblivious to how affected Tom was by the way she looked and moved. His gaze wandered from her neck down to where her cleavage peeped modestly from the neckline of her crisp white cotton blouse. Any residual tension between them dissipated away as the effects of the claret took hold. Her full lips tempted him more as she reapplied more lipstick.

'You're so beautiful. You should smile more often.'

She let him take her hands in his.

'You're not bad yourself.' She reached forward and placed a soft kiss on his lips.

The band members rocked back and forwards as they played guitar, their long hair a contrast to the clean-shaven executives Annie was accustomed to rubbing shoulders with. The two willowy backing singers swayed like synchronised cobras, harmonising and hypnotising men in the audience.

At the end of the first set, Tom's friend bowed to enthusiastic applause, jumped lightly down from the stage, and youthfully ambled over to where Tom and Annie were sitting.

'Hi guys, so glad you could make it. Wondered whether you would because we had a bit of a moment on the way down - a tree down on the North Circular.' He took Annie's hand affectionately in his. 'And you must be Annie – it's great to finally meet you. I hope this is your sort of scene.' He sat between them on a low stool, talking to Tom about gigs and pedal boards, a world that Annie knew little about.

The man was rugged, in his late fifties, with a beaming smile and expressive brown eyes. Drenched with perspiration, his hair tumbled into wet chocolate brown curls either side of his face. He was charismatic and had dominated the stage. Annie surmised that he would have many tales to tell of drink, drugs and wild parties, and that he would probably lose all zest for life if he could not perform. After a few moments, he got up.

'See you later guys.' He leapt lithely back onto the stage, beckoning the rest of the band who were gathered at the bar. The backing girls shook off their admirers and provocatively strutted to the stage again, much to the pleasure of their male fans.

After a few more songs, a young woman was introduced to the audience, entering from the side of the stage: her hair a mass of unkempt golden waves. Her piercing blue eyes fleetingly reminded Annie of someone, but the moment was quickly gone. The girl's powerful voice suddenly filled the room, silencing the audience.

'Wow! I've got goose-bumps,' said Annie, when applause had died down.

'Great, isn't she?' agreed Tom.

The young woman left the stage, blending humbly in with the audience.

Leaving Tom to chat with other friends in the audience, Annie stood up and went in search of the toilets, her head whirring from the effects of the wine. On entering, she passed an older woman neatly folding paper towels. She looked up as Annie entered, looking startled and hurriedly making the sign of the cross across her chest with her hand.

The red wine that had warmed Annie's body suddenly lost some of its potency. Feeling hot, she splashed some water on her face and looked at her reflection in the large mirror above the washbasin, conscious that the woman was watching her intently with beady eyes. Pretending not to notice, Annie turned her attention to the décor.

A small fountain with coloured lights was situated in a corner of the washroom, illuminating the bottom of a small rock pool. Iridescent tropical fish darted amongst pebbles and shells. In the bottom of the pool coins twinkled. Making a wish on a penny seemed alive and well. Polished wood panelling, brass fittings and marble columns reiterated the decor a few floors above.

Finally the woman stood up and left. At the same time, two girls entered, laughing and chatting to each other. Annie blinked and wiped the water from her eyes. The girls were well spoken, but Annie noticed their conversation seemed strangely old-fashioned. She remained next to them at the washbasins. Their reflections were pale and ethereal. Annie splashed her face with more water and blinked the water away so as to see more clearly.

The first girl to speak was agitated.

'Oh, what will Daddy say if I take Edgar home? Do you think he'll approve? I couldn't bear it if he sent Edgar away.'

'Oh I shouldn't worry, he'll be more interested in asking questions about what's going on at the Front than the fact you've been walking out with him and sending him love letters,' said the second girl.

Neither girl seemed to notice Annie.

Sighing deeply, the first girl whimpered.

'Oh I do hope you're right Gladys. I have no idea when Edgar will be on leave again. All that waiting and worrying – it's more than I can bear.'

Fascinated by their quaint way of speaking, but not wanting to appear nosy, Annie studied their reflections in the mirror. Both in their early twenties, their pallor made them appear older. Both sported very dated hairstyles: the taller of the two, who had been the second to speak, had red long hair tied up with a ribbon and a small bunch of artificial daisies. Her dress, a shade of emerald green with fitted long sleeves, was a complete and striking contrast to her flaming curls.

The other girl, who had been talking about her boyfriend, was shorter, with brown shoulder length curly hair. Her dress was a similar style to the other girl's, but red in colour, with a small bow on both hip pockets.

Amused by their strange clothes, Annie made an instant assumption that they were on their way to a fancy dress party. She retouched her make up so that she could spend as long as possible listening in to their conversation.

'What do you think of the shade of my face powder, Gladys? It's brunette. I think rose peach would suit you, don't you think?'

'Oh, are they Tokalon's new shades? Margaret mentioned them when we were all in the shelter. I rather like them. Would you like to try my lipstick?'

'Are you going to a party?' asked Annie, her curiosity getting the better of her.

Geraldine turned around and searched the room, appearing to look straight through Annie.

'Did you hear something, Gladys?'

Gladys shrugged and carried on preening herself.

Annie began to feel odd: disorientated and separated from the real world. The temperature drop was uncomfortable, and not dissimilar to the sudden chill she had felt in the lift at work. She wanted to speak again but felt detached from the environment around her.

A low whining siren percolated through the washroom Tannoy.

'Oh not again, this is so tiresome. Just when I was having a good time!' said Gladys. 'Come along, maybe we'll only have to take cover for a short time for once!'

'Mustn't forget these,' said Geraldine, snatching two square canvas bags from the washstand.

Grabbing their coats and pocketing their make-up, the girls jostled out of the washroom pulling grotesque, goggle-eyed rubber masks from the square bags without giving Annie a second glance. The spot where the two girls had been standing had turned icy cold. Annie shuddered.

There was a sudden loud knock on the outer door.

'Annie. It's me - Tom.' He pushed the door open and peered round.

'Didn't you hear the fire alarm? There's been a bomb scare.' He grabbed her arm and pulled her through the doorway, into the throng of anxious clientele, bar staff and band members.

'I heard a siren, but it didn't sound anything like this,' said Annie, noticing that the deafening sound in the rest of the pub was a contrast to the eerie wailing in the bathroom. 'Those girls must have found a quick way out,' she continued, feeling crushed and claustrophobic in the scurrying crowd.

'What girls?'

'The girls that came out of the loos just before me. The ones in fancy dress.'

'No-one else came out before you.'

'They had strange rubber masks.'

'I knew we should have gone easy on the wine,' said Tom.

'You are kidding?' asked Annie, trying to keep up with Tom in the surge of people.'

'Been seeing ghosts again?'

A shiver ran down Annie's back.

Chapter 7

Annie woke up the next morning, glad to be alone in her own bed. Tom had not protested when she had asked to be dropped back at her flat instead of spending the night with him. She lay staring at the time changing on the digital display of the bedside clock, thinking about the peculiar events of the night before.

After being hastily evacuated from the pub, she had continued to search the fire assembly point and car park for the two costumed girls. Somehow, despite it being dark and blustery, she had thought they would have been visible in their vibrant clothes and bizarre masks. However, they seemed to have slipped away unnoticed. Why had Tom not seen them inside the building? In the light of a new day, Annie was still slightly perplexed. Tom was insistent that he would have noticed the girls come out of the bathroom and that, as he hadn't seen them, they were no more than another product of Annie's overactive imagination. He had declined to mention to the venue manager that there could still be two girls inside the building. Feeling patronised and slightly embarrassed, Annie had changed the subject quickly.

She turned off the alarm and got out of bed, going through her usual daily routine on autopilot. Her head pounded and, despite having had very little to drink the previous night, she felt hung-over. Opening the chrome bathroom cabinet door, she fumbled for painkillers amongst prescription bottles and expensive brands of cosmetics. Studying her face in the mirror, she prodded the fine lines around her eyes and then gently applied cream to the areas that concerned her the most. Once again, she thought back to the previous evening and the dark-haired girl's strange hairstyle, before noticing her own hair sticking up: an irritating kink needing firm persuasion.

'I think I need a holiday,' she said to her reflection. 'What do you think?'

The comical reflection stared back, large blobs of moisturiser still in need of attention.

Annie tried on different outfits before settling for a variation of her usual black jacket and skirt. Her business suits were made-to-measure. They hung in a crisp line inside her wardrobe like a queue of funeral mourners. She selected a change of clothes for the evening, remembering that Tom had asked her to go to a fireworks display by the river when she had finished work.

Annie's headache made her feel bad-tempered.

'God, what a big kid he is,' she complained aloud to the full-length hall mirror on her way out. She began to think that she should not string Tom along, but that his childish glee at the simple things in life distracted her and she knew she needed to let someone in. She just was not sure that he was that someone. Nevertheless, Tom's antics sometimes made her feel warm inside, and the face in the mirror was so much more attractive when she thought kindly things.

Slamming the door on the way out, a sense of shame still lingered. It took courage to admit it. Leaving the plush apartment, she thought about the power she had possessed over all the men she had ever dated. She longed for something more. It would be nice to be in love.

A session with Dr. Edwards sprung to mind. She needed an ally. He always listened, passive and thoughtful, trying to get beneath the layers of the brick wall she had erected over the years.

'Why am I still so unhappy? I thought I'd moved on.'

'Grieving is a slow process, Annie.'

'I know, but it's more than that. I can't quite put my finger on it, but I feel like I'm looking for something else.'

'Terrible though it is to lose your grandfather, in my opinion your depression is far more deep-rooted. You were very young when your parents died.'

She was sinking fast. It was like drowning in a sea of mud, where the more she struggled, the quicker she was sucked downwards. She would have to tell Dr. Edwards that she had been seeing and sensing people close by that no one else could see. At least he had seen worse cases than her, whereas Tom, despite his reassuring words, must surely be thinking Annie was a lost cause.

Conscious that she had been drifting, Annie forced herself back to the day at hand, and continued on her way to work, walking again her familiar route as she had the previous day. Having taken the same route for several years meant that there were familiar faces as well as many new ones. Over time, she had made up little stories about the people who passed her by: what sort of lives they lived, how happy they were and how many were lonely like her. Detached from the people around her, Annie lived in a permanent feeling of limbo and loss.

By the time she reached work, she had compartmentalised her personal worries and had started to focus on work issues instead. As she approached the front of the office building she noticed Samuel, the door attendant, talking to a passer-by. The man moved on and Samuel turned to face Annie. He smiled.

'Morning ma'am.'

'Good morning,' replied Annie, taken aback at her own friendly tone.

Samuel seemed more surprised. He seized the moment.

'Fresh today, isn't it ma'am? It should be nice later though.' He rubbed his gloved hands together in a vain attempt to warm them whilst stamping his frozen feet on the ground.

'Umm – sorry, I've forgotten your name,' said Annie.

'Drayton. Samuel Drayton, at your service ma'am.' He doffed his top hat in his usual way.

'We've never spoken before have we?' asked Annie, feeling slightly embarrassed.

'No ma'am, I don't believe we have, but I'm sure you're a busy lady and you have more important things on your mind,' he added, as if to excuse her past ignorance.

Scanning Samuel's uniform from top to toe, Annie was drawn to the long row of medals on his chest. Noticing her scrutiny, Samuel humbly dismissed them.

'That was a long time ago, ma'am. I was just doing my job like all the others.'

'Just like my grandfather,' commented Annie, studying Samuel's heavily lined face for the first time. She cupped one of the medals gently in her hand to examine it in more detail. 'He was a pilot.'

She noticed that despite Samuel's smart appearance, one of his leather gloves was worn: several of his fingers were peeping out from the tips of the gloves and were blue from the cold. She was about to continue the story of her grandfather when she noticed that she was being watched from the reception desk inside Carlotti's.

'I must go,' she said abruptly. 'I'll be late.'

'Yes ma'am. Have a good day.'

Samuel took off his top hat as Annie disappeared inside the building, scratching his head in disbelief.

As Annie crossed the foyer, the receptionist was chatting to the security guard as he leant on the clear glass counter.

'Did you see what I just saw?' whispered the security guard to the receptionist.

'Did she just acknowledge Samuel?'

'It must have been a trick of the light,' added the guard.

Both sniggered behind their hands.

Continuing across the remainder of the foyer, Annie considered her last experience in the lift. The lift attendant stood in his usual place. She hesitated before stepping into the confined space, but eventually forced herself inside. She closed her eyes. The lift sailed

75

smoothly up to the eleventh floor, delivering Annie safely to her office. She breathed a sigh of relief, ready for another day's work.

This was not just another day though. She did not want to be on the eleventh floor. It occurred to her as she walked past hostile eyes that no one probably cared whether she was there or not. It had not mattered before, but somehow it did matter now. Adept at covering her personal insecurities with a tough suit of armour in the office, she had courted this hostility with an opinionated and aloof attitude amongst her colleagues. Now the tables were turned, her armour did not seem so impenetrable and she felt extremely vulnerable. She realised she had only herself to blame. Scurrying towards her office, any residual confidence drained away with every step. Her feet felt heavy, as though encased in lead boots, and the corridor stretching in front of her resembled a tightrope from which she dared not fall.

Disgruntled customers and colleagues plagued the day, making every small issue seem like a major problem. She knew it would only take one mistake to send Sir Frank into a rage: she had seen it happen with other colleagues. Seeing her boss marching with intent past well-ordered desks was a sure sign that someone was about to get a reprimand.

The afternoon was nearly over when Annie heard the sound of Sir Frank's unmistakable footsteps. He did not stop at the open plan office, nor turn the sharp ninety degrees outside Annie's room to march down the long corridor to the boardroom. Instead, her door shook on its hinges as he slammed it behind him, making his entrance. The unexpected storm he brought with him shocked her so much she dropped the papers she was holding, scattering them across the normally spotless and well-ordered desk.

He loomed over her like an eagle looking down at its captured prey.

'What the hell are you playing at, young lady? I expect mistakes from all the other imbeciles that work for me, but not from you!'

Annie sat motionless, stunned into silence for a few seconds. Sophie crouched down behind her computer screen and pretended to work.

Sir Frank paced the office waving his arms in the air.

'It is your job to get things right, not to create problems!'

'I'm sorry sir...I don't understand,' protested Annie, standing up to face him.

'Listen Annie, it simply won't do. Clients have been complaining all day. Some have even received the wrong contracts: you have mixed up strictly confidential documents and God knows who has hold of them!' He raised himself up to full height.

'It must be a mistake sir...'

'Are you calling me a liar?'

Annie blushed.

'Oh no...I wouldn't dream of...'

'I should think not!' he interrupted.

He looked as though he was about to burst as his face turned a livid red.

Sir Frank had never spoken to Annie in that tone before. Glancing through the glass in her office door, Annie was painfully aware that all eyes were trained in her direction. She slumped back down into her chair and let out a deep sigh.

Sir Frank turned on his heels.

'Go home, Annie. Take some time off. Your mistakes could cost us millions!'

'But sir...'

He turned to face her again.

'Enough. I'll send word when...and if, you can come back.'

As Sir Frank strode out of her office, Annie could hear the thump of his stick slamming on desks as he passed.

'Get on with your work! This isn't a circus.'

The shocked silence of the office reverted to the general hubbub of typing, shuffling of papers and muttered comments.

Sophie sprung to her feet and closed the door quietly, shutting out the enquiring eyes of the general office. She gathered up the scattered documents, trying to restore some semblance of order.

'I'll deal with these. Don't worry Annie, it'll get sorted out – one way or another.'

Annie remained slumped in her chair.

'Don't you move, I'll get some coffee,' added Sophie.

If Annie had been asked later how the rest of her day had gone, she would have no detailed memory of it. She refused to accept responsibility for all the things Sir Frank had accused her of but had no choice. She added the prospect of unemployment to her list of problems and resigned herself to the stressful and restless weeks stretching progressively further ahead of her.

Chapter 8

Annie did not leave immediately, choosing to stay and tie up loose ends: replying to last minute emails and arranging paperwork into neat piles, as she always did at the end of each working day. For a while, things were going to be very different.

After putting on her coat, she stood for a few minutes by her office window and watched the stream of yellow headlights in the street below, converging from opposite directions like two duelling centipedes.

Sir Frank had not returned for a second onslaught. His message was clear and she had already come to terms with his ferocious outburst and what it might mean if she were not allowed to return to her post.

Sophie had been a godsend, patrolling the office door like a guard dog when anyone tried to enter. Annie added a mental note to her spinning brain to treat Sophie better in the future. Without Sophie's company the rest of the day would have been unbearable. The constant whisperings from the office pool sounding like a pit of hissing snakes had almost sent her over the edge.

Standing at the large window looking over the magnificent London skyline, Annie briefly marvelled at the vibrant purplish orange fog created by the fireworks illuminating the night sky. Here and there, rockets pierced through the canopy, leaving behind them trails of red, gold and silver as they arced through the darkness.

Turning on her heels and closing her office door behind her, Annie marched to the lift. Although it had only been a day since she had been stuck between floors, nevertheless, it wasn't in her character to run away. Watching the floors slip slowly by on the illuminated monitor, Annie grasped the polished brass handrail with one hand and her recharged torch in the other, her thumb hovering over the power button every time the lights in the ceiling dimmed briefly or the lift shuddered.

The chance of meeting the ghostly figure from the night before was right at the forefront of her thoughts. He did not appear in any guise, which was just as well: as her nerves were frayed and she could only cope with so much in one day.

As soon as Annie stepped out of the lift into the foyer, it became obvious that news had travelled fast. The security guard and receptionist smiled nervously as she passed by, but said nothing. Annie found it difficult to maintain composure; her shoulders and neck stiff with the tension of the day and her limbs feeling heavy and weak. She was beginning to wonder whether maybe the chain of events was her karma for all the people she had mistreated or ignored, but immediately dismissed such a ridiculous thought. It was a result of over-working herself to the point of collapse, nothing more.

Samuel was in his usual spot. He shifted his weight from one foot to the other, unconsciously polishing his shoes on the back of the legs of his trousers. Annie looked down at his feet and managed a smile.

'I believe you're wearing a hole in the step.'

He smiled.

'I've been here a long time, ma'am.'

'That you have,' she acknowledged.

'I hope you don't mind me saying ma'am, but word got down here earlier and I wanted to say...er...I get a strong feeling it'll all sort itself out. By the end of this year I reckon you'll be flying.'

'Flying - what do you mean?'

'I mean flying - as in happy and on cloud nine.'

'Oh I see. Strange you should say that though, I spent a lot of time in my grandfather's plane when I was younger.'

'Really?'

'He taught me the basics. He was in the RAF.'

'You were in safe hands then.'

Annie stood thoughtfully for a few seconds, seemingly with her mind drifting off to another place again.

'Anyway, must be on my way.'

'Goodnight, ma'am.' Samuel watched her walk off, noticing that her stride was not as purposeful as usual. In his opinion, one could tell a lot about a person by the way they walked.

Considering what a dreadful day it had been, Samuel's words had lifted her mood. She found herself reflecting about what he had said as she got further away from Carlotti's.

Snuggling her face deep into her mother's lilac angora scarf, she felt secure, like an unborn child in the womb. She tried to recapture the memory of her mother's perfume. Imagining the scent of roses, she was back in a garden, surrounded by a riotous display of Busy Lizzies,

Hollyhocks and climbing yellow roses, which grew around the front door. An icy gust of wind woke her from her happy daydream, leaving her mother in the perfumed garden until next time.

She took her time walking to the tube station. It occurred to her that she had not called Tom to tell him about what had happened and felt no need to do so now. It was irrelevant. He could not change the outcome. She continued to reflect on happier times for the duration of her journey to the underground, her heels echoing on the wet pavement.

Although not raised in London, many elements of it reminded her of when she was young; in particular, the old market hall she passed through regularly after leaving work. This dissected the middle of a department store, remaining open when the store had closed for business. Quaint shops ran the full length in the style of a mock Georgian street. The tiled mosaic floor boasted original advertising within its swirling patterns.

Saturdays had always been the day she looked forward to: there was an order to the day, come rain or shine. Donning polished sandals, with shiny hair in plaits, she would walk to town with her parents past the huge parish church; out of which sometimes a happy bride and groom would emerge, the bride dressed like a fairy princess.

Then there would be a trip to the fruit and vegetable market, in the aptly named Market Street. She could hear the traders competing with each other.

'Juicy oranges come 'n get yer juicy oranges, pound to you, love.'

'Narnas, bunch of narnas, come on, fill yer basket sweetheart.'

In the depths of the market was a pet shop. The building was long and narrow. It looked like the filling in a sandwich, the two large pebble-dashed shops either side resembling thick slices of brown bread. It was one of Annie's favourite places. The deeper one went into the shop, the narrower it became. Becoming friendly with the little kittens in cages had been a mistake. The following week Annie would run to their cages only to find they had gone to new homes.

The fish shop was the next stop. The kittens seemed fortunate compared to the dead fish lying on a cold slab: mouths wide-open, eyes cloudy and staring. The smell of the fish shop had made Annie feel sick, but this was soon forgotten when she reached the arcade, similar to the one she was walking through now.

The arcade of her childhood was like Aladdin's cave. High in the wall had been a giant clock, which chimed every hour. She would wait patiently for the wooden figures on rails, to appear through one door as each hour chimed and disappear through another. There had been plenty of treasures to see: candy floss spun in big metal drums, miniature perfume bottles lining the shelves of an exotic Eastern stall, and a line of donkeys, each with his or her name on a headband. For ten pence, Annie could ride the length of the arcade on one of these donkeys at a leisurely pace, peeping into the little shop windows at tempting sweets, colourful ribbons and wooden toys.

On the long walk home her mother and father would pick up the weekly food shopping from their favourite delicatessen. The assistant standing at a marble counter was plump and cheerful, and wore a striped apron over a crisp white tunic and white trousers. He was adept at his job: patting butter into rectangles with ridged wooden spatulas, which he would then wrap with greaseproof paper and string, and cutting large slabs of cheese with a thin piece of wire. It was possible to choose between brown or white eggs from the high shelf behind the ruddy-faced shopkeepers.

Annie put her memories behind her. It was a ten-minute walk to the tube station, so she quickened her pace to get warm. When Tom had enthused about the fireworks display, reminiscing about the straw-filled guys he had built with his schoolmates, Annie had felt sad that she had lost the enthusiasm for family-orientated events. She had tried to think of every possible excuse not to go. Despite the breath-taking spectacle of the fireworks, she did not like the crashing and banging noises that accompanied them. Whilst most children screamed with excitement, she watched, her whole body tense, terrified that one might spin off and hit her.

With this in mind, and the sound of whizzing and screeching increasing in volume above her, she walked quickly: past designer boutiques, along cobbled mews and alleyways. This small backwater of London retained its timeless charm. Old gas lamps on top of ornate iron lampposts remained in situ, converted to electricity many decades before.

Just as Annie reached the safety of the underground, an almighty explosion caused her to jump as a display of white light illuminated the night sky above her. A rocket crackled, fizzed, and then descended to earth with a whining scream. She scuttled hastily down the first few steps, not wanting to hang around in case the rocket landed too close for comfort.

Inside the tube station, the noise of the fireworks was suddenly much quieter, muffled by the thickness of the walls. Littered with leaves deposited there by the persistent blustery wind, the metal strips on the edge of the steps glistened, defying any traveller to reach the lower levels without slipping. Apart from a small amount of wear and tear, the station had escaped vandalism and graffiti, and still retained its original Victorian tiles, architectural features and advertising boards.

The station seemed deserted. Normally Annie shared the stairway with a handful of people, and paid little attention to the surroundings, but on this night there was no one in sight. The modern advertisements at the upper end of the stairs had fallen victim to a leaking ceiling and were peeling away from the walls. A polite notice, glued adjacent to the offending posters, instructed the public about impending repairs. She studied the adverts running the full length of the stairway. The lower she descended the more dated the adverts became, some of them illustrating branding that, as far as she could recall, no longer existed. Models demonstrating the products were also from a different era: women dressed in overalls and strange turbans, and RAF pilots standing proudly next to vintage aircraft stared back at her. Slogans such as "Britain Needs YOU" were plastered across the images. Annie made the assumption that the adverts were promotional material for the Imperial War Museum, and made a mental note to mention them to Tom.

She reached the foot of the stairs and crossed the foyer; which was deserted, taking her ticket from her purse. Stopping at where the automatic turnstiles were normally located, she was disorientated for a few seconds. In place of the turnstiles, a wooden structure similar in size to a red telephone box had been erected. Leaning on the handle of a broom next to the hut, an elderly man wearing the semblance of a dated railway uniform stared back at her: cigarette in mouth and cap cocked to one side of his head.

'Ticket please?'

She approached him tentatively, holding out her ticket for him to inspect.

'Where's the automatic barrier?'

He scratched his head, and stubbed out his cigarette on the floor with a worn out boot.

'Automatic barrier? What's one of those then?' he asked, with a quizzical expression.

'I usually put my ticket in a machine.'

'I don't usually work at this 'ere station, miss. Maybe one of them bombs has damaged it.'

'Bombs?' exclaimed Annie. 'Oh my goodness, I didn't know there had been a bomb scare.'

He scratched his head again and lit another cigarette.

'Don't make me laugh girl, there's been hundreds of bleedin' bombs.' He looked at her suspiciously. ''Ere - how come you ain't heard the bombs then?' he said, gesticulating back towards the stairs.

'Maybe I missed them,' she humoured him, deciding that he was a bit unhinged. She thrust her ticket at him. 'Hurry please, or I'll miss my train.'

'There ain't no bleedin' trains tonight, I'm just 'ere clearing up,' he answered, beginning to sound irritated. He turned her ticket over and examined it. 'What sort of ticket's this then?'

'It's my Oyster card.'

'I can't let you through with this. Where d'yer get it?' He thrust it back into her hand.

Annie looked at her ticket and back at him in disbelief.

'And what did you mean – no trains? Is it because of the bomb scare?' she suggested, not wanting to argue.

''Ere, you're acting real strange. You'd better not be a bleedin' Jerry in disguise,' he said looking at her through narrowed eyes.

'I don't know anyone called Jerry. I'll be getting on now.' She turned her back on him and started to walk briskly away.

'Oi, I told you there's no bloomin' trains,' he shouted. 'Come back 'ere or I'll fetch a bobby!' he shouted again, his voice fading as she walked hurriedly on.

As Annie reached the last flight of steps, she looked over her shoulder, hoping that he was not following. He seemed to have shuffled off somewhere and was nowhere in sight.

At the foot of the stairs, the platform Annie was familiar with was cordoned off with a frayed rope tied between two metal posts. She followed diversion signs to another platform and sat on a wooden bench, leaning her head against the wall, tired and agitated. She looked around for something to distract her, believing that a train would arrive. A distant rumble reassured her that the old man had clearly been talking rubbish: trains were running in adjacent tunnels at least.

The platform was poorly maintained: dimly lit, filthy. Posters and a tube map were almost illegible on the walls. The tiles lining the tunnel were cracked and blackened, some having fallen off completely. Several bedraggled rats were foraging amongst litter on the train rails. She watched, as one stuck its nose inside an empty paper bag.

Annie suddenly sensed that she was not alone on the platform, although she had not noticed anyone on her arrival. She looked around and spotted a man on the platform a small distance away. He was partially in shadow. The lights crackling and flickering in ageing light fittings, made it difficult to see his features clearly. A plume of smoke from his cigarette rose slowly upwards to the vaulted ceiling. He turned slightly, and at this point, Annie could see, that what she had thought was a cigarette, was in fact a bulbous pipe, which the man was puffing on. He was in uniform, carrying a square box on a long strap over one shoulder. He remained motionless looking at the advertisements on the opposite wall, smoke billowing in short bursts from his pipe.

The square bag reminded Annie of the ones the two girls in the pub had been carrying. She darted a glance across to have another look, only to see that the man had gone. She stood up and wandered up and down, uneasy at being alone and surprised that she had not seen him leave. Suddenly, a muffled message came over the Tannoy: emergency repairs were being undertaken so passengers would need to use an alternative route.

Annie left the platform and retraced her steps, annoyed that her evening was being disrupted. The only saving grace was that she would maybe not need to endure the fireworks. Once off the platform she noticed that the rope had gone. Confused, she looked around, wondering whether she had lost her bearings. She looked back to the platform she had just left, but a bolted iron door now blocked her way.

Before she could recalibrate her thoughts, a train glided into the adjacent platform. Quickly checking the overhead announcement board was correct; she stepped into an empty carriage, the door closing smoothly behind her. Half expecting the uniformed man to come running out of the shadows to catch the train, she watched the platform slip away as the train gathered speed into a dark tunnel. She took her pick of the empty seats. Rush hour debris littered the floor. A solitary cola can rolled backwards and forwards as the train rocked gently on the tracks, clattering as it banged against metal seat legs.

The gentle rocking of the train quickly soothed Annie into a light sleep and she immediately began to dream that she was still sitting on the bench on the underground platform watching the uniformed man. She could not get a proper look at his face. She rummaged in her handbag for the little torch she carried with her on dark nights, only to find instead, some of her childhood toys: bag of marbles, a bracelet, her favourite doll. She accepted her toys as though to find them was rational, and dug deeper in the bag, uncovering a pot of bubble mixture. This too seemed rational. She removed the seal, pulled out a plastic wand and blew clusters of soapy bubbles, which glistened with beautiful mother of pearl colours as they rose to the ceiling. They floated towards the man, magically growing larger in size until they were several feet in diameter, bouncing unharmed against the vaulted roof of the station ceiling. They hung, like giant bunches of pearlescent grapes above his head.

The man looked up at the bubbles, and then he looked to see where the bubbles had originated from, finally fixing his gaze on Annie. He removed his cap so that his face was in full light. They exchanged glances, and at the instant his blue eyes met hers, Annie realised that the man was the double of the pilot depicted in the bronze memorial on the Victoria Embankment. Instinctively, she also knew that it was his ghostly presence in the lift at work. As her mind attempted to piece together the jigsaw, the gigantic bubbles began to shrink and pop and the man's image faded.

She was woken abruptly from the dream by the train's brakes squealing as it began to slow for the next stop. She checked the contents of her bag. Her childhood toys had seemed as real as the day she had last played with them, but now they had gone. Something had leaked from her make-up bag, covering her purse, phone and other belongings in a sticky mess, its fragrance similar to washing-up liquid and unlike anything she could recall carrying with her. She searched for the offending item but everything was intact. She was not frightened anymore. Bizarre though everything seemed, the only thing that troubled her was whether she would see the man again.

Chapter 9

When Annie reached the end of her short journey, Tom was already waiting for her at Putney Bridge station. As usual, he had been thoughtful enough to bring a scarf, gloves, warm furry boots and a large flask of coffee for Annie. Tom's attentions were sweet but sometimes his eagerness to please her was suffocating and made him seem a little pathetic.

Tom hugged her affectionately.

'Glad you came. It's going to be spectacular,' he added, offering her the scarf.

'No thanks, I'm not cold.'

'Sorry, I didn't mean to be ungrateful,' she said, realising she had been mean to him. 'Thank you.' Her fingers were beginning to tingle with the cold. 'I'll ignore your fashion faux-pas this time,' she went on, making a joke of it. She cringed at the eclectic collection of outerwear he offered her. 'I'll give the boots a miss.'

He gently wrapped the soft scarf around her neck.

'At least wear the scarf - the colour suits you.'

She linked arms with him, feeling vaguely ashamed, glad of his company.

As they walked to the Embankment to watch the fireworks with other Londoners already gazing up at the exploding sky, Annie fleetingly wished that they were watching from another place: she could be watching from the memorial, near to the mysterious stranger that was becoming increasingly part of her daily thoughts. She felt drawn to the spot and wanted to see the statue again.

The temperature had dropped quickly since they had began walking.

'I think the boots might be a good idea after all. My toes are numb.'

'You can be so stubborn sometimes.'

'All right, Mr Know-It-All. So you were right, for once.' Hopping around on one leg, Annie pulled on the thick woolly socks and grabbed at the boots Tom held aloft.

'Give them to me, you idiot.'

'Such politeness,' he jested, as he continued to hold them at arm's length. 'Say please, and I might let you have them.'

'Please, darling.'

'Wasn't hard was it?' He planted a kiss on her cheek before she had time to resist.

'You are such a child sometimes, Tom,' she said, feigning annoyance.

Wearing the boots, she was instantly warmer. As they walked to the Thames, Annie winced at the large explosions and crackling noises of rockets, gripping tightly onto Tom's arm. Cascading arcs of gold and silver, blue, red and green showered down, mirrored in the river. Tom joined other spectators with a show of appreciation, clapping and cheering every time a particularly bright firework peppered across the sky with a deafening bang. His boyish face was one of his finer qualities. It made Annie smile.

'I'll go and get us some snacks,' offered Tom as the fireworks began to subside. 'You wait here.'

'Nothing too greasy!'

He disappeared into the crowd.

The majority of spectators were beginning to disperse. As the firework display died down, some people went off in search of warmth in nearby cafes and bars. Annie observed couples holding hands or linking arms, thinking that, in time, familiarity and boredom would cause the inevitable demise of most of their relationships.

Tom returned with a beaming smile and hands full of fast food, interrupting her cynical thoughts.

'This will warm you up.' He ushered her to sit on a wooden bench behind them, and enthusiastically shared the burgers and cones of chips he'd managed to find.

'There wasn't much choice I'm afraid,' he replied, with grease dripping down his chin.

Annie began to pick at the chips, hunger winning the day.

'Not bad for fast food. Surprisingly good actually,' she admitted, her hunger abating with every bite.

Tom mopped her chin with a paper napkin and poured coffee from the flask.

'They didn't sell bibs,' he joked.

He slid along the bench out of reach as Annie attempted to dig him in the ribs.

The lingering smell of fireworks and a residual pink fog hung in the air. With only an occasional distant pop from fireworks let off in gardens across the river, the night sky was quiet again, illuminated only by light from office blocks and street lamps.

Annie decided to tell Tom about the events of the day. He would find out eventually, were he to call her office phone. Tom was visibly shocked that she had been disciplined.

'What brought things to such a head?'

'Quite honestly, I didn't have my eye on the ball. I made a few mistakes. Big ones.'

'That's not like you.'

'I know.'

'What are you going to do?'

'I can't tell Sir Frank about my problems. He's not the sort of person who would understand.'

'Still sounds a bit harsh suspending you. You have an exemplary record, don't you?'

'It makes no difference. I may have lost them a contract worth millions. You can hardly blame Sir Frank for blowing up,' she admitted, conscious of her own honesty. 'It's difficult working the hours I do, but I knew that when I took the job.'

'But you can go back. He hasn't fired you has he?' Tom asked, with concern in his eyes.

'Not yet. Maybe I need some rest anyway,' said Annie, thinking about the last few days.

Tom seemed to have read her thoughts.

'Those dreams you mentioned...tell me more about them.'

'So now you're my shrink?' she joked, dodging Tom's suggestion with a smile.

'Seriously, you only mentioned them briefly. Maybe we can exorcise them.'

'How long have you got?' She shifted to face him.

'All night if you need it,' he answered sincerely.

'I can't remember much about them,' she lied. She changed the subject quickly. 'Shall we go now? I'm getting cold just hanging about.'

Tom felt excluded.

'Well, you know where I am if you change your mind.'

On the way back to the underground station, they spoke more.

'I'm going to make the most of the time off,' she reiterated. 'Seems the best thing to do.'

'So when do I get to see you next?'

'Give me a week or two to sort myself out.'

'That long?'

Annie didn't reply. They walked silently, Tom resigning himself to the current situation. As they parted company, he spoke again.

'Be seeing you sometime then,' he said, hugging her briefly.

'Thanks for tonight,' she said, reaching up to give him a kiss on the cheek. She noticed the pain in his eyes. 'It was fun Tom, we should do this more often.'

He took the last part of her statement as a ray of hope that she intended to see him again.

'Yes, whenever,' he agreed, feeling sick inside. He could feel her slipping away. He hesitated, struggling for words that would keep her with him for a few moments longer, hoping to see a flicker of love in her eyes. It was not there. It really mattered to him that her feelings were not as strong as his. He was beginning to realise that no matter how much he hoped: Annie was not going to change, particularly if she was not bothered about seeing him for a few weeks.

She tossed her hair in her usual way, and with no more parting words, headed for the warmer confines of the station. He watched her until she was almost out of sight before turning from the station to walk to his car, which was parked some distance away. Thinking of those last moments, he decided the pain he felt when he was with Annie was not worth the agony anymore. He would probably never hear from her again.

Chapter 10

Annie shivered. She had enjoyed the evening but it had not taken her mind off of the day's worries. Despite the extra things Tom had thoughtfully brought for her to wear, the damp night air permeated through her clothes. Moreover, it had not been a good night to go out, her day having fallen apart so unexpectedly. The spectacle of the fireworks had done nothing to distract her. Despite having put on a reasonably brave face for Tom, she still felt wounded by Sir Frank's sharp tongue.

As she walked through the foyer, Annie felt there was something about the station that was perceptively different from earlier. She hesitated, trying to fathom out what it was. The air had its own personality, and was heavy and brooding. Although she could hear no footsteps, she had the sensation that someone was following her, shadowing her every move. She decided to brush the thought aside and moved on, occasionally glancing over her shoulder. At any moment, she expected someone to materialise out of the passageways that led off to various routes. She shuddered, imagining the sensation of breath on the back of her neck, and pulled her scarf tighter.

She reminded herself that soon she would be home, tucked up in the warm with a mug of hot chocolate. The thought of her cosy bed made her eyelids begin to feel heavy and her legs feel weak. The short nap on her outward journey had not been enough to prevent exhaustion taking hold.

Travelling downwards on the first flight of escalators, Annie studied the advertising hoardings that ran the length of the stairwell, noticing that they were all contemporary; with no trace of the retro advertisements she had seen earlier in the evening. When she reached the second escalator, several men were unintentionally blocking her way. She began to feel isolated and vulnerable. As she drew closer, her concerns were dispelled when it became apparent that they were engaged in light-hearted conversation. All of the men were smoking cigarettes or puffing on pipes. She wondered whether smoking a pipe was becoming fashionable again. The men were well spoken and wore long winter greatcoats, polished black shoes and carried canvas kit bags.

'Could have blown me over with a feather when he pointed that damn thing at me.'

The other men chuckled.

'Thought he was going to blow my head off for sure,' continued the first man.

The chuckling turned into raucous laughter.

'Not like you to exaggerate,' said the shortest man in the group.

The rest of the group added their comments.

'That'll teach you to go hunting with the lads from Weybridge,' said a gangly man in his early twenties.

'Hear, hear,' said another. 'Stick to shooting at the Jerries. You gave those chaps a good'un on your last op!'

The rest of the group guffawed. They did not seem to notice Annie trying to squeeze by, making no effort to make room for her as they continued with their conversation. As she passed through the middle of the group, she noticed a sudden drop in temperature, but dismissed it as her anxiety teasing her senses.

Descending the last set of escalators, she was alone again, the group of men remaining where they were. Their conversation and laughter faded into the distance, becoming nothing but a distant echo distorted by the acoustics of the underground. Annie had not really grasped the essence of their conversation; as being assaulted had been uppermost in her mind, but their manner of speech somehow had reminded her of how her grandfather used to talk.

The lights lining the length of the vaulted ceiling flickered. Annie stopped for a few seconds and looked up at them, willing them to work properly. The incident in the lift entered her mind again, and she felt in her pocket for her torch. To her relief, history was not about to repeat itself: the lights quickly regained their original brightness, making a noise like angry bees.

Once on the platform, Annie found it hard to stay awake whilst waiting for her train, and knowing that if she sat down, she would allow sleep to engulf her, she remained on her feet. Leaning back against the cold station wall tiles, she tried hard not to close her eyes. The bright lights of the firework display were still etched on her retinas and she enjoyed the memory of the vibrant colours lighting up the sky. Hopeful that she would be joined on the platform for her return journey by other commuters, she wished with hindsight that she had insisted Tom accompany her.

Carried on the draught from one of the tunnels, an overpowering smell drifted towards Annie. Her eyes began to water. Overcome by the smell of burning, she covered her mouth and nose with her gloved hand. She felt nauseous and considered that it might be wise to leave the platform and find an alternative way home if the smell lingered for too long. Half expecting to hear an announcement that there was a fire on an adjacent platform, she wondered whether Tom was still in the vicinity. Before she had time to make a decision as to what she should do for the best, her train pulled in to the platform.

She got on and was surprised to see that there was no one else in the carriage. She glanced out of the window as the train doors closed, wondering why, and startled in horror, forcing herself against the back of her seat to be as far away from the person standing on the platform. The uniformed man she had encountered on her outward journey was staring at her from only a few feet away. She opened her mouth to scream, but the train began to move, gathering speed as it entered the tunnel.

'I'm going mad,' she called out to an empty carriage, her words drowned by the clattering train. 'I can't take any more.'

The only audience was her pale reflection in the train window. She wondered: had he been waiting for her all that time, and if so, how did he know when she would be returning? Or had he followed her to meet Tom?

Thoughts began to pervade the corridors of Annie's troubled mind. She could not understand why the uniformed man was becoming part of her life. Even though with each passing second, distance between her and the platform she had just left was increasing, the feeling that someone was watching her would not subside. Nevertheless, she succumbed to the gentle rocking motion of the train, which eventually soothed her nerves and lulled her into shallow sleep again, until the train began to slow.

As the train approached the next stop, the lights of the station were not as bright as usual. Annie cupped her hand against the window to see more clearly. The station platform was full: crammed with people of all ages. There was no obvious explanation for such large numbers, there being no theatre or cinema in the near vicinity. It seemed that these people were not waiting for a train; the majority of the crowd huddled in groups like rows of sardines, snuggled under worn blankets on the cold platform floor. The station platform had the look of a makeshift dormitory. Others sipped drinks from large tin mugs or played cards. A solitary boy of around eleven or twelve sat cross-legged playing a harmonica, precariously close to the edge of the platform. His clothes were threadbare and his holed trousers revealed muddy knees.

Kneeling on the cold floor, changing a towelling nappy, a young woman was singing to calm her baby. The infant flailed its arms and legs wildly in the air. The whole scene was surreal in its silence. No one looked up to acknowledge the approaching train. It sped up again, leaving the station behind on its onward journey.

'Wake up, miss. You shouldn't be on this train. It's not allowed. You should be shelterin' wiv the others.'

Annie woke with a start and tried to focus on the face in front of her.

'What? Why?'

'Why them bloody raids, miss. Night after bloomin' night and this one's no different. My house has taken several bleedin' hits.'

The old man's ramblings made no sense.

'I've heard nothing on the news,' said Annie, gathering her things together. 'What's been going on, a riot you say?'

'Gawd blimey, what planet you on?' said the guard. 'London's on bleedin' fire.'

'Have you been drinking? You shouldn't go round making up stories like that,' protested Annie, leaving the carriage hurriedly to get away from him.

The guard muttered something under his breath.

Annie made her way up the stairs to the exit, checking yet again that she was alone. As she left the station, a thick fog greeted her, its icy fingers reaching in through the entrance and swirling around her.

The guard's words resonated in her head but there were no fires blazing or signs of looting from shops.

'Drunken fool,' she muttered to herself.

The air still smelt of fireworks, only slightly more pleasant than the acrid smells a few hundred feet below ground. Annie was glad when she finally reached her own front door and turned the key in the lock.

Chapter 11

'I don't know what's going on,' admitted Annie, her aching head lowered, sitting opposite Dr. Edwards the following morning. 'My boss has insisted I take time off. I'm losing control.'

Dr. Edwards dexterously twirled a pencil between his fingers as he observed Annie's body language, uncharacteristically withdrawn.

'What made him say that?'

'I've made too many mistakes recently. It's not like me at all.'

Dr. Edwards stopped twiddling the pencil and placed it on his desk.

'Why do you think you've been making mistakes?'

Annie fidgeted in the swivel chair; first looking out of the window at the view across the park, then back at Dr. Edwards.

'Lack of sleep?'

Dr. Edwards waited for Annie to continue.

'None of it makes any sense.'

'What about the dreams and visions you were having? Has anything else happened?'

Annie stopped fidgeting and looked Dr. Edwards in the eye. When she finally answered she watched closely for his reaction.

'Am I going mad?'

'What you are seeing may be linked to what is troubling you.'

'I don't really want to talk about it. It makes them more real.'

'Denial won't help you. Facing your demons will do far more good in the long run.'

Annie sighed deeply.

'If it helps, close your eyes.'

Annie laid back and allowed her thoughts to wash over her. A few minutes passed by with the only sounds being the ticking of the clock in Dr. Edwards' office and the muffled drone of traffic outside.

Dr. Edwards switched on his voice recorder.

'Are you ready?'

'I think so.'

'Good.'

'Do these dreams bother you at all during the day?'

Annie shifted uncomfortably in the leather chair, running her index finger along a rough tear in the fabric.

'I think I'd rather keep my eyes open if that's alright.'

She resembled a frightened child.

'It's not unusual for stress to trigger our minds into inventing unusual things. Your condition is caused by a chemical imbalance in the brain, and that could be what is making you think this way,' Dr. Edwards reassured her.

'It doesn't explain what happened last night though.'

'Tell me more about it. Take your time.'

Dr. Edwards listened intently, and then took a large book from his bookshelf. He began to turn the pages.

'What's wrong with me, Doctor?' asked Annie desperately, as if naming the condition would somehow make it go away.

'Annie, has your boyfriend, or anyone else for that matter, told you anything about how the underground was used during the war?'

'No, and if they had I would have glazed over, I'm sure. It's Tom that's obsessed with it, not me.'

'But surely you've learnt a few facts about the war from films, TV, school, the Internet?'

Annie recalled absconding from history lessons so she could smoke with her friends in the school toilets.

'Apart from the few things my grandfather told me, I'm quite certain I haven't.'

'Londoners used the underground during bombing raids as a place of refuge and a place to sleep. Did you know?'

'Sounds horrendous.' She was silent and thoughtful for a few seconds. 'When I was down there last night, it smelt a hundred times worse than a public toilet. I've never smelt anything so awful.'

Dr. Edwards reflected for a few seconds.

'There weren't adequate toilet facilities in the underground during wartime.'

Annie's unease gathered momentum. She put her hands in her coat pockets to stop herself from biting her nails.

'What has the war got to do with last night though? Why do you keep mentioning it?'

'You were describing a scenario that was common in the war.'

Annie laughed.

'If I didn't know better I would say you are suggesting I've been in some sort of time machine.'

Dr. Edwards smiled.

'That's an interesting concept, but I was suggesting that you have recalled something you might have learnt at school and projected it into your thoughts.'

Annie's fingers closed around an object in her pocket. She removed it, realising it was the button she had picked up after her ordeal in the lift. She dropped it onto Dr. Edwards' desk and it rolled towards him. He picked it up and held it up to the light, studying the detail on its front face.

'Where did you get this?'

'I got stuck in the lift at work the other day. It felt like there was someone in there with me...I could hear them breathing, but I was alone. This was on the floor when I managed to get out.'

'Annie, this is an RAF button.'

'So how did it get there?'

Dr. Edwards seemed thoughtful. He wrote more notes.

'Your grandfather was in the Air Force, wasn't he?'

A deep breath.

'Yes.'

Dr. Edwards offered no explanation and watched her silently from his side of the desk.

'I did sense there was someone in the lift with me.'

'So you said.'

Annie had not connected the button on the foyer floor with the man in the lift until now. A flash of a uniform jacket with big buttons tripped through her thoughts.

'Has it occurred to you that the person you thought was in the lift might have been your grandfather?'

'He's dead and I don't believe in ghosts.'

'Trouble letting go of our loved ones can manifest very powerful images.'

Annie took a tissue from her bag and dabbed at her eyes.

'So these things I keep seeing are related to him?'

'It's something to think about until I see you again.'

'It was a much younger man. It wasn't my grandfather, I'm sure of it.'

'Nevertheless, I think we should consider that this person could possibly be a messenger from your subconscious.'

Annie picked up the button and caressed it gently with her fingers.

'I still remember how I felt when mum and dad died. It feels like yesterday. Now it's happening all again, but this time I have no one left.' She dabbed her eyes again and placed the button gently back on the desk. 'I need some fresh air. If it's alright with you, I think I've had enough today.'

'You've done very well. I feel we are making good progress,' said Dr. Edwards, his voice dripping with that well practised, professional reassurance. 'Same time next week?'

'Yes, same time next week,' replied Annie, a touch of lethargy creeping into her voice.

She left with more unanswered questions in her head.

Chapter 12

Annie mulled over the time spent with Dr. Edwards. She strolled through the park near to his office, with no particular plan for the day. It felt unsettling to have so much free time.

On the opposite side of the park, iron gates led to a cobbled square, where a small café sat between an antiques shop and a florist. Annie had passed by the café many times before on her way to and from work, but had never bothered to venture inside. With no need to get to work and the appealing aroma of freshly ground coffee tempting her to cross the threshold, she decided to give it a try. Although a welcome sanctuary from the cold weather, it took Annie by surprise that the café was nowhere near as smart as its neighbouring shops, and was in need of a major refurbishment. Nevertheless, its faded interior had a quaint appeal and made it less likely that her colleagues would drop by on their lunchbreak.

She chose a table near enough to the window to have a good view of the park, but to be out of sight to any passers-by. A young, fresh-faced girl took her order for coffee and a Danish pastry. Annie took a newspaper from a rack on the wall and flicked through, paying little attention to any of the articles, whilst waiting for her order to arrive. She was quickly bored by headlines from the previous day, so turned her attention to the interior of the café. She studied their collection of large black and white photographs, poorly framed, which had been carelessly arranged on burgundy painted walls. Characters in pinstriped suits from gangster movies of the 1920's glared back at her: cigarettes in mouths, machine guns balanced on hips. Brash gangsters' molls were draped on the arms of the criminals, their smouldering, pouting lips daring Annie to try her charms on their men.

'Cappuccino and Danish,' announced the waitress.

'Thank you.'

'Will there be anything else?'

'No, that's all thank you.'

'If you change your mind, top-ups are free with a main meal.'

The waitress hummed gently to herself as she cleared the few used tables.

At the front of the café, two plaster life-sized mannequins occupied a cramped space next to the shop window, which had misted over with condensation. Marilyn Monroe posed provocatively in a low-cut dress: pouting from her gilded chair whilst Elvis played guitar, dressed in a glittery gold teddy-boy jacket. The figures looked mismatched and equally out of place as they grimaced at the people passing by cocooned in scarves and coat collars, battling against the weather.

Annie made an attempt to read the papers again but gave up, pushing them to one side. A flyer fell from the pages and fluttered to the floor. She picked it up and read its suggestion: to fill a day with an educational visit to a London museum. With the exception of the Imperial War museum a few days previously, she could not remember having taken time out to visit one. She needed to continue distracting herself, and pictured the disappointment in Tom's face when the possibility of opening a bottle of wine entered her mind. She paid the bill, wrapped up warmly like the army of workers and shoppers outside, and ventured out into the gusty street.

She stepped into a black cab and warmed her hands on the interior heater, thinking that the weather had no intention of changing. It boasted a spirit much the same as her mood: icy, restless and relentless. Tattered leaves tumbled and spiralled, trapped within the folds of the wind's billowing cloak.

Blown over by a sudden gust, an elderly woman was being helped up by two charitable young men in business suits, the contents of her upended shopping trolley still rolling around on the pavement. The stooping figures Annie had observed from the café moved in groups, reminding her of Lowry's matchstick figures. They leaned into the wind, hands stuffed into their pockets. A homeless man sheltered in an alleyway between two shops, sharing a tattered blanket with his pet mongrel. Annie watched as a woman offered him a hot drink and a baker's bag. The man offered his dog some of the food before taking a bite himself. His selflessness intrigued Annie.

'They must be freezing,' she said.

The cab driver looked at her in his rear view mirror. 'What's that love?'

'I said it's cold.'

He tried to make polite conversation.

'Rough weather, init? Feels like there's summat brewin.'

Lost in her thoughts, Annie continued to watch the weather doing its worst, pummelling Londoners with strong gusts. The driver mumbled something inaudible and turned his radio on to fill the silence. The chill of the wind forced its way under the sill of the taxi doors, the inefficient heater barely compensating. Annie's toes tingled with the cold.

'Can't you do something about this heater? I'm freezing back here.'

'If you want to pay me more I'll get a new one,' he laughed.

She closed the partition window and rubbed her hands together for warmth.

Normally so immersed in herself, it occurred to Annie that she actually felt concern for the anonymous people the taxi passed by: the lady who had stumbled, the tatty mongrel and his owner, the Salvation Army band playing on a street corner. The brass instruments appeared fused to the musicians' lips, which were turning blue with the cold. Branches of trees high above the buses and cars waved wildly in the gale, threatening to fall.

As the taxi passed a German Christmas market, installed early for the season, the sweet aroma of mulled wine reached Annie's nostrils. She felt instantly warmed, though none had passed her lips. The log cabin stalls were crammed with sweets, hand-blown glass animals, colourful woollen jumpers: a cacophony of sights and smells. Eager shoppers struggled with their bags, full of early Christmas purchases.

Alongside the market, a temporary ice rink had been set up much earlier in the season than usual, in order to attract children on half term as well as visitors on the run up to Christmas. Teeming with novice and experienced skaters, the rink occupied a large paved area outside a faceless grey stone office block. Annie pondered the possibility of joining the skaters over the next few days, aware that she fell into the novice category. She would maybe ask Tom to accompany her, so that he would feel obliged to protect her from eager young skaters ducking and diving around the less able. At one end of the rink a band of musicians was performing. She opened the cab window a crack to hear the music, closing it hurriedly again as the cold air mercilessly blasted her.

A few moments later, the taxi pulled up at the costume exhibition. Paying and stepping out of the taxi, Annie laughed into her scarf, wondering what Tom would think when he found out that she had spent time at an exhibition through choice. He would most likely be annoyed that she had gone without him. She ran from the taxi to get out of the cold, up the stone steps and through the museum's revolving doors. It was not much warmer inside.

The foyer boasted high ceilings, in the centre of which was a stained glass dome. The coloured glass in the dome camouflaged the true colour of the wintry sky. The floor of the entrance hall was as impressive as the ceiling: colourful mosaic tiles covering the full length of vast corridors, which stretched away in different directions like the points of a compass. Still shivering from her journey in the draughty taxi, the cold tiles did not help Annie's toes to recover.

She left her coat on, bought a programme guide, and joined the small queue of visitors as they made their way to the first exhibition hall.

Each exhibition covered a different decade of the twentieth century. Costumed mannequins stood out against their soft pastel backdrops. Dimmed lighting and high arched windows covered by fine muslin blinds protected the fragile costumes from sunlight. Glass eyes set in porcelain faces stared lifelessly at the occasional visitor stopping to reminisce.

The nostalgia attached to the fashion of her teenage years proved too much for Annie's current frame of mind. She moved into the next hall where a more sombre display greeted her: mustiness and the smell of mothballs reminding her of her grandparents' house. The lights had been dimmed. Annie found herself lingering longer this time. Studying the snapshot of a troubled decade, when Hitler tried to quash the world, she remembered Tom telling her how differently things could have turned out. As she went from mannequin to mannequin, observing a time she knew so little about, she came to realise that Tom was right and that she should be more grateful and reverent to the war veterans who secured her future.

As Annie circled the hall for a second time, her enthusiasm to move onto the rest of the exhibition evaporated. She felt a need to befriend the very essence of such a turbulent period in British history. She lingered by the exhibits and studied the household artefacts, which had been displayed in tall glass cabinets. Having always shut Tom's wordy explanations out, she had not before appreciated the level of deprivation that people had suffered year after year. The drab colours, frugal use of material and ugly footwear of fashion by necessity both fascinated and depressed her.

A square canvas handbag attracted Annie's attention. She dug deep into the corners of her mind and suddenly remembered that the man on the platform and the girls in the pub toilets had all possessed something very similar. Annie recalled the grotesque masks the girls had pulled from their bags. As she peered through the glass of the display cabinet at the stained and cracked gas mask, she felt overwhelmed by an uncanny familiarity, far more reaching than her recent sightings of the gas masks.

A strong sense of curiosity was stirring in her mind. Snapshots in her daydreams and nightmares of World War Two were just a small taste of the camaraderie and bravery surrounding her in the static groups of mannequins.

Around the hall, several seats had been placed for visitors to sit and sketch, converse or to observe the artefacts and costumes. All were empty. Annie chose a bench that allowed her to see the mannequins as one large group. She was alone in the hall. Sunlight crept through tiny gaps in the muslin blinds; the only sounds that of distant traffic, hushed chatter and noisy shoes on hard stone floors. A solitary blackbird sang its song outside the museum, casting its shadow on the muslin blinds as it sat on a window ledge outside. The warm sun caressed Annie's face. She sat for a while, observing the light as it moved across the windows, casting a soft glow on the faces of the faded mannequins.

She considered how the human form in different guises had presented itself to her, having a profound effect in such a short space of time: people on the street, bronze statues, plaster figures in a café, and finally a group of ageing mannequins. All had provoked different reactions: from sympathy to envy and aggression to compassion. Pondering over these thoughts, she left the hall with all its comfortable familiarity, taking one last look at the figures behind her.

Chapter 13

Over the next week, solitude was Annie's closest friend. There were very few moments that passed when she did not think about people she had known or lost.

Respecting Annie's request to stay away, Tom kept his distance, making no attempt to contact her. Nevertheless, she had left him with the smallest grain of hope - that they might pick up where they had left off if and when it suited her, but not before.

Annie's time spent in the costume museum, had given her time to reflect on her needs. She was still uncertain as to whether Tom's silence bothered her. Nevertheless she realised that she was feeling the need for love and intimacy with someone, but it wasn't actually Tom she was missing.

At the stroke of midnight on the following Wednesday, the phone rang just as Annie was nodding off to sleep in front of her brand new flat-screen television. Certain that no one else but Tom would dare to call her at such a late hour, she was in two minds as to whether she should pick up. Now a week had passed she was lonely.

Before the phone had time to stop ringing, she leapt up to answer, tripping over the footstool in her hurry. She composed herself before speaking.

'Hi Tom – how are things?'

A timid voice answered.

'Sorry it's so late. I just wanted to check you're okay. How are you?'

Annie ignored his question.

'I thought you would have called sooner.'

'I thought you wanted some space.'

There was an embarrassed silence from Annie.

Tom quickly changed the subject.

'Must be weird being off work.'

'It's good to have some time to think,' she dropped in, realising it was good to hear his voice.

'Not missing me then?' laughed Tom nervously.

Annie dodged the question.

'I've been really busy planning things,' she lied.

'Hope you haven't organised anything that'll clash with Friday. Don't forget we won't be back until late Sunday.'

'Sorry, what's happening Friday?'

'The air show, remember? We arranged it a while ago.'

Annie tried to think of an excuse.

'You mean you arranged it a while ago. I didn't realise we were definitely going.'

'I have the tickets now. Anyway, it will be good for you. Get you out of your flat.'

'It's not a flat, Tom! It's a very exclusive apartment.'

'If you say so.'

Annie went to the window and looked out into the darkness. The Thames sparkled in the moonlight, reflecting the office lights from the buildings opposite.

'Annie, are you still there?'

With no miraculous excuse springing to mind, Annie resigned herself to Tom's plans.

'Yes – I'm still here. What time do you want to pick me up?'

'You'll still come? That's great – pick you up at five.'

'Tom, I'm only agreeing to come on one condition!'

Tom pretended not to hear.

'I'll come straight from work.'

'Tom - listen to me! Don't pressure me into talking about my problems while we're away.'

'Hopefully your problems will all be forgotten...and I'll take you shopping in Oxford Street when we get back.'

'If you're bribing me, it won't work.'

'Not even if I tell you I have a pleasure flight booked for you?'

'Really?' A warm feeling filled Annie's heart as she recalled flights with her grandfather.

'You'll get a chance to take control too.'

'But...'

'Sorry – the line's breaking up 'I'll pick you up at five – with costumes! Bye.'

Tom hung up.

Annie looked at her phone in disbelief. Had Tom hung up on her? She stared at the phone, wondering what she had agreed to. She continued to stand at the window, gazing at the activity on the river. A boat passed by, leaving a silvery wash in its wake. A few smaller vessels were also making their way up and down the river, carefully navigating in the darkness. The hustle and bustle of London's nightlife accentuated Annie's loneliness: despite a momentary loss of control, she realised that she was looking forward to her flight. Friday could not come too soon, regardless of where he was taking her. She lay in bed that night wondering where they were going.

Tom's enthusiasm continued into the next day. He rang early the next morning. Cocooned in her duvet, Annie had slept well for once, having allowed the repressed thoughts of her grandfather to dominate her dreams, putting a stop to haunting thoughts from taking over. She unravelled herself and reached for the phone, knocking over the alarm clock and an empty glass. The bedside lamp rocked backwards and forwards before righting itself.

She answered from beneath her duvet.

'Hello.'

'You sound like you're under water,' speculated Tom. 'I can barely hear you.'

Annie picked up the clock, looked at the time and thumped it down again.

'I'm still in bed. Can't you ring me at a decent time?'

'It's ten o'clock. Some of us have done a day's work already.'

'Thanks for the reminder. Some of us have no choice in the matter.'

'Sorry – that was thoughtless of me. How did you sleep? Any more bad dreams?'

'Not that I can remember.'

Annie sat up and focused on her face in the large mirror opposite her bed. Her reflection boasted a haystack of chestnut hair and yesterday's eye makeup. She squinted in the bright sunlight, having forgotten to close the curtains the night before.

'What are you doing today – spending more money?'

'Shut up', murmured Annie, stretching like a cat.

'What was that?'

'I said I'm up,' she lied.

'Good. I'm glad you're not just mooching about. Just a few more details about the weekend.'

'Oh yes – tell me, what was that hurried comment about costumes last night?'

Tom sounded excited but a bit hesitant.

'I just wanted to tell you...a lot of people will be dressing up.'

There was an awkward silence as Tom waited for a torrent of objections. Instead, Annie remained reasonable.

'You're a big kid. What are you going as, Peter Pan?'

Tom laughed.

'It's a secret.'

'As long as I'm not the back end of a pantomime horse, I'll consider it,' answered Annie, picking up a box of chocolates from the floor.

'Fetch out some silk stockings if you've got any. You'll look greeaat!'

Distracted by the chocolates, Annie reached the second layer and turned on the television, phone sandwiched between her ear and shoulder.

'Mm hmm.'

Tom seized the moment to avoid Annie's objections and ended the call as promptly as the previous night.

'Can't wait. See you tomorrow.'

Annie reluctantly got out of bed, took a shower and dressed with none of her usual care.

The phone only rang twice during the day. Annie chose to ignore it, preferring to sit by the window and observe London whilst flicking through fashion magazines. She ignored the urge to surf the Internet for anything related to the cause of nightmares and hallucinations, deciding that she would leave that to Dr. Edwards. He could work for his money and hopefully there would be a resolution when she saw him next. She picked up her phone messages later in the day, listening to them as she prepared her evening meal.

Sophie had filled her in on all the work gossip: the office girls had been overjoyed at Annie's dressing down by Sir Frank, although loyal Sophie had kept her mouth shut when interrogated by the harpies. As word had passed from mouth to mouth, the story had grown completely out of proportion: Annie having had a rampant affair with Sir Frank. It had been passed around the office that Annie was after Sir Frank's job as well as attaining bigger shares in the company in return for services rendered. Apparently, he had already moved on to a new and equally sordid affair with a much younger new girl in HR. Annie was not to return for a couple of weeks, leaving Sophie and Sir Frank time to appease the clients that Annie had angered.

The second phone call from Dr. Edwards interested Annie far more. He had done as he promised: researching the brass button that Annie had picked up from the lift floor, confirming that it did indeed belong to an RAF uniform. Not sure whether she felt reassured or alarmed by this revelation, Annie rummaged in a kitchen drawer for a pack of cigarettes. Her mind raced as to what Dr. Edwards' findings might mean. She had not touched a cigarette for two years but she kept a packet just in case of an emergency. Her hands trembled as she fumbled with the matches. Sitting at her breakfast bar, looking out towards the Houses of Parliament, she thought about the implications attached to Dr. Edwards' findings.

It was difficult to form any sort of opinion or verdict. She could not put all the strange occurrences down to stress and tiredness anymore. If that were the case then everyone would be seeing hobgoblins and fairies every time they had a crisis in their life. She was also not buying into her own supposition that her hallucinations had been manifested because of a war-obsessed boyfriend either.

The phone rang one more time just as Annie was finishing her cigarette.

'I forgot to ask your dress size,' asked Tom, without saying hello.

Annie stubbed out her cigarette forcefully.

'You really don't know me that well, do you?'

'I'll guess then, shall I?'

'I'm a size ten. And, if you are thinking of buying me clothes, then go to that little boutique in Cyril Street. The owner Kate knows what I like.'

Tom coughed nervously.

'Okay. I'll see what I can do – if I have time.'

Annie did not hear from Tom again until Friday afternoon, when he turned up earlier than arranged.

'Hey, only me,' said Tom through the intercom. 'Shall I come up and help you with your bags?'

'You're early. I'll be down in a few minutes.'

'Well hurry up, it's bloody freezing down here.'

'Wait in the foyer then - it'll be warmer.'

When Annie reached the ground floor, Tom was jumping up and down inside the foyer to keep warm, with his usual boyish grin lighting up his face.

'I managed to finish early – bet you're pleased.'

'Of course.'

Annie was surprised at herself. She was rested, her demons had stayed away and she realised she genuinely was looking forward to a weekend away with him.

Tom opened the glass foyer doors for her.

'Wow – time off work has done you good. You look great.'

'Are you saying that I look like a hag normally?'

'Of course not. I'm just used to you looking like you're spoiling for a fight.'

'Very funny.'

Annie caught sight of her reflection in the glass doors to the apartment block. Tom was right, she did look more relaxed.

'Well of course, it could be that your radiance is due to the excitement of spending a weekend with me,' Tom added, still with a broad grin on his face.

'It's not the first time you've said that.'

Tom wrapped his arms around her, expecting resistance.

'I'm so looking forward to this, even though it took some organising. We're going to have such a great time.'

Annie relaxed into his arms, savouring human contact after the solitude of the last week.

'I can't wait to see you in your costume. Bet you'll look really sexy.'

'Costume?' said Annie, pulling away. I thought you'd changed your mind and were buying me something from Kate's shop.'

'I think there's been a small misunderstanding. I distinctly remember mentioning a costume on the phone.'

Annie raised her eyebrows and crossed her arms in defiance.

'Just what are you expecting me to dress up in then, Tom?'

Tom opened the car door for her.

'Let's get in the car where it's warm. We can talk about it on the way.'

'I really would like to know what I'm letting myself in for.'

Tom laughed.

'Did you think I had something a bit raunchy in mind?'

Annie pretended to look cross as she opened the boot of Tom's car and scrutinised the contents. He had hidden the costumes in the depths of his suitcase, far from Annie's prying eyes.

'Relax Annie. You've got the wrong end of the stick. It's nothing like that. I promise.'

'I'm warning you Tom. I might refuse to dress up at all.'

Tom pulled a convincingly straight face.

'If you really hate the pantomime horse that you suggested in the first place, you can be the front end instead.'

Annie looked horrified.

'You've got to be joking!'

'Of course I am, though I would at least have the pleasure of staring at your bum all day.'

Chapter 14

Despite winter having well and truly arrived in London, Annie felt a hint of optimism for the first time in months. She savoured the crisp afternoon air as she stepped into Tom's car.

'I feel much better, it all seems quite distant now.'

'You mean the lift episode?'

'And the weird stuff at the memorial.'

'Try and put it to one side,' suggested Tom. 'It would be a shame to let it spoil the weekend.'

'I will.'

They settled into their car seats and began their journey. A beautiful pink and orange mackerel sky was fading fast over London: replaced by shades of purple and indigo. Once out of the private gated road leading to Annie's apartment block, Tom took a back route to avoid commuters leaving London early for the weekend, driving through residential streets. Only a few leaves still clung onto skeletal trees that lined both sides of the avenues flanked by red-bricked Victorian houses. Most of the terraced properties had been renovated by city workers but had at one time been homes for flat-capped tradesmen and their extended families. As they were crawling along behind other frustrated drivers, Annie casually glanced in through the windows of the houses they passed. Large television screens dwarfed tiny front rooms. Eventually reaching the main road, they got on their way quickly to free themselves of the city, and joined the army of commuters escaping London.

'Would you like some music on?' asked Tom.

'Something mellow would be nice.'

Annie leaned back and enjoyed watching the sky as it partially turned an unusual shade of cobalt blue. She closed her eyes as the music filled her ears, unconsciously putting her hand on Tom's knee.

'Thank you for bringing me away for the weekend.'

'It's a pleasure.'

'I feel a lot better already. Just going somewhere different helps.'

'Even if you do have to dress up?'

'Strangely yes, even if I do have to be a horse,' she laughed.

Tom joined in, pleased to see her happy.

'I'm sorry I have been a bit up and down.'

'It's okay, you've had a lot on your mind.'

'I'll try harder,' she added, glancing across at him, noticing that he looked markedly relaxed. She suddenly remembered a similar expression in one of the photos of Tom that graced his family home. The image of him as a young boy in short trousers popped into her head.

'I bet you were a right little swot when you were young.'

'What brought on that change of subject?'

Teasing Tom seemed suddenly a good sport and a way to make the journey go quicker. She ignored his question.

'I bet you and your dad used to go train-spotting.'

'So what if we did?'

'Perched on little stools with flasks of tea and ham sandwiches were you?'

'Yes actually, and it was great fun. Boys do that stuff, you know.'

'Only swots and boys with knobbly knees.'

'You've got me there. I admit that I did excel at school and my knees are not my best asset.'

'I'm only teasing.'

'Yes, I realise that. But it's almost worth hearing you taking the piss just to see you smile.'

'I'm sure you could dig up embarrassing stuff about my childhood,' said Annie, feeling a flash of regret at the mention of it. 'But maybe we shouldn't be talking about the past today. I promise to focus on the weekend.'

'I'll second that: a new adventure, a beautiful sunset, a fast car and a man who adores you.'

Annie smiled at him, sensing a note of desperation in his tone.

'Give me time, Tom.'

'I will,' he said, placing his hand on hers.

Leaving London behind, tall buildings were quickly replaced by tall trees, bare branches reaching upwards like gnarled fingers. The sporadic evergreens were the only splash of colour to punctuate the approaching hard winter. As traffic started to flow more smoothly and the traffic gathered speed: a blur of parks, derelict warehouses and cemeteries all blended into one.

In the distance, Annie watched the lights from aircraft approaching Heathrow airport.

'The planes are really close together tonight.'

'They're actually a few miles apart,' he reassured her. 'They just look close from this angle, that's all.'

Annie continued to watch the aircraft, noticing a group of three planes that had broken away from the rest cross the road some distance ahead. They were flying fast and low.

'Wow – look at those planes. They must be on their way to the air show.'

Tom scanned the sky.

'Where?'

'In front of us, look.'

'Nope – still can't see them.'

As the road straightened out, the planes made a sudden and tight turn.

'They're coming this way really fast. I think they're small jets.'

'Damn, the trees are in the way. I still can't see them.'

'They're coming right over our heads - any second now.'

'They're not allowed. It's a built-up area,' exclaimed Tom, trying to concentrate on the road and scan the darkening sky at the same time.

Annie's fascination suddenly turned to horror. She grabbed Tom's hand, dangerously jerking the steering wheel and causing the car to swerve.

'They're going to crash!' she screamed hysterically.

Tom wrenched her hand off his in an attempt to regain control.

'Jesus, Annie!'

Waiting for the impact, Annie continued screaming as Tom pulled onto the hard shoulder, cutting up several angry drivers in the process. He braked hard, undid his seatbelt and turned to face her.

'What are you playing at? You nearly got us killed!'

Annie peered through her fingers at the sky and the road ahead.

'They were coming straight for us! Are you completely blind?' she shouted.

'What are you talking about - what was coming straight for us?' he asked, still very angry. 'There's nothing!'

Annie struggled to string her sentences together.

'They were so close...not jets...German markings on them...like the ones in your model collection.' She desperately searched the sky in every direction.

'If this is your idea of a joke, it's not very funny!'

'Why would I do that?'

Tom inadvertently looked through the windscreen. Stuck firmly on the outside of the glass were three large squashed insects.

'Oh good God Annie! What you saw were a few dead flies.'

'I'm not blind Tom. Don't patronise me. I can tell the difference between an insect and a plane.'

'Clearly not! What you thought you saw and what was really there are two completely separate things.'

'I know what I saw,' said Annie adamantly, wiping the tears from her face.

'Try this for an explanation. 'I'll simplify it for you. Relative movement of background and particles, in this case the flies were the particles.'

'Relative what?'

'Oh, what's the point, you wouldn't understand.'

Shocked at Tom's aggressive tone, Annie buried her head in her hands. Tom fastened his seatbelt again, looked in his mirror and pulled out into the flow of traffic. They sat in silence for the remainder of the journey.

Chapter 15

Annie was desperate to believe Tom's logical explanation, but she was also angry at his reaction to her fear. Nevertheless, try as she might, she could not dismiss the thought that the German planes had seemed alarmingly real. If they were yet another hallucination she could not fathom why they should appear now when she was off for a weekend trip with Tom in a much better frame of mind.

The events of the last few days began to loom large again, not quashed as Annie had decided only a few minutes previously. She sullenly struggled to comprehend the invasion of World War Two into her life. She remembered Dr. Edwards saying that her visions may be connected to her grandfather, but the clues still left her juggling the pieces of a puzzle that wouldn't fit. Without the missing pieces she felt as though she was peering through the mist: unable to see the full picture.

She thought ahead to the flight that Tom had booked - what was going to happen to her in a setting so familiar from her time with her grandfather? Tom's stony silence gave Annie time to think about how she was going to salvage the weekend. Despite his idea of the air show not being her idea of fun, she preferred to be with him rather than at home, where she would be alone with her frightening visions. The weekend stood no chance unless she apologised for nearly causing a major accident. It would not be easy. She felt foolish.

Struggling to find a way to break the ice, Annie took a deep breath.

'Tom, I'll understand if you tell me to shut up, but I think we need to talk about what's been happening to me.'

Tom was clearly still angry.

'I thought you didn't want to discuss problems while we're away.'

'What happened earlier...you're right...I clearly imagined it. It must've been that theory you were trying to explain.'

Tom stared at the road ahead, as though Annie's words were not enough to appease him.

Annie tried again to engage him.

'I don't want to spoil this weekend for either of us.'

'Well that's a start I suppose,' replied Tom, with a hint of sarcasm. 'But now I come to think about it, you have been acting strangely.'

'Yes, I know.'

'Half the time, it's like you're on another planet.'

'Tom, I'm frightened. I really am. I don't know what's happening to me. I know you think I'm still grieving for grandad, but it's more than that.'

'If you want to talk, that's fine, but can we try and enjoy at least some of the weekend?'

'If I can just get it off my chest, then I'll be fine, I promise.

'Go on then. Tell me everything.'

Annie recounted everything that had materialised at the Battle of Britain memorial, the lift at work and finally in the underground. She sensed a heavy black cloud lifting as each minute detail was brought out into the open. Tom remained silent and attentive.

'Do you think grief could cause all this to happen?' she asked finally, searching Tom's expression for his reaction.

Tom hesitated.

'My head is telling me yes.'

'And your heart?' she asked.

His tone softened.

'I'm a bloke remember – I don't have a heart.'

'Have you any other thoughts on the matter?'

'It's odd, I'll admit that. You could almost write a book about it. In fact - getting it down on paper might exorcise it.'

'Dr. Edwards suggested I do that.'

Tom glanced at Annie's worried face and decided it was time to lift the mood of the conversation.

'Come on Annie – I'm sure it'll pass. It's nothing but ghosts and goblins.'

'Who said anything about goblins?'

Tom patted her knee.

'You might just as well have done. It couldn't get any more far-fetched.'

'I was really beginning to think like you: that I was living in a different world.'

'Oh come on Annie, you're much more sensible than that.'

'I thought so too.'

'It's my fault as well, I suppose. I've talked about my family background a lot. Maybe I've planted information in your mind.'

'You mean the war stuff? That goes in one ear and out the other. I'm always telling you how much it bores me.'

'Subliminal input – that's all it is! If I'd been talking about Egypt and the pyramids, you might have imagined you were Cleopatra. The mind plays strange tricks when we're under stress.'

'I suppose,' agreed Annie, despite her nagging doubts.

Tom smiled and affectionately patted her knee again.

'Just remember that I have a stressful job too, and I don't go around imagining I'm Father Christmas.'

Annie laughed, feeling that despite the lack of any romantic feelings towards him, she could still enjoy the weekend. Tom would do his best to make sure they had a good time. Uncharacteristically, she took his hand in hers and relaxed a little, looking out of the windows at trees arching over their heads from both sides of the road, illuminated by sporadic streetlights. They descended into a valley. The sky was the shade of royal blue ink as Tom lowered his window a little to let in the cool evening air. The aroma of damp grass, moss and wild roses immediately filled the car. They slowed down to a walking pace, as roads became narrow lanes with barely enough space for vehicles to pass each other. Eventually they reached a narrow unkempt lane, almost invisible as it forked off from the road they had been following.

'How did you find this place? It's so quiet...magical even.'

'It does feel a bit like that doesn't it? I lived here as a kid. Mum and Dad couldn't bear to sell the place so we still use it as a holiday home.'

'You've never mentioned it before. It's lovely.'

Before Annie had the chance to ask any more questions, they arrived on the outskirts of a quaint English village with the equally quaint name of Appleby Magna. A battered pick up truck with poor lights trundled towards them in the dark, scattering dust and wood shavings from its load as it bumped and clanked on its way.

'Here we are,' announced Tom excitedly, pulling up at a junction.

Immediately opposite, an old village shop vied for space between ancient cottages: its illuminated windows filled with large glass sweet jars.

'Mmm, an endless supply of chocolate! I love this place already.'

'Sadly we don't own the sweetshop, but you won't mind that when you see the old house.'

Tom negotiated a narrow gravel driveway squashed between the sweetshop and a red-bricked stable block, stopping on a cobbled area tucked behind the shop.

'Wow, this is a well-kept secret.'

A sixteenth century house nestled between the other old buildings: gnarled oak timbers, looking barely strong enough to support its walls, bowing outwards with age. The reddish brown bricks and leaded windows were partially hidden by ivy and red-leafed climbers, which appeared to tie the crumbling brickwork together. The moss-covered roof resembled an undulating sea swell: its clay tiles distorted and cracked. A hotchpotch of different periods, the oldest part of the house looked as though it had been extended over the course of several centuries. The upper branches of two giant conifers guarded the house like sentries, tickling the upstairs windows as their branches swayed gently in the night breeze.

'I can smell flowers,' said Annie, noticing several different fragrances. 'I didn't expect that at this time of year.'

'The garden does well all year round. It's very sheltered. I think nature gets confused.'

Annie's warm breath left a momentary mist on the window as she peered through the mullioned glass of the front door. An outside lantern turning on suddenly illuminated the house and garden: activated by a movement sensor. Several bats simultaneously appeared from the darkness and flitted round above Tom and Annie's heads.

Tom unlocked the heavy oak front door, reaching inside for the light switch. The door creaked on its dry hinges, almost with a voice of its own, welcoming the visitors in. Annie stepped eagerly into the long and narrow hallway noticing that a musty smell lingered in the air.

'There's a mouse,' exclaimed Annie, as a small creature disappeared through a crack in the skirting board.

'You'll have to get used to that. The house is full of them.'

'And spiders too, I see,' added Annie, brushing a cobweb away.

Tom dropped their bags on a large plump armchair. A small plume of dust rose up as the bags plopped down.

'That's okay. My grandfather had a farm. It was rife with spiders and mice,' Annie added, thinking that she had witnessed far more scary things over the last few days.

Tom ducked to avoid a particularly low oak ceiling beam.

'No one's stayed for a while, so the creatures have taken over.'

Annie followed Tom from room to room, each door groaning and ancient lights flickering.

'What is it with me and flashing lights?'

'What's that?'

'I just said that the lights are a bit hit and miss.'

'The place needs some tender loving care. We could do with a rewire.'

'It's lovely though, and so peaceful. I feel as if the house is wrapping itself around me like a fluffy blanket.'

Tom laughed.

'It has that effect on most people. Once you've been here a few days you'll feel like you've been tranquilised,' said Tom, closing curtains.

There had been no attempt at modernisation: the charm of Tom's childhood home magnified by an eclectic collection of beaten up old furniture.

'The farm was in Polegate. I still remember giant squishy armchairs and a high bed. I used to have to climb up into them using blankets for ropes.' Annie reminisced about the heavy eiderdown and deep feather mattress on her Nan's bed.

Tom opened the creaky door to the kitchen. A cream and black range dominated the room, warming not only the kitchen but also the rest of the house. A huge copper kettle shone brightly on the hob.

'Is that fresh bread I can smell?'

'I told Artie and Anne next door what time we'd be here. They always bake a loaf when they know I'm coming.'

'I'm starving. Can we have some?'

Annie sat herself down at a round wooden table in the middle of the flagstone floor and Tom lit the oil lamp that hung above it. The light cast a warm glow on the walls and ceiling. He opened the oven door and took out a bulbous white loaf.

Annie took in a deep breath savouring the aroma.

'There's no way I can resist, even if it does mean I'll put on a few pounds.'

'Don't worry, I'll help you!' Tom flashed one of his cheeky boyish grins.

He made tea and sliced the loaf into thick slabs, spreading each warm slice with butter that instantly melted.

'How often do the family come here?'

'Not that often, as you can see from the mice, but I try to come up now and again. Artie and Anne pop in to water the plants and give it the once over.'

'I can see why you like it so much. It's a great place for getting away from the rat-race.'

'If I had a choice to work here or in London there'd be no competition.'

'You'd up sticks and move here?'

'Without a doubt.'

'It's very quaint, but I'd need time to adjust, being in the middle of nowhere.'

Tom gave Annie a reproachful look as he poured more tea.

'My great-grandparents first discovered the place. The previous owner hadn't got a clue; he'd covered up all the oak beams and boarded up most of the fireplaces. Makes you wonder why he bought the place to begin with. Still, it left us lots of treasures to uncover. We even found a hidden room upstairs.'

Annie shivered.

'You're just trying to scare me.'

'No, I'm serious. We discovered it when we were doing some decorating.'

'That sounds a bit spooky. Did you find any skeletons in there?' Annie joked.

Tom laughed.

'No, nothing that sinister, just an old rotting bed with a dead crow nailed to the headboard.'

Annie looked at Tom wide-eyed.

'You're kidding, right?'

'Gotcha! Yes of course I'm kidding.'

'Thank God for that. If the bit about the dead crow had been true, I'd have been out of here like a shot.'

'And go where exactly, now that night is closing in and bats, owls and other creatures are on the prowl?' Tom mimicked a zombie, contorting his neck and shoulders into a strange position.

Annie shivered again and stirred her tea ferociously.

'Good point!'

Now that darkness had completely enveloped the house, the ancient beams seemed to groan and creak even more, making the place seem like a living breathing organism.

'It's like the house is speaking to us,' said Tom.

'Stop it, Tom. I don't need any more nightmares.'

Chapter 16

As Annie drifted off to sleep that night, she immediately found herself wandering lost on a disused airfield amongst derelict buildings. Wrecked planes littered bomb-cratered runways: some of the planes blackened and charred skeletons, others still burning ferociously. Using the brightness of the flames to help her navigate her way along a trodden path, she suddenly spotted her grandfather's farm through the thick black smoke. As she reached the airfield perimeter gates, ghostly pilots appeared from nowhere and floated right through her body, leaving a chill that seemed to penetrate deep into her bones. One of the pilots stopped. She began to chase after him, calling out to him to wait. A sense of horror gripped her as he turned to face her. He was instantly recognisable as one of the pilots from the memorial, but unlike the bronze figures he was painfully thin, pale and ethereal. His eyes were sunken and transparent: no longer the blue that she had visualised. She backed away, half expecting the ghoulish pilot to attack her, but she was saved by her dream receiving a new visitor, in the form of a young girl. Aged around seven or eight, she skipped around the other pilots, now joined by their emaciated comrade, trying to keep pace as they ran to their planes. The young girl reminded Annie of herself as a child. Dressed in a smocked summer dress, white lace-trimmed ankle socks and brown sandals, she laughed loudly, her plaits swinging from side to side as she skipped. Just as the little girl reached out to grab the hand of one of the pilots, he slipped out of her grasp, dissolving instantly into a swirling mist along with his comrades. Left alone, forlorn and clutching a dishevelled rag doll, the girl began to cry as she squinted into the murky distance. Annie approached to console her, but as she bent down to comfort her, she too disappeared like a ship lost in a thick sea fog.

Tom did not sleep well either, aware of Annie having a restless night. He lay awake for a while, gently stroking her hand as she tossed and turned, unable to understand why she was crying out in her sleep and reaching out for something to grasp. He thought he could hear her shouting for help several times. At around three in the morning, he gave up trying to settle for the night and slipped quietly out of bed. He did his best to get comfortable, plumping up the cushions of an armchair by the open bedroom window and gazing thoughtfully out into the darkness.

Tom thought about how he loved his childhood home and the surrounding village. Tom knew too, without giving it much thought that Annie was right: she would go mad living in such a place. Nevertheless, he would not give it up for any woman, no matter how much he loved her. He looked across at Annie and his heart twinged as he reminded himself that her feelings were not mutual. Annie sighed deeply and turned onto her side, throwing off most of the covers on the bed. The worst of whatever had disturbed her sleep seemed to have passed and her breathing settled into a natural rhythm. Tom sat for a few minutes admiring the curve of her body beneath the one remaining sheet.

When morning came, Tom woke with a stiff neck, slumped in the chair by the window. His last memory had been the sound of crates clanking as the milk float arrived at five in the morning, and the whistling of the milkman as he walked up next door's drive. Tom stretched his back and legs. The chair seemed nowhere near as comfortable as it had in the night. Hearing the grandfather clock in the hall chime seven, Tom slid his feet into his old misshapen slippers, put on his striped bathrobe and went downstairs to make tea and toast.

The kitchen was warm and inviting. The Aga, the beating heart of the house, was pumping out heat relentlessly. Tom laid a tray in the fashion his mother had taught him: with an embroidered cloth and small glass vase, which he filled with flowers from the dewy border beneath the kitchen window ledge. He was buttering the toast and pouring the tea from a large painted teapot when the kitchen door creaked open. Annie poked her head round the door, squinting in the morning sun.

'Morning, thought I could hear you moving around.' She ran her fingers through her messy hair and stretched her back as she entered the room.

'You look beautiful.'

'And you look like an old man in that bathrobe.' Then laughing, she placed a kiss on Tom's cheek and took a bite of toast. 'I'm ravenous, and this bread is so moorish.'

'We don't have time to bake more, unfortunately.' Tom changed the subject. 'You were very restless last night.'

'Really? The bed was so comfortable. Sorry, did I keep you awake?'

'A little, but I drifted off in the end,' he replied, aware that his neck had not loosened up yet. He beckoned to her to sit.

Annie noticed the flowers.

'Tom, you're so sweet. I'll pretend you brought me tea in bed.' She picked up the posy and smelt it.

'Lovely.'

'I think you were having more of your dreams. You were talking in your sleep.'

'Yes, more of the same I'm afraid. I woke up a couple of times and didn't have a clue where I was.'

'I thought of waking you, but you settled down after a while.'

'I dreamt about the figures from the monument again, and then I smelt burning and woke up at one point thinking the house was on fire. It was really a horrible smell. Made me feel I was choking. And a girl - there was a young girl.'

Tom could see how talking about her nightmares changed her mood dramatically: her brow was deeply furrowed.

'Well let's put that behind us shall we? It's a lovely day, so let's make the most of it.'

'Yes, absolutely!' Annie sipped thoughtfully from a large china teacup. She noticed delicate dust particles floating lazily in the warm sunlight.

Much to Tom's amusement, Annie continued eating until nearly all the fresh bread had gone. He gently wiped melted butter from her chin.

'I see a lack of sleep has not affected your appetite.'

'That bread was the best I've tasted in ages.'

'None of your shop-bought rubbish while we're here.'

Several cups of tea later, her mood elevated, Tom was convinced that the house had worked its magic on Annie's unpredictable mood swings.

'I'd like to explore the village.' She had not failed to notice the pub when they had arrived. 'Perhaps we could have a look before we go back to London?'

'Of course – if we've time. Don't forget, not only have I booked you a flight, we've got an action-packed weekend to get through first.'

'But...'

'But nothing - it'll be fun. The more you can fill your head with other things, the more likely your bad dreams will stop. If we get back from the show late, we'll have to save the village tour for next time.'

Annie wondered fleetingly whether there would be a next time.

'Okay, but don't forget our other agreement.'

'What agreement was that?'

'Have you forgotten already? You'd better not go back on your word. You said you'd take me shopping if I came this weekend.'

'Oh yes, of course. But you have to make an effort.'

Annie crossed her arms in pretence of defiance.

'I don't remember any conditions attached to the deal.'

Tom ushered her out of the kitchen.

'You should have read the small print! Now go and get ready.'

Knowing that there was no way that Tom would accept any deviation from his carefully thought out timetable, Annie went upstairs to shower, getting lost immediately in the maze of rooms.

Tom scurried round the kitchen, returning it to its homely state, and then joined her upstairs. He shouted through the frosted glass door of the shower room.

'Your costume is on the bed.'

'What was that? I can't hear you.'

'Your costume's on the bed. Don't be long, it'll take you a while to get into it.'

By the time Annie had finished in the bathroom, Tom was standing in front of a long mirror dressed in full RAF uniform, adjusting his tie. Her heart fluttered for a few brief seconds at the sight of him: smart, upright and manly, but the feeling passed quickly when she saw her costume: a drab wool jacket, teamed with the longest skirt she had seen since her school days.

'What the hell is that? Couldn't you find me something a bit sexy?' She shoved Tom out of the way so she could see herself in the mirror, holding the Women's Auxiliary Air Force uniform up against herself.

Tom burst out laughing at the look on her face.

'What's so funny? I look like a right frump.'

'I'm not laughing at the uniform. It's your face. It's a picture,' he said, trying hard to control himself.

'Oh and I see you supplied stockings too, pervert.'

'Got to be authentic. And I'm not a pervert.'

'Did women really have to wear this stuff? It's so dreary. And what was the point if they weren't flying the planes?'

Annie begrudgingly started to dress, pulling faces like a displeased child as she took each item from its hanger.

'Well, that's where you're wrong. Women did fly, though not in combat. The ATA risked life and limb in all weather, delivering planes from factories to active airfields.'

'Really,' said Annie, glazing over. She was more interested in staring at herself in the uniform.

'In fact there were a handful of women who were qualified to fly four-engine bombers. Bet you didn't know that,' Tom added, admiring Annie's legs in seamed stockings.

'Spare me the history lesson please.' Annie continued to look at herself from different angles in the mirror.

'You look bloody sexy!' Tom advanced on Annie with a wide grin. 'Maybe we could go a bit later after all.'

'Get away from me, you idiot,' Annie smiled, giving him a playful slap.

She opened a hatbox that had also been left on the bed and prodded the curly wig that she found inside. She pushed the box to one side and tried on the hat that went with the costume. Her own hair dangled loosely below.

'You're going to have to try a bit harder than that.'

He pulled the wig from the box and tried to manipulate it onto her head.

'Ouch, that hurt. Let me do it.' She pushed him away and tried to adjust the wig unsuccessfully, realising quickly that it seemed to have a mind of its own.

Tom tried not to laugh.

'Let me at least fix your hair for you.'

Finally, Annie relented and sat on the dressing table stool.

Tom pushed hair grips into place.

'It worries me that you're so adept at that,' said Annie, eyeing him suspiciously.

'There - now you look the part. That's a forties hairstyle if ever I saw one. Just one last detail left!'

Tom handed her a gas mask bag. She hesitated before putting it over her shoulder, running her hands over the canvas fabric, finding it somehow familiar. An image of the costumed girls at the gig flashed through Annie's mind, but she pushed the thought aside as she stuffed her phone and contents of her handbag into the gas mask bag. She slipped black shoes on to her stockinged feet and laced them up.

Tom made another attempt to grab at her.

153

'You seem to be adjusting to the role quickly.'

She turned away from his advances, put on her hat and looked in the mirror so she could make final adjustments. A woman from a different decade looked back at Annie. To Annie's surprise, Tom was right: she looked the part.

'Don't spoil my hair,' she protested. 'And don't start getting any ideas about role-playing. I've agreed to wear the uniform. Isn't that enough?'

'Spoilsport! I'll have to get you drunk then, won't I?'

'Best not. You've been telling me I drink too much as it is.'

'Well maybe a little tipple won't hurt when we get back.'

'I can see I'll need to keep my wits about me, Mr Darcy.'

Chapter 17

Annie climbed awkwardly into the passenger seat of Tom's car, trying unsuccessfully to pull her skirt down over her knees. Despite looking the part, the fabric was coarse and unforgiving and she could not help but notice a slightly musty odour. She tugged at her jacket, which was squashing her chest and making her feel slightly short of breath.

'This wig's making my head itch,' she complained, scratching under the hairline of the wig with a long acrylic fingernail. 'This uniform is making me hot too - I feel like a trussed up chicken ready for the oven.' She opened the window to let in some cooler air.

Tom laughed and changed the CD to something more in keeping with their day out: trumpets and saxophones of Glenn Miller's big band instantly filled the car.

'Bit different to a corporate suit isn't it? Might toughen you up and teach you a few things,' suggested Tom playfully.

'I'm tough enough already - and what do you mean, teach me a few things?'

'Just that it might make you realise what these amazing women put up with, that's all.'

'Go on, enlighten me then,' groaned Annie, wriggling in an attempt to get comfortable.

'Do you ever listen to anything I say? I told you when you were getting changed.'

'Oh yes, you said some women flew planes occasionally. It sounds like fun, but I'd never go up in this skirt!' Annie remarked flippantly.

'Are you mad? It wasn't all fun and games for them. The ATA girls flew in all conditions, with no radio or modern navigational aids and often in dreadful weather. I'd have hired you one of their uniforms, but they're extremely rare.'

Annie seemed totally disinterested. She examined her new set of fingernails and took out a file from her gas mask bag.

'Seems a bit stupid going out in all weathers if you ask me. They should have waited for a sunny day.'

'It wasn't meant to be fun. They were delivering planes for the RAF.' Tom turned up the music, shaking his head in disbelief.

'Sometimes I despair.'

'What was that?'

'Nothing.'

As they bickered, Tom had retraced the route they had taken to enter the village, this time passing villagers along the way. He wiped the windscreen with the back of a leather-gloved hand to clear the condensation that had formed overnight.

Once out onto a slightly wider road, Annie closed her window.

'It's not as mild as yesterday. We will be watching the air show from inside won't we?'

'Afraid not, but it'll brighten up soon. There's plenty to keep you occupied anyway - even shops!'

When little droplets of rain began to fall, Tom looked up anxiously at the sky.

'Think I spoke too soon. I hope this doesn't close in.'

'I hope so too. I'll look like a damp terrier if there's a downpour. Either way, there's no chance of me flying in this get-up.'

Their journey through quintessential English countryside was dramatic: low hills in the distance stretching out to east and west as far as the eye could see. By the time they reached the vicinity of the air show, the landscape had flattened out considerably and they slowed down to join a procession of other cars crawling along the perimeter fence. The smell of aviation fuel and the roar of jets displaying overhead, made Annie shiver at the sudden memory of days spent at airfields with her grandfather, wary of what reviving those emotions might do.

Cars, vans and motorbikes were shepherded in through the large imposing iron gates by marshals in fluorescent jackets and were directed to temporary car parks in the surrounding fields. First out of the car, Tom hurried round Annie's side and opened the car door for her.

'Let's hurry, I don't want to miss the first display.'

Annie carefully swung her legs out, attempting to extricate herself from the car: her skirt catching on the seat adjustor.

'When can I change back into my own clothes?'

'When we get back.'

'I've got a change in the boot.'

'Forget it. Try and get into the swing of things. You might even begin to enjoy it.'

'I hope I do,' she said, still affected by the familiar sounds and smells of old aircraft.

Tom changed the subject.

'The sky's cleared. Only a few small clouds in the distance.'

Annie was suddenly aware of a group of teenagers pointing and sniggering.

'Never mind the weather - what's going on? Why are we the only ones in costume?' Dismayed that people close by were getting out of cars in everyday clothes, she hid behind Tom.

'What are you doing? We'll be in a club enclosure. You won't feel out of place. Everyone will be in some sort of get-up.'

'How far have we got to walk dressed like this?'

'It's close, I promise. Only a minute or so.'

Despite Tom's reassurance, Annie grabbed her long winter coat from the boot of the car, put it on quickly and stuffed her hat roughly into a pocket. Before she had time to camouflage herself completely she caught sight of the same group of teenagers pointing at her seamed stockings and flat black shoes: still sniggering behind their hands to each other. She took a deep breath and, with her nose in the air, marched off defiantly in the direction that Tom had indicated.

'Give us a hand, Annie.' Tom trailed in her wake, loaded down with a picnic basket, binoculars and an assortment of seemingly useless junk that he had wanted to bring along.

Annie stumbled on the uneven ground as she negotiated tyre marks and furrows.

'Not bloody likely! I need to find somewhere to hide.'

Feeling agitated and flustered, Annie joined other visitors walking in the direction of the public viewing area: to her relief, she finally spotted others dressed in similar costumes. Waiting for Tom to catch up, she concealed herself in the doorway of a large deserted hangar.

Tom joined her, breathless and red-faced.

'There you are! Give me a hand with some of this.'

Annie took one of the lighter bags.

'What's the matter with you? You went off without me like a rocket.'

'Nothing,' she whispered. 'I just didn't like the way people were staring at me.'

'You look fabulous, they were just gawping at your sexy legs, that's all.'

'Yeah, right. I practically broke my ankle in the mud. And I've already had a bunch of kids laugh at me,' she added.

Tom thrust some umbrellas into her hands.

'Do you think you could manage these?'

Annie took them begrudgingly.

'We won't need them. I intend to watch from somewhere dry.'

She walked closely behind him as he made his way between more deserted huts and aircraft hangars, until the sound of music, laughter and animated conversation could be heard somewhere ahead. Rounding the corner of one of the derelict hangars, a completely different scene greeted them. A large group of air show enthusiasts had congregated in an enclosure, all of them costumed for the event. Immediately outside the enclosure was a line of vintage cars, neatly parked in an orderly line behind a rope fence for spectators to stop and admire.

Tom stopped and spoke pleadingly to Annie.

'You know this could be fun, so try and join in.'

'I'll try,' she said, feeling less sulky now she could see people enjoying themselves.

'Good. Let's go and mingle.'

'Anyone you know going to be here?'

'There'll be a few familiar faces I expect. They'll be getting into the spirit of things by now.'

They approached the area, which was about the size of a tennis court, surrounded by a white picket fence, thronging with the costumed people laughing and talking. At one end, a white marquee faced a wide area of turf. Beyond the grass, small planes were landing and taking off on a narrow concrete runway. A breeze whistled through the open door of the marquee, causing the roof to occasionally balloon upwards.

Two young women dressed in black skirts and crisp white blouses were greeting people as they arrived at the entrance to the marquee: one offering glasses of champagne to guests, the other girl ticking off the names on a clipboard.

The ground had been carefully manicured, the grass short and neat. Wicker chairs and tables were evenly placed around the edges of the marquee, with a gap for a bar at one end. In the centre, surrounded by the tables and chairs, a temporary dance floor was full of dancing couples in costume. At this point Annie noticed big band music playing faintly in the background, almost drowned out by the buzz of conversation and laughter.

'See! I told you there was nothing to worry about,' remarked Tom. 'You'd look out of place if we hadn't bothered dressing up.'

'I was beginning to think the whole thing was a joke, just to make me look stupid,' she admitted, mellowing a little. 'I must admit - it does look colourful. Plus there seems to be free champers, so that's a bonus!'

Tom gave their names to the girl with the clipboard.

'Pace yourself, remember you've got that flight booked later.'

Squeezing through a gap in the crowd, Tom turned to check Annie was behind him, only to see her balancing a full glass of champagne in each hand; umbrellas precariously tucked under one arm.

'I think I'd better take those before you impale someone. And why two glasses? Are you trying to cause trouble?'

Annie raised a glass to Tom with a broad smile: a smile that indicated she would do the opposite to whatever he suggested.

'In answer to those two questions, I'm thirsty and no, I'm not!'

'Please Annie, go easy. The pilot won't be happy if I let you turn up for your flight half-cut.'

Annie took a particularly large gulp of champagne.

'I'll do my best. Where shall we sit?' she asked, slamming an empty glass down on a silver tray being carried by a young waitress.

A look of disappointment briefly clouded Tom's face.

'Over there.' He pointed to an empty table in a corner of the marquee. Weaving in and out of the gathering revellers, Annie followed Tom, dropping her coat onto one of the vacant chairs.

'This will do nicely.' Annie drank the champagne from the remaining glass as quickly as she had the first.

Tom sat down opposite her, a nervous smile on his face.

'Are you cross with me?' she asked, noticing his expression. 'I'm only having a couple to help me chill out a bit.'

'No, just concerned, and keep your voice down a bit. People are looking at you.'

'You are cross, I can tell. Anyway, a minute ago you seemed pleased people were looking at my legs.'

'Please Annie...'

'Stop worrying, I'm fine,' she said loudly, feeling the effect of the champagne kicking in already. She looked around at the marquee, scanning the people in it.

Tom asked the waitress for a jug of water.

'Well now you're here, what do you think?'

Annie looked around at men, women and children, enjoying the party: some in uniform or civilian dress from the forties.

'I admit I was wrong about today, this is fun.'

A few women dressed similarly to Annie were dancing with men in uniform. Others in stylish clothes accessorised with hats, gloves and stiff leather handbags decorated the edge of the dance floor. Some of the children that had accompanied their parents had even dressed the part: a boy in baggy shorts and a knitted tank top played with twin girls wearing identical buttoned coats and flat shoes.

Tom thumbed through the programme he had picked up from an attendant. A boyish expression returned to his face.

'If the weather stays like this, and the wind doesn't pick up then everything should fly to schedule.'

Annie had begun to scratch her scalp again, whilst eyeing up a group of men in their mid thirties seated nearby. Dressed similarly to Tom and drinking beer, one of the men sensed Annie's eyes on him.

At that moment, Tom looked up from his programme. The man winked at Annie.

'Great, we've only been here a minute and you're flirting already.'

'He's just having a bit of fun.'

Tom looked at the programme again, aware that the man and his friends seemed to be sharing a personal joke: their conversation interlaced with bursts of raucous laughter. Annie tried hard to conceal a snigger.

'Would you like me to book you both a room?' Tom asked suddenly, slamming the programme down on the table. He looked over at the man and shot him a warning glance.

'Tom, don't be ridiculous.'

Tom returned to his reading.

The man was handsome, his brown hair flecked with grey at the sides. He wore his RAF cap at a jaunty angle dipping over his forehead. His eyes were dark, his face tanned and rugged. He leaned back in his chair, rocking slowly backwards and forwards, so that he could get a better view of Annie, finally taking off his cap and raising it to her. At that point, Annie noticed that he was wearing a wedding ring. She immediately turned her attention to Tom. She had learnt her lesson about the dangers surrounding married men several years previously.

'I'm sorry if I gave you the wrong impression. Guess I was just getting a bit carried away by the occasion.'

'And you've had two glasses of champagne in less than ten minutes. Here – drink this.' Tom poured Annie a glass of water. 'Let's forget about it, okay?'

A waitress approached their table with a selection of light snacks, and then passed to the table where the group of uniformed men were sitting. Annie noticed the girl looking very awkward, turning bright red as one of the men reached up to put his hand on her bottom. She hurried away, almost dropping her tray of cakes. The men laughed loudly as they watched the young girl scuttle off.

'Idiots,' said Tom, watching the whole thing unfold.

Annie glared at the group, a little bruised that the handsome guy could divert his attention so quickly to another possible conquest. She suddenly felt glad she was with Tom, or glad he was a gentleman at least.

'You shouldn't have encouraged them, Annie. They might have left that poor girl alone if you hadn't flirted in the first place.'

'I doubt it. They're obviously finding it good sport. Had too many beers by the looks of it. Anyway, I thought we'd moved on from those guys.'

'Just making a point.'

Annie changed the subject.

'Tell me the order of the day.'

Tom scanned through the programme again.

'Some of this might not be your cup of tea, the modern jets are ear-splitting. I'll understand if you don't want to be around for those.'

Annie seized the opportunity to escape for a while.

'Good point. Let me know when they're on and I might take a wander and look at those shops you mentioned. There are shops aren't there Tom? It wasn't a ruse to get me here I hope!'

'Wouldn't want you to miss out on an air show T-shirt.'

'Is that it - just T-shirts?'

'Well, you might be able to pick up some nice sunglasses.'

'Sunglasses? It's the middle of winter!'

'That's a bit of an exaggeration, and it is quite sunny. You might need them.'

Annie huffed and rolled her eyes in disbelief.

'I suppose it's worth a look, but something tells me I will not be coming back with a designer dress.'

Tom was feeling irritable, his patience with Annie running out. Her constant complaining and wandering eyes were becoming too much to endure. He was beginning to think that he stood more chance of enjoying the day if Annie wasn't there. With such thoughts running through his mind, the roar of high-powered red jets appearing suddenly from high above made him jump. Red, white and blue smoke appeared scrawled across the sky in the wake of the jets as they disappeared into the distance.

Annie clapped her hands over her ears.

'I thought you were going to warn me.'

'It's the Red Arrows. You don't want to miss them, do you?'

The audience, startled by the sudden noise, scanned the sky. Most rushed forward to the open side of the enclosure and Tom joined them. Hemmed in by the excited onlookers, Annie called to Tom, but the rumble of the jet engines drowned out her voice. She remained in her seat like a spoilt child, furious that Tom had gone off without a thought for her.

Chapter 18

Before the spectators had finished cheering, two of the jets appeared again, this time from each end of the runway, slicing through the sky, leaving a deafening roar and blue and red smoke in their wake. They climbed steeply to join the other jets displaying above and the group then fanned out in perfect symmetry. As the display continued, the planes made low level passes and spiralled around each other, creating the illusion that they were only a few feet apart. Finally they performed complex passes across the sky, causing most adults to gasp and children to squeal with excitement, cupping their hands across their ears to muffle the noise. The opening display seemed to be over almost before it had started: the jets arcing upwards and forming the shape of a huge heart pierced with an arrow, before disappearing towards the horizon for the last time, the only evidence of their flight path, patriotic red, white and blue smoke blazed across the cold autumn sky.

As quickly as the crowd had surged past Annie, people returned to their seats babbling excitedly about what they had just seen. Tom joined Annie, oblivious to the fact that she had remained in her seat and therefore not seen anything of the display.

'We were really lucky there. If those clouds had come over, they might not have been able to fly at all.'

Annie was still annoyed.

'Enjoyed that, did you?'

'Wasn't it fantastic?'

'How the hell would I know?' bellowed Annie.

Several people, including the man Annie had been eyeing up, turned to look at her.

'I didn't see a thing. I was mobbed by all these rude people pushing past me,' she added, glaring at the individuals who had started to stare back since her outburst. 'And what are you looking at?' she barked at the handsome man on the next table, becoming more agitated when she saw him nudge the person next to him.

Tom reacted immediately, whispering in Annie's ear.

'Please don't embarrass me like that,' he pleaded, looking around at the sea of faces all fixed on Annie. 'Let's not spoil the day.'

She huffed and glowered at him.

'I need another drink.'

Tom moved his chair closer to her so bystanders might not overhear the rest of their conversation. 'Why don't you just sit back and relax, try and enjoy yourself?' He sat down again, smiling nervously at the few people still watching their row unfold.

Annie suddenly stood up and hissed in Tom's right ear.

'I can't do this anymore. I'm sick of your obsession with all this stuff.' She waved her hand towards the sky. 'I'm going home. I'll make my own way back to London.' She grabbed the gas mask bag that she had been carrying as a handbag and stormed off, not noticing her mobile phone slip out as she yanked it from the table.

Tom did not attempt to stop her. He realised he was glad she was going. She needed to cool down in the comfort of her own home. He looked across at the man that had made him jealous, but he averted his eyes quickly, pretending to be in deep conversation with his friends.

Annie did not care that she might have embarrassed Tom; all she knew was that she needed to be far away from him as soon as possible.

It was not until she was almost out of the marquee that Annie realised she had left her coat with Tom. She hesitated for a second and debated what she should do. She was already beginning to feel ashamed at her outburst and frustrated that with each passing day she was becoming more volatile but could do nothing to stop it. She had even surprised herself by laying into poor Tom for something so minor, but she could not face returning to him. Part of her had really been looking forward to the flight Tom had booked, but she knew that if she went back now, everyone would be watching her and assuming she had gone back with her tail between her legs to apologise.

Having lost the chance to fly, she began to think back to the last time she had taken the controls of her grandfather's plane. Nostalgia washed over her as she recalled the day trips she had taken with him as a teenager over the Sussex countryside. He had eagerly encouraged her to learn to fly, sometimes taking his hands off the controls, allowing her to take over. He was a maverick but she had loved his cavalier personality. It had amused him to see her face change from one of horror as the plane started to bank over to one of jubilance when she had managed to stabilise the plane again. He was the reason she had finally flown solo. She had often wondered whether he had wished for a grandson instead. He would be disappointed if he were alive and could see her now. She suddenly remembered that she had insisted to Dr. Edwards that she had no knowledge or interest in the war, which in the light of day was blatantly untrue: the time with her grandfather when she had listened to his wartime experiences had been compartmentalised to deal with his passing.

Being hemmed in by aviation paraphernalia had somehow recalled the memory of him and his stories. She felt an impromptu twang of guilt that material things, such as money and status, had become more important in her life than the people that surrounded her. Trying to put her grandfather to the back of her mind, Annie resumed her hurried pace, and marched off through the centre of the merchandise stalls, along a path worn in the short grass.

Suddenly she realised she had taken a different route back and was completely lost. Fewer people were passing by and she could not see any exit signs. She stopped and looked back the way she had come, hoping that Tom was going to show up any minute, running after her and begging for forgiveness. She opened the gas mask bag to check to see if there were any messages on her phone, but after rummaging through the bag and not finding it, she wondered if Tom had confiscated it. She grimaced, wishing she'd had the presence of mind to hide it better. She glanced back over her shoulder once more to see if Tom was following, but he was nowhere to be seen: she'd have to go it alone.

As Annie walked on, she took deep breaths to allow her racing heart to settle into a natural rhythm again. Her face felt hot and flushed and she was feeling ashamed of her behaviour: she had allowed her unhappiness to overwhelm her and cause havoc. Although she knew that she did not love Tom, she still did not want things to have ended between them in that way.

There were still no apparent direction signs for the main entrance. The droning and buzzing of aircraft taking off and landing were still audible, but they seemed to be much further away now. Reaching a gap in a hedge, Annie stepped through and made her way along a well-worn tarmacked path, adjacent to a row of old corrugated metal buildings, hoping to start seeing familiar parts of the airfield. She began to feel panicky and started to cry. She wiped the tears that had begun to fall and continued on.

Flanking corrugated buildings with grimy broken windows, weeds and nettles were battling for space and sunlight. Rows of saplings, almost completely bare of leaves, lined the path that Annie had chosen. She approached a clearing. A two storey rectangular building sat alone: concrete walls almost completely obliterated by rambling ivy. At the top of the structure, a rusting handrail creaked precariously in the breeze, having come detached from all but one of its brackets. A wooden sign hung from the railings sign. Keep Out. This Watch Office is Unsafe. A solitary kestrel landed lightly on the handrail and lazily blinked at Annie, perching majestically as if to claim ownership.

Beyond the dilapidated building, the path began to narrow. Annie noticed how the further she walked, the wilder the terrain was becoming: tufts of grass and thistles had seeded themselves, forcing the tarmac upwards into bulging bubbles resembling a volcano about to erupt. She began to worry about how far she had strayed from the path, but pride forced her onwards rather than back to Tom and the laughing partygoers. Shielding her eyes from the bright sunlight with one hand, she carefully picked her way across the uneven surface. Ahead, the road came to an abrupt stop, blocked by a pair of high iron gates, which, although closed were clearly not locked. A rusted padlock hung open, perhaps broken by trespassers, neglect or disuse.

Annie listened for ferocious barking as she approached the gates, suspecting there might be guard dogs waiting to pounce on the other side. Hearing nothing, she stood on tiptoe and squinted through a letterbox, but the metal catch tray on the other side restricted any view. Despite her heart pounding in her chest, a growing curiosity was urging her to investigate further.

She threw caution to the wind, and using all her weight to push against the heavy iron gates, shifted them open just enough to poke her head around for a better look. The gate had shuddered and creaked noisily on its dry rusty hinges, resisting her attempts. Was it a sign perhaps that she should turn around and walk away? She gingerly peered through the gap. Looking around for signs of movement, she was finally convinced that there was no vicious dog snarling on the other side and she pushed harder, her feet sliding in the mud, until she could squeeze her slight body through the gates.

It became immediately obvious that this part of the airfield had not been used for quite a time. Annie likened it to stepping into The Secret Garden as she entered the deserted yard. Brambles that had woven their thorny stems through both gates and scratched her legs, instantly made large holes in her stockings, and irritated her skin. Finally managing to extricate herself, Annie brushed leaves and thistles from her clothes and pulled out the offending thorns.

She stood still, feeling uneasy and trying to acclimatise herself to her surroundings. The birds had gone quiet and the distant planes could barely be heard. Scrutinising the shadows, she remained on alert, still listening for footsteps or guard dogs, should she need to make a quick escape. Stepping forward, her shoes broke the near silence as she trod on broken glass.

The large yard was crammed full of twisted and tangled metal: old cars, large wooden crates and unrecognisable paraphernalia, which had been abandoned and left to rust away to nothing. A narrow road allowed vehicles to come in and out: evident from deep lorry tyre tracks around various huts and buildings.

Huge twisted chunks of metal pointed up into the sky from the mud; an abstract sculpture.

Annie walked carefully through the tangled wreckage. As her eyes became accustomed to the lack of sunlight, the contorted shapes began to make some sense. Abandoned aircraft from a bygone age had been deposited there, left to rot and decay: nearly all semblance of their original purpose reclaimed by the weeds and brambles mercilessly forcing their way through cracks in fuselages. Annie recalled childhood stories of castles surrounded by deep forests as she stared at the brambles that had wrapped themselves around rotting wing spars. She wished she could retrace her steps, but as usual had proceeded to ignore her surroundings.

The wings of a large aircraft had been chained to the perimeter fence, rivets missing from the panels that formed their massive span. The chains had over time, eaten into the thin metal skin, perforating their once graceful structure. Annie thought it ironic that a once powerful aircraft was manacled firmly to the earth.

Abandoned where the main body of the aircraft should have been, was a shop mannequin, covered almost entirely with green mould, and with empty sockets where his eyes had once been. Dark holes stared blindly back at Annie. He sat menacingly above her; the aircraft wings extensions to his body, like an abstract version of the Angel of the North. He had no limbs and his lower half was clothed in a sodden pair of suit trousers that hung limply with no legs to fill them. Annie felt hypnotised by the green man's face: his lifeless expression making her think fleetingly about the figures in the Battle of Britain memorial. She imagined for a second that he let out a long and deep sigh but immediately told herself it must have been the wind merely whistling through the metal fuselages surrounding her. Feeling overcome with fear, Annie backed away, eager to get away from this place and back to the crowds of people at the event. In her haste, she stumbled back and fell against a door to a deserted hangar.

Annie wanted to run, but as she looked back at the entrance to the scrap yard, shadows seemed to grow longer and darker. Just as she plucked up the courage to make a run for it, the heavens suddenly opened, pelting both her and the tin roof of the hangar with freezing hail. As she stood in the doorway, a flash of lightning illuminated the darkening sky, suddenly heavy with rolling grey clouds. The only safe haven seemed to be inside, so she opted to use the hangar as a temporary refuge.

The interior smelt musty and rancid. Her eyes began to adjust to the shadows. Puddles had collected on the ground under the leaks in the roof. From floor to ceiling, old packing cases had been stacked as substitute shelving, threatening to collapse at any moment under the weight of their contents. Rows of black and chrome dials and gauges were balanced precariously on these makeshift shelves.

Annie made her way tentatively along the corridor immediately ahead, noticing the muted sound of music playing and faint light at the far end of the building. She dodged oily puddles as she followed the sound, hoping to find someone who could direct her back to the air show. The wind whistled through gaps in the corrugated metal walls, disturbing dust and debris, which floated down from above like the fine drizzle that often precedes rain. She could still hear the hail hammering on the roof, punctuated only by the resident crows and an occasional scuffling noise in dark corners. Despite the gloom and her earlier panic, there was something incalculable about the place that made her want to go deeper into its corridors rather than retreat to daylight. Curiosity spurred her on towards the light at the end of the building, the music getting slowly louder as she ventured down narrow passages.

Her aviation knowledge was sufficient for her to appreciate that almost without exception everything on the shelves belonged to an aircraft of some type. The high shelves continued the full length of the building, interrupted only by a faded black and white photograph of a pilot standing next to an old plane riddled with bullet holes. Annie glanced at the picture on passing, somehow nostalgic for an era she never knew.

Daylight was beginning to fade, and Annie was forced to start considering her options. The door she had entered by had slammed shut due to a sudden gust of wind that also disturbed more dust and cobwebs from the shelving. With nothing now but dark shadows behind her, she continued, turning another corner expecting to see more shelves.

Instead, a wooden workbench cluttered with tools nestled in a small corner, a wooden stool tucked beneath and a single illuminated light bulb on a frayed flex above. Above the bench, a small window looked out onto the scrap yard. A dusty old radio was perched on the window ledge: big band music playing softly. Female voices sang the words of an unfamiliar song in close harmony.

'Don't sit under the apple tree with anyone else but me, anyone else but me, anyone else but me...'

A calendar from 1941 was nailed to the wall, the picture of the month a black and white photograph of a scantily-clad girl posing over a classic car. The pages of the calendar were faded and torn.

Realising the hangar was empty and that she had come to the end of the workshop, Annie turned to retrace her steps. She moved quietly and cautiously towards where she hoped, she would find the door she had entered by, but each passageway disappeared into near darkness like a blackened maze, with nothing to light them but the pinpricks of light from above. Disorientated, Annie very quickly realised she had taken another wrong turn. She suddenly wished that she had stayed with Tom, amongst the noise and crowds.

Panic began to mount, her stomach tightening into knots. She stumbled, half running and half walking to where she could see a shaft of light from a hole in the roof, knocking things over in her haste. She felt a searing pain in her shin as she passed by something sharp. The more she hurried the more her panic gathered impetus, her jacket sleeve snagging on the metal edge of a tea chest, cobwebs clinging to her arms and hair.

Just as she was beginning to think she would never find a way out, a doorway suddenly came into sight, but standing against it and blocking her way was a tall broad-shouldered figure. She let out a scream, which echoed through the passageways. There was a deafening clap of thunder, which echoed through the hangar, causing the whole building to tremble. The crows flew from their perch outside, complaining loudly. A flash of lightning forced its way through gaps in the corrugated walls, illuminating the dark passages before plunging the hangar into semi-darkness again. Annie turned and blindly ran back the way she came, not knowing what direction she was taking. There was no escape route. She stumbled again. Putting her hands out in front to guide herself, she unexpectedly found a gap in the corrugated walls. She squeezed through, landing heavily on her knees in a deep muddy puddle. The hail stopped, and the puddle began to shimmer in the sunlight, which now beat down on her from a blue sky.

Still terrified, but exuberant to be in the open air once again, Annie scrambled to her feet, her leg now throbbing with pain, and staggered away from the dark tomb behind. Primal instinct made her continue running: the urge to get away far more powerful than the need to inspect her wounds. Putting distance between herself and the scrap yard, she spotted an alternative gate, unimpeded by brambles that had fortunately been left open. As she passed through it she glanced over her shoulder to check she was alone.

The ground began to vibrate as a deep rumbling noise resonated in the sky behind Annie. Two Hurricanes raced over her head and disappeared beyond a line of buildings, followed by another aircraft: unidentifiable due to flames engulfing the whole front section of the fuselage. Barely clearing the roofs of one of the buildings, and rapidly losing height, it was flying dangerously close to nearby trees. Its engine stuttered, the plane subsequently clipping the roof of one of the buildings with its undercarriage, causing a large section to shear off. Annie instinctively followed the path of the ill-fated aircraft. A small group of men in overalls emerged from a blister hangar close by: shouting and jumping onto a moving truck. It sped along the grass runway after the stricken plane, which eventually belly-flopped onto the grass, slewing sideways until finally coming to rest. Several more trucks tore along the grass, as the two Hurricanes flew off, joining other planes, circling, dipping and diving high above.

The trucks reached the burning plane well before Annie, arriving to rescue the pilot who was trying to climb out of the wreckage. He was struggling wildly, his clothes blackened and on fire. Annie stood well back as the heat from the burning plane became too intense to withstand.

Someone approached Annie unexpectedly from behind and grabbed her firmly by both shoulders. Totally mesmerised by the crippled plane and injured pilot,

Annie had been oblivious to the man who had been running after her from the scrap yard and she jumped in surprise. Fighting against his grip, she attempted to shake herself free.

The man tried to restrain Annie.

'Hey, calm down, why are you running away?'

Annie continued to struggle.

'Get off me you bastard or I'll...'

'Or you'll what?' he interrupted, releasing his grip.

'Or I'll beat the crap out of you,' retorted Annie, backing away from him.

'That's no way to talk to a Squadron Leader, especially one who has come to your aid.'

Annie looked up, sweeping her hair away from her face with grazed and bleeding hands, realising that the air temperature had changed and it was suddenly as hot as a summer's day. The storm clouds had cleared and the sky was blue as far as the eye could see. The man was silhouetted against brilliant sunshine, his features barely discernible.

Annie's body ached from her ordeal. She looked at the burning plane and the crowd of men gathered around a man lying motionless on the grass. Her heart raced and her head swam. She fainted and fell limply against the Squadron Leader. He instantly swept her up into his arms before she hit the ground and Annie's last thought was that the feel of his uniform buttons against her fingers felt strangely familiar.

Chapter 19

Annie woke a few moments later, the gentle motion of the man's long stride soothing her as she rested her head on his chest.

Aware that she had regained consciousness, he spoke softly.

'Don't worry, we'll have you fixed up in a jiffy.'

Annie was too traumatised and weak to argue.

'Where are you taking me?'

'The sick bay.'

'I need to find Tom.'

'Who is Tom, your sweetheart?'

'Sweetheart? How quaint.'

'Well, sweetheart or not, we need to get that leg patched up as soon as possible.'

'Whatever you say,' answered Annie, dipping in and out of consciousness.

The man chuckled.

'Gladys looks after all the boys like she's mother to all of us. By the way, my name is Hill. But you can call me Lenny.'

'Lenny...that's a nice name. Quite old fashioned.'

'Do you think so? I know a couple of Leonards, but no one calls me that.'

Acrid fumes from aviation fuel filled the air once again as a four-engine bomber flew overhead, making Annie feel nauseous. Overwhelmed by the pungent smell, she slipped into darkness once again.

When Annie awoke, she was recumbent on a lumpy mattress, aware of whispering by her side. She kept her eyes closed so as not to alert them to the fact that she was listening in.

'Why is she wearing WAAF uniform?'

'Beats me, Gladys,' replied a stern male voice. 'We're not expecting any WAAFs today, only another batch of ferry girls.'

'Did you see her fingernails, Harold? Bright red and they don't even look real. Her hands are as soft as a baby's bottom. Doesn't look like she's done a day's work in years.'

'Maybe she went to a party last night.'

Annie was aware of her hand being examined.

Gladys sounded suspicious.

'Where did you find her?'

A third person spoke, the calming voice of the man who had saved Annie.

'I found her in the stores. Followed her out and she ran off like there was no tomorrow. She was very upset about seeing that chap die.'

'You'd think she would have seen plenty of that.'

'I wish I could stay until she comes to, but the CO will wonder where I have got to.'

The last hour flooded back into Annie's muddled brain like a raging torrent.

'Don't you worry, Len. We'll clean her up and give her some tea or soup.'

'Thanks Gladys, you're a poppet. Must dash, but I'll pop by later. Are you coming, Harold?'

'Yes, best be off. Thanks for the tea Gladys. Cheerio.'

Lenny and Harold left the room. Despite the lumpy mattress and uncomfortable pillows, Annie drifted off into restless sleep still thinking about their strange conversation, occasionally regaining consciousness as her carer bustled about in the small room. She wondered why they had found just cause to question her uniform and acrylic nails, especially with so many people in costume on the airfield that day. The death of a pilot seemed far more worthy of discussion, but they had practically dismissed it.

When Annie finally opened her eyes, she was surprised to see that so much time had passed. The sun was already setting, creating silvery lines around the edge of the clouds. Pulling herself up into a sitting position: her head spun, the bed groaned beneath her.

'How long have I been asleep?'

A woman had been sitting on a wicker chair beside Annie's bed. She jumped up and fussed around Annie, plumping up her pillows.

'You mustn't sit up too quickly dear, you'll make yourself giddy again.'

'I've got to get back to find Tom and get back to London.'

The woman ignored Annie's comment.

'I'm Gladys, dear, the nurse here. Would you like a glass of water or a cup of tea?'

'Yes please. I'd love a cup of tea,' replied Annie, realising she was in no fit state to go hunting for Tom.

Her leg throbbed and she felt as though she had a hangover.

I don't know if you take sugar but I'll put some in anyway, dear. It will give you some energy.'

'Thank you.'

Annie noticed that Gladys was wearing a very old-fashioned nurse's uniform and flat black polished shoes.

'I see you've dressed in costume too. Everyone's gone to so much effort.'

Gladys looked down at her uniform, appearing perplexed.

'It's not a costume, dear. It's my uniform, I wear this every day.'

Annie laughed weakly.

'I see you're really taking the whole re-enactor thing seriously.'

'You really have got yourself in a pickle haven't you? Now try and relax.'

'I can't believe one of the pilots has died.'

'He's the third one this week. Dreadful business.'

Annie was stunned at Gladys' acceptance.

'Are there usually this many accidents at an air show?'

Gladys looked quizzically at Annie.

'Air show? You really did get a knock on the head didn't you dear?'

Annie felt her head for bumps.

'I may have done, but that doesn't alter the fact that this game has gone a bit too far.'

Gladys went to speak but changed her mind.

'I'll just go and put the kettle on next door. Sorry I can only give you one biscuit. Can't be seen to be favouring you.'

'What do you mean, favour me?'

'The boys are always starving when they get back from France.'

Gladys closed the door softly behind her, leaving Annie confused, looking around the small room for clues.

It was bleak and damp, the walls painted a washed out shade of green, the only relief a couple of simply framed photos: one of the Queen Mother when she was much younger and the other a group of men in uniform standing in front of a large plane. Each window had tatty black curtains partially drawn across. The room was furnished in a utilitarian manner: metal framed bedstead, desk and chair, medical screen and the wicker bedside chair on which Gladys had been seated.

Annie could hear Gladys humming and clattering around in the adjacent room, but after a few minutes, she heard her talking to another woman. Seconds later the door opened and Gladys entered carrying a cup and saucer, followed by a younger woman in her late thirties, dressed in a similar uniform to Annie's, but in a darker shade of blue. The younger woman was tall and slender: grey eyes, mousy hair arranged similarly to the wig that Annie was wearing.

Gladys busied herself at her desk. The tall woman approached Annie and held out her hand.

'Hello,' she said. 'I'm Margaret Bowhill. We were expecting six girls today. With you that makes seven.

185

Perhaps you can enlighten me.' Her piercing grey eyes searched Annie for clues.

'What's your name?'

Annie shook hands with the woman.

'Annie Winter.'

'I have no such name on my list.'

'I got lost on the airfield. I am definitely meant to be here. It was planned weeks ago.'

'Well that doesn't matter now. At least you have arrived, though the circumstances are a little odd.'

The woman spotted the confusion on Annie's face and filled the silence.

'Where is your luggage?'

Annie tried to think of what to say.

'I'm sorry?'

The woman continued to grill Annie.

'And the uniform...can you explain why you are wearing WAAF uniform?'

'Did Tom put you up to this? It's really not funny anymore.'

'This is not a joke. You need to rest, and then everything will come back to you.'

Annie was taken aback. The woman seemed genuine. If she was acting, she was very authentic. Annie decided to play along until she could trip her up.

'I'm sorry. It's coming back a little now. It was what I was given to wear. Can't stand the bloody thing, not my choice at all. Very itchy.'

The woman raised her eyebrows disapprovingly, making Annie wonder what she'd done.

I'm going to kill Tom when I see him, she thought.

'Miss Winter, I will not tolerate foul language in my ferry pool. We will sort this out in the morning. I've arranged somewhere for you to stay with the others. You'll be well looked after, but it's too late to take you to the farm now. Unless we get any injured pilots returning tonight you can stay here for the night.'

'I ought to phone someone.'

'The phone is for emergencies only. Rest now.' Before Annie could think of what to say in response, the woman turned and left the room without another word. Annie noticed her seamed stockings.

Gladys handed Annie her tea.

'Who the hell does she think she is, ordering me about?'

'Don't you worry dear, her bark is worse than her bite. Once you get to know her you'll find that she is very protective of all her girls.'

Gladys patted and stroked Annie's hand reassuringly and encouraged her to drink the sweet tea and eat the unexciting biscuit.

'I want to go home.'

'Well you can't dear, at least not today. You've had a nasty shock and it could be dangerous for you to be walking about.'

There was something peculiar going on: of that, Annie was sure. She drank the tea and obediently ate her biscuit: amazed that she could really taste the tea and the biscuit in what was clearly a dream. It would all stop soon, and she would wake up. Tom would be there, forgiving as ever, ready to take her home.

'Tom will be in the hospitality tent. He'll definitely be wondering where I am.'

Gladys appeased Annie.

'Yes dear, but don't you worry about your beau. You rest now and we'll get a message to him.' Gladys wrote in her accident book: Possible concussion due to a fall. Confusion. Delusional. 24 hour Observation.

Annie knew Tom would not be worried about her, not under the circumstances in which they had parted, but she wanted him more than she had ever wanted him before.

'I'll go and sort out some fresh clothes for you while you have a bit more sleep.'

As Annie watched the hours tick by on the wall clock, she tried to imagine what the man who had scooped her up looked like. She wished she was at home tucked up in her own bed, but eventually drifted off, dreaming about the shadowy figure in the scrap yard. She was chased, by menacing figures that materialised out of thin air. No matter how fast she ran, her legs were weighted down, feet glued to the floor.

She woke early in the morning, disturbed by a commotion that appeared to be coming from outside the building. The room was so warm that she pulled back the covers. Opening the black curtains she realised it was still early. She pressed her face to the dirty window to get a better look at what was going on.

The sun was beginning to rise and the sky was changing from dark blue to shades of pink and orange. The grassy field stretched away into the distance, lined on two sides by trees. She noticed that men were pointing into the distance at a small speck in the sky. As it got nearer, Annie could see that it was an aircraft in trouble. It wavered unsteadily, dipping first one wing and then the other. Grey smoke was billowing from one engine. Just as the aircraft appeared to be landing, it veered away out of view. Seconds later there was a loud explosion. Trucks raced along the grass.

She closed the curtains: confused as to why there had been two disasters in the space of a few hours.

The door opened.

Chapter 20

Lenny breezed through the medical room door. Annie's mouth dropped open as she saw his face properly for the first time. She remained like that for a few seconds as she absorbed everything about the man standing in front of her, hands casually stuffed into his trouser pockets. He looked familiar, but at that moment she was unable to place his frame. The man in uniform on the platform? Her eyes scanned his rugged face.

'How are you feeling now?'

Annie remained mute, realisation still kicking in.

Lenny held out his hand.

'It's me. Lenny. It was me that brought you here. You do remember, don't you?'

Her fuggy mind drip-fed her half-pictures: more vivid pictures from the past two weeks, the lift, the Underground, those girls in fancy dress...

'I remember your voice, but apart from that everything else is a bit sketchy.'

'You were very upset. You fainted.'

Lenny was the epitome of masculinity: tall and broad shouldered, with defined upper arms, which strained against the sleeves of his blue uniform jacket. As Annie tried to piece together her reason for being where she was, she was conscious that she was still staring, mesmerised by Lenny's physique and his piercing blue eyes. His hair was dark and wavy, with the first signs of greying at the temples adding a distinguished air to his appearance.

The silence between them stretched out awkwardly, Annie sensing that at any moment it would give way under the tension, and catapult her into his arms.

'You don't say much, do you?'

Annie composed herself.

'Oh sorry, I'm just a bit confused, that's all.' She noticed that despite Lenny's rugged complexion there was tiredness about him: a look of strain that only disappeared when he smiled.

'You look better than when I found you. Gladys has looked after you well. I popped in to check on you during the night but you were sparko.' He took off his cap and smiled confidently.

'I do feel a little better.'

The pieces fell into place. The pilot in the memorial...could it have been a relative of his? The resemblance was uncanny, but she thought it untimely to question him.

'You were running around like a headless chicken in the stores yesterday afternoon. How on earth did you end up in there?'

'I was lost, and now I'm beginning to wish I had never agreed to come to this place.'

'You mentioned someone called Tom just before you keeled over. Can't say I've met him. Thought I knew everyone here. Maybe he's off on a pick up.'

'Pick up? What do you mean?'

'Gone to pick up a Spit perhaps.'

'How disgusting! Why would Tom want to pick up spit? He's not a cleaner.'

'Uh?' said Lenny, looking puzzled. 'Oh I see,' he said at last, realising Annie's mistake. 'I mean Spit, as in Spitfire.'

Annie decided that whatever anyone said to her, it wasn't going to make any sense. Dreams are like that. So she let Lenny ramble on: about how lucky she was not to have been caught up in the trouble yesterday, how she should follow safety procedures on the airfield and how she should be more careful about losing all her luggage. She began to feel light-headed again.

Noticing that she had gone pale, Lenny reassured her.

'Oh don't worry. I don't quite know what they'll do about your luggage, but they'll do stringent checks just to check you're not a German infiltrator.' He laughed raucously at his own joke and Annie pretended to laugh with him. 'Still, as long as you can fly a plane, that's all that matters.'

Annie swallowed hard at his suggestion. She considered her reply.

'It's been a long time. I flew my grandad's plane a fair bit, but that was a while ago.'

'You wouldn't have been invited here if you weren't up to it. Once you've got your wings, there'll be no looking back. Most of the other girls are struggling with so many different planes. Some of the damn beasts are a handful for the men, so beats me how you ladies manage to fly them at all. Plucky lot, aren't you?'

Annie interjected.

'Women are every bit as capable as men at flying planes.'

Lenny raised his eyebrows.

'You think yourself as good as the best of us, do you?'

'I know I am.'

Annie pressed her lips firmly together to stop an outburst, and deliberately looked out of the window. Lenny followed her wistful gaze and stood beside her.

'You've got your colour back in your cheeks. I must remember to spar with you more often.'

Annie resisted the urge to look him in the face. His presence made her feel she was on the edge of a precipice. At the same time she disliked him for his sexist remarks.

Lenny appeared oblivious to Annie's unease and took out a shiny brown pipe from his pocket and banged it on the tiled window ledge, dislodging a small pile of burnt tobacco. Then he filled the pipe with fresh tobacco, poked and prodded the contents with the end of a teaspoon and then lit it with a silver cigarette lighter. After several attempts, a bright red glow appeared. Annie watched his endeavours with a slightly bemused expression.

Lenny continued the conversation puffing in between every sentence.

'So apart from flying, tell me about yourself.'

Annie felt suddenly challenged, uncertain of which facts would fit the surreal situation she found herself in.

'There's not much to tell really. I was born in Surrey, but until recently I worked in London.

'You must have been through a tough time up there.'

'Things haven't exactly gone to plan.'

'Made sense to get out while you could.'

'I love London. My flat looks over the Thames. It's a beautiful view.'

'I'm surprised you think that. You must have had a prime view of the carnage the bombs have created.'

Annie looked at Lenny and then out of the window again contemplating when, if ever, she would wake up. She suddenly wondered whether she had suffered some sort of head injury that first day at the monument: everything else therefore could just be what she was dreaming in her hospital bed.

Lenny noticed that she seemed distracted, but mistakenly guessed she was thinking of something else.

'You're thinking of the chap yesterday aren't you? Poor bugger didn't stand a chance. Still, just got to move on and not let it get to you.'

Annie went along with Lenny's assumption to avoid difficult questions.

'How can you be so matter of fact about a man bursting into flames? It's not like you see it every day.'

'Listen,' said Lenny gently. 'You arrived at a bad time. No one finds it easy, but you will have to toughen up if you want to survive.'

'This really is a stitch-up isn't it,' said Annie suddenly. 'Tom's for it if he ever comes and gets me.'

Lenny seemed suddenly unsympathetic.

'I'm not sure what you mean by a stitch-up, but you can deal with this Tom as you feel fit. For the next few days however, your CO has said you can stay at my aunt's farm.' He held out a small worn leather suitcase, which Annie had not noticed him carrying.

'There are a few bits and bobs for you here until we can locate your bag. My sister Betty dropped them by at the gatehouse just a minute ago. She heard what a state you were in.'

'I'll get ready then,' said Annie, feeling helpless and lost, but planning her escape.

She started to remove her WAAF costume. Lenny coughed nervously, turning his back to allow Annie some privacy. Not used to such chivalry, she continued to undress, struggling to absorb the realistic story Lenny was recounting.

He talked about the farm that he lived on with Betty and the chickens that were reared there primarily for their eggs. A rare treat according to Lenny. Not many people got fresh eggs for breakfast. That was the bonus of living in the country. For the most part, women ran the farm as the men were all on active duty. Two female ferry pilots lodged there already. By the time Lenny had explained all of the farm history Annie had selected some clothes from the case, inspected them suspiciously and put them on. It was obviously another joke expecting her to dress in yet more fancy dress. Tom was probably outside with his camera and his friends, all who would be waiting to shout 'Surprise!'

She was too tired to question anything, but Tom and his air show were taking this re-enactment thing just a bit too far. Either that or the hospital needed to wake her up from her coma.

Trying to retain some normal thoughts, Annie looked at Lenny as he had stopped talking and was poking around in his pipe again. He had been friendly, but he possessed an air of authority and sexism. He was an amazingly beautiful man: the contrast between his eyes and dark hair was striking beyond measure.

She was fascinated.

'Come on,' he said suddenly, puffing again. 'I'll take you to the gatehouse. Betty will be waiting for you there. I've got to get back to the mess but I'll see you back at the farm.' As he plucked up Annie's discarded costume and stuffed it unceremoniously into the suitcase, she thought of asking what sort of mess he was talking about. He was so immaculately turned-out that she couldn't imagine him having to clean. Remembering the burning pilot she had seen the previous day, she assumed the mess he was referring to was the aftermath of the tragedy.

Annie followed Lenny down narrow corridors, as bleak and characterless as the room they had left. Once having left the building, Annie looked around expectantly for Tom as they crossed a large tarmacked area passing uniformed and civilian personnel on the way. Both men and women saluted Lenny as they passed.

Annie was perplexed as to how it could be so hot again. It had been bitter at the air show. Today was more like summer: grass borders running the length of the brick buildings a lush green, trees in full leaf. Maybe Tom had never called for her two days ago. Maybe she had fallen asleep on her sofa whilst waiting for him to turn up. Any moment, the doorbell would ring and she would wake to normality.

But the doorbell didn't ring and instead Annie began to recognise where she was, only everything was different. Leaving the red brick buildings and hangars behind, they were approaching the outer perimeter of the airfield. Adjacent to the field were a couple of prefabricated buildings and the gatehouse they had passed on the way in. There were a handful of vintage cars and trucks parked, but no modern vehicles. Tom must have left.

'Bastard,' Annie muttered.

As they approached the gatehouse Annie heard the roar of a powerful engine, and jumped out of the way just in time as a motor bike and sidecar came screaming through the gates, squealing to a halt next to them.

A young woman was astride the motorbike. Her hair was windswept and the colour of marmalade. Annie was surprised to see she wore no crash helmet. She cut the engine, climbed off the bike and flung her arms around Lenny.

'Hello, Lenny darling.' She turned to face Annie. 'I'm Betty. I've heard how Lenny found you.'

'I got lost,' said Annie, fed up with repeating herself.

'Sounds more like you materialised out of thin air.'

Betty's smile lit up her freckled face. She was attractive, with pale skin and golden eyes: totally different to Lenny. Annie could see no likeness between them, but in this dream nothing added up anyway.

Betty spotted the worried look on Annie's face as she looked nervously at the rusty bike.

'Oh don't you worry. I'm as much an ace on this bike as Lenny is in the air.' She slapped Lenny on the back with such force that it caused him to stagger forwards.

'Steady old girl! I'm on ops tonight. I won't be much good if you dislocate my shoulder, will I?'

Betty laughed loudly.

'Well, hop in. Lenny says you have nowhere to stay, so you can come back to the farm.'

Annie looked at Lenny for reassurance. He smiled and gestured to her to get in the sidecar.

'I hope I'll get a chance to come back before ops, but if not Betty will look after you.' He winked at Betty, touched Annie lightly on the arm, tossing her suitcase into the back of the sidecar.

Annie waited until he had turned to walk away and then clumsily climbed in. Before she had a chance to make herself comfortable, Betty jumped on the kick-start and accelerated out of the gates as fast as she had entered, with Annie hanging on for dear life.

Chapter 21

Annie squashed herself into the misshapen leather seat, keeping her head low in an attempt to shelter her face behind the fly-splattered plastic screen.

Reaching into a pocket of the sidecar with one hand, whilst precariously steering with the other, Betty passed Annie a pair of battered old goggles, the lenses covered with more squashed flies.

Betty had to shout to be heard above the sound of the engine.

'Here, put these on!'

Annie shouted back.

'Don't you need them?'

'No, I'm fine. Anyway we'll be there in a jiffy.'

All care of her appearance forgotten, Annie wrestled to get the goggles on. Betty laughed. Although Annie could see little through the smeared lenses, they stopped her eyes from watering, and the leather strap helped secure her wig, which was beginning to part company with her head.

'You'll need to sort your hair out when we get back. By the way, why are you wearing a wig?'

Annie lied effortlessly. Making things up was becoming easier.

'Fancied a change in colour. Thought I'd try it for a few days before I dye my own.'

She chose not to go deeper into the reasoning as conversing whilst travelling at high speed was near impossible: fear of an imminent collision at the forefront of her mind. It scared Annie that the high-speed ride was convincingly real. Air was being blasted into her face at high speed, the goggles and screen offering little protection. Hedgerows and trees were becoming blurred as Betty confidently tore along the country lanes, hooting repeatedly when approaching blind bends. The deep throaty roar of the bike's engine drowned out all birdsong, and the brackets and springs connecting the bike to the sidecar protested noisily at every bump in the road.

Just as Annie thought her teeth were never going to stop rattling due to the vibration, Betty mimicked the earlier manoeuvre at the airfield, almost getting the bike and sidecar sideways as she rode through an open farm gate. A large family of chickens, pecking at the ground, scattered in all directions, clucking their protest as they flapped redundant wings. Having heard the commotion, a black and white border collie came bounding out of a barn to their left, barking and bucking in an attempt to round up the panicked birds.

Betty slowed down considerably and rode the bike into a large barn, coming to a stop between high towers of straw bales. She leapt effortlessly off of the bike and beamed at Annie struggling to extricate herself from the narrow sidecar.

'You'll have to get used to travelling like this. It's the sidecar or a bicycle,' she laughed, taking Annie's hand to help.

'Ooh, I feel a bit wobbly.'

Betty picked up Annie's case.

'It's the fresh air. Do you live in a big town?'

'Yes, I do. London.'

'Well that explains it then. Should think you can hardly breathe, what with all that smog and blessed debris everywhere. I'd hate it.' She affectionately stroked the dog's head as it ran excitedly around her in circles. 'Hello girlie.'

Annie held her arms above her head as the collie approached and sniffed at her ankles before backing off on her haunches, whining softly and hiding behind Betty's legs.

'That's a bit unusual. She usually rolls over to show you she's friendly.'

'Does she bite?'

'She won't hurt you unless you try to steal eggs. She guards the chickens like they were her puppies.'

'That's a relief.'

Betty walked quickly towards the farmhouse. Annie still felt unsteady as she tried to keep pace. Tess followed Annie across the yard adopting a slow slalom motion, as though she were herding sheep. She eventually sloped off back to the barn.

The farm was set out in a U-shape. Betty and Annie had approached it from the open end of a courtyard. The farmhouse was large and imposing, and built in red brick, which had faded with age to a soft terracotta colour. Single storey outbuildings were attached to each side of the farmhouse, their slate roofs in need of some urgent repair. Here and there, cracked tiles had slipped down into the guttering, weeds and moss filling the holes where the tiles had once sat. The courtyard within the three-sided structure was unevenly cobbled. Betty and Annie had to dodge deep potholes. Around the perimeter were stacked barrels and all manner of farm machinery.

Betty waved to the farmhands going about their duties.

It struck Annie that Lenny had not exaggerated: most of them were women. Workers smiled as they passed. Betty opened the top half of a stable door, which led into a large kitchen with a low-beamed ceiling.

'Anyone around?'

At first, no one answered, but then a silver-haired woman appeared through a door in the far corner of the kitchen with a basket over her arm, brimming with potatoes and carrots. Betty pushed the door open and entered, with Annie following close behind.

The woman spoke in a soft, motherly tone.

'Betty love, I see you found her then.'

'Auntie Lillian, this is Annie, the new ferry pilot Lenny told you about.'

Lillian held up muddy hands.

'Nice to meet you Annie. You won't mind if I don't shake hands will you?'

Lillian went over to a deep porcelain sink and washed her hands, scrubbing roughly at the earth, caked on from digging for the vegetables in her basket. Betty and Annie sat at the over-sized kitchen table, which dominated the centre of the kitchen.

'What's for tea, Auntie?'

'Mutton stew, dear.'

Annie winced at the thought.

'Ooh yummy, my favourite! Do you want any help with the vegetables? Annie and I can help. You don't mind, do you Annie? We all muck in here.'

'Er...no, of course not,' said Annie, concerned for her immaculate nails.

The pine table was already simply laid for a meal for a large party of people: a huge warm loaf and a big pat of butter placed in the middle. There was no indication of wealth on the big farm. Mismatched cups, saucers and plates, which had seen better days, were laid out on the table.

Lillian bustled about chatting about the weather, the chickens, and how she was fed up with the planes coming over the farmhouse so low during the night. It was only when she sat down at the table with a giant teapot in her hands and looked at Annie properly for the first time, that Annie saw she had the same blue eyes as Lenny.

She was still a very attractive woman, in her late fifties, with an air of dignity about her. She had well-defined cheekbones, a slightly aquiline nose and her silver hair was tied loosely back, styled into a low bun. She had obviously lived much of her life outside. Her skin was tanned and her hands were chapped and dry, showing the signs of someone who had worked manually for many years. The family resemblance between Lillian and Lenny was not just about the piercing eyes: it was something indefinable.

The three of them sat and talked for some time over copious cups of tea: Annie wanting to leap onto the table and devour the mouth-watering warm loaf. Every now and again, its smell wafted over her way.

'Annie was found wandering around the airfield, Auntie. All confused she was, didn't even know why she was there.'

'Goodness deary, whatever happened to you?'

'I think I fell over and banged my head.'

Betty poured the last of the tea into odd cups.

'Lucky for you our Lenny was there. We can always count on Lenny. He's always there when we need him, even now he's got our boys to take care of up there.' Betty looked at Lillian knowingly.

Annie was glad the conversation had switched to Lenny. There had as yet been no questions demanding too much explanation. Even Betty seemed to have come to the conclusion that Annie had turned up for duty at an unfortunate time during an air raid.

Betty put her fingers to her own lips.

'Shh! Mustn't talk about all those hush-hush flying trips. Careless talk costs lives, remember.'

Annie nodded in agreement, pretending that she completely got the gist of Betty's cryptic statement. The situation was almost manageable until Betty mentioned the words 'air raid' in conversation. It was at this point that Annie's struggle with her situation became too much. She pinched her leg under the table hard so that it hurt: hoping that the pain would wake her up. She let out a loud yelp.

Betty put down her teacup.

'Are you alright?'

'I don't belong here and I don't know how to get back.'

'Golly, you must have really hurt yourself.' She put her arms around Annie. 'The nurse told Lenny you were confused.'

'I thought I would have woken up by now and everything would be back to normal.'

Betty and Lillian glanced at each other. Lillian put her hand on Annie's.

'I shouldn't worry too much, dear. You've had a nasty shock so I've heard. A few days on the farm and you'll be as right as rain.'

'Yes, I'm sure you're right,' replied Annie, not believing either of them.

She looked round the room for clues, expecting at any second to see the room ripple and dissolve into nothingness, and the hospitality tent to reappear, complete with Tom and the crowd of re-enactors. Whilst Betty and Lillian talked about other things, Annie sat stunned into silence alone with her thoughts, their voices nothing but a distant murmur.

Certain things seemed set in stone. The air show had happened. She had been there with Tom. But something inexplicable must have taken place that day and it had happened suddenly. Maybe a plane had crashed and people in the audience had got hurt, including her. She must therefore now be unconscious as she had already surmised, and all the things that were happening were fanciful hallucinations shaped by the event she had been attending with Tom. She just had to bide her time. She would get better. The doctors and specialists would not give up on her, and, more importantly, Tom would be at her side talking her back to the real world again.

A voice spoke from far way.

'Annie dear, can I get you anything? You look dreadfully pale.'

Annie returned from her faraway thoughts to the comfort of Lillian's kitchen.

'I'm so sorry. You must think me rude. It's so cosy in here that I was just drifting off to sleep.'

Lillian smiled.

'Not at all. Don't you worry yourself. Just take your time to adjust to our ways.'

Lillian's words resonated with Annie. She would stick to a sensible plan: go along with whatever it was that was controlling her thought processes. She reaffirmed to herself that she would soon be able to recount all of this to Tom. And that Dr. Edwards would love it. She would be analysed, counselled, prescribed pills and be right as rain in no time. Tom might see things differently though. She chatted more readily, prepared to accept her route to recovery, no matter how long it might take. If she used some aptitude, she could probably manipulate the dream she was experiencing and steer her way back to her life in London.

When a group of people noisily spilled through the kitchen door from outside, Annie calmly put her cup down and began playing the game properly for the first time.

Chapter 22

'If I have to collect another egg again I swear I'll start clucking! Either that or I'll grow feathers!'

The rest of the group following behind burst into laughter.

The woman that had spoken plonked herself down immediately opposite Annie at the table. She was young and blonde: apart from a few stray wisps, her hair swept up under a turban made from a colourful patterned headscarf. The sleeves of her lilac blouse were rolled up to the elbow, her tiny waist exaggerated by a man's leather belt buckled tightly over voluminous khaki dungarees. She lunged at the loaf of bread and tore off a large chunk before the others had sat down.

Lillian scolded her.

'Daphne! Where are your manners?'

'Sorry, but I'm so famished I could eat a horse right now!'

Two other girls, one blonde and one dark-haired, and dressed similarly to Daphne sat down either side of her. The dark-haired one dug Daphne in the ribs with her elbow.

'You're so greedy, Daphne. Leave some for the rest of us!'

The rest of the men and women found chairs and stools around the table and politely waited for Lillian to finish bringing food from the oven. As the large party jostled for space, Annie decided to be attentive and absorb as much information from these new characters. Whatever she learnt now may prove useful later.

To Annie's right sat two boys in their late teens: both with blue eyes and dark hair, how Annie imagined Lenny might have looked fifteen years earlier. They whispered between themselves but said little to the other diners. Opposite the two boys and next to Lillian sat a quiet man with a leathery face and thinning grey hair. Lillian dished his food up first and poured him a mug of tea before serving herself, which indicated to Annie that he was probably Lillian's husband. Conversation ceased. Apart from Daphne, who was still chewing on her piece of bread, all eyes were on the older man.

He lowered his head and said grace.

'For what we are about to receive, may the Lord make us truly thankful. Amen.'

Immediately, everyone started talking at once. The bowls of steaming potatoes and mutton stew seemed not to get any smaller despite the hungry workers tucking in enthusiastically. Lillian made a point of including Annie, who seemed less than impressed with the stew, in the conversation. Annie chewed on chunks of unrecognisable meat politely, washing it down with gulps of water.

'It's a shame the girls are away today. Nice girls. Beats me how they do the job they do, when it's men's work really.'

'Auntie's talking about the other ferry girls Annie. I think they're flying back from Castle Bromwich today.'

Daphne put her teacup down noisily and raised her eyebrows, looking across the table at Annie. Then she addressed Betty.

'Is this another one of them then?'

Betty glared at Daphne.

'Her name is Annie, actually, and yes she is as a matter of fact!'

The dark-haired land girl tried to placate Daphne.

'Leave it be, Daphne. No sense in causing trouble.'

'You stay out of it, Hilda.'

Daphne mumbled something under her breath and took a small round compact mirror from her dungaree pocket, admired herself and put it away again. She glared at Annie as she blew a stray wisp of hair from her forehead.

Hilda stood up and leant across the table to shake Annie's hand.

'Don't take any notice of Daphne, she's just jealous that you get to do the glamorous bit. She'll get over it!'

Daphne gave the girl on her other side a warning glance, as if to say she had better not follow Hilda's example.

Betty joined in the conversation.

'I hardly think it's glamorous, Hilda. Those brave girls risk life and limb doing their duty for king and country you know!'

Hilda nodded in agreement.

'You're absolutely right. I wouldn't do their job for toffee!'

Lillian silenced the table.

'Let's all keep our peace and thank the Lord that we are all here together.'

'But...'

'But nothing, Daphne. I'll have no more bickering at my table thank you very much. Annie is our guest, so please make her welcome.'

Temporarily put in her place, Daphne quietly ate her food, glancing up at Annie from time to time with a thunderous expression. Annie pretended not to notice, continuing to dunk her piece of bread in the gravy, avoiding the lumps of meat. The meal soon over, one by one the diners began to get up from the table, thanking Lillian before filing out the same way they had come in. Annie was certain she did not imagine her chair being knocked against by Daphne as she passed by.

Soon the only people left seated were Betty, Annie, Lillian and the older man who Lillian finally introduced as her husband Cecil. He nodded politely to Annie, put his cap on and excused himself from the table. Once he had gone from the room, Lillian explained his silence.

'Our Cecil finds it hard with two sons away at war and the girls working in the factories. He isn't the man he used to be. He hardly smiles at all these days.'

Betty added a few words of comfort to Lillian and then changed the subject to distract her from her melancholy mood.

'I'll show Annie to her room, Auntie.' She got up from the table and hugged Lillian. 'Everything will turn out fine. The war will be over soon, just you wait and see.'

Lillian wiped tears from her eyes and went to the sink to wash the pile of dishes.

'I do hope you're right my love. I can't take much more of this.' She looked wistfully out of the window.

Betty beckoned to Annie.

'Leave the dishes, Auntie. I'll be back downstairs soon to help.'

'That's all right love. Best I keep busy. You look after our new family member.'

Annie felt saddened by Lillian's tears.

'Thank you for putting me up, Lillian. It's lovely here. I wish I could stay but I need to get home at some point.'

Lillian remained facing the window to hide her tears.

'Well our home is your home for as long as you need. Don't feel you have to leave on my account, dear.'

Annie contemplated the possibility she might never find her way back.

'You're very kind.'

'Come on Annie. Let's get you settled in.'

Betty picked up Annie's case again and beckoned her out into a hallway. They climbed a flight of stairs, which led to a galleried landing, overlooking a large living area below, which was furnished with large comfy armchairs and dark oak furniture. The stair carpet was worn and threadbare in places. The stairs groaned, reminding Annie of Tom's family home in Appleby Magna, complete with its cobwebs and dark mysterious corners.

Once upstairs, Betty showed Annie to a small room in the eaves at the end of the landing.

'I hope you will be comfortable in here. I turned back the bed to air it for you.'

Annie looked around the room, which was basic, with no modern frills.

'It's lovely. Thank you.'

Betty put Annie's suitcase on an ottoman at the foot of the bed.

'I hope you don't have to go home soon. I think we could be jolly good friends.'

Annie felt suddenly torn between the two worlds.

'By the look of things, nothing's certain. I may be here for a long time.'

Betty was understandably oblivious to the real meaning behind Annie's words.

'I ought to go and check that Auntie is all right. I'll be back in a jiffy.' She bustled off, leaving Annie alone.

The room was bright and airy, the walls decorated with yellow floral wallpaper. The double bed was huge, filling half the room: metal bedstead, deep mattress and a quilted eiderdown resembling pink fluffy clouds. Annie sat on the edge of the bed, kicked off her shoes and pulled off the wig that was becoming unbearably hot. She lay back on the bed. Sleep came almost immediately. As she drifted she was no longer afraid of her demons. There were more pressing problems to deal with.

The sounds of laughter, cheering and the loud revving of motorbike engines disturbed her slumber several hours later. She opened her eyes, taking a few seconds to remember where she was, swung her legs over the edge of the high bed and went over to the window. The sky was still bright blue. With the exception of sporadic clouds there was nothing to suggest that the weather was about to change for the worse.

She looked at the cluster of buildings surrounding the farmhouse. The yard below was flanked by an assortment of large timber-framed barns in varying states of repair. Chickens roamed freely, pecking at the ground. Beyond the barns farmland stretched away as far as the eye could see, to hills that hugged the horizon from east to west. Between the pastures and the barns a large clearing had been fenced off: the ground worn away by deep tyre treads. Leaning against the fence facing away from Annie, a small group of people were pointing and clapping. Annie climbed on a chair and pulled the top of the sash window open to get a better view of what was going on. Clouds of dust rose high into the air as several motorbikes raced around the clearing.

At that second there was a quiet tapping on the bedroom door.

'Come in.'

The door opened a crack and Betty's face appeared.

'You're awake. I looked in earlier but you were out for the count. Settled in?'

'Oh yes, thank you. The bed is so comfortable!' Annie got down from the chair. 'I thought I saw you in the field.'

'Not me for once, but come and have a look anyway. The boys are playing high-jinks as usual.'

Annie slipped on a cardigan and followed Betty back down the stairs, to the rear of the house where all the commotion was. They joined the group of spectators. Betty straddled the fence, cupped her hands to her mouth and bellowed encouragement to the men on motorbikes as they continued to tear around the field, their faces and hair caked in dirt thrown up by their antics. Their shirtsleeves were rolled up to the elbow, trousers tucked into knee-length leather boots, but none of the riders wore any form of protective clothing or crash helmets.

The ground in the field was cratered. Deep furrows had been etched into a big oval by the motorbikes: the damage evidence that the boys frequently chose to amuse themselves and entertain other people at the same time.

The group of people at the fence hooted encouragement at the boys.

'Come on Arthur!'

'Come on Raymond!'

'More brothers?'

'Second cousins.'

There was nothing to choose between them as the riders battled for the front position, jumping and weaving across the very uneven ground.

Betty shouted the loudest, gripping onto the fence as she jumped up and down. The rest of the onlookers dared the men to push their bikes harder and faster.

Suddenly, Betty leapt lightly from the fence and raced back towards the farmhouse, disappearing from view, minutes later appearing again astride a bike. She careered through a gap in the fence: red hair flying behind her, laughing loudly, opening the throttle wide, which caused the rear wheel to spin and shower the boys with more dust and debris. It occurred to Annie that Betty's courage and ability made the journey back from the airfield seem like a leisurely affair. She wondered when the sidecar was going to part company with the motorbike as it flew over bumps: bucking and crashing down again. The men gave hot pursuit.

Annie was having fun and was so preoccupied that she did not at first notice one of the spectators pointing at the sky. All at once everyone at the fence, with the exception of Annie, started running for the farmhouse. Deafened by the sound of his own motorbike, Raymond spotted the group running and looked instinctively upwards. An ominous group of bombers with escorting fighters were swarming across the sky in perfect formation, casting long shadows across the fields. Raymond leapt off his bike waving his arms furiously at Betty and Arthur as they made another circuit. They stopped abruptly; looking up at the direction in which Raymond was pointing, and hastily abandoned their bikes. By this time, Annie was frozen to the spot, hypnotised by the approaching swarm almost eclipsing the sun.

Betty grabbed her arm.

'Run, Annie! Get inside the house!'

In her panic, Annie stumbled and fell as the aircraft drew nearer, the sky above alive with noise: darker as shadows flickered across the grass. Strong hands reached down to grab her, Arthur and Raymond spurring her on.

The first bomb reached its target just as everyone bundled into the kitchen. The house trembled: clouds of particles dislodged from the ceiling beams. The men scrambled under the table, pulling Annie and Betty in after them.

Arthur was the first to speak.

'That was a close one! The Jerries are right overhead!'

'They're heading for the airfield,' responded Raymond.

Annie remained curled up in a foetal position with her head tucked tightly into her knees.

'What's going on?'

Her question was only half-answered by Betty.

'You'll have to get used to that if you're staying here.'

The group huddled under the table until the danger had passed, the droning of the aircraft slowly getting fainter.

Betty spoke again.

'I wonder if the boys got the planes off the ground in time. That was too close for comfort.'

Raymond and Arthur looked worryingly at Betty.

No more explanation was needed. Annie knew that she was trapped in some sort of parallel world. For now she had to live or die with that knowledge.

Chapter 23

After the bombers had gone, Betty grabbed Annie's hand.

'Where are we going?'

Betty whispered to avoid the rest of the family overhearing.

'Up to the attic.'

'What for?'

'Stop asking questions. Just follow me.'

Betty led Annie up a narrow staircase that Annie had not noticed before, hidden from view by a faded green velvet curtain at the opposite end of the landing to her own room. At the top of the stairs a door led to a large attic room that stretched the full length of the main farmhouse. The walls were panelled with stained pitch pine boarding and at one end, a leaded-light window looked south towards the Downs.

'This is why I brought you up here: to get a better vantage point of the sky over the airfield.'

'Why didn't you want anyone else to hear you in the kitchen?'

'I don't like the boys coming up here. They might go and tell Auntie. She's upset enough without them telling her how many planes have been shot down.'

'I see. How far away is the airfield?'

'About five miles by road, but nearer three as the crow flies.'

The attic was stacked to the ceiling with old trunks and boxes covered in a thick layer of dust, the floor littered with old furniture partially covered with dust sheets. A tailor's mannequin and a wire birdcage on a stand stood in the shadows. The four corners of the attic were in total darkness: the only light permeating the musty space coming from the small window. Annie negotiated the narrow spaces in-between furniture and personal belongings, still grasping onto Betty's arm as she tried to acclimatise her eyes to the low light.

A fleeting memory of the ramshackle buildings at the air show flitted through her mind.

'I'm not sure I like it up here.'

'What are you worried about? Apart from a few mice and birds, I'm the only one who comes up here.'

Annie shivered.

'Let's not stay long though, if that's alright.'

'Is it the dark you don't like?'

'Let's just say I recently had a scare in a place a bit like this.'

'Alright, we'll only be a jiffy.'

Betty led Annie towards the window and wiped it with a piece of dust sheet.

'Look over there – as far as you can see.'

Annie peered through the small window at the panorama. An aerial ballet was taking place over the Sussex Downs: planes soaring and wheeling like birds catching thermals over sea cliffs on a hot day. It was too far away to distinguish between enemy and allied aircraft, as they performed arabesques against the vast blueness. The planes sparkled like diamonds, reflecting the sun as they silently circled: seconds later the diamonds' lustre gone, replaced by showers of debris and dark trails of smoke spiralling towards the earth. Annie felt completely detached: as though she were watching a silent movie and not a real life situation unfolding before her eyes.

Betty weeping, wiping her eyes on a white cotton handkerchief, broke the silence of the aerial dance.

'I never get used to it - I have friends up there. It's all so senseless.'

Annie felt helpless and suddenly very humbled. Her own life seemed inconsequential.

'Then maybe we shouldn't watch. Let's go back downstairs.'

'No, I need to do this. Coming up here, seeing our brave boys, I feel as though I am willing them on.'

'But it's so distressing.'

Annie continued to look at the planes being literally knocked from the sky, as though a fly swatter had annihilated them. She suddenly realised that she had been so comfortable in her own privileged life that she had not bothered given the past a second thought. She had never considered the suffering of the young men in front of her. It was easy not to think about it at all unless Tom reminded her. She looked out at the sky one more time, before turning to console Betty. Most of the planes had either been shot down or were almost invisible: tiny pinpricks on the horizon as they left for France. Residual trails of smoke and vapour remained: a temporary imprint in the blue canopy.

Betty wiped her eyes and tried to regain her composure.

'Is it over yet?'

Annie felt overwhelmed with admiration for Betty and her caring nature.

'Yes it is.' She reached out for Betty and did something completely out of character, pulling her close and wrapping her in her arms. 'I'll be your friend, Betty.'

Betty stifled another tear and gathered herself up. She looked like a fragile China doll.

'I'd like that. You won't ever leave me, will you?'

Annie thought for a second about her predicament.

'I'll do my best.'

'That's all I can expect I suppose, with this horrid war going on. Here today and gone tomorrow if you know what I mean.'

'Yes, I do know what you mean. It's ghastly.'

Betty changed the subject.

'Let's go and find Auntie. She'll still be shaken up by all this.'

Annie was relieved to leave the attic. When they got back to the kitchen, Lillian was bustling about with a seemingly brave face, humming a happy tune as though everything was all right with the world around her.

'There you are, girls,' Lillian half-smiled. 'I'm going to have a nice cup of tea if you'd like one. It'll take more than those Jerries to keep me down for long.'

'Yes please, Auntie.'

Annie looked around the kitchen as sunlight poured in through the open window. The over-sized kettle boiled lazily on the range, the mouth-watering smell of baking bread wafted from the oven and chickens clucked contentedly in the yard. The contrast to what she had just witnessed was surreal: almost as though it was nature's way of deliberately masking the horrors of war. Nevertheless, the tranquility belied the reality. Lillian's hands trembled violently as she poured the tea.

Betty took over.

'Let me, Auntie. You sit down and rest.'

Lillian flopped down into a chair.

'You're a good girl. I don't know where I would be without you and your brother.'

Annie wanted to ask unanswerable questions, but knew she would appear unhinged. Moreover, she wanted to tell Lillian and Betty that everything would end up in Britain's favour: that Hitler and the Germans would not win the war, Britain would be rebuilt and that life in the twenty-first century would be, for most people, quite good comparatively. Nevertheless, life had not seemed that good to Annie back in her money-orientated world. Despite a privileged place in society, she knew she had just been going through the motions of an existence. The money counted for nothing. In Betty's world, Annie felt more alive than she ever had, regardless of the fact that she was mixing with total strangers who might die at any moment. She was beginning to care for her new acquaintances, in particularly Lenny and his family. The reminder of Lenny's name made Annie's heart flutter. It had not occurred to her that he was at the airfield.

Betty seemed to have second-guessed Annie's thoughts.

'Lenny will see off those Jerries. He's one of the best we've got!'

'How did you know I was thinking about him?'

'Your expression said it all.'

'I didn't think I was that transparent.'

'Smitten more like! He did rescue you in your moment of need, after all!'

They both chuckled simultaneously. Lillian smiled from across the table, a little more relaxed now she was in the two women's company.

'Really, Betty, you'll embarrass Annie.'

Annie thought about how she would feel if on this day Lenny had not been so lucky.

'I'm fine, Lillian. I can take a bit of teasing. And anyway, I have a boyfriend.'

Betty turned round to face Annie.

'Ooh, really? Tell me about him.'

'Well, it's not serious. At least not for me.'

'That's sad. But I suppose it's best not to fall in love in war time.' Betty looked wistful. 'You'll meet your Mr. Perfect. I have.'

'I'll be happy just to come out of this alive.'

Betty nudged Annie's leg under the table as she noticed Lillian's face drop at her comment.

'Let's play a game to pass the time. How about a game of cards?'

Betty tried hard to fill the gloom and distract Lillian with her banter, but Annie noticed both Lillian and Betty watching the clock above the mantelpiece every few moments. It was a few hours before any news arrived

223

concerning casualties at the airfield. The Germans had jettisoned their bombs slightly off target: the nearest one to the farm landing only a couple of miles away. According to Arthur and Raymond it had been a 'big one'. Badgered into investigating by the two teenage boys, George and William, the four of them had found a large crater right by the edge of the road that Betty and Annie had travelled along earlier that day. The bomb had carved a crater large enough to bury a double-decker bus in. George was jubilant that the Jerries had been 'seen off' and that news had filtered through that no one on the neighbouring farms had been hurt.

Lillian scolded George and William for having sneaked out when her back had been turned, but they had insisted it was safe and that the Germans had dropped all their bombs and 'scarpered'.

Dusk was approaching before anyone returned home from the airfield. All eyes were on the kitchen door as voices were heard approaching the farmhouse: men's voices, none of which were recognisable to Annie. Betty leapt up from her chair, sending it crashing over. She rushed to the door followed by Lillian, who had stopped playing cards and had been sitting by the range rocking backwards and forwards restlessly in her wooden rocking chair.

A group of tired-looking men in uniform entered the kitchen. Annie scanned their faces, disappointed when all of the faces were unfamiliar to her and that Lenny was not with them. Betty pushed past the first three to enter the room and flung her arms around the fourth, burying her head in his chest.

The man dropped his kit bag to the floor and braced himself to prevent being bowled over.

'Now there's a welcome!'

'Oh Peter, I had a really bad feeling you wouldn't come back this time. Why didn't you phone the farm? I've been beside myself with worry!'

Betty fussed around Peter. The rest of the men laughed at her fawning all over him. She looked up at the tall willowy man with adoration.

'Annie, this is my fiancé, Peter. We're getting married soon, aren't we Peter?' She looked up again at him again like a doting puppy.

Peter removed his peaked cap and shook Annie's hand enthusiastically.

'I heard about your mysterious arrival. Settling in alright, are you?'

Annie nodded affirmatively and smiled nervously at Peter and his three companions.

'Yes thank you, everyone's been lovely.'

Betty spoke up.

'Apart from Daphne, she's been a dreadful bore. Positively nasty to Annie.'

Lillian bustled about making space for the tired men.

'Let's not worry about that now. All that matters is that you're safe.'

Lillian displayed her usual level of hospitality. Annie decided that Lillian did not seem to leave the kitchen much at all. If a path could have been etched on the floor indicating Lillian's route it would have been a deep well-worn one.

The airmen relaxed quickly, though much like Lenny they had a permanently exhausted look about them, which made them look fatigued around the eyes. There was no mention of Lenny, which Annie found strange. She resisted the urge to ask. The men hung their jackets on the back of their chairs and sat down to bacon sandwiches and tea. Betty placed herself on Peter's lap and wrapped her arms around his neck again. He kissed her affectionately on her cheek.

The group of men were obviously close friends though none of them lived at the farmhouse. They had called in en route for the cottage they shared in the village to reassure Betty and Lillian that they would live to fight another day. The conversation centred on the battle that had taken place over the airfield: Annie only half-listening to their boasts of 'kills' as her ear was trained on the door for the sound of Lenny returning to the farmhouse.

In the end she could not contain herself any longer.
'When will Lenny be back?'
The conversation stopped abruptly and nervous glances were exchanged between Betty and Peter.
'He'll be back soon.'
Peter looked across the table at his male counterparts, who stopped eating when Annie had spoken.
'That's right, isn't it chaps?'

The men nodded in unison, choosing to return to eating their sandwiches rather than comment.

Betty lightened the conversation.

'I think Annie has a crush on Lenny, and she's only just met him.'

Annie felt her face colour up as one of the men opposite nudged his neighbour.

Lillian intervened.

'Really Betty, I told you not to embarrass poor Annie earlier. Look, you've made her blush.'

Everyone looked at Annie, but her embarrassment was dispelled as the door opened and Lenny walked casually in, dropping his kit bag on top of all the others. Annie's heart raced as he kissed Betty and Lillian, merely glancing across at her.

Lillian hugged Lenny and patted a cushion on the chair by the range indicating that it was his for the taking. He followed the example of the other men in the room, removing his jacket and loosening his tie, before sitting down and resting his head on the soft backrest.

'What a day!'

The men nodded in agreement.

'I'm starving! That bacon smells good.'

Lillian started slicing bread, but by the time she offered Lenny a plate full of sandwiches, he was fast asleep.

Annie's relief at Lenny's safe return had changed in the blink of an eye to disappointment. He had barely acknowledged her presence, while his friends had each in turn received a playful pat on their shoulders as he had passed behind them to get to the chair by the fireside. She envied the men feeling the touch of Lenny's hand, but tried to put it to the back of her mind, involving herself with the group as actively as she could as they told their stories.

After a while, Annie made an excuse about needing fresh air. It was much too early to retire to her room. She opened the kitchen door and stepped outside into the remains of the evening sunshine. The sun was sinking into the sky in the west and huge streaks of orange stretched right cross the sky as though they had been created by an artist's brush. The sweet smell of honeysuckle filled the air, but not being a gardener, the fragrance gave Annie no indication of the time of year. It could be spring or it could be late summer judging by the mild temperature. She walked away from the farmhouse: far enough away so that the voices were almost inaudible. A solitary blackbird sang its beautiful song, perched on a washing line post. Wood pigeons cooed repeatedly from somewhere nearby.

She walked around to the back of the farmhouse to where the bike race had taken place and stood looking into the sky where the enemy bombers had first appeared. A different scene revealed itself to her than the menace of impending attack. As the sun sank below the horizon, the faint outline of the moon became visible in the changing sky. She watched nature come alive in the surrounding fields as rabbits appeared from bushes and undergrowth sniffing at the evening air.

'You shouldn't be out here alone you know,' said a voice from behind Annie. 'You can never be too careful!

The occasional Jerry turns up, hiding in farmers' outbuildings.'

Annie turned quickly to see Lenny standing right behind her, a bemused expression on his face.

'Where did you appear from? I didn't hear you coming!'

He smiled broadly.

'Stealth! An essential tool against the Hun! Without it we'd all be...' He stopped mid sentence and drew a line across his throat with his finger.

Annie shivered, her peaceful encounter with nature somewhat diminished by the thought of Lenny with his throat cut by an intruder. Lenny laughed and lit his pipe, studying her reaction intently.

Chapter 24

It would be several days before Annie was called to the airfield. Likening it to sitting in the dentist's waiting room listening to the sound of the drill in the next room, she tried to ignore the fact. Nevertheless, she began to accept her fate: whether it was a dream or a reality was irrelevant. She was trapped and had to make the best of her situation, spending several days at the farm amidst all the hustle and bustle of people coming and going.

The general mood amongst the family and farm-workers was one of optimism. There was no talk of defeat at the hands of the Germans, nor grumbling about rationing and deprivation forced upon men, women and children by the war. It was the same picture painted by whoever Annie talked to: adopt a stiff upper lip. Though she had often heard this from her own grandparents, the expression in the eyes of most on the farm told a different story: that of sorrow and loss.

The farmhouse was cleaned from top to bottom in anticipation of Betty and Peter's wedding, which was to be a modest affair. Apprehensive, and with time to kill, Annie involved herself with the preparation, finding dusting and sweeping a mindless way to pass the time.

Lillian seemed to be able to conjure up something out of nothing, spending the dark evenings sitting by an inefficient paraffin light, cutting up old curtains to make tablecloths, napkins and bunting for the special day. Annie watched her dexterous fingers as she lovingly crafted table decorations made from bits of lace, glass beads and dried flowers.

The hours of darkness were the most perilous for all on the farm. The rumble of planes passing high above, or so low that the house trembled, woke Annie repeatedly. Too afraid to sleep in complete darkness, she adjusted the gaslight tap on her bedroom wall, turned it down to a bare minimum, and made sure the blackout curtains were tightly closed.

Occasionally, forced to abandon sleep altogether, she took a hot drink of milk up to the attic and sat on a Victorian travelling trunk watching the night sky through the leaded window. She would rarely be alone, more often than not sharing her seat with Betty, who would be anxiously waiting for news of Peter's safety after nightly ops over France.

In the distance, searchlights surrounding the airfield pierced the velvety blue sky with tunnels of white light, planes ominously cruising through the circle created at the top of the beam. Flak illuminated the sky with vertical flashes of silver and white. Annie wondered at how the men on the ground could pick out a target and be sure they were not firing their anti-aircraft guns at British planes. Notwithstanding the horror of the nightly raids, she found the aerial battles hypnotic and theatrical, with no two performances being the same.

To pass time, Betty and Annie spent their time in the attic talking about happier topics, Betty's forthcoming wedding being at the forefront of conversation. A wedding dress and veil hung expectantly on the picture rail in Betty's bedroom, waiting for the leave that Peter had been promised. The honeymoon would be at Bembridge on the Isle of Wight, a modest room booked for two precious days together before Peter's next round of duty.

Annie talked about her own background, manipulating her circumstances so as not to arouse suspicion during conversations with Betty. She talked freely about family, friends and boyfriends, tailoring the finest details so as to create a pseudo-identity for all who may show a passing interest. Annie discreetly asked questions about the local area and began to recognise the names of towns and villages from her childhood.

On one particularly bad night of heavy activity above, Betty pointed out a red glow in the sky approximately thirty miles north of the farm. London was apparently taking a real bashing. Betty had seemed particularly anxious that night: pacing the bare floorboards in the attic, clutching a comforting mug of cocoa and going over and over her wedding plans.

It was the following morning that the news arrived. It was Betty's day off from the munitions factory. She was standing at the kitchen sink washing up, chatting happily to Annie. The next second she stopped quite suddenly and turned deathly pale: dropping the soapy plate she was holding. It crashed to the floor smashing into a thousand pieces.

'What is it, Betty?'

Annie anxiously followed Betty's gaze through the open window. Lenny was walking towards the kitchen door.

'It's only Lenny. That's good isn't it?'

'No, I don't think it is good.'

'What do you mean?'

'Something's wrong. I know it.'

Betty didn't stop to dry her hands, but backed away from the door as it opened, still covered in soap bubbles.

Lenny stepped through the door and immediately took his cap off, looking nervously at both women.

Annie spoke first.

'What is it, Lenny? What's happened?'

Lenny wrung his cap between his hands, his knuckles turning white as he spoke.

'I'm sorry Betty...'

She did not let him finish his sentence.

'No, no, no, not Peter!'

Lenny caught her as her legs gave way beneath her and she sobbed uncontrollably.

Much later, Lenny took Annie to one side, whilst Betty was in her room, and told her what had happened.

'I was flying through thick clouds and had lost sight of most of the others. The next thing I knew was that Peter's plane was on fire, spiralling towards the ground.'

Annie wanted to hold Lenny, but sat close to him, so her hand brushed his. Electricity ran up her arm.

'It sounds like there was nothing you could do.'

Lenny stared at the wall.

'I should have warned him sooner. It's my fault. If it weren't for me, he would be here now.'

'You can't be sure of that. It must all happen so quickly.'

'It's my responsibility to bring my squadron back in piece. How can I ever look at myself in the mirror again knowing I killed Peter?'

'You didn't kill Peter. You loved him.'

'You can't afford to love anyone in this damned war.'

Annie felt a sudden spasm of emptiness at Lenny's statement. It was as though the words were directed at her.

'Right now you have to love Betty.'

'Do you think I don't know that? But once she finds out how I let Peter down, she'll never want to talk to me again.'

'That's rubbish. Give her more credit than that. She would never even begin to think it's your fault.'

Lenny sat at the kitchen table quietly cleaning out his pipe whilst Annie watched him. He eventually got up and went towards the door.

'Keep an eye on Betty for me. I have to get back.'

'I'll do that, but it's you she needs.'

Lenny turned and placed a light kiss on the top of Annie's head, causing the area to tingle.

'Thank you for listening.'

As he closed the door behind him, Annie sat for a few moments, her fingers caressing where Lenny had gently placed his lips, her heart divided between sorrow for the loss of Peter and the stirring emotions she had for Lenny. The kitchen clock seemed to tick more slowly, as if it too was grieving.

Betty stayed in her room for the rest of the day, the sobs of a broken woman clearly audible to anyone close by. She finally emerged: her eyes reddened and puffy, her normally pale freckled complexion as white as alabaster. Her red hair seemed less vibrant and hung lankly around her shoulders. Lillian wrapped her in a thick blanket and sat her in the rocking chair, which Raymond and Arthur had carried outside into the sunshine for her.

Chapter 25

Annie had been helping Lillian in the garden when Cecil called out to her from the house.

'There's someone here wants to see you.'

'Best you go and see who it is, dear. I'll finish off here.'

'I'll be as quick as I can.'

'Don't you worry about that. We've enough vegetables for tonight.'

As Annie walked towards the house she passed Betty, a little colour back in her cheeks, hanging out the washing.

'I wonder who that can be then. It might even be your young man...Tom was it?'

Annie's response was well-rehearsed.

'I doubt that. He'll be in London.'

Annie considered Betty's words and how strange it would be if her two worlds were to collide with each other: Tom magically materialising through some sort of portal into the world she had unwillingly been dropped into. If he had decided to look for her on that fateful day, he might have ended up in the same place. Some nights she had dreamt he was talking to her. Could that cement the possibility that she was laying in a hospital bed somewhere and he was by her side trying to wake her?

With these thoughts circling her mind, Annie went into the kitchen with her basket laden with the vegetables she and Lillian had harvested.

Sitting at the table were two women Annie had not met before, drinking tea and nibbling on slices of toast and butter. Lillian followed Annie into the kitchen.

'Oh, how lovely to see you back safely, girls. It's nearly a week since we heard anything from you.'

The prettier of the two, a petite girl with honey gold hair and blue uniform stood up and hugged Lillian.

'We've had a hell of a week - so many planes to get allocated.'

The other girl, with hazel eyes and dark brown hair plaited around the back of her head, remained seated.

'Shocking news about Peter,' the second girl exclaimed.

The first woman went across to the door and gently pushed it closed.

'Bertha, be careful. Betty's just outside. She doesn't need reminding.'

'Oops, sorry.'

Lillian intervened.

'I should introduce you to Annie.'

'Nice to meet you, my name's Nina,' said the blonde, sitting down again.

'I'm Bertha,' said the dark-haired girl. 'Sorry we couldn't be here sooner. As Nina said, it's been a rotten week.'

'Nice to meet you too.'

Cecil got up from his seat, folded his newspaper and shuffled out of the kitchen, doffing his cap in respect as he left.

Lillian tutted at Cecil's lack of words.

'Nina and Bertha are two of the pilots you'll be working with.'

Annie sat down, pins and needles in her arms and legs, her heart beating much faster than normal. The sarcasm in her reply went unnoticed.

'I can't wait.'

Nina was the more talkative of the two.

'You're jolly lucky you didn't get thrown in at the deep end like the rest of us.'

'I'm not sure I know what you mean.'

'Well normally as soon as you arrive, they've got you up for a flying test. Then Bob's your uncle.'

Annie gulped her tea.

'I think I've changed my mind. About the flying, that is.'

'It's too late for that I'm afraid. We need good pilots and by all account you've enough hours under your belt.'

Bertha pushed a brown paper parcel tied up with string towards Annie.

'This is for you.'

'What is it?'

'Uniform. We were asked to bring it along. Normally, you'd need to get your wings first, then get measured up.'

'So why have I been given it now?'

'One of the girls had to leave. She hurt her arm quite badly, and as you're an experienced pilot, you might as well try it for size.'

Annie tore open the parcel and took out the blue uniform and black lace up shoes.

Nina went on.

'I heard you lost your luggage, so you'll need to get your civvies sorted out too.'

'Civvies?'

Lillian inadvertently helped Annie out.

'Betty had a few bits and bobs she's lent Annie to wear. I've a few yards of inexpensive fabric. I'll make up a dress or two in her size.'

'Thank you Lillian. You've done so much for me.'

Annie's brief respite was over.

Nina explained the current situation.

'Planes are stacking up at the factories. There's a terrific backlog of planes to pick up from maintenance depots too.'

'So I'll still be doing the flying test?'

Nina laughed.

'I'm afraid not. We'll have to skip the formalities on this occasion.'

Annie wished she could forget.

'You'll be coming up north with us tomorrow to pick up a Lanc.'

'Will I be piloting it?'

'Good God, no! Don't try and run before you can walk. There's only a handful of us qualified to fly the four-engine jobbies!'

'What will I be doing, then?'

'You can practise your map-reading skills, unless something else comes up.'

Bertha spotted Annie's worried expression and suddenly spoke.

'Don't worry Annie. Quite a few girls have got far less experience than you, and they've managed to worm their way in. You'll be fine!'

Annie felt sick. She was out of her depth, her stomach turning over and over. Soon she would be discovered and she had nowhere to go and hide. She was about to be placed in a situation that would prove too much for her to cope with. She felt like Alice falling down the rabbit hole.

Nevertheless, she reminded herself that she could maybe with a little effort, change the course of this dream, and fly any plane with the basic skills she already possessed just by commanding her subconscious. Her attempts to convince herself that she was making this entire dreamscape up did not ring true somehow. She excused herself from the kitchen and took the brown paper parcel to her room.

The uniform fitted like a glove, and looked like the WAAF uniform she had been forced to wear to the air show, only a much darker shade of blue. She looked fondly around the bedroom as she left, wondering whether after a day's disastrous flying, she would see this place again, the cosiness of the farm and all the people in it, the one part that she did not want to surrender to her dreams.

Bertha and Nina were both waiting outside in the courtyard saying their goodbyes to Lillian when Annie came downstairs again. It was a glorious day and there were only a few fluffy white clouds in the sky. Nina and Bertha had both taken their uniform jackets off and were sitting casually on a couple of upturned beer barrels smoking. Annie felt the intense heat as soon as she walked into the open.

Betty had been putting on a brave face. An open book was on her lap and she turned to smile at Annie as she approached her chair.

Annie crouched down and grasped Betty's hand.

'I have to go and do some work, Betty. I'll be back soon, then we'll go into town.'

Betty looked wistfully up at the sky.

'Perhaps you'll find Peter.'

Annie was lost for words. She looked to Lillian for a clue as to what to say, struggling in her own way with what to say.

'There'll be news soon. I'm certain of it.'

Betty's face lit up.

'Do you really think so?'

Annie felt overwhelming sadness for Betty and was relieved when Nina broke the chain of conversation.

'Sorry to rush you, but the CO will be waiting.' She grabbed her jacket and stubbed out her cigarette on the ground with her foot. 'Come on ladies, we must go. There's a lot of work to do and the weather isn't going to last.'

Annie was uncomfortably aware that her shirt was sticking to her back, her neck already sore from the tight collar. She followed Nina and Betty out of the courtyard towards the barn where Betty's bike was in its usual place between the straw bales. She worried about how she too was going to cope with the unknown as she climbed into the back of an open top truck parked outside the farm gates.

Chapter 26

The drive in the sunshine was leisurely, unlike the white-knuckle ride in Betty's sidecar a few days previously. Nina and Bertha sat in the front of the truck and Annie in the back on a pile of tyres covered with a tarpaulin sheet. She felt sick. Today was the day she would surely be found out. Explaining herself would be impossible. She could not turn round to the commanding officer and say, 'Sorry, I'm from the future. Please excuse me whilst I slip back the way I came.'

A comment like that would guarantee that she would at the very least be laughed off of the airfield, labelled as a lunatic, or imprisoned for being a spy, in which case she would never see Lenny or her new-found friends again.

Bertha turned around in her seat to speak to Annie, noticing that she seemed elsewhere as she looked across the open countryside.

'You look worried.'

'I'm fine. It's just that it's been a while.'

'They'll start you off on something basic. We've all worked our way up to the big ones!'

'I hope I'll get the hang of it again, at least get a few hours in before I'm expected to fly anything bigger.'

'Think yourself lucky. You could be working in a dingy old bomb factory or packing parachutes.'

'What about the Lanc you mentioned?'

Bertha laughed.

'Is that what you're worried about? It's a piece of cake really, though the last one we picked up was a bit of a handful!'

Nina added her words of reassurance to the conversation.

'Bertha's right! In six months you'll be able to fly anything they throw at you, as long as you work hard enough.'

Bertha nodded in agreement.

'We'll look after you. All us girls have to stick together. Can't have those men thinking we're not up to it.'

Annie spent the rest of the journey playing virtual flying games in her head, trying to remember the cockpit layout in her grandfather's Tiger Moth and hoping that the other new recruits to the Air Transport Auxiliary ferry pool were feeling as apprehensive as her.

On arrival at the airfield, the truck was cleared to enter by the duty guard at the gatehouse. Nina parked the truck outside ATA headquarters, close to where Annie had spent the night. Nina seemed to sense Annie's reticence to enter the building.

She stopped and put her hand reassuringly on Annie's shoulder.

'You'll be fine. I promise. Come on, let's see if chief's about.'

'Chief?'

Margaret Bowhill, the commanding officer. You met her briefly when you were in the sick bay.'

'She was in charge? If I'd known, I would have at least saluted. I was very confused. I don't think I impressed her.'

'It's all very informal here, no airs and graces, so you'll soon feel at home.'

Margaret was in her office, sitting at her desk, the door open wide so anyone could walk in. Annie watched Bertha and Nina carefully for clues to etiquette when greeting Margaret, hoping that her nervousness did not show.

'Hello ladies. Please sit down.' She turned her attention to Annie. 'How are you feeling after a few days at the farm?'

Annie's stomach was in knots.

'Much better, thank you.'

'That's good. You should take your flying test straightaway. However things have changed overnight so I really don't have time to go through all the usual formalities.' She shuffled papers around her desk as she spoke. 'This is really quite unsatisfactory, but I'll check your credentials and proof of identity when you return.' She looked up at Annie. 'You didn't lose those as well as your luggage did you?'

Annie was caught off guard. To not possess any paperwork would undoubtedly instigate unanswerable questions, but she could not conjure them up when they had never existed in the first place. She took a gamble with her reply.

'No, I had those with me.'

'Good. You'll need to keep them with you at all times, so be a bit more careful this time.'

'Yes ma'am.'

Margaret's face softened.

'Please call me Margaret. We're one big family at this ferry pool.' She handed a piece of paper to Nina. 'One of the Ansons is waiting for you.'

Still anxious that she would be discovered as a fraud, Annie tried not to let any cracks in her behaviour show. She sat on her hands to stop herself from biting her fingernails.

'I've sent Avril up to the Midlands already today. She only joined us last week. Nice girl, a bit shaky to start, only three hundred flying hours under her belt.'

Bertha turned to Annie.

'See? You're not the only one nervous on their first day.'

Margaret addressed Annie again.

'How many hours do you have?'

Annie lied, thinking that she should claim more hours than Avril.

'Four hundred hours thereabouts.'

'You'll be fine then. I don't know what you were so worried about on the way here,' said Nina.

The phone rang. Margaret picked it up.

'Bowhill speaking. Yes, I'll be there right away, sir.' She placed the receiver back down, and hurriedly grabbed her jacket from the back of the chair.

'Look, I'm sorry about this, ladies. I have to attend a meeting. Be ready to leave in half an hour and be sure to remember your overnight bags. The weather isn't looking too promising up north.' She rushed out.

Annie was not sure whether the intervention of the telephone call made any difference to how she was feeling. She reluctantly followed Nina and Bertha along corridors with green walls and highly polished black floors. They eventually arrived at a spacious room, lined with grey metal lockers along two opposite walls and a table at the far end. A long wooden bench had been placed in the middle of the room between the lockers. Annie felt as though she were in an invisible bubble, Nina and Bertha's friendly chatter distant and muffled. Nina unlocked one of the lockers and handed the key to Annie.

'Things being a bit hectic, you've come up trumps. Margaret has allocated you the kit from the girl who left the other day. You should find everything you need in there.'

'Thank you.'

Annie watched Nina and Bertha lay out their kit, and followed suit, trying to appear as though she knew what she was checking for. There seemed to be so much to consider.

Nina held up a one-piece suit.

'You might need this if the weather turns colder.' She slipped off her skirt, exposing a pair of pretty silk cami-knickers, and put on a pair of dark blue loose fitting trousers. Annie pulled a pair of trousers from her pile of clothes and followed Nina's example.

Nina caught sight of Annie's thong.

'I say, they're a bit saucy! I can't honestly say I've ever seen a pair of knickers like those. Not much to them, is there?'

'You'll catch your death of cold in those.' Bertha hoisted up her skirt, displaying a voluminous pair of drab knickers. 'I prefer these any day!'

Nina raised her eyebrows.

'Well, at least if your parachute fails you'll have a second option.'

Simultaneously, the three women started to giggle. They packed their surplus clothes into kit bags, still laughing at the comparisons between underwear. By the time they got outside, the knot in Annie's stomach had subsided a little.

The weather had disintegrated: fluffy white clouds replaced by ominous grey ones over the airfield, which was bustling with activity. Annie scanned the whole scene, likening it to a film set. Imagery of her normal life with Tom was beginning to feel a little hazy around the edges. She startled, her thoughts interrupted as a loud wolf-whistle pierced the air. She looked towards where the sound had appeared to come from. A group of three men in greasy overalls, sleeves rolled up to their elbows, were working on an aircraft inside a hangar. One was standing under the wing of a Spitfire, the second man kneeling on the wing talking to a man in the cockpit.

Nina reproached the man crouched on the wing.

'Hey George, behave yourself! You don't want to scare the new girls!'

The man winked at Annie and blew Nina a kiss.

'You'll have to get used to that I'm afraid!' Nina took Annie's arm and carried on briskly.

Annie had noticed nearly every engineer had a cigarette behind his ear or one hanging from his mouth.

'I see they're not bothered about Health and Safety regulations.'

Nina seemed confused.

'What do you mean?'

'Everyone knows it's dangerous to smoke near flammable materials. One spark and it could all go up.'

'They need something to calm their nerves. You try hosing down the blood and oil after ops!'

Annie shuddered as an image of Lenny being pulled from a plane destroyed by cannon fire flashed through her mind.

Passing out of the busy hangar housing some seven or eight planes in a state of repair, the three of them continued on past several dispersal huts placed in an orderly line to the side of a grass landing strip.

Lounging on the soft grass or relaxing in wicker chairs were a large group of airmen in various states of dress: the brave men that Tom often enthused about. The men's demeanour surprised Annie. There did not appear to be any suggestion of fear in their faces, although most of them were pale and fatigued from another night of aerial combat. Those that were not asleep, laughed and chatted as though they were spectators waiting for the start of a football match. Some smoked pipes or cigarettes, others played cards or read magazines as they relaxed in the warm breeze that blew across the airfield ruffling the grass. The occasional comment was uttered by the pilots as Annie, Nina and Bertha passed by, although less sexually explicit than the catcalls Annie was used to when strutting through the streets of London. She scanned the aircrew for Lenny, disappointed that he was nowhere to be seen. Just as they reached the end of the row of dispersal huts, she spotted him sitting a bit apart from the other men.

Nina noticed Annie's face colour up.

'You're keen on him aren't you?'

Annie played down her flushed cheeks.

'It's just good to see he's safe.'

'Don't waste your time, we've all had a crush on him at some time or another.'

Bertha looked up at the sky.

'He's more interested in being up there.'

As they approached Lenny, Annie realised that he had been sketching. He looked up as Annie cast a shadow across the page.

Bertha leant over to examine his drawings.

'Morning, Lenny. I see you haven't lost your touch.'

Lenny nonchalantly dropped the sketchpad on the grass.

'Helps pass the time.'

Annie looked down at a detailed pencil drawing of an airman, which had been sensitively rendered. Lenny chatted freely with Bertha and Nina, not realising that Annie had taken the opportunity to pluck his sketchbook from the grass. She turned the pages slowly, studying scribbled poetry, notes and observations of people and planes: absorbed in the sensitivity and skill of Lenny's art.

'Do you mind? That's private!' Lenny snatched the notebook from Annie.

'They're good. I couldn't help but look at them.'

'You can draw me anytime,' said Nina, trying to pose provocatively, but not quite pulling it off.

Lenny seemed a little uncomfortable with Nina's playful pose. He abruptly sidestepped the suggestion, continuing his previous conversation. Oblivious to his embarrassment, Nina and Bertha listened intently, Annie tried hard to understand the logistics of his nightly missions. Sensing his need to replenish his energy levels for whatever was to come that night, Nina suggested to Annie and Bertha that they should be getting a move on.

As Bertha and Nina moved off, Annie whispered in Lenny's ear.

'Will you paint me a picture?'

Lenny pushed his cap back and looked straight into her eyes.

'Maybe.'

Their eyes met for a few seconds, but Annie could read nothing of his thoughts: nothing at all. She turned away to catch up with Bertha and Nina and looked over her shoulder, hoping that Lenny might be looking her way. He was sketching again.

Chapter 27

As the Anson gained height, it banked over and circled, its large windows allowing Annie a panoramic view of the airfield stretching out in all directions from the cluster of hangars, dispersal huts and other nondescript buildings. Annie used her time wisely, meticulously studying the landscape in an effort to memorise the countryside below for future reference.

Trees and hedgerows lined the perimeter of the airfield with the exception of a well-defined gap through the flight path and where the main gatehouse was situated. As well as the trees, matchbox-sized buildings outlined the pentagon shape of the airfield, the runways slicing through the middle. Aircraft were parked on the side of the concrete and grass runways in small circular bays adjacent to the long concrete airstrip: the bays resembling seedpods hanging from a long grey plant stalk. Adjacent to the runways, pilots were still assembled outside dispersal huts: a cluster of small dots the size of ants. By the time Annie had located the spot where Lenny had been seated, the Anson was beginning to turn away from the airfield, skimming the underneath of white marshmallow clouds.

Annie continued to commit landmarks and anomalies to her memory. A silvery river, glistening like millions of diamonds, coiled around the airfield perimeter like a sleeping snake, and offered pilots a watery landing should they misjudge their landing.

Annie's reticence to accept her bizarre situation was no longer her prime concern. All that was necessary now was that she fitted into the role that was expected of her. To achieve this, her ability to not alienate those people she would be working alongside, was of paramount importance. Gleaning information from the other girls could help her appear a more convincing character. Finding her way back home to Tom was beginning to take second place, and in any case, she was completely clueless as to how she could achieve that goal.

Breaking off from her conversation with the pilot, Bertha helped Annie out with orientation.

'You'll find this an easy airfield to land at. Have you flown from here before?'

'I don't think so. There's nothing I recognise from up here so far.'

'You'll be able to land blindfolded once you've done it a few times. If you follow the railway, you'll know you're home as soon as you see the remains of the abbey.' She pointed out of the window.

True to Bertha's description, a railway ran quite close to the abbey, which resembled a giant stone iceberg. As Annie wondered at the stone monolith, a steam train chugged past its crumbling spire, grey smoke billowing from its funnel. The train briefly kept pace with the Anson as it flew low over the patchwork of green fields and small villages dotted here and there.

Annie kept an attentive ear open so as not to miss snippets of important information, but rested her head against the window, closing her eyes, and enjoying the heat of the sun. The fumes from the two engines were beginning to permeate into the cockpit, making her feel queasy. Exasperated by turbulence, which caused the plane to emulate a carriage on a roller-coaster, the feeling gathered in intensity. Her stomach churned as the Anson was lifted on warm thermals as it passed over a line of hills with a chalky outcrop running along the summit.

Nina laughed at Annie's expression.

'Gosh, you've turned grey. Amazing how just a few weeks not flying can make you feel bad, isn't it?'

'The last time was on an Airbus to The States.'

'What was that?' asked Nina, struggling to hear above the banter between other passengers.

'Last time I felt like this was on a bus. I was a right state.'

'I don't travel too well on buses either. Never mind, we'll be there before you know it.'

Annie bit her lip to stop herself from tripping herself up again by saying something that would be like a foreign language to Nina. Just when she thought she could take no more and was about to vomit, the plane began its descent. The weather was deteriorating, storm clouds accumulating in the sky above the Anson. Fine drizzle deposited dirty streaks on the windows. To Annie, it felt a few degrees cooler than in the southern counties. She shivered as the plane began its final approach to the airfield that lay straight ahead. Despite the gathering gloom, the Anson touched down lightly, bouncing gently, and taxied into an almost empty hangar.

Corrugated hangars and red-bricked buildings lined either side of the concrete runway: the buildings separated only by narrow roads leading to other parts of the airfield. Outside the hangars, long lines of planes were parked, some of which were being worked on by groups of mechanics. Used to travelling business class and having all her needs met by an air stewardess with a fixed smile, Annie almost made the mistake of handing her bag to Bertha to carry.

The pilot taxied the Anson back out into grey mist that was now forming and made his way back to the runway. Annie almost wished she were going back with him. Nina and Bertha were friendly enough but she felt guarded and defensive: worrying all the time what questions they might put to her or what they might ask her to do. Apart from that, Lenny would most likely still be back at the airfield. The three of them stood just inside of the hangar doors and watched the Anson take off. It disappeared into the distance, keeping just below the angry clouds.

Bertha broke the silence.

'I didn't spot a single aircraft on the way up, did you?'

'There's nothing much happening,' replied Nina. 'Did you see any, Annie?'

'I was too busy feeling sick by the time we got here.'

Nina smiled.

'It's completely different when you're not in control, isn't it? I used to be just like you.'

Bertha looked up at the angry sky.

'Right now ladies, my biggest concern is staying dry. We'll have to make a run for the office.'

The rest of the ferry pilots bunched up behind them.

The drizzle had been replaced by torrential rain, immediately soaking Annie and the other ferry pilots to the skin as they stepped outside of the shelter of the hangar. Any evidence of a blue sky had evaporated within the space of half an hour. Heavy grey clouds hung over the entire airfield as far as the eye could see. The Anson had been lost in the murk within only seconds of taking off.

Bertha grumbled.

'He'll be for the high jump when he gets back, whereas I refuse to risk my life in such conditions.'

Nina agreed with Bertha.

'He should have waited, but at least no one expects us to fly in this weather.'

'That's as maybe, but look what happened last week. We lost two pilots who thought they ought to have a stab at getting to White Waltham.'

'What happened to them?' asked Annie.

'One ended up in the drink and the other one hit a barrage balloon.'

'Oh my goodness.'

'The trouble is if we follow the rules, the men will call us sissies. How can we be expected to get all these planes back south without flying above the clouds?'

Nina intervened.

'Don't you take any notice of what the men might say. It's completely different for the RAF boys. They have to go up in all weathers. We just have to get the planes home safely.'

There was no one nearby with a vehicle that could maybe offer them a lift the last hundred yards to the main cluster of buildings. They huddled together with coats over their heads, and ran, struggling not to drop their overnight bags. By the time they reached the main buildings, rain was coming down in sheets and Annie's feet squelched in her black rigid shoes. She hated the fact that she was not looking her best.

The commanding officer seemed oblivious to Annie's damp appearance, and was more engrossed in going through formalities with Nina as to what planes they were taking back south.

'There's a change of plan. I've informed Margaret Bowhill.'

'Why's that then?' asked Bertha.

'One of your lot arrived here earlier than expected, so I allocated one of the planes you should have picked up. She took off successfully before the weather closed in.'

Nina leant across the counter and fixed the commanding officer with a stony stare.

'And what are you implying by your emphasis on the word she?'

He coughed nervously.

'I didn't mean anything. Although your girl Avril didn't seem too confident.'

'That's alright then,' said Nina.

'Nonetheless I'm not prepared to let you girls take off until the skies clear a bit. It would mean my guts for garters.'

Bertha protested.

'I was going to the pictures tonight. I wanted to be back by six at the latest.'

'If you're that desperate you could go the Regal Cinema five miles away. Gone with the Wind is showing.'

Nina scowled at him.

'If I were a man, we wouldn't be having this conversation, would we?'

He raised his eyebrows at Bertha, turned his back and left the room mumbling. 'There'll be someone here to take you to your digs in five minutes, young lady.'

Nina paced the room, huffing and puffing, whilst Bertha remained at the counter, tapping her fingers. Annie had wanted to punch the commanding officer on the nose, but spent the next five minutes furiously rearranging her belongings, which had become waterlogged in the short dash from the aircraft hangar. She was relieved that the heated conversation had not been witnessed by anyone other than the other ferry pilots they had travelled with, as the humiliation of being regarded as only suitable for domestic servitude infuriated her beyond belief.

They did not have to wait long for their ride back to their digs. A timid young man sheepishly poked his head round the door, looking as though he was expecting to have something launched at him by one, if not all of the three cross-looking women that were waiting. His demeanour suggested that he was already familiar with the commanding officer's sexist undertones causing ripples amongst female ferry pilots. Nevertheless, he proved himself a gentleman, hoisting all of their belongings onto his shoulders, his legs buckling under the weight. Nina and Bertha tittered between themselves as he staggered red-faced to a truck outside and dropped all of their kit into the back. He was silent during the short drive to town and appeared glad to leave them at the front door of the terraced house where they were to stay that night. As soon as they had collected their bags from the back of the truck, he drove off hurriedly, still with a red face.

It was clear that the weather was set for the night. The rain poured down and beat against the windows, which incessantly rattled as the wind picked up. Annie missed her large flat screen television and fluffy pink slippers and had no interest in listening to the small radio that sat in the sitting room emitting the dulcet tones of music from a bygone era.

The house was small and basic, with a cobbled backyard and outside toilet. There were no frills but Annie was the only one to notice it. Going to the pictures would have been a welcome relief from being cross-examined by Nina and Bertha, but Annie managed to escape scrutiny as they all sat together in the small sitting room. Nina, being the most talkative and self-assured, related her complete life story. Annie felt more empathy with both women when she discovered that they came from well-to-do families with similar social standing to her own. She continued to shape her background to suit, omitting anything that could lead to suspicion as to her origin.

Knowing that they had an early start, they drank cocoa and settled down for the night, Nina and Bertha sharing the one small bedroom upstairs. Annie tried to get comfortable under a knitted patchwork blanket on the sitting room settee. When she awoke, it was dawn, the rain had stopped and the sky was almost clear. As she gathered her thoughts together, her stomach tightened at the thought of the impending day. Nonetheless, she felt that if she could get through the next few hours, anything that followed would be manageable.

Chapter 28

Annie had only just dressed when there was the sound of a vehicle hooting repeatedly in the street outside. She had woken with a stiff neck from sleeping in an awkward position and the unforgiving sofa springs digging into her side. Just as she pulled the blackout curtains to one side to look out, a sudden loud commotion erupted from the bedroom above, followed a minute later by the sound of thunderous footsteps coming down the steep staircase. Bertha and Nina burst through the door: both having hurriedly thrown on their clothes.

Nina looked dishevelled.

'Are you ready, Annie?'

'Just about.'

Hastily grabbing all their kit, still damp from the previous day, the three of them left the house and greeted the man who had driven them the day before. He seemed even more timid: his complexion pastier and his mousy hair greasier. Even his uniform did not disguise his slight frame or make him appear manlier. As soon as they spoke he turned bright red.

Nina winked at him.

'Hello, sweetheart. Aren't we the lucky ones seeing you again?'

He smiled nervously and doffed his cap, mumbling a greeting under his breath.

Nina spent much of the short journey back to the airfield flirting and teasing him mercilessly, taking great pleasure in watching him squirm. Sitting next to him, she

261

pouted at him every time he looked out of the corner of his eye at her. Bertha was less cruel.

'Really Nina, you're so unkind. You're making the poor boy blush.'

Nina winked at him again.

'You don't say much, do you?' Am I embarrassing you, darling?'

'No ma'am, I've had worse.'

'You can call me Nina. What's your name?'

'Timothy, ma'am.'

'Well Timothy, don't you mind me. I'm just joshing with you. We're all very grateful for you coming out so early, aren't we ladies?'

'Of course, but maybe Timothy would prefer if next time I sat in the front,' said Bertha.

'We'll be there soon. I'm sure Timothy can put up with me for a few moments longer, can't you Timothy?'

'Yes ma'am.'

Timothy made no further comment.

Annie sat quietly in the back of the truck trying hard to ignore the knots in her stomach. Nina's sadistic jibing and Bertha's sniggering had just been background banter: hardly a distraction for Annie's gathering trepidation.

The airfield was bleak and unrecognisable, the previous day's driving rain having turned everything the same shade of charcoal grey. As they entered the main gates, a stream of trucks and cars followed them in and filtered off in different directions to other destinations around the airfield. The truck pulled up at the same place that it had collected them from the day before.

Nina blew Timothy a kiss.

'Bye Timothy. See you next time, perhaps.'

'Bye.' He doffed his cap and drove away as quickly as he could to escape any more of Nina's barrage of innuendos.

Inside the office the same man was behind the wooden counter that had made masked comments the day before. The office was crowded with other ferry pilots all chatting loudly to one another as they waited for their flying chits. The commanding officer was tapping his fingers on the counter as he impatiently looked up at the clock on the wall.

He held out a piece of paper to Nina.

'You're five minutes late. Do you think you can manage to fly this one?'

Nina looked at the chit of paper.

'Of course. With my arms tied behind my back. Could you?' She glared coldly back at him.

He mumbled under his breath: something about women and cooking and dusters and left the room as he had done last time.

Nina glowered after him.

'That man...I could slap his face! Right ladies, let's fire up the Lancaster then!'

'The Lancaster?' The tips of Annie's fingers began to tingle.

'My favourite, and a good initiation for you!'

Nina pushed her way through the crowd and swept out of the door with Bertha and Annie jostling to keep up with her.

The moment had arrived. Annie knew her good memory and aptitude in such a difficult situation were the only assets that might save her skin.

'Annie, you can navigate as you haven't qualified on bombers as yet,' instructed Bertha.

'I haven't qualified on anything since I joined up.'

'Only theoretically!'

'I'm glad I've been spared going solo.'

Nina reassured her. 'You'd manage if you had to. It's pretty much as the crow flies to get home.'

'I'm not so sure.'

'I expect you'll be asked to bring a Spit back from here soon,' commented Nina. 'They're turning them out so fast we can't keep up. You're fine with that, aren't you?'

'Yes, absolutely...can't wait,' Annie lied, with her heart in her mouth.

They walked briskly to the aircraft hangars past a variety of planes that were completely unfamiliar. Annie ticked off in her head the ones that most resembled the marques her grandfather had owned over the years, instantly dismayed that ninety-five percent were alien to her. As they approached the iron doors of one of the larger hangars, two men dressed in overalls came out of a small door set within the bigger hangar doors.

One of the men held out a greasy hand to shake.

'Hello ladies.'

Nina introduced them to Annie.

'Hello Archie. This is our new girl Annie. Annie – this is Archie. He'll always try the greasy handshake trick on you. Whereas Bob is more of a gent, aren't you Bob?'

'Good to meet you. Nina's right. I'm definitely the gent out of us two.'

'Oh you think so do you?' scoffed Archie. 'All the ladies love me, if you must know.'

Bob raised his eyebrows.

'She's all ready for you.'

The two men put all their weight against the heavy iron doors and with difficulty pushed them open. All the planes Annie had just passed seemed instantly insignificant in comparison to the gargantuan plane standing inside the hangar, with four powerful engines, and vast wheels almost the same height as her. She likened it to a crouching pterodactyl waiting to surprise its unsuspecting prey. Transfixed to the spot, she wondered how the massive wings, which almost brushed each side of the hangar, did not buckle under the weight of the huge engines.

Bertha laughed at Annie's flabbergasted expression.

'Anyone would think you'd never seen a Lanc!'

'I haven't.'

Nina seemed surprised.

'That can't be possible.'

Annie realised her blunder.

'Well, of course I've seen them, but not at this close range. It's enormous.'

Nina seemed easily fooled.

'Let's get on with it, shall we?' she said casually, as though flying a Lancaster was something she did as often as cleaning her teeth.

Annie pulled herself up to full height and took a deep breath.

'Yes, let's!'

Out of the blue, Annie sensed someone approach from behind.

'Need some help flying that?' asked a drawling female voice.

Nina, Bertha and Annie turned simultaneously. Standing with both hands on her hips was a strikingly glamorous woman, with a mane of peroxide blonde hair, which was fighting to escape from her forage cap. Her makeup was immaculate: eyebrows dark and arched, lips full and scarlet. Another equally stunning woman stood confidently next to her, equally as curvaceous but everything else about her a striking contrast: jet black hair and skin a deep shade of chocolate.

Nina's usually friendly manner immediately evaporated, replaced by an irritated tone.

'Hello Glenda.'

Glenda continued in a judgemental American drawl, eyeing Annie up and down with complete disapproval.

'Who's this?'

The two women continued to scrutinise Annie, the dark- haired woman choosing not to speak but to chew gum instead. She smirked at Annie's obvious discomfort. For a second Annie empathised with the girls in her office and how they must have felt when she looked down on them. Bertha stepped closer to Annie, as though to give her moral support. To Annie, it felt like a Western saloon shoot out as she sensed the tension building between the four other women.

Nina reluctantly introduced the two Americans.

'Meet Glenda and Joyce - our American counterparts!'

Annie could not help but notice that the two Americans, though no more attractive than Nina and Bertha, were way ahead in the glamour stakes: not a single hair out of place, and uniform so figure-hugging that it left nothing to the imagination. They wore silk stockings, which glistened in the sunlight, and although Annie thought it was probably against uniform regulations, their shoes were impractically high-heeled.

Glenda spoke again, this time almost hissing like a snake.

'Well? Do you need help flying the Lancs? It might be a bit more than you country girls can handle!'

'I think we can manage thank you, Glenda dear,' said Nina curtly. 'We've had a bit more practice than you. Why don't you just concern yourself with keeping up with us on the way home!'

Glenda did not take the bait but sneered as she looked defiantly back at Nina.

'Come on Joyce, let's go and find those inferior little Spitfires we have to fly.'

Joyce fleetingly looked Annie up and down again before turning away, walking slowly and gracefully like a gazelle, her high heels making no noise on the hard ground.

'Ouch,' said Annie, finally breathing normally again. 'If she were any more up herself she'd disappear up her own backside.'

Nina burst out laughing, followed by Bertha and the two engineers who had said nothing during the shootout.

'Well I never,' exclaimed Nina, once she had composed herself again. 'You have an odd way of expressing yourself. I've never heard that one before, but if by that turn of phrase you mean that she's a bit big for her boots, I'm with you there.'

They all laughed again, Annie realising that by standing her ground, she might finally have made some genuine friends within the strange world in which she was trapped. As they slipped into their flying clothes and repacked their bags in the privacy of a quiet corner of the hangar, the atmosphere between the three women took on another dimension: Glenda and Joyce mimicked and ridiculed during the few minutes it took to change.

Nina and Bertha finally climbed up a short metal ladder to board the Lancaster and reached down to help Annie. All of her fear had been forgotten as a result of the last few minute's fun. She climbed into the plane, taking care not to graze her head on the sharp metal doorframe. Strangely, the fumes from the Lancaster's fuel and oil supply filled her nostrils like a favourite perfume. She breathed the fumes in, struggling with no avail to connect the familiarity of these smells with something from the

268

past. Nina strapped herself into the pilot's seat, and Bertha sat in the flight engineer's seat to her right. As Annie settled herself in the navigator's seat she knew that even if she were afraid, there was no going back. She had the easiest job of all. She saw Nina and Bertha in a new light, with a sudden sense of admiration and respect: a feeling that until now had only been reserved for the family no longer with her. Their familiarity with the plane was second nature: performing pre-flight checks, with Annie watching attentively, both women dwarfed by the sheer scale of the Lancaster. Their hands on the four throttles looked like doll's hands, too delicate to push against the hefty levers.

As the plane began to taxi out of the hangar, Annie could feel the guttural rumble from the engines vibrate deep in her chest. The wheels clunked as they passed over cracks in the concrete runway, cleared for take off, the gigantic plane gathering speed. Annie's whole body trembled with the vibration of the four Merlin engines and their massive propellers, an unexpected excitement coursing through her body as the plane thundered down the runway, fuselage and wings quaking furiously. Once in the sky, she quickly gathered height and flew like a giant bird of prey, huge wings slicing through the sky. The roar of the enormous engines seemed to impress upon Annie that there was no way they would let her down. In the air, she seemed untroubled by her colossal weight and size, and seemed to float almost unaided. Annie wondered at the uninterrupted visibility from different vantage points, likening it to looking upwards through the glass panes of a metal-framed greenhouse. As well as this, the unflustered voices of Nina and Bertha reassured Annie that all was well as they discussed their route with her. Annie plotted the course on the chart, using protractor and rule, taking into account sideways drift due to a crosswind. She called out headings.

Nina spoke to Annie from the pilot's seat.

'What do you think? She's wonderful isn't she?'

'I can't believe you can fly her.'

Bertha laughed.

'You sound like one of the men talking.'

'I didn't mean it like that. It just looks like a handful. I couldn't do it.'

'Yes you could, with practice. And anyway, it's not about brute strength. Treat her like the lady she is, and she responds like a purring kitten.'

'That commanding officer – do you come across many like him?'

'Not really, do we Bertha?'

'No, I've only come across one or two. They're best ignored. We're very bit as good as them.'

'Even Lenny asked me if I thought I was as good as the men.'

Bertha laughed again.

'Lenny likes to tease. He has huge respect for the lady pilots really.'

Annie felt a sudden surge of happiness at the thought that the further south they flew, the nearer she was getting to Lenny. With him in mind, it only seemed like a fraction of time before the plane was coming in to land, the wheels touching down on the runway, squealing as they cushioned the weight of the huge aircraft.

Annie felt euphoric. The day she had dreaded for over a week had been one of exhilaration and sisterhood. She no longer felt isolated from those around her. She had relinquished her life in the twenty-first century, protected by the pluckiness and skills of like-minded women: women who refused to be tied to the kitchen sink and domesticity.

Chapter 29

When they had finished with the formalities of delivering the Lancaster, the Anson was waiting to take them to their next collection point. This time the Anson was full to capacity, with two male ferry pilots on board as well as a bevy of chattering females. As the Anson taxied towards the runway, Annie caught sight of Glenda in the front passenger seat of a stylish saloon car, Joyce in the back seat, being driven out of the airfield at a leisurely speed by an RAF officer.

'Where do they think they are going?'

Nina tutted.

Glenda and Joyce always expect special treatment. When there's a chance of a lift with a handsome man they'll always take it.'

'It's alright for some.'

'They're certainly getting other pilots' hackles up, as well as doing a damn good job of alienating themselves from the rest of us.'

Bertha joined the conversation.

'It will take them much longer than us to get to the next pick up point.'

'That's if they bother to turn up.'

'They'll get their comeuppance. There'll be hell to pay if they're late again,' added Bertha. 'Margaret's not impressed at all with their behaviour.'

The Anson made good time as they headed north again to pick up a second Lancaster. Once they arrived, despite a lengthy delay on the ground due to thick cloud rolling in, Glenda and Joyce were still unaccounted for by the time the cloud had lifted. Nina and Bertha had already done their in-flight checks and had been cleared for take off when the two Americans arrived.

When Nina landed the Lancaster back at base it was evening and the light was fading. As they taxied towards the hangars, Annie cupped her hands to the window, peering towards the spot where she had last seen Lenny. Pin-prick dots of red light from cigarettes and pipes, flickering in the gathering darkness like thousands of fireflies, were the only evidence of people moving around outside dispersal huts. As they disembarked from the Lancaster, the chill of the evening air hit Annie squarely in the face. It had not been cold in the Lancaster, although her clothes still had a lingering dampness about them from the run across the airfield in torrential rain the previous day.

Nina, Bertha and Annie made their way past hangars in the semi-darkness. As they got nearer to the dispersal huts, the sound of laughter welcomed them. It was a strange thought that their joviality would dissipate in seconds if the pilots were called to scramble. Annie shivered, this time not from the cold, but at the terrifying thought that Lenny might be among the pilots who would lose their young lives tonight.

Nina led the way past the first of the huts. Just as they drew parallel with the first, a small group of RAF pilots spilled out into the gathering darkness. Snatches of light, conversation and laughter permeated the dusk as the door swung behind them.

'Have they been drinking?'

'I hope not. It's strictly forbidden before ops,' said Nina. 'Afterwards is different. They often go up to London if they get a chance. Heaven knows what they get up to...I dread to think.'

'Ladies! I do hope you'll be joining us this evening?'

'Not tonight boys, we've got to get back home. We're missing the village dance,' replied Bertha, dodging a man advancing on her with open arms.

'Come on darling, how about a kiss?' said a second man.

'You'd best not have been drinking, Gordon. You'll be for the chop if you're caught,' said Nina as he grabbed at her arm.

As they left the men behind, Annie caught a whiff of alcohol on Gordon's breath.

'He's had a few.'

'There's always one that flouts the rules. I suppose it's understandable,' replied Nina, with a touch of resignation in her voice.

'It's not in their interest though,' added Bertha. 'They need their wits about them.'

There was really nothing more to say. Annie took one last look at the young men in the gathering darkness, thinking how tragic it was that their life expectancy was so short. Then she turned and followed Nina and Bertha to the locker room, where they changed out of their flying clothes and back into civilian clothes.

'Everyone will be at the village dance by now,' said Nina. 'Are you both keen to go?'

'Hopefully Betty will be there,' added Bertha. 'The family will have dragged her along to distract her from Peter.'

Nina looked at Annie.

'I expect Lenny will be there too – it's his night off.'

Annie tried to avoid looking at Nina, feigning indifference with regards to the dance. She had already assumed that if Lenny were there, she would not be on his mind for one second. She wished that she could get back to the farm and change into something more becoming. Smoothing down her dress, she felt plain and unattractive. Only a few weeks ago she would have refused to wear such an understated garment and flat clumpy shoes. She brushed her hair vigorously and attempted to style it as best she could, splashed her face with cold water and put on the only item of makeup she always carried: her expensive lipstick.

'Can I borrow some of that?' asked Nina. 'I forgot to bring mine.'

'Of course.'

Nina examined the slick lipstick casing and applied it carefully.

'This is a bit posh. I don't know this brand, black market I bet!' She looked at her reflection in a small mirror on the locker room wall, pouting as she did so. 'You'll have to tell me where I can get some.'

'Well don't keep it to yourself,' said Bertha, taking it from Nina. 'I can't have you two showing me up.' She followed suit applying the lipstick with practised finesse.

'Nina's right,' she added, eyeing up the gold-coloured case. 'This must have cost you!'

'It was a gift,' said Annie, to avoid awkward questions about a product that wouldn't be manufactured until the twenty-first century.

Bertha handed the lipstick back.

'Come on ladies – are we ready? Let's knock 'em dead!'

Despite Annie still being none the wiser about the world she found herself trapped in, for the first time since she could remember, she had an overwhelming sense of self-worth. Nina and Bertha had begun to make her feel like she was a valued friend and colleague. With a growing feeling that she could do nothing but accept her plight, she jumped eagerly into the truck that had carried her to the airfield the day before. Only twenty-four hours had passed since trepidation had gripped her, yet so much had changed in that short space of time.

She sat back, shielded her legs against the cold with an old blanket, and closed her eyes for the short bumpy ride back to the village. Although she was exhausted, she did not want to sleep. She spent the short journey constructing a mental picture of what was happening at the village hall, slightly suspicious of how Lenny might be behaving off-duty. Competition between her and other women had never been a problem until now. She could not recall a time when another woman had stood in her way. Nevertheless, feeling that she was not looking her best and that Lenny had not shown that much interest in her, Annie could not settle or relax.

As they approached the village, the sound of music was vaguely audible from somewhere close by. Nina parked and they picked their way along a gravel path using the light of the moon to guide them. The hall was in darkness, blackout curtains drawn against the outside world. A few people arriving at the same time followed them towards the hall, which sat hidden by a privet hedge to one side of a Norman church. It took considerable effort from Nina and Bertha to push open the heavy oak doors.

Bright lights, loud music and garbled voices greeted them: a complete contrast to the darkness outside. Annie squinted, trying to accustom her eyes to the light. All three squeezed their way through the crowd, keeping close to the edge of the dance floor. The sheer volume of people packed tightly into the space warmed them instantly. Most were dancing, others were seated on the chairs around the makeshift dance floor or were congregating in front of a long bar area. The air above the crowd was full of tobacco smoke creating a heavy haze, the fog tinted pink by soft light emanating from a few simple lamps that hung from wooden rafters on long flexes.

A stage dominated one end of the hall. A small swing band was entertaining the partygoers. The lead vocalist had a stunningly soulful voice, her jewellery catching the light as she swayed rhythmically to the beat.

Dancing couples circled the room in a clock-wise direction: some in uniform and others in modest civilian clothes. Nina nudged Annie with her elbow and shouted above the music.

'Look who's here.'

Annie craned her head over the crowd expecting and hoping to see Lenny. She frantically searched the throng for his face.

'Who?'

'Why, Glenda and Joyce! Who else?'

Right in the middle of the crowd, Glenda's peroxide blonde hair shone like a beacon. Both women had found time to change out of uniform and were locked close in embraces with airmen.

Annie tried to hide her disappointment.

'How did they make it here before us?'

'Friends in high places, I should imagine.'

As well as Glenda and Joyce, a few of the workers from the farm including Daphne and the other land girls were dancing in a group. Daphne spotted Annie and shot her a withering look from the dance floor.

It suddenly struck Annie how the atmosphere in the hall was a complete contrast to what was going on in the skies over the southern counties. The dance was nothing but a welcome respite for pilots on leave, but offered little compensation for the high price they might have to pay. Annie wanted to jump up onto the stage and shout out at the top of her voice that the war would be over in a couple of years and convince the men and women in the hall that there was a glimmer of hope for their future. She had become so absorbed in this daydream that it took someone calling her to jolt her back to the dance.

'Annie! We're over here.'

Betty was frantically waving and jumping up and down to attract Annie's attention. She pushed her way through the crowd of dancers and threw her arms around Annie as though she were greeting a long lost friend or sister. Annie pulled away to get a better look at her. The transformation was incredible.

'Annie, he's okay, they've found him! He's alive. Isn't that wonderful news?'

'Oh Betty, that's marvellous news.'

They hugged again as Betty broke into sobs that were a mixture of joy and relief.

'Come and dance with us, Lenny's here too.'

Annie's heart thumped at the mention of his name. He appeared suddenly from amongst the crowd, precariously balancing two glasses of wine above his head, clearing a path through the dancers like Moses parting the Red Sea.

Annie felt uncomfortable with the knowledge that Lenny's presence stirred her so easily, and that she had fallen for him so quickly: especially as he had shown no sign that he might be feeling the same. She wished it would take him forever to cross the hall so that she would have had a fair chance to compose herself. Captivated by his blue eyes, the unfathomable expression within them made her feel immediately vulnerable. The closer he came, the more strikingly magnificent he seemed. She wanted to turn and walk away, as she couldn't bear for him to laugh at her adolescent blushing, but there was no time to find a hiding place. Taking a deep breath, she waited for his greeting, hoping that the sound of his voice would not cause the redness in her cheeks to intensify.

'Let me help you with those,' said a young woman appearing from nowhere, lithely slipping in front of Lenny as he approached. Two slender arms reached up to relieve him of the wine glasses. A jubilant smile lit up Daphne's face.

'Here - take these,' she commanded Betty and Annie, thrusting the wine glasses at them so forcefully that they both had to step back to avoid being deluged with red wine. 'You don't mind do you?' She fixed both with a sly smile.

With no chance to protest, Betty and Annie stood in silence, stunned as Daphne whisked Lenny onto the dance floor. Pouring herself into his arms, she peered over his shoulder at Annie, still with the smirk etched onto her face. Then she reached up and kissed Lenny on the cheek.

'Well I never!' said Betty when she had regained her composure. 'The nerve of the woman! He was clearly on his way to see us.'

Annie pretended not to care, forcing herself to smile artificially at Daphne as she waltzed around the room with Lenny. He hadn't protested, nor even glanced back at her. He seemed comfortable in Daphne's arms.

Betty sensed Annie's mood.

'Don't upset yourself over her. He's just being polite. I'm sure he'll ask you to dance once he's got rid of her.'

Despite Betty's reassurance, half an hour passed and Daphne held on to Lenny for dear life, resting her head lovingly on his shoulder for the slower dances.

Annie did not see the stranger approach.

'Excuse me ma'am, would you like to dance?' He towered above her and spoke in a Canadian accent. 'A pretty lady like you shouldn't be left alone,' he said charmingly, touching the front of his cap.

'Go on,' said Betty, nudging Annie with her elbow.' I'm going to get another drink anyway.' She conveniently sidled off leaving Annie to make a decision.

'The name's Dan by the way. And you are?'

'I'm Annie.'

Annie fleetingly studied him. He was attractive, with dark brown eyes and cropped fair hair. He wore his cap at a jaunty angle. Lenny was no longer visible.

'I'd love to.' She put down her glass and offered him her hand.

He pulled her towards him, slightly too eagerly for her liking, but she immediately reminded herself that she could handle any over-zealousness on his part.

'I noticed you as soon as you arrived. You're the best-looking dame here. Where's your boyfriend?'

'I don't have a boyfriend at present.' She regretted her statement as soon as she said it.

Dan locked her into an inescapable embrace.

'Well aren't I the lucky guy?'

Annie decided to use Dan's unwelcome attention to her advantage, allowing his muscular arms to remain wound about her slim waist, engaging him in light conversation as they circled the floor. She looked around occasionally for Lenny, dismayed to see him dancing with as many women as he could accommodate in quick succession. He seemed oblivious to her and her handsome partner. She might not get a chance to dance with him after all. Already tired of Dan's vice-like grip, she wanted to go and find Betty. She was about to make an excuse, when the tall Canadian spoke first.

'It's kinda hot in here. Do you want to get some fresh air?'

'Okay, but only for a few moments.'

She was content to have a brief interlude in the cold evening air as her dress was sticking to her skin in the heat of the packed hall. A moment outside would also free her up from the clutches of Dan, flattering though his attention was. She felt sure he was just another homesick pilot, missing his friends and family.

At that moment Lenny and his current partner danced slowly past. Annie spoke louder so that Lenny would hear.

'You can tell me all about yourself while you walk me home.'

Dan grinned from ear to ear and linked arms with Annie.

'Well you don't waste time,' he said, looking pleased with himself. They left the hall and stepped outside into darkness.

Chapter 30

A stiff breeze had sprung up in the short time since Annie had arrived with Nina and Bertha, but she was still glad to leave the uncomfortable heat of the village hall. She was also relieved to be out of sight of Lenny dancing with all and sundry.

Dan stopped outside the double doors and took a thin silver cigarette case from his jacket pocket.

'Cigarette?'

'No thanks.'

He took one out for himself and tapped it lightly on the case before taking out his lighter and flicking it open. He appeared thoughtful and said nothing more, lighting his cigarette and preferring to stare into the darkness whilst he took long deep drags.

The pleasant coolness of the air had turned to an icy chill. Annie shivered.

'It's much colder than it was earlier,' she said, filling the awkward silence and thinking Dan rude for not offering her his jacket straightaway. 'Maybe we should go back inside.'

'No, let's go for a walk,' said Dan, putting his arm around her shoulder. 'It's stifling in there, and anyway, I'll keep you warm.'

Annie wished she hadn't tried to stir up jealousy in Lenny by feigning an attraction towards Dan. Nevertheless, she allowed him to lead her away from the hall to a more sheltered spot within the porch of the Norman church. They were still near enough to hear the music and laughter they had left behind. Millions of twinkling stars peppered the night sky and lilac clouds tinged with golden edges partially obscured the moon.

Dan finished his cigarette and immediately lit another. Annie used the opportunity to study his features briefly in the flickering yellow flame from his lighter. His eyes seemed devoid of any emotion. They reminded Annie of a shark's eyes: deep dark pools measuring her up.

She manufactured a conversation to break the silence between them.

'So where are you from?'

His answers were guarded responses.

'Canada.'

'What part?'

'Nowhere you'd know. A small town in the west.'

'Have you been in England long?'

'A while.'

Annie was quickly losing interest.

'I think I'll go back in. My friends will wonder where I've got to.'

He moved in front of her and blocked her way.

'You'll be fine with me,' he said firmly, fixing his icy gaze on her again.

'No, really. I'm too cold.'

He stubbed his cigarette out on the flagstone steps of the church, and moved closer to her. 'I thought you were expecting me to walk you home.'

She could feel his breath on her neck.

'I've changed my mind.' Annie pulled away, igniting a terrible fire in the man's eyes. His hands clamped onto her, one on the hip, the other on the wrist.

'Too bad,' he replied, in a matter of fact way, deftly twisting her arm up behind her back.

'Please Dan, stop,' she pleaded, struggling against him as he pushed himself against her. Her back impacted on the cold, hard stone of the church doorway, a broken brick digging into her ribs. Annie winced with the shock of the pain, almost in tears. No one would normally dare use her like this. A wave of anger rose inside her.

'Don't touch me.'

Annie wrenched her arm free and took a swing at the man. She made an attempt to run, but he saw it coming and blocked her way. He took hold of both her wrists in one of his huge hands and pinned them against the wall above her head, lifting her off of the ground.

'You're a feisty little dame!' he mocked, his other hand on the buttons of her dress.

Dan's strength astounded Annie. There seemed to be nothing she could do. She closed her eyes as his hand found her breasts. The air was thick with the smell of his sweat and stale breath as his lips grazed her neck and shoulders. Annie started to sob. He fixed her with a merciless smile and unbuckled his belt, breathing heavily.

The music that had been emanating from the village hall began getting louder, and raucous laughter permeated the still night as people left the dance.

Dan froze but kept her firmly in his hold.

'Don't say a word,' he muttered slowly through his teeth.

The group of people laughed and joked and her shouting seemed unnoticed by all of them: with the exception of Daphne. Annie could make out the people leaving the hall: Lenny, Betty and a couple of others she did not recognise.

Daphne scanned the darkness.

'What is it Daphne?' asked Lenny, as she halted in her tracks.

'Oh it's nothing,' she said, glancing up at him with a false smile. 'Just your little friend having a bit of fun with that chap she was dancing with.'

Lenny gave a deep sigh and mumbled something as he stormed down the path into the darkness.

Daphne shouted after him.

'Don't waste your time on her!'

'That was a bit mean Daphne. For all you know he might be very fond of her,' commented Betty.

'I doubt it, but so what if he is? Better that I warn him now what she's like.'

'Daphne! Really, you should mind your own business!' scolded Betty as she walked off in the direction of Lenny's car, leaving Daphne following a few steps behind.

Dan tightened his grip on Annie again.

Desperation filled Annie's very being and she began to sob uncontrollably. Dan ignored her tears and wrestled with her dress, ripping it open with renewed urgency. Afraid of what Dan might do if she tried to fight him off,

Annie resigned herself to her fate. Any remaining strength drained from her. She screwed her eyes up tightly to avoid seeing the expression of pleasure on Dan's face as he exposed her.

Just as she felt his hand slide up the remains of her dress, he was suddenly lifted from his feet and thrown backwards so violently that he crumpled instantly: his body hitting the wall opposite. He had no time to gather his senses. A strong hand grabbed his jacket collar and pulled him effortlessly up from the ground where he lay, as though he weighed no more than a feather.

The two men squared up to each other like gladiators in a ring. Annie shivered, freezing cold and brimming with fear, as she shrunk to the floor, vainly trying to pull the shreds of her clothes around herself.

'What do you think you're doing?'

Lenny pinned Dan firmly back against the wall, his face right up against Dan's and his arm across his throat.

'Hey man, calm down. She suggested we take a walk,' protested Dan, who although bleeding from his nose still managed to smirk. He held his hands up in a gesture of surrender.

Lenny tightened his arm across Dan's throat.

'Did she suggest you take advantage of her too?'

'Well, she did seem...'

Lenny lifted him off his feet as effortlessly as if he had been a small kitten.

'I don't want to hear it. Get out of here.'

He rammed Dan repeatedly in the chest, causing the man to stumble backwards down the steps of the church.

Dan walked briskly away, disappearing into the shadows as Lenny turned back to Annie huddled in the darkness. Proffering his hand, he pulled her to her feet. She shied away from him, very aware of what she must look like. He took off his jacket and gave it to Annie, giving her a brotherly squeeze on the shoulder as she wrapped it around herself.

'Come on. I'll take you home.'

'What about him?' asked Annie, looking into the darkness.

'I'll deal with him tomorrow. I know where to find him. Right now it's you we care about.'

'I didn't encourage him. We only came outside for some fresh air.' She felt the need to convince Lenny, and more than that she wanted Lenny to be the last lover she would ever have.

'Why did you come to find me?'

'I just sensed there was something wrong.'

Lenny supported her as they walked slowly back to the car where the others were waiting for them.

Betty burst into tears at the sight of Annie's torn clothing.

'Darling, what happened?'

'Someone got a bit heavy-handed,' said Lenny, to save Annie any explanation. 'Fuelled by alcohol no doubt.'

Betty made Annie comfortable in the car and wrapped her fur coat around her.

'Don't you worry, we'll have you home in a jiffy, and then we can clean you up.'

Betty turned her attention to Lenny.

'Did you catch whoever did this, Len?'

'Yes, and I'll make sure he pays for it.'

Betty seemed satisfied.

Dan was nowhere to be seen as they pulled away. Daphne feigned a sense of concern for Annie in order not to alienate Lenny and Betty, chatting to Annie as though they were good friends.

Once back at the farm, Annie sat in Lillian's chair comforted by the warmth from the kitchen range that had been stoked up for the night. Hot embers glowed in the tray underneath, glistening like a treasure chest full of rubies. Betty fussed around, the noise of cups and saucers just a distant noise in Annie's ears. Lenny stood by the kitchen door with the top half open onto the courtyard, puffing thoughtfully away on his pipe, a look of determination on his face. For a second, his actions reminded Annie of Dan quietly smoking his cigarette, as he planned his attack. Daphne's concern for Annie seemed short-lived, as she disappeared off to bed with very little more to say before she left the kitchen.

Betty made tea for the three of them. A strange phenomenon thought Annie: how the British considered that a cup of tea could right all wrongs. In this era, there seemed to be two nationwide solaces for those enduring any degree of hardship: tea and talking about it. She wondered what comfort they had indulged in before the advent of tea. It was indeed comforting sitting in Lillian's farmhouse kitchen, sipping from chipped china cups with the only two people she trusted; two people she had only known for a handful of days.

She rested her head back against a tapestry cushion, which had been painstakingly stitched by Lillian on long winter evenings. It would have been relatively easy to be lulled to sleep rocking backwards and forwards had she still not been suffering from shock due to her ordeal at the hands of Dan. Instead she felt jittery, and the slightest noise from outside caused her to look towards the door where Lenny had been standing.

'Best we get you to bed,' said Betty, after they had all drunk several cups of tea. 'You've got another long day ahead.'

It had completely slipped Annie's mind: in a few hours time she would be on her way to pick up more planes from around the country. The company in the Anson would no doubt be a distraction on her way to her destination, but there was the worry that she would be expected to fly solo over the next few days for the Air Transport Auxiliary. If her first experience were to be in a Tiger Moth, she was sure she would soon remember everything her grandfather had taught her only a few years previously. Finding her way home without getting completely lost was a different matter.

She knew she would want to just stay in bed the next morning, curled up on the soft mattress with its thick eiderdown. But even if she could, she would probably lay there thinking about this life or the one she had come from. This was not the same as being at Carlotti's. She couldn't just phone in sick.

She pulled herself out of the chair and realised that now the initial shock was abating, she was in pain. Her arm ached as a result of Dan twisting it behind her back, and her shoulder was stiff from being forced into an unnatural position. Aware of a dull thudding headache, she touched the back of her head. There the beginning of a swelling, inflicted by the wall Dan had thrust her against. She had always thought her self fairly tough, and as Dan had said, 'feisty', but she was beginning to realise that she was as vulnerable as the next woman with regards to men.

'Lenny – thank you for what you did tonight.'

She still wondered what Lenny's opinion of her was. Did he think she had been too willing to go off alone with Dan? If he did, then there was every possibility that his opinion of her was permanently tainted. In his eyes she was at the very least a flirt, and at worst promiscuous.

'He won't bother you again.' He fiercely prodded the tobacco in his pipe, but didn't look up.

Annie desperately wanted to see the expression within his eyes, but her pride prevented her from lingering much longer. His lack of emotion pained her.

'Goodnight,' she said meekly, as she moved quietly towards the door.

Betty reassured her. She hugged Annie warmly. 'We've grown very fond of you know.'

A lump formed in Annie's throat and she looked at Lenny for confirmation of Betty's last words. He continued to forage around in his pipe, stirring the burnt tobacco with the end of a spoon handle.

'Thank you Betty – you're very sweet.'

'It's the least I can do. You go up, I'll look in on you soon.'

Annie turned to look at Lenny one more time.

'Goodnight Lenny.'

He finally looked in her direction, and she imagined she saw his eyes sparkle for a second as he looked into hers.

'Goodnight. I hope you manage to sleep.' He turned away again and lit his pipe.

She limped through the door, realising that her thighs were bruised too. Climbing the stairs seemed more of an effort than usual. The temptation to eavesdrop at the kitchen door was overpowered by the call of her warm bed. On reaching her room she removed the remains of her dress and, repulsed, threw it into a corner. She examined her reflection in the long mirror that hung on the inside of the wardrobe door. In the struggle one of her bra straps had been broken. She stood at the washstand and scrubbed at her skin with a flannel and soap to remove all evidence of Dan's touch, but no matter how hard she tried, she still felt soiled by him. She slipped on a nightdress and crawled under the covers and lay there for a few moments wondering whether Dan would appear to her in her dreams, joining the rest of her demons. His menacing face stirred familiar thoughts until sleep overcame her. All she remembered the following morning was that she had fallen asleep before Betty had come up, and that she had dreamt or imagined that Lenny had come into the bedroom during the night to check on her.

When Annie awoke the following morning and rolled onto her side, she realised the bruises inflicted by Dan hurt much more than the night before. She winced with the pain as she tried to make herself comfortable. The pain was affirmation that she was not dreaming: the world around her was real and not just a figment of her troubled mind.

There was no sign of activity in the house or the yard apart from the sound of a cockerel crowing loudly below her window, so she assumed the household was still asleep. The sun peeked through a crack in the blackout curtains, which brutally contrasted against the surrounding floral wallpaper. Annie lay on her back for a few minutes gazing at the fine cracks in the ceiling as she tried to gather her thoughts together.

Although it still took a moment to adjust to her surroundings on waking each morning, it no longer felt alien living in a different era. Nevertheless on this particular day she was scared. In only a few hours time her flying skills would be under scrutiny and she was uncertain as to how much she would remember when tested. One mistake could be her last: she might find herself flying into the side of a hill or ditching in the sea.

Despite such thoughts tripping through her mind, her emotions were nonetheless tinged with a sense of exhilaration: she felt more alive than when she had lived and worked in London. Even if she were to wake up tomorrow back on familiar territory in the twenty-first century, she would know that she had to make radical changes in her life and start living every day to the full. That life seemed dull and uninspiring compared to the one she was living now. For the first time since being dropped unceremoniously into the nineteen-forties, she realised that there must be a reason for her being here. Whatever that reason was, she still had to find out, but for now, no matter what lay ahead, she wanted to let it run its course.

She stretched and winced again as the pain of her bruises took her back to the previous evening. The thought of Dan tearing at her clothes like a wild animal nauseated her and despite trying to shut him out, the image of his cold calculating eyes kept popping into her head. She made a concerted effort to concentrate instead on the memory of her rescuer Lenny, effortlessly lifting Dan off of his feet. She wished Lenny would use that energy on her instead, and carry her lovingly back to his warm bed. The unlikelihood of that fantasy becoming reality and happening cut deep. The fact that Lenny did not see her in that way had begun to torment her.

Carefully sliding her legs over the side of the bed she tentatively put her feet on the floor, half-expecting more aches and pains to trouble her; but they didn't. Her head no longer throbbed, but as she brushed her hair the area that had made contact with the church door hurt every time she ran the bristles across it. She longed for a shower so that she could allow warm water to wash all evidence of Dan away. The comforts of a modern home were one thing she still struggled to manage without. She poured cold water from a large jug into a porcelain bowl and managed the best she could, dabbing at her face and neck with a rough flannel. She was thankful as she pulled on clean underwear and a fresh starched blue shirt that her face was unmarked.

She opened the curtains to allow the sunshine into the room. The sun was still low in the sky and although early, there was now plenty of activity outside: animals being fed and horses groomed. Chickens scuttled freely around the cobbled yard pecking at corn and seed being scattered by one of the land girls. Several farm-workers were chatting and smoking while they rolled cigarettes and went through the repetitive ritual of lighting pipes. Daphne seemed to be the centre of their attention. She lounged provocatively against a farm gate, dressed in a pastel shirt over which her dungarees had been belted tightly to emphasise her curves. Her hair had been bundled up with finesse in her usual turban, a few wisps having escaped, softening her heart-shaped face and helping her retain an air of femininity amongst the other workers.

Annie studied the scene. It gave nothing away that might suggest it was anything another than a peaceful day in the English countryside. The only thing placing the scene in the past was Daphne and the workers' clothes. The men were dressed in well-worn cast-offs: baggy serge trousers, collarless shirts rolled up to the elbow and scruffy tweed jackets. All were smoking. It seemed a national pastime, with no restrictions on where or when.

Daphne suddenly looked up, sensing Annie looking down at her. Annie stepped back, too late to avoid Daphne's glare. She broke off her conversation with the farm-workers and continued to glare upwards, taking slow thoughtful drags on her cigarette. Annie turned away from the window and took a deep breath. Daphne was intimidating at the best of times. There was no point in trying to befriend her: she was intent on getting Lenny, and Annie was in her way. The chance of her and Daphne ever becoming friends was diminishing day by day. Girls in the office were just the same: it was astounding how jealousy could change a person. Annie didn't think that Lenny had a clue about her growing affection for him, but women possessed sixth sense and Daphne had picked up on Annie's body language. The previous night would have added to Daphne's hatred, Lenny's show of concern for Annie most likely still consuming her.

Annie backed away from the window, hoping that Daphne had not realised she was being scrutinised. She took her uniform from the back of the door and slipped it on and gathered her essentials together, packing them in her overnight bag in case the weather closed in and she had to stay away again. Taking one last look at herself in the wardrobe mirror, satisfied that there was no visible evidence to suggest she had been through a struggle, she went downstairs for breakfast.

Nina was already waiting in the kitchen chatting to Lillian.

'Well today's the day,' said Nina, smiling. 'Are you all set?'

'Yes I think so. A bit nervous, but I'm sure it'll all come back to me,' she lied.

'There's no need to worry. You'll do an assessment before you go off to pick anything up. It'll be a piece of cake!'

Annie thoughtfully munched on a piece of toast while Nina and Lillian resumed their conversation. Although Annie wanted to see Lenny, a small part of her was glad he was not there. It worried her that he might discover she was a fraud. The chance of being thrown off the airfield was uppermost in her mind. She could also end up homeless if Lillian took offence at her having arrived under false pretences.

Several slices of toast and cups of tea later, Nina and Annie said their goodbyes to Lillian and left for the airfield. Bertha having a day off meant that Annie could sit in the front, which was far more conducive to making conversation than shouting from her normal seat in the back. Nina seemed oblivious to the fact that Annie's apprehension was gathering in intensity and made light conversation, discussing the pick ups they might have to do that day. Annie listened intently, gleaning as much information as possible to add to what little knowledge she possessed about the ferry pool. She asked questions that she thought would be appropriate for a new ferry pilot to ask. Nina did not seem suspicious as to why Annie had such a long list, and she filled in all the grey areas as well as offering a little more of her own background into the conversation.

'I feel quite privileged really. My family are well-to-do like yours.'

'My family are all dead,' said Annie, immediately hoping that she had not given Nina more cause to dig too deeply into her background. She tried to remember whether she had told everyone else the same story.

'Oh I'm sorry. How thoughtless of me. Have you lost them all in the war?'

'Yes,' lied Annie, changing the tack of the conversation. 'But I've been lucky. My grandfather formed his own air taxi company after serving in the last war.' Annie was surprised at her own mental agility, having been forced to concoct a convincing story so quickly.

'So he taught you to fly?'

'Unofficially. My parents were furious when they found out.'

'Why were they so angry?'

Annie tried to add minimal distortion to the truth of the matter.

'He transported rich clients all over the country. I went along for the ride whenever it was allowed. Once we'd dropped them off I got free flying lessons on the way home.'

'Gosh! That's quite a story. Luckily my parents indulged me. It was in my blood from an early age. Father funded my training. I did a little ferrying for rich clients too, before I joined the ATA.'

'Regardless of how well you think I'll cope, I hope I don't have anything too challenging to fly today. I'm a bundle of nerves.'

'It's different in the ATA from other civilian flying. There's so many women joined up and we all stick together. You'll get lots of support, with the exception of Glenda and Joyce! Best steer clear of them.'

'I'll definitely take your advice about them.'

'We still get flak from men claiming we should be at home doing women's work.'

'Yes, I remember a bit of that yesterday in the Midlands. It'll be years before women are treated equally to men,' added Annie, bravely dipping into the future. 'Where I come from, there's still discrimination.'

Nina took Annie's comment as a reference to the present and the different mentality of city-dwellers.

'I hope you're right and that one day we'll be deemed equal. Anyway, let's not think about that now. We're nearly there.'

Annie tried to compose herself.

'It's now or never.'

Nina laughed.

'If you're really lucky you might get a chance to co-pilot today. Once they're happy with you you'll be on your own.'

'It all sounds a bit hit and miss. There must be a structure to the training.'

'In an ideal world there would be. Some of the ferry pools are stricter than others. We've had to cut corners however as there is such a backlog of planes to get down south and a shortage of pilots. You won't have time to worry.'

Annie took all this in, realising that Nina was there to back her up and encourage her should she have problems. Nevertheless, the chance to progress slowly through the different categories of aircraft seemed to be evaporating very quickly. She thought back to Nina flying the Lancaster, relieved in the knowledge that only a handful of women were qualified to fly the big bombers.

'I'll try and swing it so you go up with someone that will reassure you.'

Annie didn't have time to think about her nerves anymore as they had arrived at the airfield. The place was as usual buzzing with activity. Margaret had been called away. Nina left Annie outside her office while she went to find out who was doing the flying assessment. Annie stood considering whether she needed to pay a visit to the ladies' room: her stomach starting to churn. Only minutes later Nina appeared with a reassuring smile on her face.

'Well, I have good news. You're going up straight away.'

'That's good news?' questioned Annie, following Nina back out to the truck.

'Why of course. The sooner it's out of the way, then the sooner you can tell me all about it!'

They made their way to a subsidiary runway where the new pilots were briefed and tested. Nina talked non-stop in an effort to distract Annie, the truck bumping up and down across the uneven grass. They pulled up next to a Tiger Moth and Nina jumped out and spoke to a man who was checking it over.

'Hello Donald, I'm glad it's you that's taking Annie up. She's a bit jittery – not flown for a couple of years.'

Donald beamed, a cheeky smile causing his face to crease up from ear to ear.

'I'll see she's alright.'

Annie tentatively approached him.

He wiped his hand on a rag and shook her hand.

'Annie is it? I'm Donald. So you're a bit nervous are you?' he said, winking.

'A bit.'

'I'd much rather fly with you ladies than some of the fellows around here.'

'Why?'

'They think they know it all. I've been flying for thirty years and I can spot an amateur with my eyes closed.'

'You might want to keep your eyes open if you're taking me up.'

Donald burst out laughing. Annie noticed that he looked as though he had been a heavy drinker at some time in his life. His nose was typically puffy and red. Despite this, and a ruddy complexion, his eyes were bright and alert.

'Well at least you have a sense of humour. Let's get started shall we?'

Nina went back to the car and sat watching the proceedings, smoking and relaxing in the sunshine.

'You'll still need your parachute, even though we'll just do a couple of circuits. As long as you can get her off the ground, keep her stable and land without hitting the trees at the end of the runway, I'll give you a glowing report.'

Annie glanced across at the wide gap that had been carved through the trees, not sure whether Donald's confidence in her ability, helped or hindered. He didn't mention whether anyone had landed in the trees before today, and helped her on with her parachute pack and climbed into the rear seat of the Tiger Moth.

'Wear trousers next time, most of the girls do.'

Cursing herself for not changing into her trousers, Annie struggled with her skirt as she squeezed into the confined space and fastened her harness. A young man came running out from the hangar to help and stood by the propeller.

Donald shouted to Annie.

'I've made it a bit easier for you. There's a list of flight checks taped to the left of you if you need any help.'

Annie briefly scanned through the checklist.

'I don't think I can do this,' she shouted back.

'Yes you can. Believe in yourself. I won't let anything go wrong.'

Annie took a few deep breaths. Suddenly, she recalled a formula her grandfather had taught her to help easily remember the order of things.

'Okay. I'm ready.'

The young man that had come to assist firmly grabbed the propeller and waited for the call 'contact' from Donald. He swung the propeller and the engine spluttered into life. Memories of Annie's flying time with her grandfather instantly flashed clearly before her eyes; whether it was the smell and vibration from the engine or blind panic, the procedures drummed into her a few years ago all came back in a rush.

'Chocks away,' she called, raising one hand in the air. Increasing the throttle and pointing the nose of the fabric covered biplane down the grass strip towards the runway; her last flight in a Tiger Moth seeming like only yesterday, although this experience still felt surreal. Looking down at her own hands she felt as though she was looking at someone else holding the controls. Her hands and feet seemed to be operating independently, but she was still aware of the messages from her brain telling her what to do.

Despite this strange revelation as the Tiger Moth gathered speed, Annie's heart was in her mouth. Her restricted forward vision made it hard for her to see the trees ahead but she recalled that it was a short runway and that she had little room for error. Her grandfather's dogged instructions resounded in her ears in a regimental order as he had repeated on so many occasions. The wheels bumped and creaked across the grass. It seemed like it was taking too long to clear the ground. She instinctively gently pulled the stick back remembering how quickly her grandfather's plane responded, and almost instantly the bumping of the wheels stopped and the plane lifted off the ground. She knew she had cleared the wide gap in the trees as she glanced over the side and saw them rush away beneath her fifty feet below. Allowing herself to breathe properly for the first time since strapping herself in, she corrected the plane, which was dipping first one wing then the other as it gained height.

'Not bad,' shouted Donald. 'Try and keep her level and straight ahead until I tell you otherwise. Look at your altimeter, we're a bit low. Take her up another two hundred feet.'

She had forgotten how much there was to remember even in a simple plane like the Tiger Moth.

'You'll see a church spire to your left when we reach the river. I want you to bank round it keeping it in sight but don't lose height.'

Annie's sense of familiarity with the Tiger Moth increased like a fast flowing river washing through her thought processes, as she studied the very basic gauges and controls. Keeping the nose on the horizon she continued the turn until Donald shouted to her to level out.

He kept it simple for her, but she found that faced with no choice, her survival instincts were kicking in. They banked and climbed and Donald pointed out a few obvious landmarks, some of which she recognised from her flight in the Anson: such as the railway, river and ruined abbey. Donald confirmed that they were strategically important landmarks she should be able to spot even in poor conditions. She began to relax and enjoy his comments and instruction. It was a beautiful day and the green and gold patchwork of the English countryside was as rich as ever.

Just as she was beginning to feel more confident and familiar with the controls, Donald shouted again.

'Let's see how good you are at spin recovery.' He didn't give her an opportunity to protest and took control of the plane. He banked hard right and started a spin. 'You have control.'

'I'm not sure I can do this,' screamed Annie.

'You have control,' he repeated.

'Tell me what to do - please Donald. Can you hear me Donald?'

Silence from the rear cockpit.

She started to panic again but knew this was a test and that she had to get a grip of her emotions. The plane began to gather momentum and time was limited if she was to recover the situation. The ground was coming towards them much too fast.

'Try and remember,' thought Annie. 'Shut everything else out. Think with your hands and feet.'

Instinct kicked in yet again. She applied opposite rudder and forward stick, instantly stopping the spin. After levelling out she called out.

'You have control.'

'I give the commands in this plane. Let's try a landing. You have control.'

As she approached the airfield the wings were dipping again as they had on take off and the engine revs were much too high. She realised how rusty some of her flying skills were and how she needed to be a lot more gentle with the controls.

'Too fast, sort it out!'

At the last minute her panic made her forget the correct procedures and she pulled the nose up and headed off for another circuit, looking carefully for other planes landing or taking off. Thankfully apart from a few very distant dots there was nothing in sight.

'Well recovered. Now try again.'

Still banking around to the left she could pick out the airfield to the left of the nose. The engine revs seemed about right, the horizon was level and straight ahead and she had finally mastered keeping the wings level. It was now or never. She gently pushed the stick forward.

This time she realised what she had done wrong on her last approach so she settled the plane into a slower descent. There was still a mile to go before the Tiger Moth would clear the gap in the trees at the end of the runway. Two planes were landing ahead of her so she tried to keep in line a few hundred feet above them. The first landed and taxied off towards the large hangars at the far end of the airfield. The second aircraft landed heavily, sending up clouds of dust before slowing to a taxiing speed. She could not believe her bad luck on her first solo attempt at landing. Maybe she should not have been expected to fly solo so soon without more instruction.

The airfield was now less than a mile away and she was flying at about two hundred feet above the ground, barely high enough to negotiate the clearing through the trees. The airfield was still immediately ahead but not visible now she was flying so much nearer to the ground. She needed to cross the trees before she would see the runway again at which point she would only have a few hundred yards in which to line up for a final landing. The gap in the trees passed beneath, much closer than when she had taken off. The ground seemed to be coming up too fast but just as she was considering lifting the nose again, the right wheel touched down first followed almost immediately by the left and the plane shuddered as she attempted to keep it straight. With a huge sigh of relief she began to breathe normally again as she slowed, regaining some composure. She taxied back towards Nina. Her head and heart were full of opposing emotions. Tears welled up in her eyes, which she wiped quickly so no one would see her distress. Relief, exhilaration and wonderment at her moderate recall of her flying skills filled her head. She cut the engine, undid her harness and began to climb out of the plane, her legs feeling like they had turned to jelly.

'I'm so sorry it took two attempts to get her down.'

'I've seen worse,' said Donald, unstrapping himself and leaping lithely out of his seat like a sixteen year old. 'And I'm sorry I put you on the spot – it was the only way to get you over your fear.'

He dropped to the ground lightly, holding out a hand to help her off the wing.

'I thought I was dreadful.'

'Not at all. I knew from the moment you got us in the air you were a natural. You just didn't believe it yourself! A little drama was all it needed to make you remember.'

'Well I don't believe it. I could have had us both...' The words trailed away as the realisation hit her. 'My God...I got us back all in one piece.'

'That you did. A few words of advice though,' mentored Donald. 'Always fly below cloud level. Your job is to deliver the planes safely, not be a maverick. Leave that to the RAF boys.'

If she had been back in the twenty-first century, a prank like the one that Donald had just pulled would have made her livid. She would have caused a major scene and never spoken to the perpetrator again. Nevertheless she couldn't stop smiling as Donald and his engineer pushed the plane back into the hangar.

'You've done that before, haven't you?' she said, as she walked over to say goodbye to him.

'Yes I have. But the outcome was different!' He pointed at another Tiger Moth in the corner with one wheel missing.

Nina drove an elated Annie back to the officers' mess where they celebrated her initiation as an ATA girl.

Chapter 31

Although not out of bounds, the mess was not generally the place where ferry pilots met up to relax. Unchallenged, Nina and Annie wove their way through the men settled on chairs or lounging on the grass: the continuous drone of planes taking off and landing the only reminder that this was an active airfield. As the waiting pilots smoked and chatted in the sunshine, their body language offered nothing to suggest that fierce combat had taken place only hours before in the sky immediately above.

Annie's hands were still trembling. The sensation of gripping the Tiger Moth's control stick in her hand had not yet disappeared. She flexed her fingers in an effort to release the tension.

'Do you want some tea?' asked Nina. 'You deserve one after that fantastic effort.'

'I could do with something stronger, but I'll settle for tea.'

'Find yourself a chair and I'll bring you one out.'

Nina disappeared inside the mess building, leaving Annie by herself. She scanned the crowd to see if she could see any familiar faces. To her dismay, sitting nearby were Glenda and Joyce surrounded by RAF pilots. Both women, as ever, were immaculately groomed and oblivious to Annie's presence, too wrapped up with all the attention being showered upon them. Annie found a chair and looked on, quietly curious.

Glenda resembled a film star. She pouted as she put a silver cigarette holder to her lips: the considered delivery of her practised movements adding a sense of contrived glamour to the act. Her provocative pose suggested that she was inviting her male admirers to conjure up a camera from thin air and take photographs of her. Joyce reclined, eyes closed and head tilted upwards so she could feel the heat of the sun on her face. Four pilots jostled for space on seats next to them.

'Like bees round a honey pot,' said Nina, appearing from the mess hut with two mugs of tea. 'Look at them. Tailor-made uniforms and not a single hair out of place!'

'They look fit for the cover of a magazine.'

'They must carry everything but the kitchen sink in their overnight bag to do that every day.'

'I don't know how they find the time,' said Annie, remembering the ritual of preparing herself for work at Carlotti's early each morning. 'I bet they don't see the light of day without make-up.'

Nina tutted and changed the subject, turning her chair so that Glenda and Joyce were no longer in her eyeline.

'How are you feeling now?'

'A lot better thanks.'

'I doubt you'll have to fly anything other than a Tiger Moth for a while. That's normal procedure.'

'What about the backlog of planes?'

'I'm not going to lie, though you mustn't worry. Things don't always go by the book. Occasionally we're expected to fly something unfamiliar.'

'What went wrong with that other Tiger Moth?'

'That happened quite recently. My fault I'm afraid.'

'Really? Was Donald instructing you?'

'Gosh no! He took it up so for a test flight after routine maintenance and I went along for the ride. I wasn't paying attention when he told me to take over. Got in a bit of bother over that.'

'That must have been frightening.'

'I'd be fibbing if I told you I never got frightened. The first time I flew a Spit I was scared stiff.'

'I'll look forward to it then,' said Annie sarcastically.

'Don't forget you'll have your pilot's notes to help you. Good bedtime reading material!'

Annie didn't want to think too hard and long about flying a Spitfire. Flying a Tiger Moth had been one thing, but if her grandfather had been able to see her an hour ago he'd have been pretty angry that she'd let her nerves get the better of her.

Yet again Nina seemed to second-guess what Annie was thinking.

'Just take it one day at a time. No one expects you to find it easy. There's a good number of less experienced pilots than you in the ferry pool. Imagine how they feel!'

It didn't matter to Annie how the less experienced pilots might feel. All she could think of was how she might make a big mess of things. The image of a Spitfire with its nose buried in the mud flashed across her mind. An eruption of laughter from Glenda's table broke her train of thought and she turned to see what was causing the commotion.

Glenda had changed her position and was surrounded by even more airmen. Her peroxide blonde hair glinted in the sunlight. Whatever Glenda might lack in beauty, she more than compensated for with sex appeal. She knew how to make the most of her figure. She posed seductively in the champagne light of the day, a generous pout on her full scarlet lips. Joyce watched from the sidelines, smiling at Glenda's antics as the airmen continued to enjoy her performance, nudging each other and wolf-whistling. Annie thought about her own formerly inflated ego and flirtatious behaviour, realising that Glenda was not that dissimilar. Glenda remained in her pose a little longer as if to validate to herself how desirable she was. The pilots puffed out their adorned chests like a muster of proud peacocks, unused to such displays outside of their late night trips to the capital.

'This is simply unacceptable,' said Nina. 'They're puppets in her hands.'

'It's sickening. Men are so easily manipulated.'

Annie turned her attention away from the pilots shouting innuendos, to others sitting further away engrossed in conversation. Her heart jumped as she unexpectedly spotted Lenny sitting at the edge of a large group, looking down at an open book. At first glance it seemed like he was reading, but then she realised he was writing in his dog-eared sketchbook. He looked up but strangely didn't seem to notice her, instead studying Glenda's erotic pose as he drew sweeping lines across a page with his pencil. Annie wanted to leap up from her chair, push Glenda off her perch, and rip the pages from Lenny's book. There was no doubt about it: Glenda was posing for Lenny, arching her back like a cat basking in the sunshine. She was as bad as Daphne. They all wanted Lenny.

Annie's heart continued to beat hard against the wall of her chest. She imagined that her heart was visible on the outside of her body, like a pulsating entity that had attached itself to her breast. She realised she had said nothing of consequence since the conversation about Spitfires, Glenda's exhibition having distracted her.

Nina was still irritated by the American woman.

'They're practically falling over each other to get to her. I don't think I can stand any more. Shall we go?'

Annie wanted to stall for time so that she could see Lenny for a bit longer, despite being apparently invisible to him.

'Tell you what,' said Nina, not waiting for a response. 'You wait here while I check the itinerary hasn't changed.'

She left the table, making small talk with pilots and friends as she passed them, giving Glenda's table a wide berth. Annie sipped her now tepid tea. She wished that she had brought some of her ego and confidence with her from the twenty-first century, packed into a little bag so that she could get it out when she needed it. Nevertheless, she was becoming adept at creating an illusion of confidence. She shuddered, remembering Dan, and immediately tried to put him to the back of her mind.

Now that Nina was gone and there was no one she could make easy conversation with, Annie resumed her observation of Glenda's party, as she stood in the middle of the men: a fresh cigarette in the silver holder. Annie glanced across at Lenny again expecting to see him sketching still, but instead he returned her gaze.

Glenda broke ranks with the crowd surrounding her and snaked her way between the tables. Annie watched her progress and the reaction she had on all that she passed, lustful eyes following her every move. She reached Lenny's table. He looked up, closed his book and placed it on the table in front of him. She reached for the book, but Lenny firmly placed his hand on top of it. Unperturbed, Glenda attempted to work her magic on him, pouting like a small child that wants something it can't have. Still Lenny kept his hand on the closed book. She circled him several times, making her way around behind him. She put her arms around his shoulders, and whispered in his ear.

Annie could take no more. She stood up so quickly that her chair toppled backwards, the heat rising in her face, turning it beetroot red. Having spotted Annie out of the corner of her eye, Glenda smirked, her arms still around Lenny. Annie wished she could get Daphne and Glenda together, throw them into a boxing ring and let them fight to the death over him.

Leaving the bewildered onlookers, Annie walked briskly off, wanting to get as far away as possible from Lenny who was obviously enjoying Glenda's advances. Faint stirring memories of storming off at the air show after having argued with Tom shuffled through her mind. Having forgotten that Nina would be coming back with an update on the day's itinerary, she left the path to find somewhere quiet to vent her rage. Here the grass was unmanaged, still damp from morning dew. Small shrubs had been left to grow untended. Apart from birds flitting between the bushes and the drone from aircraft above, there were no other sounds.

Rounding a corner, Annie stopped. She knew instantly that she had been to this place before. Large gates and a fenced enclosure towered in front of her. Approaching the gates with reticence, she was not certain if she wanted to see what was on the other side. She paused to gather her thoughts together. A shiny new padlock hung open on a hasp. She had found the scrap yard that she had stumbled across that eventful day at the air show. It seemed so long ago. Had this been a week ago, she knew that she would most likely have entered and tried to find her way back somehow to the life she knew. Now she stood temporarily paralysed to the spot, less than a few feet away from the gates.

Finally, after what felt like an eternity, she felt able to move again and reached to push the gates open. As her hands made contact with the gates, her arms suddenly felt heavy as though they had lead weights attached. Her fingers began to tingle. Suddenly gripped by the thought that if any part of her made contact with the strange world beyond the gates, and she might be sucked back into the twenty-first century, she let her arms fall limply to her sides, and battled inwardly with her dilemma. The fear of the idea was enough to jolt her into taking evasive action. Who did she want: Tom, who was safe and reliable, or Lenny who seemed to be immune to her, but whom she had clearly fallen for?

Chapter 32

Backing away from the scrap yard, she turned and ran as fast as the uneven ground would allow, putting distance between herself and the portal. As she continued to run, elements of her childhood nightmares surfaced yet again: the sense of someone chasing her uppermost in her mind spurring her onwards to safety. Annie, unsure of what to do next, half-hoped that Lenny would have chosen to follow her, just so he could tell her that he didn't want Glenda, Daphne or any other woman apart from her, but he didn't appear.

At last, when she had almost given up hope of finding her way back to the officers' mess, the distant sound of voices and laughter reassured her that she had quite by accident found her way completely unscathed and still alone. She stopped short of the building to get her breath back, fully expecting all eyes to fix upon her as she made her appearance.

'There you are!' said Nina, weighed down with two parachute packs, Annie almost colliding with her as she turned the corner of the mess. 'Lenny said he saw you go off in a hurry!'

'Couldn't get away fast enough,' Annie laughed, hoping Nina wouldn't notice her breathlessness or gradually subsiding distress whilst relieving her of one of the parachutes. 'I had to get away. Glenda had her hands all over him, I didn't know where to look!'

'Nothing surprises me as far as that woman is concerned. I doubt he has any interest in her though. Flying's all he seems to care about!'

'He didn't put up any resistance. In fact he seemed to be enjoying it.'

'I doubt that very much. That's just Lenny being polite.'

'Not that I'm bothered who he fancies,' added Annie. 'It was just a bit embarrassing.'

'Oh well – never mind. We've more important things to think about than those irritating Americans flirting with our boys!'

'Where are we going now?'

'We're taking a Tiger Moth to Tangmere. I have to pick up a Hurricane from there. It'll give you another opportunity to get a bit more confident.'

They headed off towards the hangars again, saving Annie the ordeal of facing the bemused pilots who had witnessed her storming off for no apparent reason.

'How will I get back?'

'Most of the pick ups are already taken care of, so you're to follow me back in the Moth on your own, unless someone needs a lift. Then we'll see if there is any outstanding ferrying to do.'

'Do you think I'm up to it? It was different when I had Donald with me.'

'You'll be splendid I'm sure. Just your navigation to brush up on.'

'That'll take forever. There's so much to remember.'

'You'll soon familiarise yourself. Before you know it, you'll be flying on instinct alone. The weather's gorgeous, that should help.'

Annie looked up at the sky, both women agreeing that there seemed no indication of anything other than more glorious days to come. The occasional clouds floating high in the canopy were small, white and fluffy. The day was comfortably warm.

'My only concern is if we get stranded again,' stressed Nina. 'We've got Betty's wedding to consider.'

'Things happen so quickly around here. I'd forgotten they were getting married so soon.'

'That's war for you. No point in missing an opportunity.'

'But weddings take months to organise, and cost thousands of pounds. Where will Betty get that sort of money?'

'Thousands of pounds? Whose wedding have you been to costing that sort of money, royalty?'

'I had a very wealthy cousin,' lied Annie.

'Lillian will have everything under control. She's probably made all the dresses by now,' laughed Nina. 'I doubt the whole affair will cost more than a few guineas.'

As they took off in the Tiger Moth, Annie was taken aback at how little East Sussex's landscape had changed, the only obvious difference that the major roads between coastal towns would not be built for many years. The South Downs stretched away to the horizon like a billowing green ribbon.

The afternoon passed uneventfully, Annie confronting most of the difficulties caused by her earlier loss of confidence and lack of recent flying. Attempting to come to grips with its little foibles, she flew the Tiger Moth that she had taken up for her appraisal, remembering how her grandfather had drummed home the fact that each plane had its own peculiarities. 'Flying's like falling off a log,' he used to say, and that all her knowledge would come back to her whenever she got back in a cockpit. To her surprise, he was right and she was beginning to relax and enjoy the experience. After a long delay at Tangmere due to an earlier incident that had caused a backlog, Annie flew the Moth solo back to base, closely following Nina in the Hurricane.

The sun was low in the sky as they approached the airfield. Long shadows from the buildings stretched across the grass like long black fingers, lengthening by the second as the sun sank lower. Annie was tired but aware of a feeling of elation and an overwhelming sense of achievement. She had not realised her premonition of nose-diving into a hill. She landed the Moth so lightly that it seemed to her as though she were still flying just inches above the grass.

Once back in its hangar for the night she left the Tiger Moth to be checked over for the following day.

'Well, how was it?' asked Nina.

'I can't believe I managed it, to be honest!'

'Well normally you would have received your wings first, but like I said earlier, nothing goes by the book while we're stretched for pilots.'

Adrenalin and fatigue fought as Annie strolled back to headquarters with Nina. It seemed implausible that only a few weeks previously, at this time of day, she would normally have either been nestled on her leather settee in front of her flat screen television or in the city on a night out. Thoughts of Tom and her everyday existence in London seemed like fading snapshots of someone else's life.

'A penny for your thoughts,' said Nina.

'Honestly?' Annie paused, sighing deeply. 'I'm just relieved today is over.'

'You really surprise me Annie, you're just as good as most of the other new pilots. You just need to get in as much flying time as you can.'

As they changed out of their flying kit and packed it all away, Annie began to consider her praise. Nina was right: she was a good pilot. The anxiety she had experienced over the last few days was already beginning to evaporate. She was now officially part of the war effort. She laughed.

'What's so funny?' asked Nina.

'Oh nothing really, it's just I was thinking how radically my life has changed in the last few weeks.'

'I'm sure it can't have changed that much. We're all in the same boat.'

'Believe me – it has!'

'You'll have to tell me more about it.'

'I'm not saying it was exciting,' said Annie, trying to disengage Nina before she asked too many probing questions. 'In fact, my life was mundane compared to this.'

She smiled inwardly, with the knowledge that Nina was completely unaware of the bizarre truth behind her statement.

Chapter 33

Driving back to the farmhouse was a calming experience. Annie reached out of the open window, allowing her fingers to caress the long grass on the verge flanking the country lane. Dusk had already descended upon the patchwork of fields but the heady fragrance from wild flowers still lingered. The white cottontails of droves of rabbits bobbed through the verges in the gathering darkness.

'We'll only just make it before dark,' commented Nina, squinting into the distance.

'Don't your headlights work properly? They're very dim.'

'Have you forgotten there's a war on?' exclaimed Nina incredulously. 'We'll be for the high jump if I take the covers off!'

'Blame it on a long day. I'm not thinking properly,' Annie excused herself. She scanned the fields over the low hedgerows: her error punctuated by the lack of visible lights from cottages and isolated farms. Their journey along winding country lanes was precarious to say the least, the way lit only by a full moon. It explained to Annie why Nina's face was almost touching the pockmarked windscreen in her effort to see ahead.

'Tell me if you spot anything coming the other way or an animal crossing the road. I'd never forgive myself if I hit anything!'

'I'm as blind as you.'

'Two pairs of eyes are better than one.'

Annie cupped her hands around her eyes to block out the light from the moon, making it marginally easier to see a short way ahead. As they approached tight bends in the lane, Nina slowed to a crawling pace knowing full well that she would have little warning with only blinkered headlights to guide her. The truck bumped along on the uneven road surface drowning out all sound apart from the loose stones bouncing up and making a loud clattering against the chassis of the truck.

They had just rounded a particularly tight bend when Annie screamed out.

'Nina! Look out! What's that?'

Nina peered at the road ahead.

'I don't know. It's much too big for a badger!'

A large dark shape had emerged from a gate at the side of the lane less than a hundred yards ahead. It moved slowly towards them, hugging the hedgerows.

'It could be a loose sheep,' added Annie. 'It looks big enough.'

Nina slowed to a stop.

'Maybe. We'll wait here until it finds another gap in the hedge.'

Darkness had now enveloped everything it touched. Nina sounded the horn expecting the animal to react and turn back, but it stopped where it was.

'Do you want me to get out and shoo it off?' asked Annie, hoping that the answer would be no.

'That's probably not such a good idea. It may be a bull.'

Annie didn't know why she should be frightened of a farm animal, but she was uncomfortable being stationery in a beaten-up truck in the darkness. She instinctively reached down to find a non-existent central-locking button to secure the doors. Looking ahead again, she noticed that the creature was on the move again. Halving the distance between itself and the car, it was now only fifty yards away.

'I don't know why, but I've got a really bad feeling,' whispered Annie, grabbing Nina's arm for some sort of comfort.

'Me too. Hang on!'

Nina roughly manhandled the gear stick, the gearbox wailing and clunking its objections before engaging. Looking over her shoulder, she reversed as quickly as she could with nothing but the moonlight to guide her. Annie gripped her seat tightly as Nina attempted to negotiate the first tight bend in the lane.

The noise of the truck on gravel did nothing to scare the creature away. Instead it suddenly reared up to full height, doubling in size, and began to run towards them.

'Bloody hell, it's a man!' screamed Annie as the sprinting figure was finally caught in the camouflaged headlights. 'Go faster, he's catching up!' She sensed that this was not a farmer or local wanting to hitch a lift in the dark.

Nina was still looking over her shoulder to see where she was going: the rear lights of the truck pathetically inadequate.

'Damn! I can't see a bloody thing.'

Snaking down the lane, catching small branches as she reversed, Nina continued cursing.

As the gap between the man and the truck closed to only a few yards, Annie pressed her body back into her seat as if to get as far away from him as possible. His face was now just visible: a gritted determination in his expression. Just as it seemed their predicament was dire, Nina violently swerved the truck through a ninety-degree angle up a dirt track, slammed the gear stick into first and raced off in the opposite direction.

'That was close,' said Annie, turning in her seat to see if the man was following. Much to her relief, he had abandoned his pursuit and had melted away into the darkness.

Nina wiped the perspiration from her forehead, releasing her tight grip on the steering wheel.

'Good job I know this route so well,' she said, slowing to a respectable speed. 'And it's a damn good job you spotted him when you did.'

'But who was he?'

'A German I should think, hiding in the woods. He must have bailed out around here.'

'Does that happen often?'

'Now and again there's the odd one lurking around. More often than not they're captured.'

Nina spoke with little empathy for their plight.

'Don't you think it's quite sad?'

'What do you mean?'

'They must be scared stiff.'

'You have to be a bit more thick-skinned than that Annie. What do you think he'd have done if he'd caught up with us? He might have slit our throats to get the truck.'

'What if he was injured?'

'Do you want me to turn round and go back for him?' said Nina sarcastically.

'No.'

'You have to have your wits about you. Maybe it's a good thing this happened. Once you've got your own transport you might think twice before stopping to offer strangers a lift.'

Annie began to fear for her own safety and vowed not to leave her bedroom window ajar at night. Nevertheless, a sense of sorrow for the German and others like him still clung onto her thoughts. She imagined him alone in the woods night after night, hoping for rescue or the very least some food and water.

Nina took an alternative route home, barely speaking, which Annie put down to the shock of the confrontation rather than irritation at her naivety. She felt much the same as Nina: the peace of what had started as a tranquil drive through lovely English countryside had been abruptly shattered by a desperate young German.

Chapter 34

On arriving back at the farm, Annie's vulnerability resonated within her due to the drama that had just occurred.

Nina backed the truck into the same timber barn that housed Betty's bike at night. She lit a Hurricane lamp, lifted the bonnet of the truck and removed the battery, stashing it under an upturned bucket.

'Why are you doing that?' whispered Annie, still slightly shaken by their experience.

'Out of necessity I'm afraid,' Nina whispered back. 'We always disable the vehicles at night just in case.'

'Just in case of what?'

'Like I said earlier, that young German chap won't be the only one trying to get home. She gestured to a foreboding copse of trees situated the other side of the lane. 'One of them might be watching us right now.'

Annie shuddered as she looked from the copse into the darkest corners of the barn.

'We could be murdered in our sleep then!'

'Oh Annie, don't be so daft! The dogs would raise the roof if there were the slightest sniff of an intruder. Listen – they're all asleep, so there's nothing to worry about,' she reassured Annie.

Annie wasn't so sure.

'What if they offered the dogs some food?'

'Do you really think those starving men would give up what little food they've managed to steal? And anyway, they'd be stupid if they didn't realise there are men on the farm who are a good shot.'

'I hope you're right.'

Whether she was right or wrong, Annie still continued to scan the dark shadows as they made their way across the courtyard to the welcoming farmhouse kitchen.

Despite the blackout curtains hiding all signs of light from within the kitchen, the ageing windows seemed to offer little protection from who might be lurking outside waiting for an opportunity to break in and raid the larder. Nevertheless, once inside with the heavy iron bolts on the kitchen door drawn, Annie felt instantly safer. The kitchen still held the heat of the faithful old stove, but was lit only by a few glowing embers that had dropped into the hearth beneath. Nina lit an oil lamp, flooding the kitchen with a mellow light. She opened the range door and threw on chunks of wood. Within seconds the fire began to burn brightly again, dancing shadows creating patterns on the faded kitchen walls.

Although not that late in the evening, the house was quiet with no sound of movement from the rooms above. Everyone seemed to have retired for the night. The peacefulness struck Annie. She thought back to her London flat, where if she opened her window she could hear the constant drone of cars and the unrelenting tramp of work-bound feet. To a certain extent, she had become immune to that type of background noise.

'Cocoa?' said Nina, tearing Annie away from her other life.

'Yes thank you, that would be nice.'

'A penny for your thoughts.'

'I was just thinking of home.'

'It's difficult at first, but you'll soon get used to it.'

'I'm sure I will, given time.'

A sense of tranquility enveloped her and she allowed it to wash over her as she sank back into the soft cushions of the rocking chair. Closing her eyes, she listened to the gentle hiss of the kettle on the range. Sitting with Nina, it didn't seem necessary to fill the silence with conversation of any sort. The sound of gentle tick-tocking from the grandfather clock in the hall, Nina setting out cups and saucers, and the crackling from the fire were all she needed. She couldn't remember a time when she had savoured such a welcoming environment. Nina was no longer just a transient acquaintance. She was a friend.

Annie suddenly wondered whether time occurred at the same speed in parallel worlds and whether she had been away long enough for anyone but Tom and Sophie to be concerned. Whatever the truth, there were too many unresolved aspects, none of which she could discuss with anyone without being labelled insane. As well as this, there was also no value in fretting. Depending on her outlook, she was either trapped or been given a second chance in an alternative life, bizarre though it might seem to even consider the latter. Disregarding the attack by Dan and the sudden appearance of an unknown man in the lane, the alternative life was looking to be her preference.

Moments spent with Lenny began to flood into her thoughts. Although her initial challenge had been the mastery of unfamiliar planes, she now realised that the hardest thing so far, had been resisting the urge to fall for someone that was not willing or able to reciprocate her feelings. Her invisible wall of defence had been breached before she had a chance to resist. She was frustrated that Lenny had not expressed anything other than gentlemanly concern, the expression within his piercing blue eyes giving nothing away.

Nina took the saucepan of milk from the range and stirred in the cocoa. Annie opened her eyes and looked around the kitchen, absorbing the moment. During the day, she had not paid much attention to specific detail, distracted by the hustle and bustle of daily activity as people came and went. She noticed that the interior was as aged and faded as the outside: its walls reminding her of the sun-bleached buildings that bordered the canals in Venice. Just like the towering facades that bordered the Grand Canal, the sun had kissed the farm buildings: bricks, wood and stone mellowed by hot summers and weather-beaten by winter gales over the course of three hundred years. For years, Annie had plodded on through her monochromatic version of London, the loss of parents and grandparents and the lack of passion that she felt for Tom compounding her lethargy and view of the world. Accumulative forces had finally deadened her senses, making one day seem much like the next. Only now did she realise just how deeply unhappy she had been.

Nina sipped her drink and sat back in her chair. She turned to Annie and asked an inevitable question.

'Tell me about your boyfriend. Have you heard from him since you arrived?'

Vaguely surprised at Nina's directness, Annie chose her words carefully, somehow managing to be just about honest in what she revealed.

'I've not mentioned him much to anyone. I think coming here ended anything between us,' added Annie, realising there was finality in her voice. 'I doubt he has a clue where I am now.'

Nina seemed to understand.

'It's hard to maintain a relationship at a time like this. Do you miss him though?'

'Maybe a little, but I'd been having doubts for a while,' admitted Annie. 'Once I was dropped here out of the blue, it seemed inevitable it was over. My life has transformed so radically.' Inwardly she was enjoying the rhetorical game she was playing with Nina.

'That's sad, but maybe being here and being so busy will help. At least you're not working in a factory like poor Betty. You are very privileged.'

'I couldn't stand it,' agreed Annie, the thought of working in a noisy and dirty environment amongst industrial machinery a million miles away from what she was used to.

'I don't know how she manages to come home every night looking so clean and healthy,' added Nina.

'Maybe it's the ride from the factory on her motorbike that puts the colour back in her cheeks. One thing's for certain, now that Peter's been found alive she's a bundle of joy! It's taken no time at all for her to recover.'

'Thank goodness Peter wasn't badly hurt. I think he was suffering more from exhaustion than anything else.'

Looking around the farmhouse, the gradual transformation it had been undergoing in preparation for the special day was fast becoming apparent. Homemade paper chains had been suspended from lampshades and curtain rails and the black kitchen range had been polished until it gleamed in the light from the oil lamp. The Welsh dresser and over-sized pine kitchen table smelt of beeswax polish, the dresser boasting Lillian's best matching crockery neatly displayed on its shelves.

Although Annie was happy for Betty, she sat wondering whether she would ever marry. Although this was not a new thought, it hadn't mattered quite as much as now, prosperity having masked her unhappiness. Now however, a week of living frugally had stripped all the outer covers away. She wondered whether if she had faced her demons sooner instead of struggling on, her mind would have still played tricks on her, inventing her current existence. She scanned the kitchen again looking for anything to suggest it might not be real.

Despite Annie not asking, Nina began to talk about her family and the few dates she had been on with men from her own village. She made no secret of the fact that she found RAF pilots intimidating and too forward. Annie thought her naivety quaint and outdated. On a more negative note it made her feel a little too experienced and worldly, so she decided that she would not divulge too much about her past success with men. It worried her that Nina might consider her promiscuous having lived such a sheltered life herself. She wondered again whether Lenny had judged her in that way after her willingness to go outside the village hall with Dan. Once Nina had finished describing her innocent relationships, Annie asked her about Lenny, casually dropping him into the conversation in the attempt to sound nonchalant.

'Do you know who puzzles me Nina? I just can't work him out.'

'Who's that then?' Nina stared at Annie excitedly.

'Lenny – he always seems so distant. I know you said his flying was what mattered, but it seems odd that he wasn't interested in Glenda. All the other pilots couldn't take their eyes off of her.'

Nina chuckled.

'Maybe she's just not his type.'

'What is his type, do you think?'

'Beats me. I've never seen him giving any of the girls a second look. Perhaps it's the war. Does strange things to you. It's a bit dangerous falling in love when you know you could be dead tomorrow.'

'I see what you mean.'

She closed her eyes, trying to get a better picture of Lenny in her head. A number of situations flitted about in her mind, real, imagined, tragic and euphoric.

She didn't feel Nina tap her on the arm to wake her, or hear her making up the fire for the night and turn the wick on the oil lamp down so that it barely lit the room. By the time had Nina put a blanket over Annie's legs and slipped out of the room, she was already asleep dreaming of nights locked in Lenny's arms.

When she awoke sometime later, the temperature in the kitchen had dropped a little. She sat for a few more moments listening to the old beams react to the change, creaking and groaning in the same way that they had in Tom's old cottage. The thought of her time with him in Appleby Magna filtered into her thoughts. She wondered if he was worried about her.

Sitting in Lillian's kitchen seemed surreal, especially with the thought of another day's flying being only a few hours away. With a respite from coping with bitchy office staff, there were only Glenda and Daphne to consider. She could handle a little female rivalry if necessary.

Sleep got the better of Annie once more, and she sank deeper and deeper into a world filled with graceful planes soaring through the sky on a summer's day. This time she was not piloting one, instead she lay in a meadow of poppies and long grass looking up at the planes spiralling around each other. There was someone next to her. Her face was hot from the heat of the sun, as real as a summer's day when she was awake. The man stood up, blocking out the sun as he bent over her and swept her up effortlessly into his arms. She rested her head on his familiar chest, listening to his strong heartbeat.

In the morning she woke up and turned over to see the morning sun peeping through a crack in the blackout curtains. She was in her own bed, still clothed and with no memory of how she got there. A smile danced across her lips.

Chapter 35

Annie didn't want to get out of bed the following morning. She had slept well and awoken elated as the result of Lenny having featured in all of her dreams. Fanciful romantic notions of them as a couple: swimming naked in the sea, walking through bluebell woods, and making love in his warm bed still flooding her senses as she tried to focus on the day ahead. She felt like a teenager again. She was in love for the first time.

She dressed reluctantly and went downstairs, still savouring her dreams before they had a chance to evaporate. The kitchen was empty when she arrived, the hissing kettle the only sound to greet her. Breakfast was still laid out for latecomers. The door to the outside had been left wide open. Tess was excitedly attempting to herd the frightened chattering of chickens, whilst Lillian forcefully pushed washing through a mangle in the courtyard. Annie stood momentarily at the kitchen door sipping tea and watching the activity. Puzzled that there were no others waiting for a ride to the airfield, she went outside.

'Hello dear,' Lillian greeted her, smiling broadly. 'Did you sleep well?'

'Yes thank you, I had a very peaceful night,' said Annie, trying not to blush as she recalled her dreams.

'I expect you're wondering where everybody has got to? There was a bit of trouble last night - I'm surprised you didn't hear the kerfuffle. The bombers scared all the animals again.'

'Where is everyone?'

'The boys must still be at the airfield dealing with the chaos, but Nina and Bertha should be down for breakfast soon.'

Annie went back into the kitchen, and nibbled at some bread and butter whilst she waited for Nina and Bertha to appear. Her dreams had already faded to just a few lustful images. She decided it was probably for the best that she dismissed them from her thoughts, as none of it was ever likely to happen. Why be reminded of what would never come to pass?

Bertha arrived first with Nina on her heels.

'Morning. Have you eaten?' Bertha asked Annie.

'I'm not that hungry.'

'You'll regret it later.' Bertha took three fresh rolls from the table and wrapped them in a clean white tea towel. ' No time to stop, we can eat these on the way.'

'We'd better go and see what the damage is,' added Nina.

'Do you know if anyone's hurt?' asked Annie, wanting to mention Lenny's name as she scurried out of the door behind them.

'Apparently it's a bit of a state down there. Some of the planes didn't get off the ground before the Jerries arrived,' replied Nina, not directly answering Annie's question.

Nina was less careful than usual driving the truck as she negotiated the twisty country lanes, making no effort to slow down in anticipation of oncoming cars or farm vehicles. As they approached the airfield, black plumes of smoke were visible, rising up from behind the perimeter trees. There was a flurry of vehicles tearing in and out of the main gates. By the time they had parked up, Annie felt nauseous, as though she had been on a fairground ride. The truck had collected a fair amount of greenery from the hedgerows: twigs and leaves wedged firmly into gaps between the chassis and the wheel arches. The pungent smell of burning rubber and kerosene filled the air. A large group of ferry pilots were gathered outside the ATA headquarters smoking and talking in low voices, signs of concern on their faces.

'Any news?' Nina asked one of the pilots.

'Not as many losses as they feared. We're just waiting for the all clear.'

Annie wondered whether the mention of losses implied aircrew or planes, but she was afraid to know the truth. She followed Nina and Bertha to the front of the crowd where a handwritten sign had been pinned to a notice board.

All ATA pilots wait here for briefing. Thank you.

'Oh well, best do as it says,' said Bertha, lighting a cigarette.

'We'll know soon enough,' added Nina.

Before Annie had a chance to think too much more about what the plumes of smoke represented, the group fell silent as a man came out of the building and addressed them.

'I'm afraid I have some bad news. The RAF lost three pilots on the airfield early this morning.'

A murmur went up from the group.

He continued.

'I can't as yet inform you as to their identities. They were attempting to take off but unfortunately the Jerries got here first.'

His words silenced the group again. Annie's heart began to thump and the sickness she had felt during the journey to the airfield took on another level.

'The runway is still being cleared of debris, then you will be cleared for take off to do your daily pick ups. Please report back here in one hour. Thank you.' He turned abruptly away just as a female pilot approached him to speak and disappeared back into the building.

Nina put her arms around Bertha and Annie pulling them close so that she could speak without being overheard.

'I can't wait around here wondering who the casualties are. Let's go to the mess and see what we can find out.' Unnoticed by the other ferry pilots, Nina beckoned them down the side of the headquarters into a building that Annie had never visited before.

'I know a short cut. Follow me but keep your voices down,' said Nina.

The maze of corridors was so complex that Annie was sure she would never remember the route if she were to use it again. The building seemed almost deserted with only the occasional clattering of typewriters through glass doors punctuating the silence.

'We're really not meant to come through this way,' whispered Nina. 'Just try and look like you know where you're going. Say you're delivering a message if you're challenged.'

They weren't challenged however, and in no time at all they were back out in the open again behind the dispersal huts. A shiver ran down Annie's spine as she spotted the heavy gates that led into the scrap yard. As they rounded the corner of the dispersal hut where Lenny had sat sketching, Annie was shocked by what she saw. There was no laughing or sense of frivolity about the sight that met her eyes.

The men that had been chatting, laughing at each other's jokes and smoking the last time she had seen them, sat silently in their wicker chairs staring across the airfield towards the plumes of smoke that had been visible from the road. Several fire tenders and trucks were parked next to the stricken aircraft: burnt-out skeletons smouldering on the runway. They stood abreast still in the positions they had adopted as they had tried to take off.

Nina approached the pilot nearest to her and gently put her hand on his shoulder. He smiled weakly and tried to gain control of his obvious grief. Bertha approached another pilot who was seated with his head in his hands. This wasn't how Annie remembered pilots in the war films that she had watched with her grandfather. Pilots were valiant heroes and didn't show their emotions so readily. The British stiff upper lip was nowhere in sight amongst the men gathered in front of her. It was almost as though they were staring death in the face for the first time. She felt useless, unable to know what she could say or do. Leaving Nina and Bertha to console the men, she made her way through the group of pilots, not allowing herself to linger on the thought that Lenny might be in one of the charred planes. He did not seem to be amongst the group. She looked out at the plumes of black smoke again. Nina and Bertha sympathetically worked their way through the lines of men, offering words of comfort.

Annie approached Nina.

'Lenny and Peter aren't here,' she whispered, feeling slightly guilty that she hadn't thought about Peter's welfare or the effect on Betty if she had to go through the same grieving process again.

Bertha's expression changed from sorrow to anguish.

'Are you sure? Have you had a really good look?'

'Yes, I've been up and down a few times.'

'Have you been inside as well?' asked Nina.

'No.'

'No one will mind,' suggested Bertha. 'If anyone asks, just say you're worried about your boyfriend.'

Annie felt a rush of pleasure at the suggestion of Lenny being her boyfriend, but anxiety quickly veiled the thought. She walked past the wall of men and dispersal huts and entered the officers' mess. The silence that prevailed outside was replaced with sombre and deep conversation between the assembled men. It was hard to see who was who in such a packed environment.

Suddenly Annie spotted Peter.

'Peter! Thank goodness you are alright,' she said guiltily, remembering her earlier thoughtlessness.

'I must get word to Betty. She'll have heard by now, it'll be all round the factory.' He looked at Annie quizzically, seeing her attention elsewhere as she darted glances around the crowded room. 'I guess you're worried about someone else?'

'Yes I am. I can't find Lenny anywhere. Have you seen him?'

'No. It's been pandemonium. We still don't know...'

Annie didn't give him time to finish as she ran towards the exit, fighting her way through the assembled officers.

'I must find him.'

Peter called after her.

'I'm sure he's fine. He's the best we've...' his words trailed away.

She burst through the double doors. Outside, the fresh air made no difference. Her world was beginning to spin.

'Annie, is there any news?' asked Nina, rushing up to her. 'Did you find them?'

'Peter's in there,' she gasped, gulping for air. 'He's fine.'

Nina took Annie's arm as Bertha disappeared inside the building.

'I think you'd better sit down for a moment. You're frightfully pale.'

'I'm alright.'

'You don't look it. Sit down,' said Nina, leading Annie to a nearby chair.

Annie sat motionless, trying to fight the overwhelming feeling that she would faint at any second. The black smoke was now reduced to a wisp of grey, but the skeletal planes still sat on the runway: a ghastly reminder that three pilots had lost their lives. Annie watched as the recovery vehicles began to remove the wreckage.

'Annie, look. Over there.'

Annie turned to see what had caught Nina's attention, but there was nothing but pilots milling about aimlessly.

'What am I meant to be looking at?'

'Look again,' said Nina.

Annie shielded her face from the sun. Behind the pilots were dispersal huts and rows of chairs, partially filled with others waiting for news.

'You still don't see, do you?'

Nina put her hands each side of Annie's head and gently turned her to face whatever it was that she wanted her to see. Walking towards her was Lenny.

Chapter 36

The tears came immediately as Annie registered the fact that it was really him. Each stride he took towards her seemed to be in slow motion. As he passed through the group of pilots assembled at the far end of the dispersal huts they turned to acknowledge him, patting him on the shoulder and exchanging a few brief words. As he drew closer it seemed to Annie that everyone around him seemed to dissolve away and fade out of sight. His parachute was slung casually over one shoulder and he wore his cap at a jaunty angle as usual. She fumbled in her pocket for a handkerchief to wipe her eyes but Bertha discreetly passed her own which was clean and pressed neatly into a triangular shape. She leant down and quietly spoke to Annie clutching her hand to offer comfort.

'You kept that quiet, didn't you? I had no idea you were smitten!'

'I didn't think I was until...well, maybe not this much.'

As Lenny drew near Nina held out her arms to greet him and hugged him briefly. Bertha followed suit but Annie didn't know how to react; wanting to do the same as them but feeling glued to the chair. She didn't want Lenny to see that she had been crying.

He acknowledged a few more pilots with a wink and a nod before dropping his parachute on the ground and flopping down in a chair opposite Annie. Bertha was the first to speak.

'I'll get you a cup of tea Lenny, you must be exhausted!' She nudged Nina discreetly suggesting that it would take the two of them to carry tea for the four of them. The excuse for yet another cup of tea had served Bertha well in giving Annie the chance to be alone with Lenny.

He took out his pipe and banged it on the table, knocking out the debris into a neat pile. He wiped the burnt tobacco off of the table with his ungloved hand. Annie noticed that his knuckles were sore and had been bleeding. His uniform was not in its usual pristine condition; there were black marks on his jacket chest and sleeves. His face was sweaty and where he had been wearing his flying goggles the impression of them still remained leaving red lines across his cheeks and forehead. She wanted to reach out and hold his hands in hers and kiss away the soreness , but she did not want to look at his face for fear of giving her feelings away. What was the point in telling him anyway how she felt when he had barely noticed her existence?

'Are you alright, Annie? You look like you've been crying,' he said, breaking the silence.

He leant back in his chair, showing off the full extent of the damage to his uniform, his cap low over his eyes, shielding them from the sun.

'Yes, I'm fine,' she answered curtly, struggling for a convincing answer. She was glad that his blue eyes were in part shadow; looking directly into them could be a recipe for disaster.

'Worried about someone?' he pried again, filling his pipe with fresh tobacco as he spoke.

Surely he hadn't guessed.

'Only Peter,' she lied. 'I wouldn't want to break the news to Betty if he had been hurt again.'

He lit his pipe slowly and blew out the match, still looking at her intently from beneath his cap. She felt like a fly caught in a spider's web, wanting to look anywhere but at him.

'Peter's fine,' he said.

'Yes, I've seen him thanks.'

'No one else then?'

'No one else what?'

'You know what I mean. Were you worried about anyone else?'

He took his cap off and tossed it on the table. It brushed against her clenched hands. She cursed herself for feeling this way, but couldn't suppress the electric tingle she felt at the touch of the coarse material.

She looked up at him, slowly and deliberately, his perfect eyes the colour of robins' eggs inviting her in. She crumbled and sobbed, unwanted, unstoppable tears burning on her face. She wiped them away hurriedly, drenching the already wet handkerchief. The sound of talking from the people around her subsided into the distance until it was only him and her left. She felt grateful that her tears made him slightly out of focus; it was easier to look directly at him.

'Well yes of course...' she stumbled on her words.

He sat up and rested his elbows on the table. She automatically leant back to put a little distance between them. She wished she was talking to him on a telephone. His face made it difficult to think straight and speak without sounding unprepared. She had to think carefully before she spoke realising that time was of the essence; Nina and Bertha would be back any minute and the opportunity might be lost forever. He might fly out to France that night and not come back, and he would never know that he was the only man she had truly ever fallen in love with.

She sat up and faced him, her arms resting on the table, their faces no more than a few feet apart. She took in a deep breath as he sat motionless looking directly into her hazel eyes.

And then she told him how she felt as he sat as still as a statue appearing not to breathe, his eyes burning into hers as she said the words.

'I've never felt this way before. I've tried hard not to but...' she garbled clumsily.

'I felt it the first time we met...like it was meant to be...oh, bloody hell. I'm so sorry, Lenny.' She hated the fact her sentences were disjointed and that her face was tearstained.

His injured hands closed around hers and he laughed quietly as he answered her.

'Don't apologise,' he said. 'Would it help if I told you I felt the same way the moment I first set eyes on you?'

She stared at him with wide eyes.

'But we have to keep it under control. Nothing is going to happen between us. How can we let it in this world? I could be gone tomorrow.'

'But I had no idea!' she exclaimed.

'That's because I didn't want you to.'

The stark blueness of his eyes continued to invite her in, but this time she allowed herself be a willing victim. They sat for several minutes in silence just taking in each other's features as he caressed her hands in his. She was hopelessly lost with no hope of recovery; and she knew now that he felt the same.

She thought back to his apparently dismissive behaviour: the time he had chosen to dance with Daphne instead of her and his scolding words when he had rescued her from impending rape by Dan. It had been his way of denying his feelings; it all seemed so obvious and as clear as the light of day.

The contrast between the horror of the smouldering planes in the distance and the intense passion that now burnt freely in her chest struck her to the core. He still sat looking at her a though he was burning with the same desire but was containing the urge to leap across the table and pull her close to him.

'Tea time!' said Nina, approaching behind Lenny and smiling at Annie as she took in the chemistry between them.

Lenny gently squeezed Annie's hands before releasing them, sitting back in his chair again.

'Thanks Nina,' said Lenny. 'I can't think of anything more that I need right now.'

He winked at Annie as he spoke. The intensity of the fire that he felt inside seemed visible on the surface to Annie and she wondered whether he could see the same thing in her. She wanted to be alone with him more than anything else, to finally be able to hold him and learn who he was beneath that veil of calm and distance. Sitting drinking tea in a civilised manner with two friends who were now aware of what was passing between her and Lenny felt awkward and ill-timed.

Nina sat stirring her tea far too many times, looking from one to the other. Bertha attempted to fill the embarrassing void, asking Lenny about the raid on the airfield. Annie felt detached as though she had just woken from a pleasant dream; she sat quietly waiting for the bubble to burst and Lenny to shut her out from his world. He sat conversing politely with Nina and Bertha filling them in on how events had unfolded whilst occasionally glancing at Annie; a warm and knowing expression on his face.

She didn't want to hear about the terrible ordeal that had occurred in the early hours of the morning; it would only be a force to remind her how Lenny's life hung in the balance. She couldn't come to grips with his view that any relationship between them should and would be kept under control. To have loved him but to have never felt his arms around her would be a tragedy and one she could not imagine coming to terms with. Would the rest of her life be worse if she had never made love to him? Or would it be better not to know what she had missed? It was the worst of two evils and one she had never had to consider before.

All the men in her life paled into insignificance compared to him; not that they hadn't been interesting, intelligent or good-looking. It wasn't about that, any of it. It was a feeling that was just there all the time. Her very being was consumed by and depended upon his existence; the way he moved, expressed his words and merely glanced in her direction left her defenceless and vulnerable. Every step that he took or sentence that he mouthed hung in her memory as crystal clear as if it had just been said or done. The physical space between them seemed charged with a magnetism and electricity.

She thought back to Tom and wondered how she had ever allowed him to touch her, let alone make love to her. She had responded with what could only be called a mechanical reaction, fulfilling their physical wants. Whenever he had said that he loved her she had always said that she loved him too, but always in response to his words to save his feelings. It had never been love and she had known it really at the time. So much in him seemed to be lacking, as it had in all of her previous partners.

She looked around at the assembled pilots who were now beginning to accept the devastation that had been cast upon the airfield. The moments that had changed a few families' lives forever would be compartmentalised in the brave men's troubled minds so that they could fight another day. Stunted laughter was beginning to emanate from small groups around her which against the backdrop of smoke and recovery vehicles had an unpleasant irony about it.

'More tea, Annie?' asked Bertha, pouring without waiting for an answer.'

'Oh, yes please,' she replied dragging her mind back to their conversation.

'I'm so glad we'll all be here for Betty's wedding,' remarked Nina, continuing to keep the conversation flowing. 'What with this dreadful state of affairs we need something to cheer us up, don't we?'

It was more of a statement than a question, but true nonetheless.

'This time tomorrow she'll be married to Peter and off on honeymoon for a couple of days. How lovely! I envy her, don't you?' said Bertha.

Of course Annie would never wish to deprive Betty of her happiness, but she thought longingly of two days and nights in a quaint little hotel room in the English countryside with Lenny. She guessed that he was thinking the same as he caught her glance across the table as Bertha spoke.

'I must go and talk to a few of these men, some of them look rough,' interjected Lenny unexpectedly. 'I have tonight off though unless something big happens. I'll see you ladies later.'

He pulled himself up from his chair, looking exhausted from the effort. He hugged Nina and Bertha lightly and looked over their shoulders at Annie. This time she knew there was no reason why he should exclude her apart from the fear that he would lose control of his resolve to remain nothing but friends. He slung his parachute over his shoulder grimacing slightly with the weight and strolled off ,disappearing amongst the group of men near to their table. The moment he was out of earshot the questions began.

'Well well, how long has this been going on?' asked Nina in an animated tone. 'You're a dark horse if I may say so! You've succeeded where others have failed, might I say?'

'Oh it's nothing really,' Annie mumbled, trying to mask the reality of her feelings.

'Oh come on Annie, don't hide it from us, we need something to brighten our days!' said Bertha.

'He just saw I was upset about what happened here today and that I was worried about Peter, that's all,' she lied.

Nina and Bertha exchanged unconvinced glances and pressed Annie for more.

'Annie, we're not blind, we saw him looking at you. He's obviously taken with you,' said Nina.

'I've never seen him so distracted, he's usually so absorbed in flying, and I saw him holding your hand!' squealed Bertha.

Realising that they were not going to let it go, Annie relented and allowed the truth to be known, eventually excited to be able to share her feelings with the two of them. Holding it in was going to be impossible, especially if Lenny was going to insist on keeping their relationship purely on a platonic level only. They sat around the table like three young schoolgirls whispering their darkest desires to each other. Annie checked from time to time that Lenny was not in earshot or watching them from close by, but he was nowhere in sight, lost in the throng of other pilots. It was almost painful to discuss the intensity of what she was holding inside, as every word describing how he made her feel caused her heart to pound and her body to stir in ways she had never felt before. Nina and Bertha sat attentively absorbing her every word and when she had finished gave her words of advice.

'Gosh, you really are in love. How difficult it must be for you not knowing what each day has in store!' said Nina sympathetically. 'War can be so unkind though Annie, you must treat each day like it's your last.'

'Well maybe you should take heed of Lenny's advice. He obviously can't cope with how he feels. Why don't you try and forget about it for now and think of Betty's wedding tomorrow?' Bertha seemed intent on distracting Annie.

'Yes, you're right.'

They made their way back to ATA Headquarters and waited with the other ferry pilots for clearance to fly. The backlog of planes could cause a problem getting back that night if flying was postponed much longer. They did not have to wait long however before it was announced they could use the second runway so they collected their belongings from the truck. Nina and Bertha left in a different plane to Annie this time and she and took off with one other ferry pilot in the Anson, looking down at the airfield at the small dots milling around.

Chapter 37

It didn't occur to Annie that on her next pick up she might be required to fly a different type of plane: her mind was in a spin, Lenny foremost in her thoughts. Back at headquarters she had glazed over as the station officer had discussed the order of the day as he handed out chits to the queue of waiting ferry pilots. Since becoming part of the ferry pool, Annie had been comforted by the knowledge that she would be expected to accustom herself to the Tiger Moth before climbing aboard Hurricanes and Spitfires, so was not surprised when she received her chit to see that she had not been asked to fly anything more challenging.

As the airfield disappeared from view, Annie continued to think about Lenny. Whether she could persuade him to drop his guard was far more important than her next port of call. In her euphoric state, it seemed as though the more distance that was put between her and the airfield she had just departed from, the more the invisible thread connecting her to Lenny was being stretched to breaking point. She sat in silence, wanting to order the pilot to turn around, looking out of the window as the other ferry pilot chatted happily with the pilot of the Anson. Annie considered how for the last few years, the world had seemed dreary from her depressed perspective, but now the fields and villages stretching away beneath appeared spectacular: sun-kissed shades of green and gold vibrant amongst glistening lakes and rivers.

The Anson had been in the air for almost an hour when it finally began its slow descent to an unfamiliar airfield. Annie quietly cursed herself for not paying attention and for being so sidetracked by her thoughts. She wisely used the next few minutes before landing to get her bearings by chatting to the other ferry pilot.

Norman, a slightly built red-haired boy, spread out his map across his knees and showed her useful landmarks to aid her on the way back to base. The weather was clear and bright. The only problem, Norman warned, was flying into bright sunlight when heading south: enemy aircraft could be much harder to spot.

The Anson dropped them off and immediately taxied out to the take-off position again. Norman and Annie made their way to the office. The queue was short on this particular morning: most of the planes reallocated to other ferry pools due to the early morning raid on their airfield.

'Afternoon,' said the station officer, Annie noting that he was far more pleasant than the chauvinist character she had encountered in the Midlands. 'I hear you've had some trouble down there.'

'Yes,' said Annie. 'They've just about cleared up the worst of it.' She thought back to the smouldering wreckage.

'Damn Jerries,' muttered the station officer, looking at his paperwork. 'There are only two planes left to deliver today: a Spit and a Moth. Do you want to toss a coin for it?' he laughed.

Annie gulped, still not having prepared herself for an unexpected change of flight order.

The station officer saved her the trouble.

'You needn't look so worried, young lady. You're taking the Moth as you're new. Not likely you'll be expected to fly much else for a few weeks.'

Annie's heart was still fluttering.

'So I've been told.'

'You'll get your chance soon enough,' he chortled. 'You'll undertake some familiarisation before you pick up a Spit!'

Annie relaxed instantly.

'I'm quite glad to be flying the Moth actually. I need to get back home as soon as I can. My friend is getting married in the morning.'

'You'll be back in a couple of hours, though you'd both better get a move on anyway. There's heavy rain heading this way.'

Annie said her goodbyes to Norman and watched him walk to the Spitfire he had to deliver to a maintenance unit: his small frame dwarfed by his large parachute pack. She studied the Spitfire's iconic shape and the unmistakable shape of its elliptical wings, wondering how a mild-mannered man such as Norman could ever master her. It stood alone, beautiful but ominous. She wondered whether she would ever reach the standard required to fly such a plane and as she thought this the image of Tom popped into her head: his expression one of total disbelief as she stepped out of a cockpit smack bang in front of him. She wondered whether he would ever recover from the shock.

A month ago, she could never have envisaged how much her life was about to change. A more pressing problem would have been the choice of which shoes to buy: black or red leather, six-inch heels or kitten heels. She chuckled at the two different scenarios, but at the same time she felt a slight sense of shame that she had been so shallow: the old life now so transparent and superficial.

As Annie flew south, the invisible thread connecting her to Lenny began to shrink and return to its normal size. Her hands and feet responded automatically to the needs of the Tiger Moth's individuality; it was slightly more responsive than the first one she had flown. She didn't need to think anymore about how to handle the little plane as it purred along, the wind flowing over its wings. She adhered to instructions as she headed southeast, flying as low as possible: a dark rolling bank of clouds fifty miles north chasing her as the station commander had promised. Nearing home, the railway line showed her she was close to the abbey ruins: the last landmark before the twisting river. As she passed over its spire and reached the airfield, she noticed there was an unusual excess of air traffic, so she circled around behind several other planes waiting to land. On the spot where the three planes had exploded into flames the grass was charred and black, although all of the wreckage had been removed. Annie followed another plane in, touched down and gave herself an imaginary gold star as she taxied to a stop and carried out her checks before getting out of the plane.

As she walked past the dispersal huts she noticed that the atmosphere was back to normal: the men relaxing in their usual seats, smoking, writing home or talking. Lenny was in his usual spot with his sketchbook open. She was about to approach him, but suddenly felt oddly shy at the thought of drawing attention to themselves. Choosing to wait until later when they might have a chance to be alone, she continued on. She handed in her chit at the ATA headquarters and headed back to the locker room, hoping that Bertha and Nina would be around to give her a lift back to the farm.

The locker room was empty. She undressed and stood in her underwear for a few minutes so that she could cool down, feeling liberated after being strapped into the small Tiger Moth cockpit in such intense heat. She studied her reflection in the long mirror that hung on the end wall, noticing that she was a few pounds heavier than she had been a month or so ago. What with strict rationing and food shortages, she hadn't thought it likely that anyone would put on weight during wartime, although Lillian seemed to be extremely capable of making a feast out of almost nothing. Had she ended up in London, it would have been a different story, and she felt an overwhelming wave of gratitude to Lillian and the family, so willing to share what little extra their farm provided them with and care for her, a complete stranger, without a second thought.

Hearing voices in the corridor outside, she snapped out of her daydreams and quickly dressed.

Glenda and Joyce appeared in the doorway.

'Well, if it isn't the new girl!' drawled Glenda in her Louisiana accent. 'Managed to get off the ground without making a fool of yourself yet, missy?'

Joyce crossed her arms and coiled her lithe brown body against the doorframe, stopping Annie from leaving and anyone else from entering.

'Cat got your tongue?' she hissed at Annie.

'Back off, I'm every bit as good as both of you. At least I respect my colleagues and those 'little Spits'. That is what you chose to call them, I recall?'

Glenda was clearly taken aback at Annie's newfound confidence and raised her perfectly shaped eyebrows in surprise. She turned to look at Joyce who had lit a long slim cigarette and was smoking it thoughtfully as she observed the confrontation.

'I do believe you are getting ideas above your station, new girl!' drawled Glenda, her nose almost touching Annie's.

'Give it a rest!' said Annie, unperturbed by Glenda's aggression. She began to place her flying clothes in her locker.

'Don't turn your back on me,' warned Glenda, poking Annie in the back. 'I'm talking to you, you stuck up bitch!'

'That's enough, Glenda!' said a stern voice suddenly from beyond the doorway.

Joyce jumped in surprise, dropped her cigarette and spun round. Glenda turned to face whoever had dared to speak to her in such a tone.

'My office, now. Move yourself!'

'Yes ma'am,' said Glenda, throwing a withering look at Annie as she followed Joyce out of the locker room past Margaret Bowhill.

'Are you alright?' said Margaret.

In looks she did not appear much of an imposing character, but her commanding voice left Annie in no doubt that she was a force to be reckoned with.

'Yes, I'm fine thank you.'

'I hear you're doing well, keep up the good work. I want you to do a refresher flight in a Spitfire in the next few days.'

Annie was about to inform Margaret that she could not do a refresher course in a type of plane she had never flown, but Margaret had already gone before Annie could protest. Annie heard her office door slam and a raised voice from beyond the glass window. Somehow she felt sure that Glenda and Joyce would not be bothering her again. She tidied her hair during which time several other pilots came and went. With no sign of Bertha or Nina she found a wooden bench in the shade of a tree outside of headquarters where she could wait for their return.

The sun still beat down on the grass verges and cracked tarmac. She closed her eyes and listened to the drone of planes taking off and landing, aware of people walking past, making the most of the sunshine before another night of combat.

Outside the medical quarters two nurses were helping a young pilot take a few small steps, one supporting him on either side. Apart from his leg being heavily bandaged and being unsteady on his feet, he was laughing and talking to the nurses, unperturbed by his seemingly minor injuries. Two other pilots were sitting on a bench watching and applauding as he took a few steps on his own. Annie watched too, as the young pilot, a man no older than twenty, struggled with his injuries without complaint. She pondered about how resilient the young pilots seemed and how people in the twenty-first century didn't have what it took to face the same level of hardship. They needed a war to sort them out.

Despite the dangers that lay ahead, Annie knew for certain that she did not want to return to that life. Being near Lenny was all that mattered. Whilst she was thinking about him again, a newfound fear popped unexpectedly into her head. Would she wake up one morning to find this life she was fast accepting had disappeared into oblivion? The sun disappeared behind a small fluffy cloud, as if to say all was not certain, and she shivered.

'Annie, back at last! Have you been waiting for me?'

Annie looked up to see Nina approaching, weighed down with her parachute pack.

'I haven't been here long. Just enjoying the sunshine.'

'I'll be out in a jiffy, let me get out of this stuff.' She disappeared into the locker rooms.

Annie closed her eyes again, enjoying the sun on her face. The injured pilot and his colleagues had gone, and for a few moments she was totally alone.

Life was good.

Chapter 38

By the time Nina finally appeared from the ATA locker room, Annie had noticed that the rain that had followed her in the Tiger Moth had finally caught up. An angry grey bank of clouds hung northwest of the airfield, threatening to blot out any remaining blue sky as it headed southeast. Despite the threat of a storm brewing, Annie suddenly felt the urge to voice her sense of wellbeing.

'Do you know how lucky we are?'

As she said this, Tom crossed her mind again, as she remembered him having made a similar comment on the Victoria Embankment on their way to the memorial. She felt a sudden pang of guilt for having rebuked him for his boyish enthusiasm.

'In what way?' asked Nina, looking at Annie quizzically.

'Having the opportunity to fly Spitfires and Hurricanes! How many people will ever get a chance like that, apart from the RAF boys of course, and I don't envy them! My friends would never believe it!' added Annie, Nina oblivious to the real meaning behind her words.

'Wait until you've flown one, you might change your mind!' teased Nina. 'Though I'm sure you'll manage perfectly well,' she immediately added, seeing Annie's face change to one of concern.

'I haven't told anyone back home that I've joined the ATA. They'd be worried sick in case I had a crash,' said Annie, hedging her words.

'Frankly our worst enemy is the weather, not a crash caused by a German pilot taking a pop at us.'

Annie shivered at the possibility.

'You can't pretend that the ATA isn't exciting.'

'It can be,' laughed Nina, seeing the sparkle in Annie's eyes. 'But might I add that I think love for a certain person is making you view our job through rose-coloured spectacles!'

Annie blushed and savoured the euphoric wave that washed over her. She changed the subject, aware that she felt like a love-struck teenager.

'The office in London is mundane compared to this,' she said eventually, playing down her position at Carlotti's. 'Now I've joined up, there's no way I would want to return to that job, at least not if I can help it,' she added, her words highlighted by the distant rumble of thunder fleetingly reminding her of the scrap yard. She wondered whether it still possessed the power to send her back to the twenty-first century.

'I wouldn't want to work in London whilst the war is on,' remarked Nina. 'It must be terrifying.'

'I've not been caught up in any of that,' said Annie, enjoying the deception she was presenting to Nina. 'There's always plenty happening to take your mind off of the war: clubs, bars, theatre and so on.'

So I've heard. The boys don't stop going on about the Windmill.'

'What's the Windmill?'

'You must have heard about the Windmill Theatre! Nothing but feathers, fans and naked women,' complained Nina.

'Oh yes, I remember now,' lied Annie. 'But that goes on all over London.'

'Really? Quite disgusting if you ask me! What sort of woman parades around showing off their body to all and sundry?'

'Glenda?' suggested Annie. 'She ought to audition!'

'Good point,' laughed Nina.

Annie smiled to herself how quaintly naive Nina was, but then considered that maybe she was lucky not to have witnessed the world seventy years later. She wondered how Nina would react to the twenty-first century if she were suddenly to wake up in a part of London inhabited by strip clubs, binge drinkers and drug addicts.

'You look like you're in a world of your own!' said Nina suddenly, waving a hand in front of Annie's face.

Annie startled and laughed.

'You have no idea how close to the truth you are. I was thinking about home.'

Nina changed the subject, mistaking the distant look on Annie's face as one of longing.

'Let's talk about something else? I bet they'll be glad of some extra pairs of hands getting ready for tomorrow.'

Annie appeared bewildered.

'Have you forgotten Betty's wedding?' asked Nina.

A sudden rush of excitement gripped Annie at the prospect of being part of Betty's celebrations.

'How could I forget that?' she scolded herself. 'Must be the talk of home.'

'Let's get a move on then, before we get collared to pick up any more planes!' she said, grabbing Nina's arm.

Back at the farmhouse a transformation had taken place. Modest posies had been attached to each gatepost with scarlet ribbon that fluttered in the breeze. The pending storm had changed direction and the courtyard in front of the house was bustling with activity: all available hands tidying and cleaning. The yard had been swept and the machinery that was normally stacked around the edge was hidden away in outbuildings. A large homemade banner with the words 'Congratulations Betty and Peter' had been strung across the front wall of the farmhouse. Trestle tables stood end to end outside the kitchen, lined each side with mismatched chairs, stools and upturned half-barrels to seat around thirty people. The sound of Glenn Miller wafted from the direction of the kitchen into the open air, shrilly accompanied by one of the farm worker's expert whistling as he helped with the preparation for the wedding. Even Daphne's mood swings could not spoil the uplifting environment of all the farm workers, as she busied herself with washing the outside of the kitchen windows. She stopped and glared at Annie through the glass as Annie entered the kitchen with Nina.

'Oh girls, I'm so glad you made it back,' said Lillian, polishing the table with beeswax. 'We're all so excited. Go and freshen up and I'll make some tea.'

Lillian refilled the ever-boiling kettle and placed it back on the freshly blacked range. The smell of home cooking was so tantalising that Annie's mouth immediately began to water. All manner of Lillian's baking creations peeped out from beneath fine muslin cloths on the Welsh dresser: scones, cake and pastries vying for space and threatening to tumble to the floor if disturbed by someone unable to resist. Annie fleetingly remembered the feast that Tom's mother had conjured up on the night that she had visited them with Tom for the first time. Lillian's baking was equally as impressive.

The rest of the house was filled with other delightful aromas. Freshly picked flowers adorned every available polished surface: roses of every imaginable colour, shade and size of bloom picked from the garden. The afternoon sun streamed through the stained glass landing windows creating a rainbow of colour on the oak panelled walls and family portraits. Lillian's blue eyes, identical to Lenny's, welcomed Annie.

'I'll see you downstairs,' said Nina, disappearing into her bedroom.

The soft music from the kitchen carried up the stairs and into Annie's room. She hastily changed, leaving her discarded clothes on a wooden clotheshorse to air, and dressed in a knee length skirt and floral summer blouse that immediately cooled her skin. Her neck was sore from where her starched shirt collar had rubbed.

Having splashed her face with cool water, she sat at the dressing table brushing her hair enjoying a few moments to herself. There was suddenly a gentle knock on the bedroom door.

'Come in, it's not locked,' she called, still brushing her hair.

And there he was again: Lenny, beautiful and perfect in Annie's eyes, standing in her bedroom doorway with his cap in his hand. Her heart immediately began to pound as she chose not to face him, choosing instead to look at his reflection, which somehow made her feel less vulnerable. He filled the width of doorway, his broad shoulders tapering gently down to his waist, his free hand smoothing back his dark hair as he spoke.

Annie noticed a slight tremor in his voice.

'Sorry if this is inappropriate, coming to your room I mean,' he apologised, his eyes mirroring the brilliant blue of the sky outside. 'I realised you were back when I heard you talking to Nina.'

'It...it's fine,' she stammered, unprepared for his unexpected arrival and the instant effect he caused on her. 'Come in. I was just changing.'

Lenny entered the room as though it were forbidden territory, ducking under the low doorframe. Annie continued to look at him in the mirror as he went to the window to avoid her gaze.

'Nice view from here,' he said, filling the awkward silence as he looked at the distant hills shrouded by a heat haze.

'I thought you were talking about me then for a second,' said Annie, joking with him to ease the tension between them.

'Oh – I see. Well, of course I meant that too,' answered Lenny, still seeming nervous to be in her bedroom. He fumbled in his pocket, took out his pipe and filled the bowl of the pipe with fresh tobacco. Annie noticed his hands shake as he clumsily lit a match, dropping it on the floor as the flame burnt his hand.

The silence stretched out as Annie resumed brushing her hair as an excuse to continue watching him in the mirror and waiting for him to speak again. Her heart continued to thump. Lenny seemed to use the pipe ritual as a tool to give him time to compose himself.

Finally he spoke.

'I'll be off then. I'll see you tomorrow at the wedding.'

He left the room quickly, covering the floor with long strides, without so much of a glance in her direction.

Had she dreamt that he had just been there? She slowly and gently put down her hairbrush, as though any sudden noise or movement might shatter the previous few moments. Looking in the mirror again, she searched for his reflection: expecting to see the image of him still standing at the window preserved in her mirror for all time for only her to see. However, the only things reflected in the glass were her pale face and the view through her window of the hills in the distance. Why had he come only to say so little and leave so soon?

The Glenn Miller music wafted up the stairs again as Lenny's footsteps receded into the distance. All that remained to prove the moment had been real was the spent match on the floorboards. As if the matchstick were all she would ever have of his, she picked it up and rolled it tenderly through her fingers. The woody smell from his tin of tobacco had already evaporated, overpowered by the scent of the flowers in her room.

Annie jumped as Nina appeared in the doorway.

'Did I just hear Lenny?'

'Yes, he stopped by to say hello.'

Nina seemed not to notice Annie's wistful look as she tidied her dressing table.

'Let's go and help Lillian, there must still be errands to run and things to do!' suggested Nina.

Lenny was nowhere to be seen when they arrived downstairs, but his earlier appearance made Annie feel self-contained, bobbing around in her own little bubble of joy as Lillian immediately commandeered her into baking, assuming she was practiced at the art of cookery.

'You don't mind helping me, do you?' asked Lillian, passing Annie an apron.

Annie put the apron on, wincing at the frills and bows. 'Happy to,' she pretended, fearing discovery: her ability to microwave ready meals as far as her culinary skills stretched.

The pounding of dough and airing of pastry seemed endless, and Annie's hands and wrists soon hurt from the effort. She had not appreciated how baking had been such a lengthy process before the advent of modern kitchen gadgets: the piles of scones and cakes amassing slowly until there were no available surfaces left on which to place them. By the time Nina had washed all the mixing bowls and utensils, tidied away recipe books, packets of flour and sugar, the sun had sunk lower in the sky and Annie felt she had done a workout at the gym.

Workers seemed to have an internal body clock, sensing that it was an appropriate time to make an appearance: hungry from their physical efforts in the yard. Somehow, as well as baking enough for an army, Lillian had managed to conjure up the usual staple meal for the farm workers: piles of potatoes, vegetables and meat pie from what little was left in the larder. She passed plates of food through the open window to the hungry workers who sat at the long trestle tables in the garden eating as though there was no tomorrow. Annie sat at the kitchen table picking at her food, hungry but distracted by thoughts of her brief encounter with Lenny, whilst Nina and Lillian chatted. As they were finishing their meal, Bertha arrived back from the airfield, having completed a short cross-country relay with four other pilots bringing a glut of Hurricanes back as replacements for the ones destroyed in the raid.

'You're just in time dear, before the others ask for seconds. Sit down and make yourself comfortable.' Lillian served up some of the leftover potatoes and vegetables and a slice of pie.

'Betty's outside,' said Bertha incidentally, sitting down and tucking in to her dinner. 'I thought I'd have to walk to get here tonight – couldn't cadge a lift from anyone. Betty just happened by!'

Betty burst in through the kitchen door rosy-faced and windswept, carrying several heavy bags, which she dropped by the door. Her hair had been separated into small tight curls pinned into place: her scarf disguising the fine net she wore to anchor the curls.

'Less than a day to go and I'll be Mrs Larkin,' she informed everyone proudly.

Lillian grinned from ear to ear as she tried to make the last bits of food stretch even further.

'Oh don't bother with that Auntie,' said Betty, grabbing a spoon from the cutlery drawer. She stood by the range and threw her manners to the wind, eating directly from the near-empty saucepans. 'I'm famished – it must be all the excitement!'

Eating as though she had been starved for days, once Betty's hunger was finally satisfied she flopped down into the rocking chair.

'I must have forgotten something Auntie,' she chattered, her wedding nerves apparent for all to see. 'I knew I should have written a list,' she added anxiously.

'Everything is taken care of my love. Don't you worry about anything. I've got Nina and Annie helping if something's slipped my mind.'

Betty leapt up and hugged Lillian, Nina and Annie affectionately.

'Thank you so much for everything you're doing. I can barely breathe, I'm so nervous,' she said.

'Betty dear, why don't you have a bath while there is still plenty of hot water?' suggested Lillian. 'The workers will be cleaning up soon, so best you do it now. It'll help settle your nerves too.'

'I think you're right,' agreed Betty, gathering up her bags. 'I won't be long.'

Once Betty had retired, Nina, Bertha and Lillian followed her example one by one, until Annie was alone in the kitchen. The evening sky was displaying its tropical plumage through the open window, turning from a flaming orange to blood red as the sun sank lower behind the trees.

Annie sat in the rocking chair, gently rocking backwards and forwards to the rhythmic sound of the clock, aware that moments spent in quiet contemplation were always tinged with a mixture of emotions: some happy and some sad. The velvety blue night slowly began to conceal the flaming spectacle of sunset, and Annie attempted to shut her demons out and welcome the more positive thoughts to filter into her mind. To her surprise, her current thoughts were unusually untroubled: replaced instead by a feeling of stability and willing acceptance of her current situation. Tinged with this came an intuitive awareness that there were still challenges to face, although she had no idea what they might be. The only certainty in the quietness of the kitchen, was that Betty would marry Peter the next day and that whatever weather was thrown at the occasion, nothing would spoil the day. Even Lenny's decision to put a block on a relationship developing between them would not be sufficient to dampen her spirits. His confession of hidden feelings at the airfield was enough to sustain and carry her onwards for a while at least.

Annie closed the blackout curtains and sat for a few more minutes enjoying the heat from the range, gazing at the hot embers dropping into the grate beneath. Unlike the consuming ravages of the fire at the airfield, watching the strength ebb from the hot coals instilled a feeling of comfort. Finally, feeling the temperature drop as the night closed in, cooler air creeping under the kitchen door, she followed the others to bed, anticipating a wonderful day to come.

Chapter 39

Early the next morning, the grandfather clock downstairs chimed six o'clock, as the cuckoo clock on the landing added its voice to the morning chorus in the trees outside. Waking suddenly, and thinking she was late for a corporate meeting, Annie gathered her senses and threw open her heavy blackout curtains. Immediately, the early morning sun bursting through the open window dazzled her. She breathed a sigh of relief, knowing that the day offered far more than a stressful day in the office. She also noted that her dreams had been far less menacing of late, although she had no idea why that might be.

Putting these thoughts behind her, Annie went to the tiny bathroom along the landing and ran a tepid bath. Forgetting she should use it sparingly, she poured a generous amount of pink eau de cologne from a crystal decanter into the warm water. Six inches of bath water, which was the house rule, was hard to get accustomed to: a deep bath brimming with bubbles was one of the few things that Annie was beginning to miss. She sat in the shallow water, washing as best she could with her minuscule ration of cold tar soap, and then patted her skin dry with a rough towel that had never seen fabric conditioner. Finally she slipped on a soft satin bath gown: one of only a few luxuries borrowed from Lillian.

By the time Annie had returned to her own room and dressed, she could hear light-hearted squabbles on the landing as to who should have priority in the bathroom. Annie poked her head around her bedroom door and was immediately greeted with a long queue of young and old family members playfully whipping each other with their towels.

Downstairs, the finishing touches had been made to the kitchen and trestle tables outside. Lillian was rearranging flowers and laying out plates and cutlery.

'Can I help?' asked Annie eagerly, feeling guilty that there seemed to be little left to do.

'Some of us got up early,' snarled Daphne appearing from the side of the house with a basket of fresh eggs.

'Do you think you could desist for just one day Daphne?' suggested Nina, appearing with wet hair by Annie's side.

Daphne swept past Nina and Annie and handed the basket of eggs to Lillian.

'Thank you dear – you've been such a help,' said Lillian in an attempt to appease Daphne's mood. 'Now you girls go and see if Betty needs any help and that the boys are not misbehaving. Lenny's gone to collect Peter. Everything is just about ready.'

Annie's heart fluttered at the mention of Lenny's name and she blushed as Nina caught her eye.

'Am I missing something?' asked Bertha noticing Annie's red face.

'I'm really hot, that's all,' replied Annie, aware of Daphne's suspicious look from the other side of the table. 'I'm not used to such a hot summer,' she went on fanning her face with a napkin, trying to cool her red face.

'Anyway, there's nothing left to do. Off you go!' said Lillian, chivvying them along with a damp tea towel, deliberately defusing a situation before it began.

Using Betty as a good excuse to escape Daphne's questioning glare, Annie ran upstairs and put her ear to Betty's door.

'Damn and blast,' blasphemed Betty from inside.

'Can I come in? It's me.'

There was a sound of rustling and things being dropped and then the door opened a crack. Betty peered round and seeing that it was Annie, pulled her in and locked the door.

'Oh Annie, thank God it's you! My hair's a disaster. I can't do my make up, and I'm not sure my dress will fit!' she blurted out in a torrent of anxiety.

Betty's hair was a mass of tumbling red curls collapsing over her face.

'Sit down and let me deal with it for you,' said Annie calmly, guiding Betty back gently to her dressing table stool. 'We've plenty of time, you'll look beautiful, as always.'

Annie gently pulled her fingers through Betty's glossy curls, teasing the curls into soft waves.

Betty began to relax.

'You know you really don't need any make up," said Annie, patting at Betty's nose with a powder puff and deftly applying a layer of coral lipstick to her generous lips.

'Now let's get you into your dress. Peter will be here soon before he leaves for church.'

The mention of Peter's name was enough to send Betty scurrying to the window wearing only her cream silk underwear and petticoat.

'Don't let him see you – it's unlucky,' said Annie pulling Betty to the centre of the room. 'Now close your eyes until I tell you to open them.'

She helped Betty step into her dress and fastened the tiny pearl buttons at the back and wrists. The sweetheart neckline showed off Betty's perfect porcelain skin and the fitted bodice hugged her curvaceous body, enhancing her small waist. Having carefully arranged the full skirt and train and helped Betty into her simple satin shoes, Annie attached Betty's veil to her red curls with cream rose buds and turned Betty to face the long mirror on the wall.

'Open your eyes, I told you you'd look beautiful. Peter's a lucky man.'

Betty opened her eyes and looked at her reflection, silenced by what she saw, the stunning woman staring back at her vaguely familiar.

'Oh Annie, thank you,' she smiled, her eyes watering. 'I do look nice don't I?'

'Of course you do, silly, you look perfect. Now don't cry, you'll smudge your powder. Save the tears for after the wedding.' Annie dabbed the tears that were starting to fall with a cotton handkerchief.

'Betty? It's time to go,' called a voice from the other side of the bedroom door. 'Peter only popped in for a moment, he's on the way to the church.'

Annie ushered Betty out of the door to where Lillian was waiting with her bouquet: a combination of cream and yellow roses and trailing greenery that reached almost to the floor.

The wedding party left for the chapel on a pony and trap, Betty holding firmly onto the arm of Cecil with Lillian on her other side. A stream of cars and trucks followed them to the village. The small chapel barely accommodated the fifty guests and echoed with the hymns and booming voice of the vicar taking the service. Between a sea of hats Annie caught glimpses of Lenny, but he only turned and made eye contact when he reached over to hug Betty as she walked down the aisle as Mrs Larkin.

Betty and Peter stood on the steps outside and were immediately inundated with small silver tokens tied with ribbon from young children, and handfuls of rice thrown by the rest of the congregation. Annie waited her turn to congratulate the bride and groom, standing back so she could quietly take in the happy scene. A sycamore tree shaded her from the heat of the sun as it blazed down on the happy crowd. The simplicity of the wedding struck Annie as far more emotional and genuine than all the no expense spared functions she had attended: Betty and Peter were totally lost in each other.

An arm linked with Annie's as she stood at the back of the well-wishers, making her jump.

'She's beautiful,' the voice said.

'Yes she is,' said Annie, trembling at the touch of Lenny's arm against hers.

'That makes two of you then,' he said softly as he turned her to face him, lifting her chin gently up to his. He pulled her close to his strong uniformed chest, locking her helplessly in his arms.

Everything and everyone around Annie seemed to evaporate as Lenny's lips brushed hers.

'But you said...' she began.

He gently stroked her lips with his fingers as if to silence her.

'I know,' he said. 'I didn't want to start a fire I couldn't put out...but it's too late. I love you.'

Annie rested her head on Lenny's chest and he ran his fingers tenderly through her hair.

'It's too late for both of us. I love you too,' she whispered.

Annie stood motionless, listening to the rhythm of Lenny's racing heart. She dared to look up into his piercing blue eyes knowing that she had indeed reached a point of no return. She was defenceless. Whether he had reacted spontaneously or planned this moment didn't matter.

The sound of cheering jolted them both back to the moment. Peter was helping Betty into the trap. Betty tossed the bouquet high into the air and many pairs of hands jostled to catch it.

'Let's not forget why we're here,' said Lenny respectfully, placing one arm around Annie's waist and leading her towards the crowd to wave to Betty and Peter as they left for the reception. As the pony and trap pulled away from the church gates followed by more cheering and rice throwing, Lenny took Annie's hand again and walked her to his car. They drove in total silence during the short journey back to the reception, his hand lightly caressing hers.

Chapter 40

Betty and Peter held each other close for their first dance: twirling around to the music playing on Lillian's gramophone. With no superficial frills to overshadow their moment, the attention of the partygoers was solely on the happy couple. Annie stood arm in arm with Lenny, quietly enjoying the festivities as she recalled weddings she had attended, when a show of wealth and status had been the things that had impressed her most. She felt suddenly uncomfortable knowing that she had been so shallow. Betty and Peter needed nothing but each other and had not even thought it necessary to compile a wedding present list. The expectation of buying their own home, equipped from top to bottom with material things, was not something Betty had even mentioned to Annie.

Lenny made no attempt to mask his feelings anymore, holding Annie's hand or continuing to link arms as they mixed with the other guests. Annie found the urge to pinch herself almost irresistible as she held on tightly to Lenny.

'Would you like to dance?' Lenny asked. 'After all, we have some catching up to do.'

'What do you mean, catching up?' asked Annie as Lenny led her to the centre of the dancing throng.

'The village dance,' he explained.' I avoided you.'

Annie remembered Daphne preying on Lenny.

'I didn't think you were interested in me, even when you rescued me from that Canadian.' She cringed at the thought of Dan's touch.

'It was all a pretence,' he went on. 'I wanted to dance with you, but I knew if we got close to each other, you'd guess how I was feeling.'

'I had no idea. You did a good job of hiding it.'

'I'm sorry. I was more concerned with the prospect of starting something I couldn't finish. God, I hate the war.'

'Don't apologise. We're here together now, that's all that matters. We don't need to think about what tomorrow might bring.'

Lenny pulled Annie close to his chest as the music slowed, stroking her hair as he had done earlier in the churchyard. There was so much she wanted to say, and questions she was eager to ask, but she chose to put them all to one side and savour the feeling of elation that pulsed through her very being. Lenny's warm breath on her forehead aroused her senses as he cocooned her in his arms. They danced slowly, the space between themselves and the other revellers like a protective cushion from the real world. The music was mellow and slow: no fast numbers playing to make them feel that they should release their hold on each other. Wrapped in Lenny's arms, Annie felt safe from all the nightmares that had been plaguing her, as though nothing predatory could get to her all the time Lenny's strong body was pressed close to her small frame.

'Well here's another reason to celebrate,' announced Betty, appearing suddenly, and breaking in to Annie and Lenny's private space. 'You crafty old thing Lenny, you certainly pulled the wool over my eyes for once!'

Lenny beamed and pulled Annie closer still. She nestled against him just in case the dream should vanish. Betty cradled them both in her arms.

'How long has this been going on?' she quizzed, looking first at one and then the other.

'Since I first set eyes on her,' said Lenny, looking deep into Annie's eyes, and showing no qualms at declaring his feelings. 'Are you really all right with that, old girl? I'm sorry I didn't tell you.'

'I'm absolutely delighted, darling,' said Betty, reaching up on tiptoe, and kissing him affectionately on one cheek. 'I'm not sure about Daphne though. She's not pleased at all, she's got a face like thunder. You know how enamoured she is with you.'

Annie scanned the farmyard, trying to appear casual, but was immediately met with a treacherous look from Daphne, lolling against the doorframe of one of the barns, a cigarette in one hand and a glass of wine in the other. Her eyes bored through Annie and Lenny. She gripped the glass so tightly that her knuckles had turned white: the glass looking set to shatter at any second, injuring more than her ego.

'Oh dear...I know she doesn't like me much, but I don't like making her feel that way,' said Annie, surprised by her own unusual demonstration of sincerity.

'Oh, don't you worry about Daphne,' said Betty dismissively. 'She's got a string of ardent admirers, she'll get over it soon enough!'

Suddenly, Betty left without another word as Peter pulled her away.

'Come on Mrs Larkin, leave the young lovers alone!' Peter winked knowingly at Lenny as he whisked Betty off to dance again.

'I hope Daphne isn't making you uncomfortable,' said Lenny, picking up on Daphne's hostile behaviour.

'I just feel a little sorry for her.'

'Don't worry, I'll speak to her. Betty's right, she'll be fine,' said Lenny as he resumed his protective hold.

Annie glanced at the other dancers. Most were paired, with the exception of a few children who ran around the dancers at high speed in a game of catch, squealing and giggling as they dodged in and out. As the morning became the afternoon, the farm became congested with the arrival of more guests: most being personnel from the airfield, still in uniform, come to join the celebrations before operations the coming night. A small group of musicians from the village set up their instruments in one corner of the courtyard and struck up some lively country music to replace the gramophone player. The sun beat down mercilessly on the partygoers, who, finding the heat too intense, abandoned their uniform jackets, caps and ties and danced in shirtsleeves rolled up to their elbows. As the pace of music and dancing quickened and the beer began to flow more freely, Lenny took Annie's hand and led her away.

'Do you mind if we go somewhere quieter?' Lenny asked.

'Do you think Betty will mind?'

'I'm sure she won't even notice we've gone.'

They walked with an unspoken understanding that they wanted to be alone. Moving around the side of the farmhouse, they reached the path that led to the muddy field where Annie had watched Betty and the boys messing around on their motorbikes. The churned-up mud had dried up a while ago in the heat of the sun: the field now parched, large cracks having formed in the deep tyre tracks that still remained. The fields beyond the enclosure were a complete contrast to the motorcycle track: green and lush with healthy crops of barley and corn swaying gently in the summer breeze. Lenny and Annie walked on still silent, feeling words were not needed, until they had put some distance between themselves and the farmhouse. The sound of music and laughter was still audible in the distance.

Lenny stopped where the crops ceased and long soft grass and wild poppies replaced them. He removed his jacket, placing it on the ground amongst the tall grass. Annie noticed that his shirt was wet with perspiration, and trembled at the first glimpse of his chest and upper arms, which were visible through the thin cotton material.

'We'd better not be away too long,' said Lenny, breaking the silence, nervous as he scrabbled for something appropriate to say.

They stood still, unsure of each other amongst the poppies, the jacket on the ground the only thing separating them. Annie stepped lightly across the jacket and took Lenny's hands in hers, helping him to overcome his nervousness by guiding them to the zip of her dress. His hands trembled as he slowly undid the zip and eased the delicate silk dress from her shoulders. It floated to the ground like a feather in a breeze, and came to rest around her ankles. She stepped out of the daffodil yellow silk, noticing how Lenny seemed fixated on her, seemingly unable to move from where he stood. His blue eyes seemed to search her soul as they stood facing each other in the meadow with no other person in sight. She lowered herself down onto the ground, pulling Lenny gently after her. His uniform jacket lining felt cool against her back. She welcomed Lenny's lips as he lost all control, kissing her passionately and repeatedly: the full weight of his body pressing her against the ground. Breathless from her excited state, she felt the urgency in him, as still trembling, he guided her hands clumsily to his shirt buttons: the scent of his perspiring body hypnotic and irresistible to Annie. She began to unbutton his shirt as she looked into his eyes. His breathing was rapid. He rolled onto his back so that Annie was on top of him, and kissed her neck and bare shoulders as she leant over him: her hair brushing against his face. He allowed his fingers to play up and down her arms but hesitated when he reached the delicate skin between her neck and breasts. She reached down to undo his belt but he grabbed her wrists and spun her onto her back again, pinning her down as he sat astride her.

'I want you as much as you want me,' he said, as though second-guessing she sensed his reticence to immediately strip her naked. 'I wanted to make love to you the first time I saw you,' he confessed, sliding her bra straps from her shoulders. She arched her back in anticipation of him reaching around the back to unfasten it. 'I love you so much.'

'I love you too.' She nuzzled his face as he leant over her. 'More than I ever dreamed possible.'

He guided her hand to the front of his trousers as he leant forwards and reached around her back with the other hand. Her bra strap released willingly.

Suddenly a male voice bellowed from a few hundred yards away.

'Lenny, Annie, where are you?' They're going to cut the cake.'

Lenny stopped and lifted his head enough to see where the voice was coming from. Annie collapsed backwards onto the grass, suddenly feeling shy, and held her bra protectively to her breasts.

The voice had come from someone standing at the edge of the dusty field with hands cupped to his mouth as he looking around for them.

Lenny sighed and dropped his head in defeat.

'Damn it, they noticed we'd gone after all! We have to get back before they discover us like this,' he uttered resignedly.

He waited until the man had gone back around the other side of the house and scrambled to his feet. He picked up Annie's silk dress from the grass, apologising as though he had been the one to interrupt their lovemaking. He was as tender with the act of helping Annie dress as he had been when removing her clothes, taking care not to trap her tumbling hair in her zip. He straightened his shirt and finished dressing.

They made their way back the way they had come, following the tracks they had created earlier in the long grass and barley. Lenny stopped several times and kissed Annie eagerly. As on their outward walk to the little patch of oasis, they did not speak until they were almost back at the farmhouse.

Just before they turned the corner, Lenny turned to Annie.

'No matter what happens in this damn war I won't...'

'There you are, what have you been doing?' asked Nina, interrupting Lenny's sentence, as she appeared from around the corner of one of the farm buildings. The colour immediately rose in Annie's face at Nina's question.

Nina noticed their embarrassed faces.

'Come on you two lovebirds, it's speech and cake-cutting time.'

Lenny plucked a piece of grass from Annie's hair. She felt as though everyone would guess she had been practically naked only a few minutes previously as they tried to subtly integrate with the noisy guests. Betty cast a knowing smile as she stood radiant at Peter's side and cut the simple one tiered cake that had been lovingly baked by Lillian.

'To the happy couple,' shouted the guests as glasses were raised to Betty and Peter.

'To the happy couple,' said Annie, first raising a glass to Betty and Peter, then to Lenny as she looked into his eyes.

Chapter 41

The dancing continued well into the evening, and apart from one dance with Betty, Lenny did not leave Annie's side. Daphne temporarily turned her attention to a young airman, wrapping herself around him for all to see.

As the burning sun finally lost its strength and slipped towards the purple and grey hills in the west, the guests began to filter away, leaving only the immediate family and a smattering of close friends enjoying the welcoming cool of the gathering dusk. Betty and Peter excitedly said their goodbyes and left for the railway station in the pony and trap. Lillian openly wept as the sound of hooves clattering on gravel faded into the distance.

As the heat from the day was replaced by a cooler night, Annie pulled her cardigan around her shoulders.

'Let's go inside. I'm getting a bit cold now the sun has gone down,' said Annie.

Lenny removed his jacket and placed it over Annie's cardigan.

'Of course.' He took her by the hand and guided her in the darkness towards the kitchen door.

'I've never been this happy. I feel like I'm dreaming.' Annie suddenly felt a sense of panic at her statement and the thought that everything related to the Second World War could all indeed be a dream she would wake up from at any moment. 'I don't want it to end,' she added, as if to reaffirm her wishes.

Lenny stroked her cheek.

'I'm going to try hard to survive this war,' he said, pretending to make light of their predicament.

'What if I'm whisked away and I couldn't tell you where I've gone?' exclaimed Annie, thinking of the scrap yard.

Lenny laughed.

'Whisked away? Where to exactly? Anyway, I have faith in the ATA and their training. You'll be fine as long as you follow the rules.'

'I wasn't talking about the flying,' said Annie, wishing she could blurt out everything to Lenny about where she had come from. Instead she changed the tack of the conversation. 'Will you come to my room,' she went on, immediately thinking that she might have come across as too forward.

Fortunately Lenny seemed unfazed by her suggestion.

'There's nothing I'd like more,' he said, as they entered the kitchen. 'But it wouldn't be correct – not here.'

'You're right. It was disrespectful of me even to suggest it,' admitted Annie recalling lustful yet clumsy instances with other men she would rather forget.

'I should have restrained myself earlier too. It wasn't very gentlemanly of me.'

'Not at all - don't apologise. I wanted to be alone with you as much as you did with me.'

'I couldn't help myself,' added Lenny, looking Annie up and down appreciatively. 'You look so beautiful in that dress.'

He escorted her upstairs and held her close for a few moments on the landing, kissing her tenderly.

'Goodnight, my darling.'

Annie trembled at Lenny's use of such endearing words.

'I love you,' he added, his lips brushing hers.

'I love you too,' replied Annie, surprised at how easily the words rolled off of her tongue. 'Goodnight.'

She reluctantly released her hands from his and backed towards her door, feeling as though she must add yet another image of him to an already crowded compartment in her memory. Nevertheless, her primary urge was to pull him into her room and finish what they had started earlier, but she chose instead to leave her bedroom door unlocked just in case he should ignore his moral stand and come to her.

She undressed and lay down on her bed, not expecting sleep to come calling, and tried to ignore the sensations stirring deep within her body. Her very being ached for his touch. She clutched her yellow dress, holding it close to her face in an attempt to recapture Lenny's scent. Eventually however, exhaustion from the excitement of the day won over and she fell into a restless sleep. Lenny featured in all of her dreams as her knight in shining armour, shielding her from the man with the flaming hair that still chased her regularly in her nightmares.

Oblivious to the knocking on her door in the early hours of the following morning, Annie clung onto sleep, exhausted by her demons. The knocking became loud and urgent.

'I'm awake now, you can come in,' she grumbled. 'This had better be important,' she added, forgetting where she was for a fleeting second. Lenny, who was still chasing her pursuer on his galloping white horse, evaporated in a puff of sparkly pink fairy-dust.

'Annie, I've been knocking for simply ages! Get up, there's been a message to get to headquarters. It's pandemonium down there,' blurted out Bertha, red-faced and breathless.

Annie squinted through half-closed eyes at the blurred figure at the end of her bed and then turned to see the time on her clock.

'Bertha, for heaven's sake, surely it can wait! It's only five in the morning,' she protested, rolling over and facing the other way.

'No, it can't wait, now get up! Our heads will roll if we're late,' Bertha insisted, pulling the covers forcibly off of Annie. 'You've got five minutes and not a second more.' Bertha left the room, her footsteps thundering down the stairs.

Then Annie remembered: another glorious day with Lenny lay ahead before his two days leave was over. Perhaps whatever was going on at the airfield could be dealt with quickly, although intuition told Annie that such a probability was unlikely. She splashed her face with cold water, hurriedly pulled a brush through her tangled curls and pulled on her clothes.

'Come on,' said Nina poking her head round the door. 'I'll tell you what little I know on the way.'

'I must say goodbye to...'

'No time for that, you'll see him later,' second-guessed Nina as she thrust Annie's uniform jacket into her hands. She helped Annie stuff her belongings unceremoniously into her travel bag, making no attempt to leave, in case Annie should decide to creep along the landing to Lenny's room.

Annie's stomach had no time to register hunger as she almost stumbled on running down the stairs. She ran through the empty kitchen, crossed the yard, and climbed into the waiting truck. Birds were already assembled on the telegraph wires singing their well-rehearsed dawn chorus. Nina accelerated away quickly, forcing the spinning wheels of the truck to send loose gravel ricocheting high into the air. The protesting birds flew off noisily into the safety of the surrounding trees.

'Orders came in overnight,' shouted Nina over the sound of the racing engine.

'What orders?' Annie shouted back, hanging onto her cap for dear life. 'What's so important that you've dragged me out of bed on my day off?'

'No idea, but all ferry pilots have been summoned urgently,' explained Nina.

'All leave's cancelled,' added Bertha. 'We all have to report at six on the dot.'

Annie sat quietly for the rest of the journey feeling cheated and slightly apprehensive. By the time they arrived at the airfield she was suffering from a bad case of travel sickness. She tried to ignore the urge to retch as the truck swerved to a halt outside of headquarters, where a large group of ferry pilots were assembled, smoking and talking.

'You can all come in now,' a voice announced, as a man poked his head out of an open window.

The ATA assembly room had not been designed for such an unlikely scenario and was not sufficiently spacious to accommodate all of the pilots. As a last minute arrangement, chairs had been removed and hurriedly stacked outside in the corridor, to make space for everyone to squeeze inside and stand as they were addressed. An hour later there was much disgruntled whispering as the pilots began to disperse, with a reminder bellowing out from a low platform at one end of the room by their commanding officer.

'Remember all of you, careless talk costs lives!' Please make sure those words are etched in your mind!'

Most of what the commanding officer had said seemed doom-laden in Annie's eyes, from the second that she had been instructed that three hundred Spitfires and Hurricanes were to be collected and delivered to various airfields before dark, without fail.

Annie could feel the trepidation grinding away in her stomach, which still had not recovered from the dash to the airfield in Nina's truck.

Annie jostled for space in the confined locker room, sardined by experienced pilots scrabbling in their lockers more eager than her to get on their way. She had no desire to be first or last to arrive at Westland, Castle Bromwich or any other airfield or maintenance depot in the UK. Her preference was to be snuggled in Lenny's arms, asleep or otherwise occupied and unaware of all the sudden activity.

The Anson she had been allocated to was full to capacity with a few familiar faces as well as some that she did not recognise. Taxiing out to the grass runway in a long procession of other taxi aircraft, it bumped along the grass runway, adding to her nausea, and took off climbing more steeply than was usual, close behind other ferry planes. At a few thousand feet the planes broke formation, fanning out and heading off to various pick up points with the blood-red morning early morning sun glinting on the fuselages.

Annie sat quietly, disengaged from the other pilots, wondering whether she was the only person on board not to have flown a Hurricane or Spitfire. She looked around the crowded cabin at the noisy pilots, all of whom were making a good show of appearing unperturbed by the demands that had been made of them. With the exception of a young mousy-haired woman who sat looking out of the window for the entire journey biting her nails, there were no visible nerves on display as the pilots laughed at each other's jokes. Annie recalled how she had felt on her first trip to pick up the Lancaster with Nina and Bertha. She suddenly realised how, that now she had become much more self-assured, she no longer resembled anything like the young girl huddled opposite. Despite this knowledge, she began to pray for a problem with the Anson, one that would not be life-threatening so as to alarm everyone, but sufficiently worrying enough to make the pilot turn back. However, the powers that be were not looking out for Annie on this particular morning. In no time at all, the plane banked over, allowing her a clear view of the airfield they would soon be touching down at.

Once on the ground, the unusually long queue of pilots took a considerable time to process their chits. The mousy-haired girl hung back and Annie found herself pitying her anxious expression.

'Are you all right? You didn't say anything up there,' she enquired. 'I'm Annie by the way.'

'I'm Rose,' the girl replied. 'Actually, I'm feeling awfully sick. I think it's my nerves. You see I was under the impression we had to undergo some sort of training.'

Rosie's words mirrored those uttered by Annie only a week previously.

'Well you must have had some. How many hours have you got?'

Rose leant over towards Annie and whispered in her ear.

'Only around a hundred or so, and that was a while ago.'

'Oh my goodness! How did you get accepted?'

'I lied, and they were so busy I slipped through the system. I wish I hadn't lied. I got carried away with the glamour of it all.'

'You'll be fine,' said Annie trying to reassure Rose. 'It'll all come flooding back, you'll see.' Annie felt instantly relieved that she was not the only one squirming.

'I hope you're right. My instructor said I was a natural. Do you think I should tell them?'

'And get thrown out?'

'Yes.'

'Just tell them you're nervous. You won't be the first pilot to feel the way you do. If it makes you feel any better, I haven't flown a Spitfire or Hurricane before.'

'Really?'

Rose moved forward in the queue alone with her thoughts. When it was Annie's turn to hand over her chit, she was about to protest to the station sergeant about being thrown in at the deep end when he stopped her in her tracks.

'Oh yes, young lady. I've had a call about you and another new recruit. We really don't have the time today, but you'll both need a few hours familiarisation before you're allowed to deliver the planes.'

'That must be me, the other new recruit,' said Rose, raising a hand meekly from behind Annie's right shoulder. 'I only joined two days ago.'

'Well girls, let me tell you, none of us expected anything of this scale. You poor ladies wouldn't be in this dilemma under normal circumstances.'

Apart from a few pilots queuing behind Annie and Rose, the rest of the pilots had already filtered off to make their usual checks and get their allocated planes off the ground quickly. Annie and Rose were sent off to the far end of the sprawling airfield to a vast grey hangar where various planes were standing ready for collection.

'What did he mean?' said Rose finally, having walked in silence until they approached the hangar.

'The CO? I think he meant we should have been up in a Spitfire before being asked to fly one this soon. I suppose they're forced to use everyone they can to get the job done.'

'Well I'm not sure I'll be able to get the darn thing off the ground, let alone keep it in the air,' said Rose, looking in dismay at the line of high-powered creatures of destruction.

A rosy-faced man in overalls, aged around fifty, suddenly appeared from under a wing of a Hurricane.

'Ready to have some fun?' he asked, laughing at Rose who was still standing with her mouth hanging open.

'I can think of other things that would be more fun than this,' commented Annie brusquely.

'Me too,' added Rose, visibly shaking with fear.

'You're in good hands. We'll have you off the ground in no time at all. Trust me,' said the man, who introduced himself as Robin. 'These planes are valuable. I won't allow you to take them unless I'm really sure you can handle them. Now pay attention.'

Annie and Rose remained silent as Robin led them through the controls and order of operation and flight checks. He was rigorous in his training methods down to every last nut, bolt and rivet, and talked about the planes as though they were friends of his, likening the Spitfire to wearing a well-tailored suit. He emphasised that the Spitfire could almost fly itself, and pilots often commented how it seemed to naturally hug one in all the right places. He made light of its little foibles in an attempt to relax Annie and Rose, making no attempt to rush them prematurely into the air, despite his earlier glib comment. His patience and methodology disguised any reservations he might have had about sending them to certain death that sunny afternoon. He stood on the wing as they both took turns to sit in the cockpit and get a feel for the controls. By the time they had mastered the dashboard, taxiing, read all the pilots notes and received the answers to their long list of questions, the last of the planes had taken off, leaving just the two Spitfires champing at the bit.

'Who wants to go first?' he asked out of the blue.

'I'd rather not,' said Rose in her high-pitched voice.

'Once you've done it once, you'll never look back. It's a piece of cake.'

'I'm not convinced,' said Annie.

'Look, like I've already said, the hardest bit is take off. Once you're up there you will love it, believe me.' He looked at his watch. 'We've got time to do take offs and bumps, then you're on your own. I want to be sure you make it well before dark.'

Rose looked at Annie for a get-out option.

'Okay, I'll go first,' said Annie, surprised at her own courage.

'Good. That's my girl. Get kitted up and we'll get you on your way.'

Rose helped Annie, talking incessantly to mask her jangling nerves.

'Good luck. See you at the other end then,' she said, self-doubt obvious in her voice. She sat on an oil drum outside the hangar as Robin cross-examined Annie: testing her on everything he had drilled into her over the last few hours.

'Perfect,' he said once he was satisfied. 'You've remembered more than most of the new pilots. 'Now let's see you put it into practice.'

As Annie checked over the outside of the plane and climbed onto the wing for a second time, she could finally appreciate why Robin had spoken the way he had with such affection. The Spitfire was perfectly put together: compact, elegant and graceful, but Annie was not naïve. She realised that the Merlin engine harboured a power she had yet to come to grips with. She recalled stories thrust upon her by Tom of his relatives' escapades in combat and the might and air superiority of the Spitfire. She wished she had paid more attention at the time, and hesitated as she climbed into the cockpit, sniggering at the thought of Tom's expression if he were able to see her now.

'What's so funny?' asked Robin.

'Oh nothing,' replied Annie. 'Just my nerves getting the better of me.'

'Well try and focus on the job in hand, and do everything I've told you so I can sign you off.'

Once inside the cockpit again and less flustered than the first time, Annie began to relate to Robin's comparison of the plane to a well-tailored suit. The cockpit was snug and the controls all within easy reach. She wondered how some of the men managed to fit in it at all; it seemed more suited to a woman's frame. Having done her checks and ready to prime the Merlin engine, and with a second check outside done, she shouted.

'Clear prop.'

She pressed the booster coil and start button simultaneously. The propeller began to turn and a feeling of exhilaration coursed through her body, all fear forgotten as she felt the rush of surging adrenalin. As she waved the chocks away the smell of the engine began to fill the cockpit. The vibration from the twelve cylinders alerted all of her senses as she let the brakes off and began taxiing. Weaving gently so as to see anything in her path, she prepared for take off. For a brief second Robin's words became a muddle of confusion in her overloaded brain: all order of things forgotten. She knew she couldn't hang around for long, remembering Robin emphasising that rising engine temperatures were not recommended: Spitfires impatient to be airborne. She pointed the nose into the wind, dictating orders out loud to herself as she opened the throttle; reinforcing her newfound knowledge, knowing that nobody could hear her above the deafening noise. The plane thundered down the bumpy runway, Annie's heart in her mouth, her body feeling the vibrations coursing through her excited steed. For a split second she hesitated, the urge to abort take off overwhelming. Before she could apply the brakes, the realisation hit her that she had already left the ground and that the grass was slipping away beneath.

The flight test was carried out with her being acutely conscious of every decision and application carried out methodically by her hands and feet, but simultaneously she felt strangely detached as though she was looking down on someone else in the cockpit operating the controls as she had in the Tiger Moth. Oblivious to everything apart from the sound of the powerful Merlin engine and the responsive controls, the bumping and taking off again felt not dissimilar to the Moth. She had no time to consider the fundamental differences as her final landing came all too soon. Robin waited with crossed arms next to Rose who looked like a tiny doll perched on the oil drum. He marched purposefully towards Annie as the plane came to a final stop in front of him and she shut down the engine.

'That's good enough to get you home,' he said as she jumped down from the wing, her legs trembling like jelly. 'Your landing needs a bit of brushing up, you were a trifle too fast coming in.'

'Yes, I did struggle a bit. I'm sure I forgot a few things.'

'You'll remember if your life depended on it,' he laughed.

'Thanks for that snippet, but I hope I won't have to make a decision based on that knowledge.'

'Well off you go, you don't need to go round again. It should take you an hour to Duxford - nice long runway there!' Robin dismissed her lightly with no further comments.

Rose seemed to shrink as Robin walked purposefully towards her, willing herself to disappear through the filler cap in the top of the oil drum.

Chapter 42

Annie was about to master what most normal people would never have dreamed possible; with only a few hours of intense instruction bolted onto her recent ATA training and flying experience from flights with her late grandfather. The Spitfire thundered down the runway for a second time, but this time Annie's new found confidence was invisibly emblazoned deep inside her chest behind her ATA badge.

For no apparent reason, a quick flash of Carlotti's entered Annie's mind. She chuckled at the comparison of her normal working week to what she was doing now. Her life in the twenty-first century was just a distant memory that was fading by the day. She immediately pushed such thoughts away as she realised the Spitfire was airborne. Instinctively, she retracted the undercarriage, placing all her trust in the worthy Merlin engine. The Spitfire seemed to climb independently of her hands and feet making adjustments to cope with a slight side wind that had sprung up. Annie compared the plane to a thoroughbred racehorse, eager to show her its true colours as it bolted across the sky.

As Annie looked down at the airfield slipping away beneath her, she gave herself a proverbial pat on the back, knowing that she could stand tall if she managed to deliver the plane safely.

She began to relax and enjoy the sensations that the Spitfire delivered, whilst closely monitoring the perfect azure sky for any other planes, friendly or otherwise. It occurred to her whilst she was doing this, that her main weakness was her lack of ability to differentiate between British and German planes at a distance. At close range, she was fairly confident she would be able to tell the difference, by which time she might be in danger.

Annie headed southeast for Duxford, reluctantly ignoring the urge to fly straight back to Lenny, leaving the Midlands far behind. She pitied Rose being the last to head south and wondered how she was getting on under Robin's expert instruction. She surmised that by the time Rose got off the ground she would need to use daylight wisely, otherwise it would be too dangerous for her to complete her journey. It was clear to Annie that Rose was a timid character who would find being alone in fading daylight a daunting prospect.

With the exception of a corridor of barrage balloons floating like giant sea creatures in the east, and a few aircraft that were so far away that they were nothing but specks in the sky, Annie's flight to Duxford was trouble-free. As she began to prepare herself for descent she scanned the countryside ahead looking for the airfield. She knew very little about her destination apart from the information she had gleaned from other ferry pilots. As a frontline airfield, suffering many attacks from the German air force, Duxford held its own, being well placed for the RAF to get off the ground quickly when necessary. Annie recalled that Robin had mentioned that it had a long runway. She wondered whether he had mentioned it partly to reassure her due to her approach speed and height being a bit misjudged earlier in the day.

Trying to keep the plane steady and level, at the same time she checked her maps for landmarks and immediately realised that she was on course: her map-reading skills having improved tenfold. Railways and rivers seemed to be in the anticipated places.

The English countryside undulated below, like a woven tapestry consisting of fields, farms and scattered villages. Cornfields and poppies competed against each other in vibrancy; their reds and yellows splashed across a metaphorical canvas with a huge paintbrush. This was England at its best on a magnificent summer's day. Annie considered that foreign travel was wasted, there being nothing to compare to the counterpane of small hamlets boasting church steeples poking sharply upwards and the meandering rivers that stretched away into the hazy distance.

She thought of Lenny again, and wondered whether he had slept well, or whether he had lain in bed and yearned for her as much as she had for him. The thought of his warm naked body teased her already heightened senses, adding to the pleasure she was already experiencing.

No other planes interrupted the unblemished and perfect sky. No clouds threatened to tumble down from the north to compromise her flight. Instead, the sun beat down mercilessly on the Perspex canopy, the fumes from the engine beginning to make her feel a little nauseous. She opened the canopy a crack and took a deep breath of summer air. Realising how easy it could be to overshoot the airfield due to her mind wandering, Annie folded the map and turned her attention back to the Spitfire as it purred through the sky.

As she took the plane down a few hundred feet, a shadow flitted across the ground below: the Spitfire perfectly etching its path with a black replica of itself across the fields of corn and wheat. Suddenly another flash of black also made an imprint on the fields below as it mingled for a few seconds with the shadow of the Spitfire. Annie meticulously scanned the sky immediately around her, shielding her eyes from the brilliant sun with her hand. With no other plane in sight, she flew on, assuming the sun had played a trick on her, distorting the shadows of trees or buildings.

In the distance the sky was busier: unidentifiable planes descending and taking off a few miles to the southeast. Annie took out her map again and checked her location. Duxford lay ahead. The landing strip was just about visible from her vantage point: a long grey strip dividing two rectangular fields a couple of miles ahead.

Annie suddenly sensed that something was amiss. Even with her inexperience, she recognised an ME109 as it came at her from out of the sun. The German plane banked over and circled around until it was behind the Spitfire. Annie realised it would take her only a few minutes to reach Duxford if she maintained her present course, but she realised that if she increased her speed she might jeopardise her landing. She felt like a sitting duck with no weaponry on board to protect herself. Feverishly searching the ground in every direction for a nearer place to put down, Annie did not notice the ME109 disappear until it suddenly appeared again, this time racing up towards her from below, arcing up into the sky in a show of acrobatic skill. It seemed as though the pilot was biding his time by taunting her and enjoying the thrill of the hunt before he opened fire. Annie realised he would have been observant and noticed that she was unarmed, so he could take his time and pick his moment.

Then as suddenly as her enemy had appeared, they were no longer the only two aircraft, more shadows appearing on the fields below. Travelling in the same direction as Annie, she instantly recognised them as Spitfires by their elliptical wings. They joined the fray. Annie could clearly see the face of one of the pilots on her starboard side, as he was perilously close. He waved his hand in the direction of Duxford as if to tell her to get on her way, and then he peeled off abruptly, banking and climbing steeply before flying rapidly away in pursuit of the German plane. The other Spitfires were already engaged in combat.

Joining in the battle was not part of Annie's job description and in any case she knew her limitations. To fly with the same skill as the three pilots who had come to her aid was something she could only dream of, and if she stayed with them she was a liability. With the airfield less than a mile away, and despite being protected to a certain extent, she began to feel panicked and extremely vulnerable. She began her descent, her control of the plane somewhat erratic as a result of her fear of the dangerous situation unfolding around her. The sound of cannon fire between the Spitfires and the ME109 was uncomfortably close. Annie sought solace in the fact that the German pilot was clearly outnumbered. He seemed to have no back up.

With only half a mile to go and five hundred feet off of the ground, the situation abruptly changed. More enemy planes appeared. In her panic, Annie had failed to spot them as they flew from out of the sun. All but one joined the battle. A German gun strafed her left wing as the pilot turned his attention on Annie with the intention of finishing what his comrade had started. Scared senseless and totally unprepared, Annie knew that he would continue to fire on her before she could reach the airfield. She could not bale out, being too low for her parachute to open. Added to this, her Spitfire felt odd and unstable now that air was being forced through the large holes in the wing making a sound not unlike a whistling kettle. Just as Annie held her breath in anticipation of more cannon fire, a gap appeared in some trees close by. Reflex responses kicked in. The gap was narrow but she dived towards it, her wing tips almost brushing branches as she rapidly lost height. Too late and with only fifty feet to go she realised that she had forgotten to put her wheels down. The belly of the plane impacted, groaning as it slewed sideways. She regained her senses and cut the engine and the plane came to an abrupt stop as the propeller buckled and dug into the ground.

Without waiting for the German to strafe her again, she hauled her bruised and shaken body from the Spitfire in case a heavy landing had ruptured the fuel tank. If she were to be fired at again, the plane could go up in seconds. The whining sound of another distressed plane came from behind the trees. The ME109 that had fired at her appeared skimming the treetops; angry flames and black smoke belching backwards engulfing the entire fuselage. Annie watched as he attempted to land. The German pilot stood no chance. Blinded by the inferno consuming his badly mutilated plane, the ME109's approach was steep, fast and erratic. Despite his wheels being down, they dug into the ground, snapping off like matchsticks with the sudden impact. The ferocity of the fire increased tenfold as the propeller twisted into a grotesque shape and the fuselage tipped momentarily onto its nose before flopping back down. The canopy was flung open and with black smoke belching from inside, a man struggled free from the carnage. Most of his upper body was scorched, his brown flying suit blackened and smoking. He fell from the wing and rolled his body around on the grass, putting out flames licking around his shoulders and head. Annie was paralysed by the shock of the spectacle, which suddenly caused her to liken the man to the orange-haired attacker in her nightmares. The German staggered away from the burning wreckage, his clothes still smoking, and badly injured, disappeared into the undergrowth.

For the sake of safety, Annie distanced herself from her own plane, and sunk to the grass. She watched the remains of the ME109 smoulder. Several of the Spitfires that had come to her aid swooped low overhead to inspect their gory conquest, executing victory rolls as they passed over Annie's head. Despite her gratitude that they had probably saved her life, she was gripped with a fleeting feeling of revulsion that they had celebrated shooting down another human being.

Still shaking and finding it hard to even walk, Annie looked around her for signs of any houses or the nearest road. Shock had set in. Her legs felt like jelly and the nausea she had experienced in the cockpit earlier returned tenfold. She knew that she needed to report her location and head for home. She hid her parachute in some brambles and abandoned the possibility of retrieving her belongings from the plane. Totally unworthy of flight, the Spitfire would remain exactly where it was. She headed for a farm gate at the far end of the field appreciating that Duxford, although only less than half a mile away as the crow flies was probably much further by foot.

Looking around for a place to rest, a ramshackle old building caught Annie's attention on the other side of the lane. Nestling derelict and forgotten in an overgrown garden, a white-washed stone cottage flanked by a variety of fallen-down outbuildings invited her in. Despite its charm, the cottage appeared to have not been lived in for years and was being used as a storage facility: bales of hay visible through the open windows. Although the building was debatably unsafe due to a gaping hole in the roof, half an hour's rest and the hope of a soft bed of hay appealed to Annie far more than a long trudge back to Duxford whilst still in shock. She opened the wrought iron gate and walked up the path.

Hanging off of its hinges, the front door was ajar. Just in case a farmer was working inside, Annie tentatively knocked on the door a few times. Satisfied that no one was around, she let herself in. To her relief, the sun streamed through the windows, which were on the whole, missing all their glass panes. As a result of this, there were no dark and sinister corners. Annie still felt very unsteady on her legs and looked around for a suitable place to sit. The stairs to the rooms above had partially collapsed and were cordoned off with a piece of thick rope between the wall and newel post. The interior smelt of hay and damp and was packed floor to ceiling with farm equipment. The room to the right of the small hallway seemed the most inviting; home to stacks of logs smelling of fir trees and a pile of relatively clean horse blankets. It seemed as good a place as any to rest until she was sufficiently recovered to go searching for directions to Duxford.

She made herself as comfortable as possible on the blankets. In no time at all she had fallen into a deep sleep, the shock of her ordeal draining her of any energy. She slept for about an hour, but it seemed to her that she had only had her eyes closed for a few moments when a sudden noise outside forced her eyes open. There was the sound of the garden gate being opened as its dry hinges squealed in protest, desperate for a few drops of oil. Whoever was walking up the path made no attempt to mask the sound of their heavy footsteps.

Annie sat bolt upright and looked for a corner to hide in, worrying whether the boots belonged to the owner of the property, and how she could justify her intrusion. Worst still, an angry farmer may have noticed the fragile front door pushed open and confront her with a pitchfork or shotgun.

She was still traumatised with the image of the burning man from the ME109 imprinted itself in her head, and was sure she could not cope with any more surprises.

With no visible place to hide in a hurry, Annie braced herself for the pitchfork attack, should she not get the chance to give the farmer a decent explanation. She realised that even if she were to take him to her crashed plane, she did not have a hope in hell of convincing him that a woman had piloted it. She imagined his words.

'Don't make me laugh, a young slip of a thing like you flying a Spitfire? Now bugger off and get off my land!'

A shadow flitted across the corner of the hallway.

'Who's there? asked Annie, aware that her voice sounded high-pitched.

Nothing in reply.

'Please, whoever you are. I can explain.'

A figure staggered and fell against the doorframe as he entered the room. His clumsiness caused the rotten door to fall apart and crash to the floor where it broke into several pieces.

'I'm sorry I trespassed. I'm only resting, I crashed my plane,' squeaked Annie breathlessly.

The light from the window silhouetted the man, causing Annie to take a few seconds to make out the grimace on his face.

'Thought you could get way from me, did you?' he growled in a deep guttural German accent.

He lunged at Annie with blistered and burnt hands that were as disfigured as his face. Bloodshot eyes bulged out of the molten skin, which appeared to be dripping from his face like hot wax. His flying suit hung charred and shredded, exposing a badly burned torso covered with angry weeping welts.

Screaming so loudly that the sound echoed throughout the cottage, Annie backed into the corner and pulled a horse blanket over her head and shoulders in a vain attempt to protect herself from attack.

'You all right, missy? I saw you come down in my field,' said a different voice, waking Annie up with a start, still wrapped in the blanket. It took a few seconds to focus on the man, who was much shorter than the one she had just dreamt about. He was not the ghoulish figure of the pilot who had disappeared into the woods, but a close likeness to the farmer she had imagined.

'You were 'avin' a bad dream. Don't know what you were shoutin' about though.'

Annie recalled her experience in the underground when the guard had woken her from her sleep.

'I'm so sorry. I'll leave straight away.'

'You stay right there til you feel well enough to move.'

Once the farmer had established who Annie was, he sat her next to him on the tractor she had wished for earlier, and took her to the nearest village. He said his goodbyes, and whilst waiting for the next train, the stationmaster supplied Annie with a cup of sweet tea and a bowl of warm water to clean the worst of the grease and grime from her face and hands.

She sat on the platform being watched by two men cleaning the platform and checking that fire buckets were filled appropriately. She pondered whether her life was to be plagued by near capture and lucky escapes, until the train pulled into the station with steam belching from its big green funnel chased such negative thoughts away. As the train pulled out of the station it passed the derelict cottage on its way to the next stop where she needed to disembark.

Annie wondered whether she was meant to survive the life she had been thrown into, or whether the unpleasant outcome was karma coming back for her.

Chapter 43

Due to Annie not arriving at Duxford, the news had quickly filtered through that she was missing, although one of the RAF pilots involved in the dogfight with the ME109 reported back that he had seen a woman climbing out of the stricken Spitfire when he had made a low level pass over the field. Margaret Bowhill had also been informed, but had decided to keep the news confidential until more details were received.

By the time early evening arrived however, Annie had been cleared fit to travel and the news that she was relatively unscathed forwarded on from Duxford ahead of her arrival.

Annie caught another train back, and with a brief stop via the airfield to verify her story she arrived back at the farm, having been given a lift by a flight engineer on his way home.

Her bruises were beginning to show and all of her body ached with the force of the impact. She thanked the engineer and limped across the courtyard, wishing for nothing more than the chance to lay in a warm bath. Noticing that the farm workers were still out in the fields, Annie slipped unnoticed into the kitchen, which was unusually deserted. Hoping for a quick passage to her room without being fussed over, she crept upstairs, trying to avoid squeaky floorboards and holding onto the banisters for support. To be asked about her lucky escape and quizzed about the badly burned German pilot was something she wanted to avoid. The vision of his panic as he fought to quash the flames would remain with her forever. As well as this, she knew that if she were to subsequently find out that he had died a lingering death alone in the woods, she would feel a huge sense of responsibility, having not gone to his aid.

Her room was cool and inviting. As Annie entered, she noticed a Red Admiral butterfly outside her window, repeatedly fluttering against the glass as though it was trying to get in. Annie remembered her mother telling her that butterflies were the souls of the dead offering reassurance and protection to the loved ones they had left behind. She opened the window to see if the butterfly wanted to enter, but after landing fleetingly on her hand it flew away. She dismissed her hope that the tale was true and that someone dear to her was trying to make contact.

She slipped out of her clothes and opted for satin against her skin, which instantly made her bruises slightly easier to bear without the weight of her uniform pressing against them. She noted how deserted the farmhouse seemed. Ever since she had unceremoniously arrived in the family's life via Betty's sidecar, the farm had as a rule always been full of the sound of people coming and going. On this evening however, she welcomed the quietness that made her feel as though a soft protective blanket protected her, cocooning her from the outside world.

She gazed out of the window, over the roofs of the outbuildings to the fields beyond. Small dots moved around the fields, digging and stacking bales, whilst birds flocked around a tractor as it trundled up and down. The scene reminded her of a traditional oil painting, romanticising life in the countryside.

Moving away from the window, she sat down on the end of her bed, ignoring the gathering pain that surfaced at the slightest movement. She lay back, thinking how safe she felt knowing that the farmhouse was partially protected from intruders by the people working on the land. As she had this thought, she realised that men from the twenty-first century suddenly seemed on the whole, less attractive. For the first time, the concept of attending a gym to get fit seemed a poor substitute compared to the hard labour that men and women endured in the factories and fields during the war. As she lay there, she struggled to think of a man she could categorise favourably with the men she had come to know in the war. As she imagined the businessmen she mixed with during her working day: working on their computers, talking loudly on their mobile phones, or driving their executive cars, she felt repulsed by their greedy lifestyles. They had no clue what it was like to struggle on a daily basis just to stay alive, and she wondered how many would fall by the wayside if they were plunged back in time.

Her thoughts switched to Tom. Even he had no real idea about hardship despite his ability to talk about the past with great reverence. That was easy to do from a distance. Hiding behind a wall of respect for dead relatives did not make him any more of a man than the business types that made up most of her address book. She realised that if she were to return to that life, it would be nigh impossible to find a man that she respected knowing what she did now. She belonged at Lillian's farm in a life she had only known for a short time. Whether she was asleep and dreaming or in a parallel dimension was of no consequence. She had made an important contribution, rather than just taken. She was unashamedly regretful of her past over-indulgence and shallow views.

Voices suddenly filtered into Annie's room through the open window, the sound of workers coming back from the fields jolting her out of her daydream. As they noisily piled their pitchforks and spades into one of the outbuildings beneath Annie's window, she continued to lay on the bed, too bruised and battered to bother to take a look. She imagined Daphne would be with the rest of the workers, and that she would undoubtedly throw a scathing glare up at her window. Annie pushed the thought away and instead considered instead how she wished she could stay where she was until the morning and dream of better things than Daphne's jealousy. Nevertheless, the urge to see Lenny was already overruling her urge to sleep, and she began to consider whether she could make herself presentable to him considering how fragile she felt.

The dialogue outside the window faded as the workers made their way round to the kitchen for supper. Annie decided to remain quietly in her room, not wanting to alert anyone to the fact that she had returned. She waited, slipping quietly in and out of a light sleep. Much later, she was woken by a sudden clatter of noisy shoes on the staircase and landing as goodnights were said and doors closed. A few moments later when all was silent again, she crept along the landing, reasonably convinced that people were settled for the night. She was eager to wash all evidence of the day from her aching body. The floorboards creaked all the way to the bathroom, as though they wanted to reveal her whereabouts, convincing Annie that her presence would certainly be given away.

The bathroom was as cool as Annie's room. It was compact, square and basic with a tiny window that had been left open by the last person to use it. The sweet smell of honeysuckle from outside the window filled the room with a heady scent. The walls were painted with white emulsion that had begun to peel away. The taps always squeaked. Annie slowly turned on the bath taps, remembering how once the water was running, the pipes made peculiar noises. She listened for movement but could hear nothing but rustling from animals in the sheds below.

Ignoring the rule that she should use the hot water sparingly, she allowed the bath to fill to capacity. Being the last to need it that night, she could indulge herself. She slipped off the satin robe and looked at her naked body in the mirror, noticing the bruises dotted all over her body, and again also how she had put on a little weight. Looking at herself from several angles, she decided that her newfound curves suited her far more than the much leaner body she used to possess. Rationing had made little impact on the quality of life in the countryside. Despite her satisfaction at the shape of her body, the strain of her ordeal showed in her face. As she studied her complexion, she could still see the fire in her eyes that Tom had mentioned. Full lips kissed her back from the tiny mirror.

As Annie stepped gingerly into the bath, immersing herself in the hot water, the smell of the honeysuckle washed over her. The lack of modern bubble bath did not seem to matter. Humming a tune she did not recognise, she relaxed back in the bath, her hair floating in the water like a mermaid's long tresses around her face. The tapping in the pipes still persisted.

She looked up at the dusty glass lampshade that hung modestly on a plaited lighting flex from an old Bakelite ceiling rose. A spindly-legged spider negotiated a single strand of silk spun from the shade to a corner of the ceiling. There was a time when she would have found its presence abhorrent and not cared if he had met a watery death, but now she felt relief as he reached the safety of a crack in the ceiling.

The noise in the pipes startled her as it suddenly got much louder and more constant.

Tap, tap, tap.

She sat up and touched the pipes, which ran along the side of the bath and up the corner of the bathroom wall, but there was no apparent vibration.

Tap, tap, tap.

She turned off the hot water tap, hoping that once the water stopped flowing that it might cure the problem.

'Annie, is that you in there?' whispered a man's voice as someone tapped again on the door.

'Yes,' she answered, taken back by the sound of Lenny's voice and realising at the same time where the tapping noise had come from. Her heart began to pound.

'Can I come in?' he asked, still whispering.

'Give me a...'

Without waiting for her to finish her reply, Lenny entered, quietly closed the door behind him. He sat on the stool next to the bath facing Annie.

Annie blushed, with no bubbles to camouflage her nudity. She instinctively pulled her knees into her chest to try and hide her breasts.

'Do you usually enter the bathroom when you know someone is in the bath?' she demanded.

'Never!' he said, with a boyish grin. 'That is, until now. Would you rather I wait in your room?'

'No you can stay,' she answered, uncertain of her own body in the harsh light from above.

His eyes ran over the parts of her that he could see. He noticed how her hair, which was much darker when wet, clung to her olive skin camouflaging her breasts.

'I heard about today,' he said, reaching forward and stroking her face. 'Those bruises must hurt,' he added, studying her purple knees and arms.

Annie was still trying to hide her nakedness and found it hard to string words together.

'I think my pride hurts more,' she admitted, making light of her injuries.

'You did well to put the kite down in circumstances like that.'

'Thanks,' said Annie, still struggling to make any conversation. She averted her eyes for fear of giving away her vulnerability.

'I hear an ME109 came down in the same place. Bit of a mess by all accounts.'

Annie shivered at the memory.

'I'd rather forget it.'

'It's jolly hot in here.' Lenny removed his jacket and tie and pushed the window open a bit more.

Annie noticed how his shirt was already clinging to his body. Tiny beads of sweat were forming on his forehead. She could see the outline of his shoulders through the shirt and she instantly wanted to invite him to take all of his clothes off and join her in the bath. He wiped his forehead with his sleeve and sat down again. His blue eyes pierced her armour as they always did. She began to cry. Instantly he fell on his knees and pulled her close, not caring about getting his clothes wet.

'What is it darling? I'm here. Nothing's going to hurt you.'

She nestled into his chest searching for his heartbeat.

'I'm sorry. I don't even know why I'm crying.'

'I do. You've been through an ordeal, my darling.'

He released his hold and gently massaged the back of her neck and shoulders with his strong hands. Then he kissed her neck and throat tenderly.

'Just imagine the consequences if you'd tried to reach Duxford. You'd have been shot down before you made it there.'

He continued to kiss her neck. Still clutching her knees to her chest, she responded eagerly, pressing her lips to his.

Annie was no weight in Lenny's capable arms as he plucked her from the bath, and sat her gently on the wooden window ledge. His sudden demonstration of strength and passion made her gasp. She abandoned her modesty and flicked her wet hair away so it hung dripping down her back.

Lenny began to kiss her shoulders and the base of her neck, slowly working his way down her body.

She let out a gasp.

'Do you want me to stop?' he asked.

'No.'

She put her index finger to his lips as if to silence him and unbuttoned his wet shirt. Trembling at the sight of his bare chest, she was oblivious to anything else apart from a fleeting realisation that before this moment she had never genuinely made love and that sex had been a meaningless waste of time and energy.

'We must be quiet,' whispered Lenny, hesitating before hurriedly removing the rest of his clothes.

Annie was acutely aware that to begin with, Lenny was holding back his emotions for fear of being overheard. As he pressed hard against her in rapid thrusting moves, he buried his face in her soaking wet hair, as if to do so would mask the sound of his desire for her. She wrapped her legs around his hips, forgetting the pain of her injuries in the few brief moments of their passionate lovemaking, positioning herself to allow him to be as deep inside her as possible. He began to tremble as the intensity of the moment gathered momentum. He gripped her thighs tightly to prevent her wet body from slipping out of his grasp, avoiding the bruises, which were clear to see. He cupped his hand over her lips to diminish the sound of her cries of ecstasy as she became lost in the final climax.

Annie cried again when the tension went out of Lenny's body and he pulled her close in a loving embrace.

'I'm sorry, did I hurt you?' he asked, wiping her tears away.

'No...I'm crying because it was so wonderful.'

'For me too,' he added, wrapping her protectively in a large towel.

After checking there was no one on the landing, he carried her to his room and lowered her gently onto his bed as though she were made of priceless porcelain. His room offered them a temporary sanctuary, as they shared moments of tenderness and moments of frenzied passion. For several hours they looked into each other's eyes making unspoken promises, before slipping into a deep sleep, drenched in perspiration, wrapped in each other's arms.

In the early hours of the following morning, Annie woke suddenly to what sounded to her like the door closing. She had dreamt of their night together and woke thinking it was just a dream. Realising that it was real, in her half sleep she reached over to put her arm around him. In only seconds it dawned on her that he was not there. She sat up quickly to see a simple brief note was propped up on the dressing table opposite.

Darling, I'll be back as soon as I can. Urgent op. I love you. Yours forever. Lenny x

She studied the words several times and moved to his side of the bed, clutching the note and falling asleep again as she savoured the space that was still warm from his body.

Chapter 44

When Annie woke again, the note from Lenny was still in her hand. She savoured his masculine scent on the sheets and pillowcases. She slid out of bed and ran her fingers across the fabric of Lenny's striped pyjamas, still neatly folded on the bedside chair.

His room was plain and functional, and much larger than hers, the walls painted a soft shade of eau-de-nil. As well as the large comfortable bed, a walnut dressing table with matching wardrobe and a green velvet Edwardian chair furnished the room. There was also a cast iron fireplace inset with art nouveau tiles that decorated either side of the unused fire- basket. On the mantelpiece, an ad hoc collection of faded sepia photographs of people Annie didn't recognise vied for space.

Annie waited until she was sure there was nobody moving about on the landing, and then she wrapped herself in the damp towel from the night before and crept back to her room, aware with every movement that she was stiffer than the previous day. She examined her bruises in her mirror and noticed that they had turned to a deep shade of purple and that she had a few cuts and grazes that she had not noticed previously. She washed and dressed, wincing with pain every time her clothing brushed against her wounds.

As Annie went about her normal daily routine, she was aware that it was a concerted effort to remember the procedures regarding ferrying planes that by now that she was well rehearsed in. Nevertheless, she managed to keep up with the busy delivery schedule, so much so that, by the time she did her third pick up late in the afternoon from Castle Bromwich, she began to feel a little less preoccupied. As she flew south again, she thought of the invisible thread that connected her to Lenny contracting again as she came into land for the final time. For some reason, she found it harder than usual to imagine, but chose to put it down to her weariness.

It was almost dark as Annie touched down, so she followed the ATA guidelines for that airfield and left her first Hurricane by the perimeter fence rather than taxi to a hangar. A few other late arrivals had already done the same: a neat line of Spitfires and Hurricanes lining the high metal fences that were topped with barbed wire.

She made her way by foot back to headquarters with her heavy parachute slung over one shoulder. The gravel crunched beneath her feet on the narrow pathways and ten minutes later she approached the first of the airport buildings. The various huts, offices and hangars huddled together in a compact area to the south of the airfield. As Annie passed Lenny's usual spot, a few other men were seated in the semi darkness, waiting for orders to scramble. They looked up at her as she passed but seemed too engrossed to make conversation with her.

Lenny's wicker chair was empty, sitting in its usual place a little apart from the others, tucked round the corner of one of the dispersal huts. Annie was always aware of an ominous feeling in the pit of her stomach that she had to force to one side whenever she passed his vacant seat. She also found it difficult to get used to the fact that there seemed to be a constant flow of new faces, replacements for those who had not come back from their nightly sorties. She looked again at Lenny's empty seat and wondered where he was and when he would be back. Without him seated on the chair sketching, the chair seemed forlorn. She dismissed the notion that a chair could have feelings and continued on.

Taking the route that Nina used when in a hurry, which was a short cut back to headquarters, Annie began to weave her way between the buildings, which were by now familiar and friendly even in the dark. As she walked through the long damp grass, soon she could make out headquarters', the slate-tiled roof glinting in the moonlight, and a tiny chink of light shining through one carelessly drawn black-out curtain. She was almost clear of the long grass when she suddenly heard a dog's deep growling close by. She froze, trying to pinpoint where the noise was coming from. She was terrified. The growling seemed to be coming from all around her, but she put this observation down to her fear. Headquarters seemed suddenly much further away, unreachable even though her path was well lit by the moon. She felt cornered. The growling continued. Annie realised that the dog was not moving either, and assumed it was considering the best moment to attack. There seemed to be no solution to her predicament. If she ran, she had no hope of outrunning what was clearly a young healthy guard dog that had slipped its lead. On the other hand, if she stood still, he would undoubtedly smell her fear. All these thoughts took only seconds to consider and dismiss. Either course of action seemed very undesirable.

'Here boy,' came a voice suddenly from the darkness. 'What's bothering you?'

Annie immediately forgot her intent to move slowly, and spun round to see where the voice had come from, which was the worst thing she could have done. Burning red eyes were firmly fixed upon her, low down in the grass only a few yards away. Loud barking poured threateningly from a mouth full of long white teeth.

'Who goes there?' demanded a man appearing from out of the shadows shining a torch in Annie's face.

'Keep still. He won't attack unless I tell him to.'

The dog raised itself from its haunches and began to dance from side to side in a peculiar display of affection for the man.

'He doesn't like you much, miss,' said the dog-handler as he attached the lead to the dog's collar, roughly stroking his back.

The dog immediately stopped leaping around, and squatted down by the man's side, his long pink tongue lolling out of his open mouth and his eyes losing the fiery look they'd had a few seconds before. He remained in that position looking at Annie.

Annie wanted to shout at the man for letting the dog off of its lead but thought better of it.

'Not a good idea to go wandering around in the dark, miss,' said the man as he approached Annie. 'Best stick to the main path where you can be easily seen.'

The huge dog stood again and cowered behind the man.

'I will next time,' said Annie. 'I was a bit late so I took a short cut.'

'Not like him to act strange. He's a softie, not much of a guard dog if you ask me,' said the man stroking the dog affectionately again.'

'You could have fooled me. He scared me senseless. Anyway, you said something about him attacking if you ordered him to.'

'I had to say that. You could have been anybody. You know the old saying, his bark is worse than his bite? That's old Brutus here.'

The dog-handler said goodnight, then turned and walked back into the shadows with the dog following, nervously looking over its shoulder at Annie. She waited until they had receded into the darkness before she set off again, crossing the remaining open space as quickly as the weight of the parachute would allow. By the time she reached headquarters, had signed off and got a lift back to the farm, most people had retired for the night or were in the throes of doing so. She hadn't seen many of the family for several days, and Nina and Bertha had been sent off to other airfields.

Annie undressed and changed into some slacks and a blouse. She lay on the bed for a few moments and closed her eyes. Unable to settle and feeling restless, she went downstairs again. She had missed the evening meal but did not feel particularly hungry after her ordeal with Brutus. She wandered outside into the courtyard, which

433

was completely illuminated by the moon, hoping to meet a friendly face of someone else returning late as she had done.

She recalled a conversation with Tom when he explained how wartime pilots dreaded a full moon. He had told her how although the moon lit their way so well, it also made the slow and heavy bombers 'sitting ducks'. She realised that she barely thought of Tom anymore, and wondered whether it counted as being unfaithful having made love to Lenny in a different lifetime. She dismissed thoughts of Tom, instead studying the detail of the moon against the royal blue sky. Pigeons still cooed in the rafters of the barn, making her feel not entirely alone. She followed the sound of the pigeons and walked around the side of the house to where the chickens roamed freely in the mornings.

Annie climbed onto the fence that faced the field where Betty and the boys had raced around on motorbikes. Beyond that she could make out the field where she and Lenny had first held each other. She looked back at the house. The rooms were all in darkness, blackout curtains carefully drawn. Slow music was playing softly in one of the rooms, its dulcet tones flowing through an upstairs window that had been left open.

Suddenly, she was aware of a light coming on in her room momentarily flooding the yard. The figure of a man appeared at the window and hurriedly closed the blackout curtains.

Lenny was back. Annie ran indoors breathless with excitement. By the time she had raced upstairs and reached her bedroom door her heart was pounding in her chest. She burst in.

'Lenny! I'm so...' she started to say, but the words trailed away as she saw the strain on his face.

He was sitting on the polished wood window seat with just a bedside light illuminating his face.

Annie stopped half way across the room shocked by his appearance.

'What's happened to you? You look so pale. Let me hold you,' she said reaching out to him.

Lenny stood up and moved away from her.

'Please don't,' said Lenny. 'Don't come any closer.'

'What do you mean, don't come any closer? I love you, and I thought you loved me too,' she said, tears welling up in her eyes.

'I've come to tell you something,' he replied.

'It's over, isn't it? It was just a bit of fun for you,' she sobbed.

'Annie, how could you think that?'

'Well you're not doing a very good job of convincing me otherwise.'

'Look, this isn't easy, believe me,' he said, not reaffirming his love for her. 'Something happened early this morning not long after I left you. I thought you would've heard. I'll be away for a while, but I came to tell you I'll be back as soon as I can.'

Annie started to feel really uneasy.

'When will you be back?' she asked quietly.

'I've already told you, as soon as I can,' he repeated.

'You're frightening me. What is it, Lenny? You have to tell me! Some sort of top secret job you have to do?' Her legs began to tremble. 'Surely we can have a little more time before you go. Please hold me,' she begged.

'That will just make it harder for both of us.'

'Alright, but please get a message to me, just to let me know you are okay,' she said, tears streaming down her face.

'I am okay. Nothing will keep me from you.'

Annie stood motionless, and then the room began to swim in front of her. For a second she thought her legs were going to give way. She sat down suddenly on the edge of her bed and immediately the room began to tip upside down.

I don't feel too good. I think I'll just lay down for a minute.'

'I'll fetch Lillian,' said Lenny.

'No, don't go. I'll be all right in a minute,' said Annie, trying to postpone his inevitable departure. 'Don't worry her.'

As the room began to spin, Annie was aware of Lenny's face close to hers and his words echoing around the room.

'I'll always be here...I'll always be here...I'll always be here...'

Then Annie slipped into darkness.

When she awoke, the room was much colder and she was still fully dressed on her bed. Lenny had gone.

She remembered his reserve when she had tried to hold him. She began to sob again, and feeling distraught,

She went along the landing to Lillian's door, feeling it only fair to tell her of Lenny's departure. She knocked gently so as not to wake up the whole household. There was no answer. She knocked again.

'Lillian? It's Annie…sorry to disturb you.'

There was the sound of someone stirring and coming to the door. It opened a crack and Lillian peered out. She looked tired and drawn.

'I'm sorry to wake you, but can you come to my room for a minute,' asked Annie, speaking casually so as not to alarm Lillian.

'My dear, you've been crying. Let's get you back to bed and I'll make us a nice cup of cocoa.' Lillian slipped on a candlewick dressing gown and followed Annie along the landing. 'When you didn't come home I thought it would have to wait till the morning as it's so late.'

'What would have to wait,' replied Annie, facing Lillian as they entered her bedroom.

'Judging by your tears I thought you knew. Lenny's missing. He went down over the sea early this morning. We received the news this afternoon.'

Annie turned away and looked vacantly towards the window at the spot where she had dreamt Lenny had been sitting. She was confused as she could still smell Lenny's pipe tobacco still lingered on the air.

'But he was here…' Annie whispered as she fainted, her head hitting the floorboards hard as she fell.

Chapter 45

When Annie awoke, she was in bed. Her thoughts were woolly and muddled; her only areas of clarity being the memory of feeling like she had been on a fairground ride just as she had fainted, and more importantly, the devastating news that Lenny was missing. She was nevertheless sufficiently conscious enough to be aware of a blur of people coming and going and the fact that her head throbbed relentlessly. She struggled to sit up, which immediately made the room spin again.

'Don't do that dear,' said Lillian rushing to her side, and gently applying a cold compress to Annie's temple. 'You banged your head, poor thing. You must rest for a while until the swelling goes down.'

A feeling of nausea engulfed Annie.

'How long have I been out? I feel dreadful.'

'A couple of hours dear, it's not morning yet,' said Lillian, continuing to apply pressure to Annie's temple. 'But you have some colour back in your cheeks now. You'll be as right as rain in no time.'

'Is Lenny back?' asked Annie weakly.

'Don't you worry about Lenny, he'll be fine,' said Lillian, instantly changing the subject. 'The doctor has been, and he's insisted that you're to stay put and get some sleep.'

'I don't want to sleep. I just want to know where Lenny is.'

Lillian dodged the subject again.

438

'Sit up slowly this time and have a sip of water.' She plumped up a pillow and placed it behind Annie's head.

Annie was still finding it difficult to focus on her surroundings.

'Thank you.' Feeling very dehydrated, she drank most of the water that Lillian had offered her.

'That's it, dear. Help you sleep.'

'Oh no, what have you given me?' protested Annie. 'I must stay awake in case there's news.'

'It's just something to calm your nerves, dear. The doctor left it for you. Just close your eyes and rest. Before you know it, you'll be up and about.'

'You will tell me when Lenny gets back won't you?' asked Annie, almost immediately feeling her eyelids becoming heavy.

'Of course, dear,' said Lillian stroking her forehead gently.

'Come and tell me if you hear anything – anything at all.'

Annie's eyes flickered closed. She drifted in and out of a restless sleep, aware on her moments of waking that her headache had begun to subside and that she no longer felt sick.

Uncertain of who apart from Lillian was watching over her, Annie realised that her carers had mistakenly assumed she was asleep and as a result been careless with their whispered words. Realising from their conversation that Lenny had not been found was enough reason to keep Annie from caring about making a quick recovery. It wasn't until late morning that she felt inclined to open her eyes. She lay on her side and looked out of the window.

Black storm clouds scudded across the sky blocking out all evidence of summer. Heavy rain lashed against her window leaving diagonal streaks. There was to be no letting up in the storm, not that it mattered to her any more. During the hours that she had slipped in and out of consciousness, she had visualised Lenny's limp body being tossed around in a choppy grey sea: alone, cold as stone and lifeless, and nothing but a tiny dot in the massive ocean. Suspended in a life jacket preventing him from plummeting to the ocean floor, she imagined him been carried backwards and forwards by strong currents and smashed against jagged rocks. She pitied some unfortunate fisherman who might eventually be the one to pluck his broken body from the foaming waves.

Annie turned over, not realising that all the time she had been daydreaming, that Betty was asleep in an armchair by her bed. She was dishevelled but beautiful nonetheless, and had fallen asleep with a row of knitting uncompleted. After all the pain and suffering that she had endured as a result of Peter's sudden disappearance, Annie thought her peaceful demeanour was well deserved, especially as there had been little expectation at the time that Peter would reappear at all. Poor Betty had turned into a mad woman during those endless days of waiting. When Peter had eventually come home, he had been reasonably unscathed physically, but how he had felt psychologically was something that probably would only be revealed to Betty.

Nevertheless, Annie was fully aware of how different in personality she was to Betty, who was wonderful, kind and totally generous with her heart. Betty's gentle nature had made her vulnerable and unable to cope with the inevitable outcome of war. Had she been made of tougher stuff she may have better endured her emotional pain. As Betty stirred, Annie realised she was kidding herself and that she was as wounded and helpless as Betty had been. Her heart was breaking.

Betty opened her eyes and immediately sat up when she realised Annie was awake at last.

'Oh darling, we have been so worried about you,' she said, stroking Annie's hair.

'When did you get back? I'm so glad to see you.'

'An hour or so ago. I came straight up when I heard the news,' said Betty, her expression instantly changing to one of sorrow.

'Do you think Lenny's dead?' asked Annie suddenly, gauging Betty's reaction by the look in her eyes. Caught off guard by such an exacting question, Betty turned and looked out of the window before replying, not wanting to give her thoughts away.

'I don't know,' said Betty weakly, eventually looking back at Annie. 'I always believed that Peter was alive. What does your heart tell you, Annie?'

Annie thought for a moment, saying nothing as she revisited the scene of Lenny in the sea. It was hard to visualise his powerful responsive body with no heartbeat and his skin as cold as marble.

'When I think of him I see can see him as clearly as though he were here now,' she answered. At that precise moment, she decided to reject the horrible images that had been replayed since the early hours of the morning.

'Then you must hold on to that hope, darling.' Annie felt a stab in her chest at hearing the term of endearment until then only used by Lenny.

'It's all you have for now. You know that you can talk to me as much as you need to,' said Betty, stifling her own grief behind a sodden cotton handkerchief.

'Tell me about your honeymoon,' said Annie suddenly, realising she had omitted to ask. 'I need to hear some happy news.'

'It was lovely, but there's plenty of time to talk about that,' answered Betty. 'It wouldn't be right to go on about me and Peter when there is this hanging over us.'

She fussed around Annie, the personal pain not masked well in either of their faces, and then went to offer the same level of care to Lillian who was locked in her room.

Within a few hours, bored with staring out of the window at a rain-stricken panorama, Annie could endure bed rest no more. Taking her time at first to find her balance, she walked slowly backwards and forwards along the narrow landing outside Lenny's empty room and the bathroom where he had lost any remnants of self-control, imagining that she could hear his voice.

Eventually after another day of patrolling the farmhouse, during which time the thunder and lightning had seemed to be lamenting Lenny's absence: the rain stopped. The sky still refused to clear, remaining dull and grey, but the wind ceased buffeting the old house. The air became still and even the birds seemed quieter than usual.

Several days after her fall, the doctor called again and after examining Annie, declared her fit enough to resume her ferrying for the ATA. On her last day of rest and recuperation, she sat on her window seat considering the certainty that her life would never be the same again now Lenny had gone. The future stretched out before her like an endless parched desert. All colour seemed to have drained from the previously stunning view outside of her window. The undulating fields no longer waved their golden ears of corn as she stared vacantly at the spot where Lenny had made love to her. Wheat, barley and wild poppies stood row after row, like grieving servicemen on Remembrance Day. The grey sky stretched out to the horizon masking the distant hills like a heavy woollen blanket, which gave the air a distinctly oppressive feel.

Finally, Annie ventured outside and walked to the lush meadow beyond the barns, expecting the place where she had lain with Lenny to be exactly as she remembered it, the grass flattened by their entwined bodies. Instead, the grass stood erect and tall as though hiding the fact that lovers had been there: a cruel reminder of how time can erase anything. She returned to her room, thinking that there was no point being stranded in the early nineteen-forties, when all to be expected was loss and uncertainty. Equally, she did not want to back to the stagnant relationship she had with Tom. She argued with herself as to which was the lesser of the two evils, and finally decided that she would rather stay where she was, to wait for news of Lenny, good or bad, to reach her.

Betty was backwards and forwards between Annie and Lillian, sensing that Annie's despair was about to tip her over the edge into a realm she could not come back from. Annie recalled how Betty had never completely given up on the hope that Peter would return, and she kept that thought in the back of her mind when daydreams of Lenny floating in a vast, bitterly cold sea threatened to overwhelm her.

Later that afternoon, Betty took Annie into town. The journey in Betty's sidecar brought back the memory of the first day they had met at the airfield. So much had changed since Betty had screamed to a halt at the gatehouse, her wild red hair cascading around her shoulders. They passed the chapel where Betty and Peter had held their marriage service. Annie was unable to avert her gaze from the hawthorn tree where Lenny had stood and told her that she was beautiful.

'He's still with you,' said Betty, reading Annie's mind. 'I'll always remember the two of you standing under that tree.'

Annie did not respond. Numbness bandaged her emotions. She allowed Betty to lead her around the shops like a puppy on a lead. As she followed in her wake, she was deaf to the conversation that Betty made with her and the people they passed in the street. More images began to take shape in her mind, of herself sinking slowly to the bottom of the ocean where Lenny had been drifting. She too was slowly drowning: slipping into an unfathomable inky blackness. As she looked up at the surface of the water, she could see Lenny, still alive but weakened by his ordeal and the weight of his parachute, attempting to swim to shore. The sunlight pierced the water, silhouetting his body. Annie stretched up to reach for him with but with no life jacket to keep her afloat, her wet clothes weighed her down. As she continued to spiral downwards into the dark and cold, Lenny disappeared from view. With these ghoulish pictures replaying in her mind, she had not realised that she and Betty were back at the motorbike. She had no clear memory of the last couple of hours.

'A breath of fresh air is just what you needed,' said Betty, as she loaded provisions into the back of the sidecar.

'Yes, thank you, I really enjoyed it,' lied Annie.

'We must do it again soon. It's best to be busy. Before you know it, Lenny will be back.'

Annie suddenly broke down.

'It's no good Betty, I can't go on,' she said behind a wall of tears.

'Yes you can, and you must try to. Lenny would want that.'

Annie continued to cry.

'I can't bear to think of him never coming back.'

'Annie darling, he wouldn't want you to suffer like you are.'

'We had so little time together. What if I forget his face, or his voice?'

'You'll never forget, not feeling the way you do about him. Anyway, there is every reason to believe he'll be found. Now come on, let's get back to the farm. You need your rest for tomorrow.'

Annie clambered into the sidecar, trying to believe in Betty's words. She knew that Betty was right and that there was a chance that Lenny would be found. With this thought still only a weak hope in her mind, as they made their way back to the farm, Annie vowed to herself to try and adopt a more positive view.

On their return, Lillian came into the kitchen just as they were about to go to their rooms. She offered a weak smile and touched Annie's hand in passing, but chose to say nothing. Annie noticed that Lillian's hair seemed to have turned a more silvery shade over the last few days and that her expressionless face had an ethereal quality about it. Annie felt a pang of guilt because she had only considered her own grief. Lillian and Betty's hearts had been broken into many tiny pieces and she realised she had offered no words of comfort to either of them. She bowed her head in shame as she left the room.

It was an effort to prepare her clothes for the following morning, in the same way that simple tasks such as brushing her hair and washing had been since the shock had set in regarding Lenny. How she could be expected to fly a plane she had no idea, and a part of her hoped that the following morning when she arrived at the airfield that she would be declared in no fit state to do so. Nevertheless, if she was expected to fly, she had little regard for her own life anymore. One lapse in concentration and in seconds her misery could all be over.

She looked out over the yard again. The weather at least had improved. It was as though the sun was saying that it was time to move on and get over Lenny. In contempt, Annie closed the curtains, but a small amount of daylight persistently forced its way through a small hole in one of the blackout curtains. Small particles of dust danced lightly in the narrow shaft of light, making patterns on the paintings and faded photographs on her bedroom wall. The scenario reminded Annie of the day after her mother's death, when the sunlight had seemed to exercise some trickery by selectively lighting up the face of an angel in a painting on the lounge wall. Although a long time ago, she remembered how the moment had offered her much comfort, as the sun had seemed intent on lingering over the angel's face. It seemed like a message from her mother, to say she was somewhere safe.

No pictures of Lenny hung on Annie's wall. Apart from his crumpled message and a spent matchstick, she had nothing of his to cherish or to keep under her pillow at night. His bedroom lay untouched since the night he had disappeared, almost like an unsaid shrine to his memory. Lillian had been too traumatised to remove the sheets from Lenny's bed or to hang his freshly laundered shirts in his wardrobe. His door remained closed, the room undisturbed as though he had just popped out for a while. Annie thought for a few moments about the sanctity of Lenny's room, but could think of no reason why she could not go pay a brief visit, as long as she showed him the respect he deserved and left everything in its rightful place. She crept along the landing, every floorboard groaning, as if to announce that someone was about to enter a hallowed place.

Once inside his room, Annie closed the door quietly and turned the key. The bed had been left untouched; in disarray as it was after the climax of the precious few hours they had spent in each other's arms. A sparse collection of clothes hung expectantly in Lenny's wardrobe. Annie sat on the dressing table stool and carefully picked up Lenny's personal belongings, holding them lightly in her hands as though they were made of eggshells. In her hands, his possessions were worth more than gold bars. Dark hairs still clung to his ivory comb and a single spare car key attached to a leather fob embroidered with gold wings lay dejectedly in a porcelain dish.

Annie plucked a few hairs from the comb and wrapped them in a clean white handkerchief that she took from his drawer. She tucked it next to her heart thinking that if anyone had been watching, they should be forgiven for thinking that she was collecting items to cast a spell to bring Lenny back.

It was in Lenny's dressing table drawer that Annie found his grey well-used sketchbook, nestling amongst some folded clothes. It was tied closed with a leather cord through which was tucked a single pencil. She cupped the notebook in her hands and stroked its cover fondly. As she untied the cord and tentatively opened it, she recalled the memory of glamorous Glenda sprawled across a dispersal hut table. Annie wondered how she would react if she were to find pages filled with the images of beautiful women.

All of Lenny's illustrations were rendered in the soft graphite pencil that had been attached to the sketchbook. Detailed renditions of aircraft and portraits of servicemen filled the pages, with their names written in meticulous italic script beneath each sketch. Each image was interlaced with notes about the person or object. As well as the sketches, a few pages hosted sensitive poetry that Annie wondered if Lenny had composed. Her insecurity concerning pictures of women was ungrounded, as the sparse sketches of females were not depicted in the provocative poses that she feared. Despite such reassurance, disappointment began to cloud her thoughts as she turned the pages, as it seemed that Lenny had not been inspired enough to portray her. As she reached the end of the pad, she was nevertheless proved wrong. A sensuous sketch of her, sleeping with nothing but a thin sheet hugging her curves, had been rendered with skilful sweeping strokes. She closed the book, moved by Lenny's portrayal, and placed the book back in the drawer. She began to weep uncontrollably. Lenny had immortalised her on paper, his love flowing freely onto the page.

As she stood up to leave, the unexpected aroma of Lenny's woody tobacco again filled the air. Fearing for her own sanity, she left quickly, feeling suddenly cold, miserable and in need of some form of comfort.

Chapter 46

Annie ran a bath. She lay back in the warm water and tried to relax, knowing full well that no amount of pampering would make any difference to her state of mind. There was no cure for a broken heart, except perhaps the passage of time, although she doubted that in her case time would make any difference. The feeling of being cheated of happiness surged through her very being.

The woody fragrance of Lenny's pipe tobacco seemed to have travelled with her, and was at its strongest in the bathroom. She sat quietly, treating the aroma as some sort of sign, with a deepening conviction that Lenny might be dead. The last month or so had challenged all of her beliefs, so although it had not altered her conviction not to embrace God, she half-expected Lenny to materialise in whatever ghostly form he was able to adopt. Annie turned off the bath taps so she could listen for any subtle movement or sound that might suggest Lenny was trying to contact her, but there was nothing but the sound of water still dripping monotonously as the minutes passed by. Laying back again and closing her eyes, it was not long before she succumbed to sleep, drifting in a swirling pool of confused memories and wild imaginings.

Once again, Annie imagined that she was sinking in an inky sea, desperately reaching up towards Lenny as he floated on the surface supported by his life jacket. It seemed that every time she thought she might reach him, strong currents would mercilessly drag her downwards. The salt water stung her eyes as she attempted to focus on unfamiliar objects and get back to the surface. When she had almost given up hope, she became suddenly entangled in some debris, which began to tighten its hold. In doing so, it wrapped itself around her arm like a boa constrictor. In her panic, the more she struggled the tighter the coils became.

With one last concerted effort, and before her lungs filled with seawater, Annie made a last ditch attempt to break free from her bonds, surfacing unexpectedly into bright light. She gasped for air. Her eyes still stung, making it impossible to focus. She startled as the snake brushed against her again, but this time it seemed peculiarly lifeless as it floated benignly beside her. Nevertheless, panicking at its close proximity, she kicked out repeatedly to push it away. It was then, as Annie's eyes finally began to clear, that she realised the snake was nothing but a shower hose that her dreams had transformed into something far more sinister.

Annie was suddenly aware that she was now reclining in a luxurious warm bath of perfumed bubbles rather than a one of tepid water. The over-indulgence confused Annie fleetingly, as she was now used to going without such things at the farmhouse. She also knew that Lillian's frugal bathroom cupboard contained no such luxuries. As she tried to work out how they had got there, slowly her eyes cleared and the bathroom came into focus. Soapy bubbles hung like bunches of grapes from the bathroom tiles, kicked there as Annie struggled to escape the imaginary snake. On the shelf above the taps sat a decadent collection of oils and lotions. Annie found the coloured bottles strangely familiar yet somehow disconnected with anything that might belong to the members of Lillian's household. Her heart began to race at the sudden revelation that she was no longer in Lillian's basic bathroom with its roughly painted walls and deep cast iron bath. She began to study the expensive taps and other fittings that surrounded her. After a few more seconds she began to orientate herself, and she realised that she was somehow, back in her own bathroom in her penthouse flat in London.

Annie froze, aware of her heart beating so fast that she could feel it pounding in her chest. She began to panic and hyperventilate, but tried to fight it, taking slow and deep breaths. She closed her eyes again and counted to ten, hoping that when she opened them Lillian's bathroom would be reinstated. Nevertheless, she could not change her surroundings back to those of the farmhouse. She repeated the process a few times more. When she realised that her actions were futile, she cried out in anguish, buried her head in her knees and began to weep uncontrollably. The minutes ticked by as she sat in the bath, praying for assistance from the God that she did not believe in, knowing that she no longer wanted to be trapped in a modern society with all its frills. Questions began to spark in her mind like small fireworks firing off in random directions.

As Annie tried to reconcile herself to her predicament, she noticed that the bathroom door was wide open and that she could hear the sound of a radio or television announcer. She strained to hear the voice of the newsreader.

'And that is the end of the ten o' clock news. The weather will follow shortly after the break,' said a male voice.

'Thank you Bill, and I've heard that we're expecting snow by the morning,' said a female voice. 'Maybe it will be a white Christmas after all!'

'Let's hope so – and it's goodnight from Caroline and myself.'

'Goodnight,' said the two voices in harmony.

Annie was acutely aware that she couldn't remember anything current. From the mention of Christmas by the two presenters, she realised that she was missing a big chunk of memory. She was frightened.

The bathwater was no longer warm and Annie started to process the fact that she had almost drowned herself. She stepped out and hunted for a bathrobe or towel to wrap around her body, finally finding one hanging on the back of the bathroom door. She found another on a hot radiator and wrapped it around her head. Her fingers and toes were shrivelled and blue. She must have been in the water for a considerable length of time. It began to occur to Annie that maybe this was what was like when you started to get old: the memory beginning to fragment into little disjointed chunks.

Her surroundings were acutely familiar, but she felt like she always did when she had been away on a tropical holiday. The house was grey and claustrophobic. She began to look for clues that might jog her memory, the first sign being the contents of the bathroom cabinet. Little brown plastic bottles labelled as various prescription sedatives gave some clue. Most of the bottles were almost empty. She closed the cabinet door again and wiped away the condensation on the mirror with the sleeve of her bathrobe, noticing as she studied her reflection an indentation on her temple. It reminded her of something. Was it a fall? A vague memory of fainting tripped through her mind, but she could not recall anything but contact with a wooden floor. Different images and sounds began to pop in and out of her head of uniformed men and women, vintage cars and planes and snatches of music from a bygone era. She had a strange fragmented image of having looked down on the world but the images had very fuzzy edges and seemed to be slipping away as quickly as sand through her fingers.

As her flat began to feel more familiar, she tried to dismiss the constant barrage of people and abstract objects that kept interfering with her normal thoughts. She reassured herself that a mug of hot chocolate and an early night would help, and that she would wake up the next day with everything feeling as it should. Before she could convince herself of this completely, the memory presented itself smartly that she had been suspended from work. Try as she might she could not remember why.

As she made herself a hot drink, Annie thought about the weather forecast on television. The mention of snow seemed bizarre. She felt as though it were only yesterday that she was basking in blazing sun, but she could not recall exactly where. Why was there talk of

Christmas so soon when she had not even taken her two-week holiday at her timeshare in Spain? She took a sip of her drink as she pondered where autumn had gone and why she could not remember it even happening. She retched and spat her drink into the sink. The milk was off. She opened the milk carton and sniffed its contents. It was foul smelling, thick and made a glooping noise as she poured it into the sink. She looked at the use by date and realised the carton was well out of date. October 2006 stared back at Annie from the wall calendar, the numbered daily boxes full with handwritten notes. It seemed that September had been a busy month. She turned over the pages in an attempt to jog her memory by remembering any of the appointments and dates. Apart from a few boxes that had been allocated doctor's and therapist's appointments, there was no mention of anything more compelling. She touched the indentation on her temple again, trying to remember how she had sustained the injury, wondering whether she could have been concussed, and therefore be suffering from amnesia. It would explain why her memory was patchy. It scared her to think that maybe it had happened in her own home, and that she may have lain undiscovered for days.

Annie backtracked to waking up in the bath. She could not even remember filling the bath in the first place or turning on the television. The dream of someone else's bathroom was fading fast. The flat was warm, clean and tidy, which gave the impression that it had been lived in right up to the present moment. This only added to Annie's confusion, as she had a strong feeling that she had been away. Wherever it was, that somewhere was still eluding her. With the voices on the television being her only company, Annie sat stiffly on the edge of the sofa. She studied the lounge, searching for a clue as to why she felt so disorientated. Everything seemed to be in its appropriate place: cushions plumped up each end of the sofa, remote controls on the coffee table and DVDs filed neatly under the large flat screen television. Nevertheless, she was dismayed to see that her collection of plants was dead. They hung pathetically over the edges of their pots on the windowsills. Brittle leaves and petals had accumulated on the carpet beneath.

She picked up the remote control for the TV and after considering for a few seconds how to operate it; she flicked through the channels restlessly. She finally returned to the news channel and suddenly heard the female announcer mention that it was the 15th December and that retail outlets had reported a rise in public spending. The statement confirmed what Annie had already questioned: weeks seemed to have just disappeared from her life. She could think of no easy explanation and tried to think of what else apart from a blow to the head could have caused such big chunks of her life to be displaced.

There was a sudden clattering sound in the hall. The noise of the letterbox rattling as letters dropped to the mat beneath startled Annie back to the present. As she peered round the corner of the lounge door towards the front door, the red answer-machine light flashing on her home phone distracted her. She approached it tentatively and pressed the play button.

A monotone voice addressed her.

Your voicemail box is full. You have fifty-four new messages.

Annie debated which to deal with first: the pile of envelopes and junk mail on the doormat or the messages on her phone. She opted to listen to the messages and began to play them back, confused as to why there were so many. She instinctively knew that it was not her style to ignore so many for such a long period. As she listened, she bent down, picked up a clutch of envelopes from the front door mat, and examined the postmarks. Some dated back to weeks before. There was a note on the pile hastily scribbled by the postman informing her that her letterbox in the lobby was full.

Message one. Hi Annie - it's Tom. I'm sorry about the argument. Call me.

Annie immediately turned her attention to the phone.

Message two. Hi Annie - it's Tom again. Look I'm really sorry it ended the way it did at the air show. At least let me know you're okay. Call me – please.

Annie dropped the envelopes.

Suddenly she remembered that she had a boyfriend named Tom and that her last memory of spending time with him, was at an air show, where they had fallen out with each other. She could neither remember why they had argued or the content of their argument, but she realised from the answer phone messages that the disagreement had caused their relationship to finish quite suddenly.

She began to feel light-headed, so she made her way back to the comfort of the lounge. Just as she reached the sofa, an image of a derelict enclosure full of twisted pieces of metal popped into her head, before evaporating again before she could try and make sense of it.

Message three. Hi Annie. It's Sophie. Just rang for a catch up. Where are you? Call me back as soon as you get this message.

Annie stared at the television as she flopped down onto the sofa. The rest of the messages punctuated the air, unheard by Annie as she tried to get a grip on reality. Outside, snow was beginning to fall and Annie was fully aware by now that her mind was a tangled mess. There was nobody she felt she could turn to that would not think she was deranged. No one could explain the images of old aeroplanes and burning buildings that were increasingly beginning to pop into her head. She wondered whether there had been some sort of accident at the air show and whether she had witnessed something so horrific that it had caused some form of post-traumatic stress disorder. The little flashes of information trying to piece themselves together were still not painting a very clear picture.

Annie thought back to her disagreement with Tom, and started to remember that she had wandered off, becoming lost. A vivid picture of a burning man exploded in her memory. She began to blame Tom although something told her that he was only a small piece of the mystery. Maybe he was there at the time of some pivotal event, and that was why they had argued and why he had left so many messages: to apologise for tipping her over the edge.

As Annie had these fragmented thoughts, the barriers protecting her mind from trauma burst open like a dam wall cracking, letting all her stored fantasies come crashing through. As the images burst into the open, Annie had the strangest feeling that they were not just fantasies, but stored memories of a past life, which was something she would have dismissed as rubbish not that long ago. She began to remember that a plane had indeed crashed, and that someone had come to her aid. Although she could not yet picture any specific features of his face, she was aware that he seemed so familiar. She vaguely recollected the man shielding her from the flames of the burning plane. Then she remembered the content of the dream she had experienced whilst languishing in her bath. In her dream state she had achieved things she would never have thought possible, things that she had no prior knowledge of, and she had executed them down to the tiniest detail. On this occasion, she had been the master of her dreams, yet it had seemed so much more than that: finite and solid.

It was eleven o'clock at night, but Annie suddenly remembered that there was someone she could call at any time of day or night. She picked up the phone and dialled Dr. Edwards' number. The phone rang in his office but the answer phone cut in.

This is Dr. Edwards. I'm out of the office until January 2nd. In the case of an emergency please leave a message and I will get back to you as soon as possible.

Annie slammed down the receiver, alarm bells still ringing in her head.

'January the second?' she said out loud. 'What the fuck is going on?'

Dr. Edwards had unwittingly rubber-stamped the fact that she had mislaid weeks of her life. She felt lost in time and space and completely out of step without whatever was happening outside the confines of her home, suddenly exhausted by the magnitude of what was happening to her. She needed to sleep and give her subconscious a chance to work it all out.

Annie closed all the blinds, locked the doors and sorted through the near empty medicine bottles and took a couple of sleeping tablets. As she slipped into her drug-induced sleep, her last conscious thought was that she would worry in the morning if she still could make no sense of the torrent of memories that was making her head spin.

Chapter 47

It was mid-morning before Annie finally opened her eyes. The tantalising essence of an alternative life was still looping through her mind as she stared at the ceiling, embedded there by dreams that were becoming increasingly more succinct. As she dragged herself out of bed, some of the crisp details were already beginning to slip away, like egg yolks through arthritic fingers. After only a minute or so, all that remained were vague ghosts of inhabitants of a country farm, uniformed personnel, and a violent confrontation as battered planes arced across a troubled sky. Annie tried to analyse the relevance of the scenes, finally concluding the fact that they all depicted elements of the Second World War was most likely due to Tom's brainwashing. Nevertheless, she could not dismiss how the images had been so detailed on waking, and that they seemed more like a collection of fragmented memories rather than just random thoughts. She immediately told herself that to think in such a way was clearly ridiculous.

She made a mug of herbal tea and sat thoughtfully on the rug by the fire, still struggling to recall anything more recent, apart from the memory of walking away from Tom after their argument. One moment she was with him, and in the next, she was waking up from a peculiar dream, alone in her bathroom.

Feeling unsettled and quite hungry, she went to the kitchen for some breakfast. After one look at a loaf that was more mould than bread, she decided to just call Sophie.

'My God Annie, where on earth have you been?' squealed Sophie, clearly shocked to hear Annie's voice. 'We've all been worried sick. I called round and spoke to that fashion designer who lives in the flat beneath you, and she said she thought you'd gone on holiday. If it hadn't been for her we were going to call the police,' she ranted.

Annie tried to remember whether she had even spoken to Ms...whatever her name was, but could recall no such discussion.

'I needed to get away,' she lied, deciding that it was possibly wiser to collaborate her neighbour's story rather than suggest the possibility of amnesia. 'It's been marvellous.'

'But you should have told everyone that you were going away!'

'Sorry about that, it was a last minute deal. Guess it just slipped my mind. Anyway, like I said, I had a marvellous time but now I'm back I can't wait to get back to work.' As Annie said these words, she realised that she could think of nothing worse than being confined to an office. A panoramic bird's-eye view of the South Downs on a summer's day flitted through her mind.

'Anywhere exciting?'

'Hmm?'

'Did you go anywhere exciting?'

'Oh, just a bed and breakfast on a farm in Sussex. I didn't want to be too far from London in case I was needed in the office,' replied Annie, plucking a remembered location from last night's dream and dropping it in to the conversation.

'That's not like you. You usually go somewhere exotic like the Maldives.'

'The weather was wonderful actually, some lovely hot days.'

'How could it have been wonderful? It's been bloody freezing all over the UK for weeks!'

'Talk about getting the third degree,' said Annie, confused and irritated by Sophie's repeated interrogation. She changed the subject. 'Let's get back to work issues shall we? Any idea when Sir Frank is expecting me back?'

'I'm not sure it's that simple.'

'What do you mean, not that simple?'

Sophie coughed nervously.

'I'm waiting, spit it out,' growled Annie.

'Oh it's nothing really,' said Sophie casually. 'Sir Frank replaced you with a temp. She's a relative, and was doing him a favour by stepping in short term. She's been useless though,' added Sophie quickly, trying to defuse any possible annoyance on Annie's part.

Annie considered her response.

'Oh well, can't say I'm that concerned. How Sir Frank can think anyone could do my job as well as me, beats me.'

'Exactly.'

'I guess there'll be all sorts of mess to sort out when I get back.'

'Nothing you can't handle now you've had a break.'

463

Suddenly Annie remembered why she had been laid off, but pushed her previously deteriorating performance to the back of her mind.

'Tell Sir Frank I'll send him a letter to arrange my start back date.'

'A letter? You mean an email don't you?'

'Of course!' Annie exclaimed, wondering why instead she had suggested putting pen to paper.

Sophie changed the subject.

'I should have asked. How are you feeling now you've had time to get away?'

'I'm in the pink, although a bit bored being stuck in the flat doing housework.'

'In the pink? That's a new one! And excuse me for mentioning it, but what happened to your cleaner? You hate housework.'

'I let her go. Gives me something to do,' lied Annie, noticing on quick examination that her nails were chipped and brittle.

On the other end of the line, Sophie was thinking that Annie sounded different, but she could not quite put her finger on whether it was the way she had phrased her sentences, whether there was a subtle shift in her manner, or the fact that she sounded as though she was hiding something. This apart, she found it odd how Annie had apparently disappeared for such a long period with no word to anyone.

Annie, on the other hand, was still struggling with the fact that she felt totally out of step with her environment, confused by the imagery of a world she had never lived in, and constantly bombarded with what felt like triggers to something indefinable. There was a mystery to unravel. As she ended the conversation, she had the sudden feeling of not being alone in the flat, but before she could analyse the fleeting sensation further, the feeling passed. She concentrated instead on the fact that it had been a relief to touch base with reality. That it was with Sophie was probably a good thing. Had she spoken to Tom, she suspected that he would have tried to dig much deeper than Sophie had dared to, Sophie operated on a much more singular level: shopping, socialising and fashion being her chief interests. Tall tales of bombers, fighters and brave women pilots would mean nothing to her. At the thought of women pilots, the sound of female laughter rippled through the room.

Annie startled but drew the conclusion that the sound she had heard must have been coming from the flat beneath.

She realised that she could not provide answers to all of the questions that were sparking in her head, and she dreaded the time when she would have to explain herself to all and sundry. All she had to go on was a collection of weird dreams, which were beginning to seem bizarrely real. She had almost convinced herself that she had slipped into a parallel world. She was in danger of losing her judgement of what was reality and what was fiction. There seemed only one way to reach a satisfactory conclusion. She would research some of the flashing images that were still replaying like a stuck record in her mind, and this would clarify for once and for all that, there was not a glimmer of truth in any of them.

She stared out of the window at the snow that had settled on every inanimate object in sight. Despite the flat being pleasantly warm, she shivered at the prospect of venturing outside. She dressed casually in jogging bottoms and a fleecy top, put on some background music and logged on to the Internet. She briefly scanned her thousands of unread incoming emails whilst she sat pondering what to research first. She began to scribble some suggestions and pointers on a notepad. The faces of the people from her dreams seemed separated from her by a thin veil, making them impossible to discern from each other.

Annie's Internet browsing history gave few clues to her activity leading up to her amnesia. At first glance, there was nothing that grabbed her attention until she reached a link to London monuments and sculptures, which she immediately assumed must have been for Tom's benefit. Her finger hovered over the delete button, but something made her stop and view the link instead.

Images of the Battle of Britain memorial almost seemed to power out of the screen at her, refusing to be ignored. Suddenly Annie's memory kicked in again as she recalled the acute embarrassment of stumbling in front of hordes of tourists by the memorial. Tom had dragged her along to see it. She clicked on more images of the sculpture. A group of bronze men stared back at her from their plinth.

Annie's fingertips began to tingle as her mind tried to piece together what else might have happened on that particular day. She continued to study the faces of the pilots fully attired in flying suits and other equipment. Her memory fizzed and popped again, as little flashes attempted to make their way to the surface of her consciousness. When they finally did reach the surface, they exploded like a cork shooting out of a shaken champagne bottle.

Lenny.

The man in the statue was Lenny - the only man she had ever loved. It was not a dream.

Annie began to shake at the prospect that she had done the impossible, as a pleasant woody fragrance, much like tobacco, filled the room. Her head throbbed with the information that was spilling into her consciousness. She likened it to thousands of newspapers spilling off a printing press. She left the images of the memorial open on her screen and went over to the fireplace, aware that the temperature in the room seemed to have dropped quite suddenly.

She glanced at the framed photographs that lined the mantelpiece. Her grandfather smiled at her from his silver picture frame, standing proudly next to his Tiger Moth. Her mind flickered like the frames of an old silent movie as images of her flying lessons with her grandfather mingled with images of her hands on the controls of a familiar yet archaic plane. She tried to harness her thoughts, picking up and studying the line of pictures one after the other. Her loving mother smiled reassuringly from her armchair. Father and grandfather stood shoulder to shoulder next to a Spitfire. She picked up the photograph that had been taken of her after her first solo flight, remembering how her grandfather had presented it to her with enormous pride. She studied the image of the old plane again; every line, curve, nut and bolt. She needed no teaching to know it inside out.

She sat at her computer again. The bronze image of Lenny stared back at her, but she could not quite equate the connection between the figure and a man that lived and breathed. The timings confused her, although his face was becoming clearer with every flashback. She woke later with her head on her desk, the printer spewing out A4 images and information from her research. She had dreamt that she had flown from a remote airfield in the Midlands to somewhere in the south of England with two other women in a four-engine bomber. Every detail of the cockpit and the sound of the rumbling engines seemed familiar. A winding river stretched below around some old church ruins. A steam train had kept pace with them before curving away to the west, disappearing in its own plume of smoke. Lenny had taken her hand, leading her to a field of brightly coloured flowers, bobbing and bowing in the summer breeze.

Annie's heart ached. A solitary tear rolled down her cheek as she tried to work out how the world she kept dreaming about resonated as real as the flat she resided in. She felt detached from the real world.

The phone rang a few times. Knowing that now word had got back that she had returned from holiday, she ignored it. Instead, she emailed Dr. Edwards, allowing her thoughts to spill onto the page and trying to type as quickly as each thought surfaced. Soon there were no cream walls visible in Annie's lounge as she frantically pinned images on every available space, not caring about any marks that she might leave. Faces, places and aircraft from a small window of time she had managed to narrow down to the early nineteen-forties stared back at her. When Dr. Edwards replied to her email almost instantly, she sensed the urgency in his words.

Annie,

sorry I am away but here is my response to your email. Let me know when you have read it.

Where do I begin? I think we know each other well enough now for me to be frank about your state of mind.

There's no doubt you have regressed somewhat since I saw you last. The fact that you have not been to see me for weeks has worried me. We'd made progress back in October. Where have you been? I've been concerned for your welfare.

I want you to use the relaxation techniques I taught you without fail, before you go to sleep each night, and I've left a prescription with my receptionist. She'll be in the office right up until Christmas Eve. The tablets will help you relax and stop your dreams from being quite so vivid. It's important you take them regularly.

Your descriptions of 'war experiences' confounds me. I've been doing some research while we've been out of touch, and going through the tapes from our conversations.

Uncannily accurate considering you were never there, and you claim you never covered it in school!

As far as a bit of self-help goes, I have a few ideas. You could begin by doing a little research yourself. Start with the statue if you like, or the history of the London underground, indeed anything connected with what has been going through your head for the last few months. You're bound to find some discrepancies between your dreams and how it actually was back then. This will help you realise that, forgive me for sounding like I am mocking you, that you have not travelled in time. Record everything – we can look at it together.

If you don't start to feel better after a few days, ask my receptionist to book you in with my colleague Dr.Greenway. He can access your records if needs be, but I'm sure it won't come to that.

Best we meet as soon as possible - I get back on the 2nd Jan.

Have a good Christmas and a Happy New Year.

Dr. Edwards.

Dr. Edwards had not said anything that she did not know already. Nevertheless, it jarred that he had expressed disbelief. His words reverberated in her head.

Uncannily accurate considering you were never there...you're bound to find some discrepancies . . .

She sat for a minute with eyes closed, her head in her hands. Then she began to laugh uncontrollably. It was the laugh of someone disturbed and coming apart at the seams. She curled up into a tight ball by the fire, hugging her knees tight to her chest. The image of a Lillian's kitchen range, a full kettle boiling away on the hotplate, popped into her head. Annie randomly picked up from the carpet some of the sheets of paper she had printed, and studying the images and read the text. Groups of people in black and white photographs stared back at her, but here was no one familiar in the few pages she glanced at that triggered anything fresh.

That night Annie dreamt in black and white for the first time that she could remember. The orange haired man that normally stalked her on most nights seemed almost harmless in shades of grey, as he blended into the landscape. The only hint of colour to break the monochrome was the blue of Lenny's eyes, reminding Annie of the inviting waters of a warm turquoise sea. In her sleep, the scent of his body was like nectar and she hungered for him. When she woke the next day, covered with perspiration, she reached out for his warm body but his side of the bed was cold. She opened her eyes with a start, realising instantly that she had to find him. There had to be a way back.

Chapter 48

Annie was conscious of the fact that she wanted to be shut away from the outside world in the short run-up to Christmas. Nevertheless, she could not wholly disguise her presence, due to the show of lights from her penthouse lounge acting like a beacon to anyone passing by in the street below. In the end, the only protagonist to disturb her peace was the postman, with an item that required her signature.

The young man smiled nervously, used to Annie's usual look of contempt whenever she snatched the morning post from him on leaving the building for work. This time, despite her desire for solitude, Annie greeted him with a broad smile as she held out her hand for the large brown parcel. Whilst signing, she wished him the best for the Christmas period, and then closed the door gently, leaving him shaking his head in disbelief.

Annie put the parcel to one side, unaware of the shift in her behaviour, and sidetracked by issues that were more important. She was finally convinced that they were not dreams. Perched above the executive flats, she felt like a princess trapped in a tower, waiting to be rescued and taken back to that other place.

As she surveyed the heavy London sky, thoughts of the countryside on a hot summer's day began to penetrate her thoughts. The urge to stroll in a meadow of wild flowers overwhelmed her as she looked across the river towards the Houses of Parliament. The lack of the fragrant smell of wild honeysuckle wafting through an open window bothered her. The bustle of London was a far cry from what she had grown accustomed to on Lillian's farm. She no longer checked herself at the suggestion that for a short period she had somehow mysteriously crossed time and embraced another life.

Word had also travelled. Each time the phone rang, Annie flinched, its piercing tone jolting her out of her daydreaming. Finally, after several pleading messages from Tom requesting a catch up, she reluctantly answered, the repetitive ringing becoming too much to handle.

A few seconds of silence ensued.

'Annie? Are you there?' said Tom.

'Yes, I'm here,' she answered; surprising herself that she was so pleased to hear his voice.

'Thank God! What's been going on? Where have you been? I've been going spare worrying...'

She cut him off mid-sentence.

'I'm fine Tom, really I am,' she pretended. 'I've just been away. I used the opportunity to catch up with some old friends, like I told you I would.'

'You should've let us know you were...'

She interrupted again.

'Yes, I know. I should have done. I've had a grilling from Sophie already.'

Tom changed his tack.

'I'm really sorry about the air show,' he said meekly. 'I should have come and looked for you.'

An awkward silence.

'I've missed you,' he added.

Annie chose not to reciprocate Tom's sentiment.

'I thought after our disagreement you weren't that bothered,' she answered, coldness creeping back into her voice.

'It's not like that,' protested Tom, in an attempt to defend his corner.

'Things had come to a head between us, don't you think?' suggested Annie, immediately softening her tone again.

'Can we at least talk about it? How about dinner?' he asked, clutching at straws.

'I don't know,' said Annie, feeling torn, the desire to be alone diminishing quickly.

Tom waited silently for Annie's decision.

Annie hesitated, remembering that she had been cruel to Tom in the past, and aware that it did not sit comfortably with her to behave in that manner anymore. It seemed heartless to suddenly ditch him so near to Christmas.

'I suppose it wouldn't do any harm,' she said finally. 'Maybe we could drive out to the country and find a nice pub.' The flash of an idyllic village green popped into her head.

'How about tomorrow then? I know just the place,' said Tom, his pleading replaced by excitement.

'Tom, slow down - you've got to cut me some slack. I've got a lot on, like making sure I still have a job!'

'Let's make it the weekend then. Is that okay?' he replied, hope for a reunion obvious in his voice.

'That's fine, I'll look forward to it,' she agreed. 'I must go now, call me later in the week.' She ended the conversation before Tom had the chance to make more demands.

Whilst Annie sat pondering whether she had given Tom false hope, Tom sat at his desk and reflected back on the conversation. Annie had not sounded much like Annie at all. It was true to say that most things about him usually easily irritated her; that fact was nothing new. Nevertheless, there was warmth in her manner and calmness in her speech that he was not prepared for. Her lack of aggression was a refreshing change; nevertheless, something about her changed persona worried him. She seemed detached. He decided that whether she liked it or not, he would call round in a day or so. He needed to see for himself what was going on at first hand.

Annie had the luxury of plenty of spare time, which allowed her to sift methodically through the hundreds of pieces of paper that were scattered all over her lounge carpet or stuck temporarily to the walls of her lounge. A sense of purpose took over her, due to the fear that the flashes of the past might eventually slip away, her activity also making her feel that she was less likely to sink into a bottomless well of depression. At the same time, she felt no cause to celebrate the impending approach of Christmas. She smiled at the thought that she was no longer a willing victim of consumerism. Thoughts of Lenny now consumed her instead.

Technology seemed suddenly to be less of a friend than it had once been at Carlotti's. In Annie's other life, she had quickly adjusted to the lack of a constant stream of texts and emails constantly arriving on her mobile. She tried to magic up images and sounds from Lillian's farm, such as the grandfather clock in the hall and the big band music playing softly on the radio in the kitchen, but try as she might, Annie felt as though she were viewing the scene through the fine fabric of a tulle veil. As she continued to glance at the pieces of paper in her hands, she refused to resign herself to the fact that modern technology dictated that her inbox would keep filling up and that big brother would keep watching. She was adamant that she no longer wanted to be part of it.

Noticing a point of interest on one of the pages, Annie began to research the details, noticing how she was finding it difficult to readily locate the letters of the alphabet on her computer keypad. It took her a few moments to familiarise herself. The keys felt alien to her fingertips. She realised that despite it only being morning, she was already tired, and that curling up on the sofa seemed like a tempting alternative. As she fought the desire to sleep, anxiety over what she might discover about her missing months as well as eagerness for the truth, battled against each other.

If none of her wild imaginings were real, then would Lenny eventually fade into the deep corridors of her sub-conscious? If that were to happen, she would never find the passion he had sparked in her with anyone else, and to settle for less was just not worthy of consideration. To find that the airfield or the cosy confines of Lillian's farm had never existed would be a grounding and mortifying experience, and one that she would refuse to accept if it came to it. Worse still was the thought that Lenny might be nothing more than a fictional knight in shining armour, created by her troubled mind to rescue her from an unfulfilling life. Had she created him in her mind to compensate for the love she craved? If on the other hand he was real, and she could prove it beyond all measure of doubt, would she be able to cross time once more and continue their life together? She was trapped within the perimeters of her own existence – one that she was beginning to despise. There was no comforting warmth in her magnolia-painted home.

She picked up a pile of papers from the carpet. Aerial photographs showed clearly what remained of scarred airfields. A grainy black and white photograph stared back at her, suddenly triggering recollections of grass runways and the smell of aviation fuel. She compared then and now images of clusters of buildings and trees scattered around various airfields, hoping that they might remind her of something. One particular photograph caught her attention. Hedgerows and perimeter fences clearly defined an airfield: long lines of aircraft parked up outside large hangars. A square control tower sat to the northwest of the runways, behind which a small copse of trees nestled. As Annie studied a snaking river that meandered its way past the airfield, and a railway slicing across its path on its route to the West Country, flickering images stirred in her mind. Shadows of clouds peppering the old photograph obliterated something that she could not quite put her finger on. She followed the line of the railway as it carved out its path across the English countryside past villages and farms dotted amongst the rectangular fields.

She sat up suddenly from her hunched position on the floor, realising she had remembered something of which in theory she should have no prior knowledge: the abbey, its spire a welcome landmark on the approach to the airfield. Something had drawn her to this particular photograph. Scrambling to her feet, she rummaged in her desk drawer for her magnifying glass. The abbey had to be on the map somewhere, proof that she was not dreaming after all.

A steam train unexpectedly lumbered through Annie's mind, thumping rhythmically in time to her heart. In her imagination, she was up in the sky on a perfect summer's day sub-consciously narrating a romantic drama. The heat from the sun burnt down on the insect splattered cockpit hood of her Hurricane, making her feel slightly light-headed. Soot and steam belched from the steam train far below her as the leviathan swept away into the distance amongst the purple and lilac hills. An iridescent river twisted through lush green valleys like a silver serpent. As she flew beneath a layer of marshmallow cloud, she scanned the ground for the abbey glinting like a foreboding iceberg as the sun refracted on the granite. The sight of its spires was a sure sign that she was nearly back at base.

Returning to the here and now, and with her heart still thumping, Annie's hand shook as she held the magnifying glass over the spot where she knew instinctively that the abbey would be. Tucked under the cotton-wool edge of a small cloud, sure enough, a solitary spire peeked out, barely visible as the cloud passed over. Annie had evidence. She knew that nothing about her life in the nineteen-forties had been a dream. She had never seen the photograph before, and had definitely never flown to that particular airfield: at least, not in this lifetime.

An image of Lenny, floating lifeless in a grey choppy sea, manifested itself, piercing her heart like a sharp needle. She suddenly panicked at the thought of coming across his epitaph if she were to search for it. In addition, the truth that might be waiting for her amongst the litter on her floor was an ordeal she was not sure she could endure. Despite this, she needed answers. It occurred to her that to find the airfield, or whatever was left of it, was what she needed to do. The ghosts that still resided there could seek her out if they so desired.

With this in mind, Annie hurriedly abandoned the debris she had created, and left the house soon after with a hastily packed overnight bag. She relished the sense of heightened excitement and anticipation, and refused to allow any doubt to creep in that she might not find a way to get back to Lenny. It suddenly occurred to her that she might be able to alter his fate by stopping him from flying on the night that he went missing. Being so wrapped up in the unimaginable, she did not consider how, and if she was going to achieve such a task. Moreover, if she did step back in time, would they all be waiting for her: Lenny, Betty, Peter and Lillian? Could she be sucked through another portal if she called to them? The concept of time travel did not seem ridiculous anymore.

Chapter 49

The wind whistled and howled in Annie's ears as soon as she stepped outside of the heated and double-glazed foyer. It seemed to Annie that the wind was trying to tell her something, and that any hidden messages were designed to help rather than hinder her in her quest. She buried her face in her familiar angora scarf and squinted as the cold north wind swept across the river, causing her eyes to sting.

The crunch of the crisp new snow beneath her feet softened the sound of her footsteps and sparkled as far as the eye could see as though thousands of diamonds had been randomly scattered on the pavements. Annie assumed that her neighbours were either at work or huddled in the warm, as her departure had gone unnoticed by all except a few people passing her by. As she reached the street adjacent to the short service road, she kept well back from the edge of the kerb, for fear of being splattered with sludge by cars and lorries. As the wind gusted along the Thames causing ripples on the river, she pulled her coat tightly around and her buried her nose deeper into the upturned collar.

Though her bag was heavy, laden with printouts of photographs and Ordnance Survey maps, and an overnight change of clothes, Annie felt lighter knowing that she was going to find out one way or another whether she had completely lost her senses. The closer she could get to where she last saw Lenny, the better she knew she would feel. If the old adage that love can cross time were true, then he would surely find a way of reaching out to her. There could be no acceptance on her part for anything less. Her life would be barren if there were only fading memories and years of wasted hope and wondering.

For a second Annie hesitated as she noticed the welcoming glow emanating from lit buildings either side of the river. She had taken a while to adjust to darkness descending on London so early after the heady summer evenings she had just returned from. The light was already beginning to fade even though it was only mid afternoon, and for a second the safety of her flat beckoned. Coloured Christmas lights twinkled and winked at her from offices and flats, almost as though they offered friendly encouragement by lighting her way as she passed by. For a second, the memory of Christmas as a child resurfaced and the smell of sappy logs burning in the open fire teased her nostrils. She was beginning to realise that to have left first thing in the morning would have been more prudent, but now she had made a decision she could think of no reason as to why she should waste any more time.

Ignoring the snow, which had drifted along the length of the Embankment and Westminster Bridge, she braced herself against the weather as it scattered constant flurries of snow directly into her path. By the time she reached the bright lights of Waterloo station, she realised that night was almost upon her.

She took the tube train to Victoria station, and once there, stood alone, thinking how, as usual, London had been unprepared for such a sudden temperature drop. Gritting the roads had not yet begun. An announcement over the Tannoy concerning the weather affecting the whole network instantly threatened Annie's mood, the fact that she might need to change trains several times making her wonder whether she should retrace her steps. Her knees were already numb. Whilst waiting for further announcements, she wandered outside to see if the weather was getting any worse. Commuters and visitors to London tentatively placed one foot in front of the other, risking life and limb on the icy pavements.

She used a nearby cash machine and then went back inside the station to buy a coffee. By the time she had allowed it to cool a little to the point that she could drink it comfortably, her train was already waiting at the platform and ready to leave, most people already having boarded. A smattering of snow from the train's inward journey had left dirty streaks down the windows, already heavy on the inside with condensation. Rows of pale faces peered out through the grime. Annie stepped on the train and scanned the half-full carriage, managing to find a seat a little separate from the other commuters. She placed her bag on the seat next to her, hoping it would discourage anyone from joining her.

The train slid smoothly out of the station, rapidly gathering speed as it sped south. Annie wiped the condensation away with a tissue and smiled at her own reflection, whilst the rest of the travellers either read their papers, listened to music or typed on keypads. Deep in their own thoughts, the sound of music leaked from those who wore headphones, making a sound that resembled angry bees. The gloom deepened outside.

Annie pitied the other passengers. Without exception, all looked as though they had not enjoyed warm sun on their faces for months. She imagined that foremost in their thoughts was the prospect of a warm carpet under frozen toes or a late dinner before rolling into bed. She however, was looking forward to something far more life changing.

Too agitated to sleep and wanting to savour every emotion that entered her head as she drew closer to her destination, Annie spent the journey idly watching the darkening night, which deepened into a pool of black interrupted only by lights on station platforms that they flashed through.

When she finally stepped down from the train an hour and a half later, the only traveller to alight, the sparse lights at that particular station flickered from one end of the platform to the other. She felt immediately as though she had stepped back a hundred years as she studied the Victorian architecture. The cold night air instantly chilled her, making her nose tingle and her teeth chatter. It seemed several degrees colder than it had in London. The train glided out of the station and immediately disappeared into a tunnel.

No one challenged her for her ticket. If not for a lone cab driver sitting in his car outside the station, smoking and reading a crumpled newspaper, she would have believed her thought from a moment before that she had travelled through a portal to the past again.

She asked the driver about hotels.

'You been here before?' he asked suspiciously, putting down his newspaper and scrutinising her hand luggage.

'Not for a long time,' she answered, hugely disappointed that the old station had not yet stirred any buried memories.

He raised an eyebrow as he got out and held the passenger door open.

'Bit late to be out and about.'

'I'm fine. I know the area well,' Annie lied, irritated by his nosiness.

The man muttered something as he put her bag in the boot. Having called ahead to check there was a room for the night, he dropped her at the only bed and breakfast for miles around.

Annie noticed that the house had no character to speak of, but as it was just a place to recoup her energy for one night, she was not particularly bothered. She slept in her clothes, spending a restless night, willing the dawn to come so she could get to the airfield as soon as daylight broke. The room was damp and unwelcoming, a musty smell pervading. As soon as the slightest hint of morning sun crept through a gap in the curtains, she packed her wash bag hurriedly, left money and a thank you note on the hall table, creeping out without breakfast or saying goodbye to her unmemorable host.

The dutiful cabbie from the night before was waiting as instructed, bemused by her secretive manner. After trying to extract her reason for visiting the area and getting few clues, he silently drove her along frosty lanes for several miles, passing farmers already beginning their daily chores. When rolling hills appeared in front of the car, Annie knew instinctively that the taxi would turn left and arrive soon at her intended destination. She did not need to look at her map to know that she was on familiar ground.

'This it, love?' he asked, as they approached the large imposing gates she recognised from her day out with Tom.

'Not quite yet. A bit further,' she answered, examining her maps.

The driver seemed puzzled.

'I thought you said you wanted the local airfield! Well this is it.'

'No I want the old airfield. It backs on to here a couple of miles down the road.'

'The old airfield? There's nothing there now, apart from the lake and a few old buildings. There's a new housing estate being built.'

Annie's heart sunk at the thought of the place she had grown to love changing so much.

'Are you some sort of researcher?'

'Something like that.'

Annie felt pensive as they passed the gatehouse. Her time with Lenny seemed suddenly all so long ago. She thought back to her experience. The scrap yard had been a considerable walk away from the air show. The driver was right. She unfolded her Ordnance Survey map and tried to get her bearings. Any of the airfields nearby fulfilled the criteria. They all sat within the landscape she had flown over many times.

It was futile trying to find the exact spot where she had first met Lenny. This was a military airport that was only opened once a year to the public. She had no good reason that would warrant her being granted access to wander around aimlessly. They drove on for several miles, but seemed to be getting further away from where she thought she should be.

'Stop!' she shouted, as they approached a bend in the road.

The cab driver braked hard.

'Blimey – you gave me a start!' he exclaimed, looking at her in the rear view mirror. 'Are you okay?'

'Sorry, but this is it. You've found the place.'

Nestling amongst a large copse of trees a couple of hundred metres away, sat a square building, its facade visible from the road.

'That's the old Control Tower,' said Annie in wonderment, stepping out of the car. 'The aviation scrap yard should be around her somewhere too.'

'You can't get to it at the moment. We've had so much rain, and now this snow...'

Annie's portal to the past was tantalisingly out of reach.

'Damn.'

'Do you want me to wait? It's a bit out of the way here.'

'No, I'm fine. I might need a while anyway.'

He handed her his business card.

'There's nothing here worth looking at. That building's been empty since the war – trashed by kids.'

'I'll call you when I've finished. Is there a phone box or a hotel anywhere near?' said Annie, putting the business card in her pocket.

'Haven't you got a mobile?' asked the taxi driver, puzzled.

'Can't stand them,' she replied, leaving the man shaking his head in disbelief.

'Mad,' he thought to himself. 'Listen, love, I'm passing back through this way in an hour, I'll keep an eye out for you.'

She turned away and tried to negotiate a path through overgrown brambles and ferns, using her small suitcase as a battering ram. Then she climbed over a metal five-bar padlocked gate ignoring the trespass sign. The cab disappeared back the way it had come.

Swathed in a motionless mist, the dilapidated control tower had been barely visible from the narrow road. She realised that she had been lucky to spot it. It seemed that no one had been curious to investigate its remains: there was no trodden path. The cab driver had been wrong about vandalism; the undergrowth had acted as a prickly sentry guarding the walls from predators. She struggled on, her clothes and shoes offering little protection from thorns and the boggy path.

Just as she reached a barbed wire fence partially surrounding the tower, she was suddenly aware out of the corner of her eye of a flicker of movement through one of the control tower's broken windows. Simultaneously, rustling noises began to emanate from the undergrowth and trees all around her. A rook cawed, complaining from its perch on a handrail belonging to the control tower's roof.

Annie stopped, too frightened to turn around. An icy chill began to overwhelm her, despite bright sunlight filtering through the trees. She stood still, listening, waiting, wishing for something to happen, no longer sure that she wanted to experience a visitation of some sort. The rustling became a rumble as the undergrowth parted. She was surrounded. He came charging towards her at speed, his eyes wide open and staring, making her lose her footing and fall backwards into the undergrowth.

Chapter 50

Unblinking glassy eyes stared directly at Annie, giving her the strangest feeling that the creature before her was warning her that something unwelcome was lurking in the shadows. Finally, after standing for a few seconds squaring up to Annie, the young deer snorted, white vapour escaping from its nostrils, and then darted into the woods. The rest of the herd followed, and soon disappeared from view. Annie picked herself up from the grass.

Despite the unexpected visitors startling Annie, the control tower still seemed to retain an air of tranquillity. Nature had excelled, masking the concrete structure with well-established ivy, which enhanced an otherwise uninteresting façade. The ivy had grown beyond the roofline, mingling with the branches of the canopy of bare-branched trees above. Nearly all of the windows and window frames of the control tower were broken or missing. On the roof there was a small structure, about the size of a garden shed, which led onto a flat roof with a handrail around the edge. The metal doors to the shed-like structure, hung off of their hinges, squeaking like the doors of a western saloon bar. The roof had at one time boasted a panoramic view of the airfield. Annie searched for an opening but could see no apparent way to get in. The ground floor windows had been bricked up with breeze blocks and all doors chained and padlocked to keep intrepid explorers such as her at bay. She skirted around the perfectly symmetrical structure, beating down the brambles that flanked the building on all sides with a stick. She wondered how the deer had found their way out.

Even though she was aware that she felt disappointed, Annie walked on, noticing that the trees were becoming sparser. Eventually, the trees gave way to a huge clearing. Annie tried to orientate herself with her surroundings, recalling from memory that the main runway was only a stone's throw away. To her dismay, a vast lake blocked her path, burying all evidence of where the main runway had once crossed. She stopped and studied her Ordnance Survey map to check she had not taken a wrong turn, vaguely remembering a stretch of water when she had wandered off after her row with Tom. Certain that she was in the right place, she glanced across the lake which reflected distant trees, its surface broken only by the ripples made by birds taking off and landing. A low mist hung atmospherically only inches from the surface of the water, as though invisible threads suspended it from above. Annie peered into the depths of the lake, realising that there was no way of judging how deep the water might be, or whether the airfield still existed beneath.

On the opposite shore beyond more mature trees, was the housing estate that the cab driver had mentioned. Between the lake and the trees, a few old buildings stood forlornly neglected; skeletons of dispersal huts, a large crumbling red two-storey building and several large corrugated hangars in varying states of repair. Annie's heart sunk at the realisation that any access was blocked

491

by the nature of the current landscape, and that so little still remained of the buildings that she had once frequented.

She turned and looked again at the control tower, concentrating on the reigning silence and hoping for a spiritual sign. Nothing came. She was alone with a camouflaged herd of deer, probably still watching her from the safety of the woods, and a flock of wild birds that seemed unperturbed by her presence. She sat on the trunk of a fallen tree and looked out across the lake. It was easy to conjure up images of plane after plane taking off from where the water now shimmered and hear the drone of their engines as they cleared the gap in the trees. She imagined that she could almost see the reflection of Spitfires and Hurricanes in the smooth mirrored surface of the lake and laughter of other ferry pilots as they traipsed across the airfield to a waiting Anson.

She was jolted back to the present by the squawking of a large bird coming in to alight on the water, using its webbed feet as brakes as it touched down on the surface of the lake. A large flock followed, clumsy and uncertain as they misjudged their vocal descent in their foray of activity. Annie chuckled quietly at the comparison of her perfect landings in various planes compared to that of the wild birds.

Savouring the beauty and tranquility of the lake for one last time, and still hoping for a sign that she might make contact with Lenny's world, Annie trudged back towards the road to wait for the taxi driver, wishing that there were a way that she could remain for an indefinite period, and wondering what to do next.

When he arrived he seemed to sense that Annie was upset, by the far away expression on her face.

'Where to, miss?' he asked, noticing in his rear view mirror that she looked tearful.

'I think I might stop for coffee somewhere.'

'How about a drop of sea air then? I know just the place, a hotel with good food and a cracking view. It's not far from here.'

'Sounds good to me,' said Annie, looking back at the control tower as the driver pulled away.

You can pick up a train not far from the hotel, he added, trying hard to make conversation. 'It's the same line you came down on.'

'Thanks,' said Annie, still looking out at the derelict airfield buildings, her flat mood evident in her voice.

The driver turned on his radio in an attempt to lift her spirits. As though to add to her heavy heart; the heavens suddenly opened. Driving rain pounded down on the roof of the car. Within half an hour, and with no sign of the rain abating, they reached the hotel that the driver had mentioned. He dropped her at the front door, repeating his guarantee of a good view and nice food. He seemed hesitant to leave her as he handed over her luggage.

'It's a five minute walk to the station from here,' he explained helpfully, pointing towards the town. 'Hope you find what you were looking for,' he added intuitively, sensing that she probably had not.

Smiling weakly, Annie paid him, and turned to climb the steps of the hotel. It was as drab and as the place she had stayed at the night before, but this time she hoped that the view would compensate. She watched the taxi disappear for the second time that day down the gravel drive, and then turned away from the unwelcoming hotel down a footpath that ran along the boundary fence.

Well before she got to the cliffs, she could hear the sea crashing against the rocks below. Rivulets of rain had forced their way down her neck, determinedly finding their way through her clothing to her skin. Her hair was drenched and had begun to stick to her face. The clouds were becoming heavier as they swept in towards the coast from the horizon, resembling rolled up charcoal-coloured blankets stacked next to each other. There seemed to be no one else foolish enough to brave the weather, but this did not bother Annie, who felt a sense of exhilaration being alone with the elements, despite her earlier disappointment. The wind buffeted against her, pushing and pulling, so much so that she struggled to remain upright. She abandoned all caution and peered over the edge of the cliff at the boiling sea, almost willing a sudden gust to carry her over so that her emotional turmoil could end. Just as she thought her wish might come true, there was a moment of calm, as the wind suddenly dropped to a whispering breeze and the sound of the sea seemed to become just background noise.

For an instant, in the corner of her eye, Annie thought she glimpsed an airliner through a small gap in the clouds. She scanned the sky to check, pitying the poor passengers enduring a bumpy ride, but there was nothing to see. Only a distant murmur gave an indication that she might be right. As she continued to look upwards to see if she could spot the plane again, the clouds began to break up, exposing small pockets of blue.

Suddenly, a large shadow appeared a few hundred feet above, just to the south of Annie, flanked by five or six more shadows of the same size flying in perfect formation. The deep guttural rumbling noise of the engines seemed strangely familiar, but at first, Annie could not place where she had heard it before. As the clouds continued to expose more blue sky, Annie's mouth dropped open at the final realisation that six ghostly Lancaster bombers were fast approaching the coast, their spectral form semi-transparent against the blue sky.

Annie began to laugh hysterically and wave her arms in the air at the imaginary pilots, oblivious to the fact that she was dangerously near to the cliff edge. Loose boulders fell to the beach below, dislodged by Annie's feet, ricocheting as they smashed against the cliff face on their descent.

'What the hell are you doing? Are you mad?' screamed a male voice from behind.

Within seconds Annie had been wrestled to the floor.

'Get off me!' she screamed, fighting to get free.

'I'm not letting go until you calm down. Nothing's worth throwing yourself over the cliff for!'

The memory of a man pinning her to a wall flashed through her head. Suddenly she remembered Dan, but as quickly as the thought entered her mind, it had gone again. She looked at the concerned face of the man pinning her down.

'I wasn't going to jump.'

The young man, attired in running kit and aged around twenty-five, helped her up.

'I thought you were,' he said, his face still pale with a look of horror.

She ignored his comment, pointing to the Lancaster bombers as they continued on their way northwards. She felt like an excited child.

'Aren't they amazing? I've flown in one,' she added, wildly gesticulating at the sky.

The man looked upwards, still holding on to her just in case his suspicions that she might jump were right.

'There's nothing there,' he coaxed, still scanning the sky.

Annie looked up at the sky again but the planes were nowhere in sight and the rumbling of the Merlin engines had abruptly ceased.

'But they were...'

'Are you okay?' interrupted the man. 'Do you want me to get some help?' he asked, uncertain of what to do.

Annie feigned some composure, realising that she was the only one to witness the planes.

'Thank you, but no. It must have been a trick of the light, or maybe I had a few too many last night,' she lied, remembering how many times she had used that excuse.

He released his hold.

'As long as you're sure.'

'Really, I'm fine, but thank you for saving me from getting blown off the edge,' said Annie, turning on her feminine charm.

'Well, best keep to the footpath next time.'

'I will,' said Annie, turning away.

The man stood and watched her walk back along the cliff path before he resumed his run. She chose not to stay at the unwelcoming hotel, arriving instead at home just after dark.

Chapter 51

Nothing was resolved, and Annie had come away from the control tower feeling cheated. She had intended to spend much longer in the countryside adjacent to the airfield, looking for familiar landmarks from the faded photographs that she had stumbled across: the abbey, the railway and most of all, the farm that she was beginning to consider her home. The knowledge that most of the airfield had been under water like the fabled lost city of Atlantis had served as big enough a shock to make her want to leave immediately. There had been hints of a past that she thought she recognised, but were too painful to see in their altered state, and now another day had commenced, she wondered whether her visions really were nothing more than just dreams.

The following morning the sun peeked timidly through Annie's blinds, but did nothing to lift her spirits. There was nothing to live for, but equally there was nothing to die for. Unless she could find another window to the past, her life stretched ahead like a dark yawning chasm. Her heart had been split in two, and she didn't think it would ever heal.

She sat on the edge of her bed for a few moments, wondering why going back to the airfield had not triggered anything pivotal to happen as it had at the at the Battle of Britain Memorial or at the aviation scrap yard. As this thought occurred to her, she suddenly realised what she had to do, and that was to go back to the beginning: to the place where all the strange occurrences had begun.

As she no longer cared particularly what she looked like, Annie dressed hurriedly in faded jeans and an oversized thick grey jumper normally saved for evenings at home in front of the television. Having called a taxi, but tired of waiting, she grabbed her cerise coat and slammed the front door behind her. A sense of urgency in the cold air greeted her as soon as she was outside the apartment block foyer, the wind immediately encouraging her to walk faster as it gusted her along with its icy fingers. Knowing that she had a fair walk ahead, she allowed the wind to assist, thinking it a sign for her to hurry. Her heart began to race with the anticipation that she might not get the answers she hoped for, but whatever the outcome, it seemed that the statue by the river was calling out to her.

As she crossed Lambeth Bridge, she had a strange feeling that strangers were all aware of her plight, thinking her deranged, and fixing her with their sympathetic smiles as she passed. Looking down at the pavement so she could avoid eye contact, she counted cracks in the pavement that glistened threateningly with winter ice. The sky was cloudless and a brilliant blue. She made her way past Victoria Tower Gardens, isolated, the sound of traffic noise nothing but a distant hum. Autumn had vanished, leaving trees naked. Despite their bare branches, Annie imagined them as inanimate sentries, standing proudly, as they waited in line for the spring to bring them to life again.

It was a fine day for walking the short distance to Westminster Bridge. On this occasion, it seemed appropriate to dismiss using the underground, giving her time to think rather than sharing a confined space on a crowded train or on a grimy platform, where a constant breeze would whisper in her ear as it whooshed from dark tunnels. It was also almost a shame not to go down to the river and sit in the sun. The parks were not so full of tourists at this time of year.

Annie noticed as she passed other people in the street, that they barely made eye contact with each other, texting or talking on their mobile phones or staring straight ahead. She switched her attention to the view ahead of the Houses of Parliament and the London Eye turning slowly in the distance.

It seemed like no more than a few days since she had walked to the Battle of Britain memorial with Tom, ignoring his conversation as she sent trivial text messages and unimportant emails. How different she felt now, despite a lot of missing pieces to the jigsaw of events. It was as though she had experienced all the emotions of a lifetime rolled up into one neat package, in the space of only a few weeks. It was liberating but at the same time depressing to know that before falling in love with Lenny, her life had been comparable to that of a caged tiger.

As she approached the northern end of Westminster Bridge, she was aware that her heart was starting to beat much faster. The statue of Boudica stood at the end of the bridge, a testament to the power that woman possessed. The Thames glistened and twinkled to her right. The memorial seemed to not get any closer with each step that she took, almost as though it were trying to keep its distance until it was ready to receive her. Annie hesitated as it finally came into sight, and reflected again on the first day that she had seen it, and the lack of respect she had shown for something that was about to change and shape her life forever. Oblivious to the impact that the memorial had made on Annie, tourists clicked away with their cameras, taking turns to pose against the bronze façade. For a few seconds the bronze effigy of Lenny and his comrades was completely obscured by a crowd of Japanese tourists enthusiastically taking pictures of their friends.

As Annie got closer, she suddenly began to doubt whether it had been a sensible decision to return to this place and expect a message of some sort to be delivered to her, as it had been on that day that Tom had dragged her along there. To hope for visions of airfields and pilots in the same manner that she had seen that autumn day, was ridiculous. Nevertheless, she knew that by showing the memorial some respect, she did hope for closure.

Chapter 52

Tom was worried. He had only just arrived at work, gone through his post and drunk a cup of coffee when he had the sudden feeling that he should check on Annie. He was still uncertain as to what had sounded different about her tone of voice on the phone: her manner was extremely odd. For the rest of the morning, he remained distracted, trying to think of an excuse to call round to see her. He fidgeted at his desk, unable to put his mind to the pile of papers that had accumulated since the day before. Anxious that she might back out of her agreement to see him soon, he suddenly leapt up from his chair, grabbed his coat from the hat stand and gave no explanation to his personal assistant as he left the office.

'I'm going out, Deirdre! Not sure what time I'll be back.'

A grey-faced, mousy-haired woman in her early sixties looked over her glasses at him.

'But I need your signature on a few things,' she protested forcefully, looking at the pile of unsigned documents strewn all over Tom's desk.

'Sorry. Something's come up. I'll sign them later.'

He shut the door quickly on his way out, before Deirdre could breathe fire at him. He valued her efficiency, but as for her character and lifestyle, he was certain that she was, and always had been, a spinster.

Deirdre pondered for a few moments about Tom, thinking that his behaviour was increasingly puzzling. Since his relationship with that high-flying business executive woman had ended a while ago, he had not had his mind on the job at all. He spent a lot of time pacing round the office or staring blankly out of the window, and generally delegating as much as he could to his entourage of war experts instead of doing the work himself.

Oblivious that his behaviour was under scrutiny, Tom pressed the lift call button several times and hearing no movement in the lift shaft, raced down the six flights of stairs two steps at a time and straight out onto the street, where he nearly bowled over several passers-by. He flagged down a taxi and jumped in.

'Where to, guv?' asked the driver, glancing in his mirror at the pale man with a mess of brown hair.

'Lassco's will do, I'll walk from there.'

The driver nodded and closed the partition window, from time to time glancing at the man in the back seat, who seemed restless and agitated. He was used to people of all types, some were easy company and made small talk, and others preferred to keep a distance. This man seemed very anxious as he repeatedly checked the time on his watch and adjusted his already straight tie.

Tom looked up at the bright blue sky as they raced through London. The morning rush hour was well over and London was awash with tourists and children on school trips. Despite this, the cabbie made good progress. It was only when they got closer to Vauxhall that Tom noticed that nearly all the traffic lights seemed to have staged a vendetta against them and that road works were more prolific than usual.

'Damn it!' said Tom under his breath as the traffic became more snarled up. Other drivers had begun to show their annoyance, repeatedly sounding their horns at workmen digging up the road. With Annie's flat no more than a stone's throw away from the stream of other cabs, buses and cars queuing at temporary traffic lights, Tom considered getting out and walking the rest of the way.

The driver opened the partition window.

'It'll take us a while to get through this, mate.'

'Why can't they do this work overnight?' protested Tom, clearly agitated. 'It's bloody typical of this country.'

'At least you 'aven't got my job,' chuckled the cabbie.

Before Tom could object or jump out to make his way on foot, the driver swung the cab round unexpectedly, choosing a route that Tom was not familiar with. He wondered whether the driver was just plain impatient and as fed up as he was with all the delays, or conscious that there was a sense of urgency in his passenger to arrive at his destination as quickly as possible. Five minutes later, Tom recognised Annie's apartment block as the driver turned into the service road.

'Keep the change,' he said, thrusting a twenty-pound note at the driver, and jumping lightly out of the cab.

The cabbie wound his window up and sat for a few seconds watching as Tom walked quickly off, disappearing round the corner, before pulling away.

Tom did not like intruding on Annie's space, but when he received no response on the intercom, he entered the code that Annie had given him on one of the many nights he had helped her home after one of her excessive drinking bouts. The door buzzed and swung slowly open and Tom crossed the foyer. He was beginning to think that maybe he should have just waited a few more days before contacting her again, but he still could not shake off the feeling that had nagged at him all morning that something was wrong. As he travelled up in the lift to the top floor, he rehearsed what he was going to say if she were there and was just choosing to ignore callers. He had driven by a few times over the last few weeks when she had stubbornly not answered his phone calls, but on each occasion, he had typically not had the courage that he had on this particular day.

He exited the lift and stood at Annie's door with his ear pressed firmly against it, listening for a sound to suggest that she was at home. There was a redundant letterbox in her door, no longer used now the foyer had been updated and post could be left in customised lockers. Tom knelt down and peered through the letterbox into Annie's hallway, wondering whether he had been right that she was shutting herself away.

There was a dreadful smell coming from inside. He pulled a clean white cotton handkerchief from his pocket, clasped it over his nose and peered through the letterbox again.

'Annie, are you in? It's me, Tom.'

He began to feel alarmed by the nature of the smell, and an image of Annie's dead body flashed through his mind. He told himself not to be so stupid and began to rap on the door. The sound echoed along the spacious corridor, followed by silence. Tom knew that Annie was a stickler for cleanliness, so strange smells coming from her flat were something he could not ignore.

He called out again.

'Annie? If you don't answer the door I'll let myself in,' he shouted with a note of authority in his voice.

Nothing stirred.

He thought about making enquiries in the flats below, but he was not in the mood for complaints from anyone about Annie's late night antics, and his sense of urgency was beginning to take over all other potential actions. He took out the spare key that he had commandeered after one of Annie's wild nights and hurriedly let himself in, feeling nervous about what he might find.

He closed the door and leant back against it, composing himself before stepping forward. Suddenly he retched at the dreadful smell, which seemed to have increased in intensity now he was inside the flat. He continued to press the clean handkerchief over his nose and mouth, as he stepped over the pile of letters and junk mail that were strewn on the floor under the letterbox, thinking that the postman must have been forced to bring mail up due to a full locker. In case he had entered a scene he was trying hard to put out of his mind, Tom chose not to touch anything, and alternated between holding the handkerchief to his nose or in his hand to keep his fingerprints from leaving their mark on door handles. He had the sudden thought that if something had happened to Annie, that he would be a likely suspect, due to their last argument. Unprepared for such a possibility, he tentatively pushed doors open.

A large fly buzzed round Tom's head and attempted to land in his hair. He swatted it aside, only to be buzzed by more flies escaping from the kitchen as he opened the door. He immediately noticed that the stench was strongest here. He quickly opened the kitchen window and leant out to gulp a few breaths of fresh air. Dead plants hung forlornly in their pots on the window ledge.

'Good God Annie! What on earth have you been doing for all this time?' he exclaimed, as he surveyed the contents of her kitchen. It looked like the flat had been taken over by vagrants. Dirty crockery and cutlery littered every available surface. An open bottle of milk had turned almost to butter on the kitchen table. The open window had done little to diminish the smell.

Tom systematically scoured the rest of the flat, starting in the bedroom in case Annie had become ill and taken to her bed. He noted that her bedroom had never been so untidy. Designer clothes spilled out of drawers like water cascading from a waterfall, and hung half on and half off of hangers in her walk-in wardrobe. Boots, shoes and handbags lay abandoned as though Annie had tried every single item on before coming to a decision. The blinds were closed and rather than turn on the light in case Annie was asleep in bed under the piles of discarded items, Tom squinted into the darkness. He shivered with the realisation that she was at least not laying dead and undiscovered, and continued to go from room to room, still with a slight morbid expectation as to what he was going to find.

He was about to enter the lounge when from across the hall, his heightened senses made him aware of the almost inaudible sound of a dripping tap coming from Annie's bathroom. His heart skipped a beat. The door was slightly ajar. He was afraid and felt a lump in his throat. Trembling, he slowly pushed the door open far enough so he could see the bath, with the image of Annie's naked dead body imprinted on his mind. He closed his eyes for a few seconds, praying that when he opened them, that Annie would not be a bloated corpse, and that she would appear instead wrapped in a towel and greet him with a welcome kiss.

The bath was full almost to the top, with no bloated corpse within it, but the overflow had been working full-time in order to stop the bath from running over. Tom felt the temperature of the water for a clue as to how recently Annie had bathed. It was stone cold. He quickened his search, fearing that he might still have a few surprises waiting for him in the lounge.

The door was closed, but as he opened it, he was suddenly certain that he would find Annie, in front of her flat screen TV watching one of her favourite films and munching her way through a box of chocolates. He would no doubt get an earful for letting himself in, but at this moment in time, the state of the flat was evidence enough that she needed urgent intervention – that much was clear. He still loved her no matter what she might feel for him and would do whatever it took to make her well again.

He scanned the room. It was empty and in semi-darkness. The sound of muted music greeted him; the dulcet tones of Glenn Miller. This choice surprised him. Annie was out. With this knowledge, the knot in Tom's stomach relaxed slightly. He turned on the light and stepped across the sea of paper littering the floor. It looked as though there had been a paper storm, as similarly to her bedroom, which had been strewn with clothes, every available surface, including her magnolia walls were covered with printed sheets of paper.

He picked up some of the paper from the floor and scanned the contents: references to airfields and RAF personnel from World War Two. He studied the images that had been haphazardly stuck to the walls. Black and white images of people and planes stared back at him, evidence of a time that held no fascination for Annie. He was perplexed. Her sudden fixation made no sense. He went to her desk. Strangely, her screensaver hadn't yet activated. The Battle of Britain Memorial stared back at him.

Tom realised that Annie was maybe suffering some sort of breakdown and had succumbed to what she had called his enthusiastic ranting about the war. This was his fault. He had inadvertently brainwashed her with his stories of heroism and long lost relatives. She had been ill already, vulnerable, broken, and somehow as part of her decline, had been sucked into his obsession. But where was she? And why had she gone out leaving the place in such a mess? He felt big pangs of guilt. Why had he not seen the signs and been there for her? He picked up her coffee cup to take to the kitchen. The least he could do was to make a start and tidy up her mess. He didn't care if she objected. He would be her protector for now.

Suddenly, Tom realised that her cup was vaguely warm. There was no doubt about it – he had just missed her. He frantically looked around for clues as to where she might have gone, but there was nothing. He went into the hall and instantly noticed that the red answer phone light on her home phone was flashing. He pressed the button.

You have one new message. To listen to saved messages, press one.

He pressed one and listened to a woman's voice.

Message today at eleven thirteen a.m. This is a call for Miss Winter. Your taxi will be late. Your driver is stuck in traffic.

Tom dialled the number on the card by the phone.

A woman answered.

'Crystal Taxis.'

'Oh, hello, I've just picked up your message for a Miss Winter's taxi, saying it would be a little late.'

'Hold on sir, I'll just check his progress,' said the woman.

A few bars of music filled the silence.

'To the Victoria Embankment, was it?' asked the woman.

'Er...yes, that's right. How long will it be?' asked Tom.

'Should be with you any second now. Sorry for the delay.'

'Thanks.'

Tom looked down to the service road below. A cab had just pulled up. He waved to the driver to acknowledge that he knew he had arrived, and then took one last look at the carnage in Annie's flat, before locking the door on his way out.

Chapter 53

'Can't you go any faster?' asked Tom almost pleadingly. 'I need to get there quickly!'

'Sorry guv, there was some sort of major incident on my way to pick you up, police and ambulances everywhere.'

At the mention of ambulances, an image of Annie being knocked over by a bus flashed through Tom's thoughts, as he imagined her in a world of her own, absent-mindedly crossing the road.

'Can you try another route?'

'Of course. Victoria Embankment was it?'

'The Battle of Britain memorial, please.'

'We'll take Lambeth Bridge. The snarl up's south of Westminster Bridge.'

The driver turned the car around and ducked through a couple of back streets, much like the previous driver had done when dropping Tom off at Annie's flat. Tom began to feel sick at every bend as well as frustrated that now that he was in a hurry to catch up with Annie, every imaginable obstacle had been sent to test his patience. He swore under his breath as mothers with pushchairs crossed the roads and cyclists adopted suicidal tendencies weaving in and out of the London traffic. Double-parked delivery vehicles seemed to have been wedged into the worst possible places, causing angry drivers to shout abuse and sound their horns.

'Drop me as close as you can to the memorial,' asked Tom as they finally swung round Parliament Square.

'Right you are.'

Big Ben chimed just as they turned onto Victoria Embankment. Tom's concern for Annie's welfare had taken precedence over anything that might be waiting back at the office. He would deal with the wrath of Deirdre on his return. It was while he was thinking about how high his stack of paperwork might be, that Tom suddenly spotted Annie, in her cerise pink coat, walking purposefully along towards the memorial.

He opened the window and shouted across to her.

'Annie, wait! It's me!'

She stopped for a second, at first Tom thinking that she had heard him calling, but then he realised that she seemed to be interested in a large group of tourists that were gathered around, taking photographs. She walked on.

'This will do,' said Tom, fumbling with his wallet. 'Stop here please.'

The driver braked fiercely and pulled over to the side of the road on the opposite carriageway to the memorial.

Tom thrust money into his hand.

'Keep the change.'

Tom leapt out of the cab, but pressed himself up against the door as the sound of a large horn warned him of a London bus bearing down on him. Looking between passing cars and buses, he tried to keep Annie in sight as she mingled with the tourists at the statue. Taking his life in his hands, he darted between moving traffic, miraculously avoiding being knocked over by a speeding motorcycle courier. He reached the pavement in time to see Annie behaving oddly through a gap in the crowd. People were gathered around her, whispering and laughing, as she seemed to be speaking to herself and caressing thin air.

Tom moved stealthily towards her, not wanting to scare her in her moment of strange behaviour. The worst that could happen would be for her to fall on her backside like she had once before, in exactly the same place. His mind was trying to grasp the relevance of that fact, when the crowds suddenly grew in numbers to view the spectacle of Annie's performance, blocking his view of her. Forgetting all courtesy, he pushed his way through the crowd towards the place where seconds previously she had been standing. She was not there. He scanned the crowds, walking from one end of the statue to the other and then back again, becoming more and more agitated with each passing minute. He stood on top of the wall between the pavement and the river in an attempt to get a bird's-eye view, in case she had walked further than he had anticipated, or retraced her steps. He ran to the edge of the river, fearing the worst, quickly realising that had she fallen or jumped into the river due to the state of her mind, people would be rushing to her aid. There simply had not been enough time for her to move off that far, even at a run. He went back to the statue and repeated the exercise, becoming more confused and concerned by the moment. He started to ask tourists if they had seen a girl in a pink coat, but to no avail. Those who may have witnessed the spectacle had already moved on. There was nothing to do but wait. Wherever she was, she couldn't be far away, as he could see for several hundred yards in either direction.

Being a logical man, Tom dismissed his fears quickly, and regained a sense of calm by using his time to familiarise himself again with the intricacy and craftsmanship of the memorial. Nevertheless, he could not get Annie's bizarre behaviour out of his head, and was struggling to work out why she had chosen to visit the monument again since she had shown it such contempt the last time. Thinking again about the craftsmanship of the sculptor Paul Day, who had been commissioned to design and sculpt the memorial, Tom realised that no matter how many times he visited it, there was always an element within its friezes that he liked to stop and admire. This sunny but blustery day was no exception.

He joined the throng of enthusiasts.

'Excuse me, could you take our picture please?' said a young Japanese girl, in perfect English.

'Of course,' said Tom, jolted suddenly out of his thoughts.

The young girl linked arms with a young Japanese man, and they smiled at Tom as they stood in front of the memorial. Used to his own camera, Tom took his time as he attempted to take the perfect picture of the couple next to a dance hall frieze.

The couple thanked Tom and moved on.

Tom wondered why he had not noticed the dance hall frieze before, that had framed the Japanese couple. He moved closer to examine it in detail. It depicted a swing band with a large brass section of musicians surrounded by couples dancing together wrapped in each other's arms. He looked at their happy faces. He looked at Annie's happy face as she danced with a handsome pilot, locked in the pilot's embrace.

The world seemed to stop turning. Time stopped. Tom felt the hairs on the back of his neck stand up. His heart began to pound, and he felt light-headed and began to tremble as he took in the face of the young woman again. He knew that without any doubt that it was Annie, cast in bronze, magically embedded into the work of art that he knew so well: happy, immortalised, in another place, another time.

Something told him that she was not coming back.

The End.